Beware...

One-night stands don't turn into forever... unless you happen to pick up a werewolf.

Brittany Hauge's life is falling apart. She's been fired from her job, her roommate deserted her, and her business partner wants to abandon their project. Britt's solution for coping with stress? A night of wild sex with a stranger—except this hook-up isn't playing by her one-and-done rules.

Werewolf Dakota Towne knows Britt is his one and only... his fated mate. But the headstrong female drives him to distraction—until he discovers she's ignorant of the paranormal world, despite being best friends with a shifter. Nor is she aware of the dangerous situation that brought Dakota to town.

Britt panics when Dakota reveals he's an undercover agent—and a werewolf. But Dakota doesn't behave like the demons her hellfire preacher father warned her about. Instead, Dakota is determined to safeguard her no matter what.

"No matter what" includes vampires, a stalker ex, a predatory politician, and dismissive cops.

As the evil around them turns deadly, Britt accepts that Dakota is her destiny. But is their bond powerful enough to defeat the monsters from her past?

Tropes/Themes/Characters: Werewolves, fated-mates (but not insta-love), shifters, vampires, supernatural, crooked politicians.

Trigger Warning: non-graphic rape scene.

Each book in the trilogy is a stand alone romance, but because of the overarching story, the books are best read in order.

Beware of the Moon
Service for Sanctuary Book 2
MJ Compton

Comptonplations Publishing

Beware of the Moon (Service for Sanctuary Book 2)

Copyright © 2019 by MJ Compton Herwood

2nd Edition

All rights reserved.

No portion of this book may be reproduced in any form without written permission from the publisher or author, except as permitted by U.S. copyright law.

NO AI TRAINING: Without in any way limiting the author's exclusive rights under copyright, any use of this publication to "train" generative artificial intelligence (AI) technologies to generate text is expressly prohibited. The author reserves all rights to license uses of this work for generative AI training and development of machine learning language models.

This copy is intended for the original purchaser of this book ONLY. No part of this book may be reproduced,scanned, or distributed in any printed or electronic form without prior written permission from Comptonplations Publishing. Please do not participate in or encourage piracy of copyrighted materials in violation of the author's rights. Purchase only authorized editions.

Cover designed by Getcovers

Published in the United States ofAmerica by Comptonplations Publishing

www.comptonplations.com

EBOOK ISBN: 978-1-959923-15-2

PRINT ISBN: 978-1-959923-16-9

This book is a work of fiction. While reference might be made to actual historical events or existing locations, the names, characters, places, and incidents are either the product of the author's imagination or are used fictitiously, and any resemblance to actual persons, living or dead, business establishments, events, or locales is entirely coincidental.

The publisher does not have any control over and does not assume any responsibility for author or third-party websites or their content.

Denise Thomas Barber

Acknowledgements

For patiently answering my questions:

Kristine Kipers, Attorney; Lawrence Brown, Attorney; Christine Wenger, retired parole officer; Walt Kaczor, retired science teacher; Elisa Konieczko, PhD, Full Professor of Biology, Gannon University

Also:

The Purples, critique group and the best of friends—Carol Lombardo, Christine Wenger, Gayle Callen, and Kris Fletcher; Walt & Andrea Kaczor for opening their home for writing retreats; Reneee Kloecker for allowing us to use her cottage in the woods.

And especially:

My husband Steve, for pizza, Chinese, and meatball subs to go. Love you!

Contents

Chapter 1

BRITTANY HAUGE SIPPED HER drink and studied the patrons of the bar. The sour stench of a decade's worth of spilled beer clung to the air. Loud music, nominal lighting, battered decor—Holsters was her usual hangout when she was in the mood for some action. Tonight, anyone who appeared remotely interesting was either occupied with someone else or had been tried before. She wouldn't want to give some poor, weak-minded man the wrong idea by giving him a second chance. One and done.

Maybe she needed to find new hunting grounds. Even her usual hurricane tasted off, as if the bartender used powdered orange drink instead of real juice.

Her annoyance with her best friend for reneging on their business plans tainted everything. Britt came to Holsters to work off her irritation with an orgasm or two. No strings attached. Forget her frustration with Selena. Now that Selena had her famous musician husband—and gee, Britt wasn't at all bitter for not being invited to her best friend's wedding...hey, at least she didn't have to buy a gift. Britt took another sip of the fruity concoction, searching for a buzz in the liquid.

"Wanna dance?" a potential one-and-done asked.

Why not? Nothing else happening.

She nodded but held on to her half-gone drink. She feared date rape drugs. As a chemist, she could cite their components and how they worked. Awareness didn't make her immune. Being a Holsters regular didn't guarantee her safety. She'd stopped being careless a long time ago.

That's why Selena's about-face on their business surprised her. If Britt trusted anyone on the planet, she would have placed her money on Selena Wolfe.

Enough energy wasted on the traitorous bitch. Time to dance. Maybe work up some enthusiasm for the pitiful specimen gyrating in front of her.

The liquid in Britt's glass sloshed as she swayed her hips in time to the music. She closed her eyes, fantasizing she was having a good time. Didn't work. She opened them again.

And saw him.

A stranger. In more ways than one.

He loomed over every other man in the room. Yet his size wasn't what made him stand out. His eyes were the key to the strangeness flowing into every cell of her body. Dark. Fluid. He exuded darkness, not only from his eyes and the longish black hair framing his head. His very presence brought midnight into the already murky space. The time could have been high noon and the effect would be the same. The impression ran deeper than his black T-shirt, jeans, and denim jacket. There was a stillness about him, a watchfulness that might have unnerved her had she been completely sober. His stare. Brooding at her.

As tipsy as she was, he proved to be her undoing.

Britt wasn't aware she'd stopped dancing until the one-and-done wannabe made some irksome comment. She handed her glass to him and headed toward the stranger. His dark gaze compelled her as surely as if he'd hypnotized her. She felt as fluid as the hurricane she'd abandoned. Half a drink should not have triggered the humming of her nerves. No, not humming. Sputtering. Rain pattering on a calm lake during a storm; water jumping, splashing, the surface disrupted, leaping, fragmented; still water, but not a cohesive whole.

She bumped her hip against someone's chair and didn't pause to apologize.

"Who are you?" She stood toe to toe with the stranger.

Not that his name mattered. She preferred anonymity.

"Dakota."

He spoke as if his name did matter. Should matter to her specifically.

"Dakota Towne."

She couldn't place his accent except to determine he wasn't native to northern Minnesota. "I'm Brittany." She never offered her surname in these situations.

"Selena calls you Britt."

Britt jerked. "You know Selena?"

"I work with Ethan." His mustache and beard beautifully framed his mouth.

"Oh. You're one of his Colorado friends. Are you in the band? Toke Lobo and the Pack?" She didn't recognize him. She would have remembered those eyes. She might have stalked him solely to have those eyes stare into hers.

"One of the bus drivers. Want to go for a walk?"

"Yes. What does a bus driver do?" *Duh!* The man splattered her brain.

"I drive the band bus when we're on tour."

He probably had a woman in every honkytonk town in the country. *Good.* He could add Holsters in Warwick, Minnesota to his itinerary.

Dakota took her arm and steered her toward the exit. Lightning crackled along her skeleton. Every hair on her body rose as if honoring his presence.

"Were you here for Selena's wedding?" Not that she was bitter.

"Wedding?" He pushed open the door. "Selena and Ethan didn't have a wedding. Not in the way you mean."

What kind of answer was that?

"I don't want to discuss Ethan and Selena," he continued. "Let's talk about you and me."

"Our wedding? Dream on." She hated pick-up lines.

He led her around the side of the tavern. The sleeve of his denim jacket brushed against her bare arm. She shivered.

She hadn't brought a sweater. Coming to Holster's was spur of the moment. Selena made her so angry—

Dakota's mouth on hers drove every thought from her brain. If his eyes were a bottomless darkness, his mouth was a storm surge, flooding her, stealing her ability to breathe, perhaps to survive. His tongue did things she'd only imagined. No one ever kissed her with such...possession. Such thoroughness. Not even in the early days with Judd—

Her senses returned. Dakota pressed her against the building's unyielding cinder blocks, his mouth on hers like that of a man devouring his first meal after years of starvation. The damp, chilly night air brushed her skin, but the places Dakota touched her were as hot as the hellfire her father preached. Her arms twined around his neck of their own volition. Her nipples tingled.

He smelled of an experimental soap she and Selena created for their business; lemon balm with a hint of basil. His impressive erection burned past the layers of their clothing and branded her belly.

Although mindless sex was why she'd come to the bar, all her senses screamed if she indulged with Dakota, the act would not be meaningless.

She averted her head, breaking the kiss. "Not here." She was a slut, not an exhibitionist.

"Not here," he echoed, his voice as rough as the cinder blocks at her back. "Do you have a place?"

Right. He was staying at Ethan's with the Colorado contingent.

Her roommate got cranky if Britt brought home guests. What the hell. Britt paid half the rent. If she wanted to fuck some random guy's brains out, she would. And she decided Dakota's brains were supremely fuckable.

"Yeah. You want to follow me?" Her voice warbled. Taking inventory, her voice wasn't the only body part caught in Dakota's disruptive aura. Her legs were barely able to support her body weight. Her heart thudded crazily in her chest. Even her respiration was off-kilter.

"I jogged," Dakota said. "Can I catch a lift with you?"

Okay. Jogging to a bar was weird. Ten miles easily separated Ethan's house on Ash Street from Holsters. The guy hadn't even broken a sweat.

Britt wasn't stupid. She usually texted a photo of her one-and-done's license plate to Selena or her roommate. Tonight would be okay to skip. Right? Dakota and Ethan were pals.

Or so Dakota claimed. He could be lying. He didn't want to discuss Selena and Ethan. Maybe he didn't know them.

As if her eyes transmitted her thoughts, Dakota pulled out a cell phone and punched in a number. He put the phone on speaker. When Ethan answered, Dakota said, "I won't be coming back to the house tonight."

"Okay," Ethan replied.

"Did he follow Britt?" Selena asked in the background. "She doesn't—"

Dakota disconnected, and tucked the phone into his breast pocket. "Shall we?"

I FOUND HER.

Dakota managed to cram his body into the front seat of the insult-to-motorized-vehicles Britt called a car. He figured the aches from the contortions would be worth the result. Next time, they'd use his SUV. For the rest of forever, they'd use his vehicle.

He'd found his mate. Finally. He'd been stunned to find he'd been matched with a sapien female. A pack's upper echelon were the ones who usually mated outside homo lupus. The Ancient Ones must have great plans in mind for him.

Part of him had questioned his interpretation of the smell lingering around Ethan's house. He'd sniffed all the lycan females before they'd returned to their homes in the forest. Not one emitted the aroma arousing his body, his brain, his soul. Tracking Britt was easier than he'd anticipated.

There she'd stood, her hair glowing like a moonrise, in the half-lit bar, surrounded by males in cowboy hats, boots, and too-tight jeans, all hoping to get laid. He'd spent too much time in similar honkytonks to believe differently. Britt's unique aroma marked her as surely as he planned to mark her as his.

The amazing miracle was discovering Britt wanted him as intensely as he wanted her. Sometimes mating was tricky with sapiens. He could smell Britt's arousal. He'd tasted her passion when he kissed her. He wanted to kiss her again, but he needed to wait until they arrived at their destination.

His mate-to-be was a dreadful driver. Maybe she was drunk. She'd had a glass in her hand when he'd first seen her. The car's flimsy floorboard barely withstood his stomping on a non-existent brake pedal. She took so many twists and turns, he wondered if she was trying to shake a tail, and he didn't mean the kind he wore in his four-footed version.

Maybe she was trying to confuse him. As if she could. He'd been blessed with an unfailing sense of direction. The gift came in handy when finding the scat-kicking towns where Toke Lobo and the Pack played in their early years. She had the rest of her life to learn all about him. He couldn't wait.

Mating fever. He'd witnessed the malaise often enough; burning in its grip was different. Way different. Humbly different.

Scat. He didn't have berries to offer her. Then again, she was sapien. Maybe she wouldn't notice he was late with the gift. She might not be aware of the mating tradition where a male werewolf was supposed to serve berries to his female.

His cell phone vibrated against his chest. He pulled the phone from his pocket and read a text message from Ethan.

Don't hurt her and make sure she's happy.

Dakota's stomach clenched. The words were standard advice to a male before he claimed his mate.

Britt's apartment was in a nicer section of Warwick than Ethan's house. Dakota approved. Not that they'd be living in her apartment. Nope. He wanted to return to Loup Garou, where trees were what trees were supposed to be, not the creepy growths in Minnesota's north woods. If Bigfoot existed, he lived there.

Unfolding himself from the car prevented Dakota from racing around and opening Britt's door for her. He managed to pry himself out. Britt waited in front of a door stupidly constructed of glass. Maybe it was leaded or heavier than regular glass, but it was still glass. She should be protected by steel.

Dakota trailed her up a dark stairwell. He waited while she fumbled putting the key into the lock. He tamped the urge to seize the key and open the door. "You need a light in the hall."

"The bulb burned out last week. I called the landlord." The lock tumblers clicked, and the door opened.

"Call him again." The stairwell light didn't matter. Her future was elsewhere. Dakota slammed the door behind him.

"Shh. My roommate might be asleep," Britt said.

"No one else is here," Dakota assured her. He would have heard an extra heart beating, other lungs bellowing in and out. They were the only two in the apartment.

"In that case—" The rest of her sentence was lost as her mouth covered his. Her fingers curled into his T-shirt. He stumbled on something as she dragged him toward what he hoped was her bed.

He was trying to figure out where to touch her first when something crunched beneath his feet right before they toppled to the bed and Britt straddled him.

He was going to lose his mind.

"Touch me." She moaned the words before her mouth descended on his. Her tongue brushed against his, imitating the rocking motion of her lower torso.

Instinct took charge. Her tank top fell to the floor, followed by her bra, both torn from her body. *Don't hurt her,* Ethan had cautioned.

As much as Dakota wanted to rip off Britt's remaining clothing and toss away the scraps, he needed to be careful. Females were delicate.

Britt's bare breasts dangled above his mouth.

What was he supposed to do? He wasn't an infant; Britt wasn't his mother.

"Touch me." Her tone was insistent. Impatient.

He was getting the impression she was more experienced at sex than he was. Not difficult since she was his first.

He licked her areola. Her nipple instantly tightened. Hardened.

"More." Her whisper was harsh. "More, damn you. Stop teasing me."

Whatever the female wanted.

He forgot to worry about hurting her; forgot to ponder his next move. All the sounds Britt made as he touched her encouraged further exploration. Her skin was as smooth and firm as a plum. Except her nipples. They'd become raspberry textured as he used his tongue on them.

At some point, Britt had unzipped his jeans and freed his cock. Her hand clasped the swollen flesh firmly. With purpose. He tried to reciprocate, but his fingers were big and clumsy as he inserted them into the waistband of her leggings. He did try to leave the garment intact . . . for around two seconds. Yanking them from her body was easier.

"Protection?" Britt asked, between panting and moaning. "From me? Sweetheart, I am your protection."

She didn't argue, and he couldn't explain.

She impaled her body on his. His brain stuttered, mimicking the cadences of his heart and lungs. Britt guided him with her rhythm and experience.

A passive bone did not exist in Dakota's body. He flipped Britt onto her back and took command.

"Yes. Oh, yes." She sank her fingernails into his shoulders and convulsed. The bed squawked as Dakota increased the intensity of his thrusts. Her knees and thighs clamped his ribs.

He flipped her onto her stomach. Her body was as limp as the sheets on the bed. He grasped her hips with his hands and raised her ass. She trembled when he plunged into her.

"I can't," she whimpered. "Not again." Yet as soon as his teeth found the spot on the right side of her neck—her mating spot—happiness flooded her. Dakota could smell her satisfaction. The way she contracted around him pushed him into the same state.

He shuddered as his happiness mingled with hers.

Chapter 2

Britt yawned and stretched before colliding with something hard and hot. Solid. Male. She groaned. A one-and-done was supposed to be gone before morning. Everyone obeyed the unwritten rules. No walks of shame. No awkward attempts at conversation. No wakeup calls.

This guy didn't follow the rules. Instead of vacating her bed, he stroked her bare hip. Yeah, the caress felt...fabulous...Oh hell, she didn't have any place else to be. She could linger. She wanted to linger.

Dakota—yeah, that was his name—was the personification of what sex should be. The experience she'd searched for with her one-night stands and never found. He was assuredly worth a repeat.

Except another go-round with him wouldn't be a repeat. If she recalled correctly, he'd been insatiable. Unstoppable. She'd lost track of where one orgasm faded and the next began.

His hand abandoned her hip and slipped between her legs. She was sore, but the discomfort was worth the result. Besides, the ache vanished after a few strokes of his magic fingers.

"Are you some kind of demon?" she asked, fighting an urge to moan.

His voice was low and wicked. "No, only your everyday werewolf."

She touched the spot where he'd bitten her neck. The nerves still tingled. "Not a vampire?"

She figured she'd offended him when he retorted, "Don't insult me when you should respect me."

Respect him? She refrained from snickering in his face. He trolled country music dives trying to hook up.

"Okay, Bus Boy, show me why I should respect you."

DAKOTA STRETCHED. HIS MATE was alone in the shower having emphatically declined his company. Imagining Britt all wet and steamy made him hard and ready to mount her again. Except he couldn't hurt her, and she'd winced the last time he'd plunged into her. Mating, he decided, was fairly straightforward. Not only was Britt happy, he was certain his newfound ecstasy would be visible to all.

Next on his agenda was to find berries for her. He could always take a cue from Ethan's courtship of Selena and locate a fast-food place offering fresh berries and yogurt.

"Why aren't you gone?" Her fierce scowl, as she emerged from the bathroom, distracted him. As did the beads of water clinging to her naked shoulders and the flimsy gray towel she'd wrapped around her torso. The ends of the towel were tucked between her breasts. She stepped across the discarded clothes at the foot of her bed.

"Maybe we can grab some breakfast before you go to work or whatever you do."

The blue of her eyes darkened. "Are the rules different in Colorado?"

Rules? The only rules werewolves followed were *find your mate, mark her, don't hurt her,* and *make sure she's happy.* They weren't really rules. They were closer to guidelines for a happy existence. "What rules?"

"Hookup rules." She sounded impatient and flung the wet ropes of her yellow hair over her shoulder.

Hookup. He'd heard the term bandied around in the bars where Toke Lobo and the Pack used to perform. Did Britt believe he was a one-time occurrence? Time to set her straight.

"I don't do hookups."

"I don't do anything else," she retorted. "Allow me to explain how hookups work. We meet in a bar, we go someplace, have sex. The person whose someplace it isn't leaves before morning. No waking up together. No group showers. No breakfast twosome. Sex. Nothing more."

"Sounds lonely," Dakota replied. "Lousy way to live a life."

"Works for me."

Ah. That explained the thunderheads gathering in her eyes. "Meet your new and improved future."

"A stalker," she muttered. "I had to go and let myself get picked up by a stalker."

He sensed she meant something other than his hunting skill. He also sensed Britt, who allegedly had been Selena Wolfe's college roommate, was unaware of a few critical facts, such as Selena's true nature, meaning Britt was also ignorant of Ethan's true nature, and by extension, his.

Her ignorance complicated their situation.

Britt slammed around her room. She shed the towel as if he weren't present. Bureau drawers opened and closed with a violence he might have found amusing in other circumstances.

Dakota recalled a time right after Tokarz, his alpha, had claimed his sapien mate. Delilah hadn't known Tokarz was a werewolf. She accused him of being a vampire. Britt flung the same slur at him.

Delilah flipped out when Tokarz revealed himself. Gone vamp-scat crazy. Every member of the Toke Lobo and the Pack touring company heard her. On the other hand, Stoker Smith's sapien mate loved Stoker's lycanthropy and was jealous of his ability to shift.

Based on Britt's current rampage against her wardrobe, Dakota was going to guess her reaction to the truth would be closer to Delilah's than to Lucy's.

Britt pulled on gray leggings and a blue shirt, checked the mirror, yanked off the shirt, and flung it to the clothes-carpeted floor.

His life mate was a slob.

While she lashed around the room, Dakota donned his own jeans and T-shirt. Locating his socks took longer.

"I suppose you want a ride back to Ethan's house." Britt didn't bother trying to hide her nasty mood.

"Not if you have to go out of your way." His calm response was meant to soothe her.

Fail.

She tugged on a greenish tank top, swiped the blue shirt from the floor and jammed her arms into the sleeves. "I might as well drive you. Maybe I can talk some sense into Selena."

Oh? Maybe she wasn't irritated with him, but with Selena and her half-baked plan to create a line of herbal beauty products for sapien females. Britt was supposed to be Selena's business partner, supplying the expertise needed to make the products. Selena originally planned to use her share of the profits to support her village.

A renegade congressman ordered the inhabitants of Ulvskog exterminated before the plans matured.

Dakota sat on the edge of Britt's mattress and pulled on his boots. "Selena is still mourning her grandfather."

"She told me." Britt's voice harbored her irritation, joined by an underlay of sullenness. She jammed her feet into black flipflops. "She's still alive. His death didn't stop her from marrying Ethan."

Selena had some serious explaining to do, but Britt's reality check needed to come from him. He'd marked her. She was his forever. The facts couldn't be avoided.

Besides, Selena and Ethan faced more important situations than Dakota's love life.

The Ancient Ones never made mistakes.

Chapter 3

Britt couldn't believe she was driving Dakota around. Her car was too cramped for the two of them. His presence stole her air. Or maybe she merely didn't want to breathe in the scent of sex clinging to him like ozone after a lightning strike. Dakota hadn't showered, while she'd scrubbed her skin raw trying to get his aroma off her. The scouring hadn't done any good. Besides, she was breaking every hookup rule she had.

A good-looking guy. A guy hung like—never mind. What she minded was wanting another go-around with him. Maybe a weekend-long fuck-a-thon. Work him out of her system once and for all.

"So what do you do with yourself?" Dakota squirmed in the passenger seat, disrupting the sparse air, sending his pheromones in her direction again.

"I'm a chemist."

No, no, no. Do not engage with him. Sex only.

"You must be smart."

Was he saying she was too smart for him? Was he going to try to take her down a peg? *Been there, donated the T-shirt.* "I'm as smart as I am. I could be smarter. Everyone could."

"I wasn't insulting you."

Dakota's calm manner infuriated her. The only time he hadn't been placid was during sex. Amazing sex. Stupendous—

"You and Selena were working on herbal healing bath stuff for females," Dakota continued.

"Are working on," she corrected. She refused to believe Selena would abandon their hard work because her grandfather died.

His foot slammed against the floor as she took the corner onto Ash Street too fast.

"You're not going to tell me I'm too pretty to be a chemist?"

"What does one have to do with the other?" He sounded perplexed, as if he meant the words.

"Never mind," she muttered. She needed to concentrate on not hitting the group of men dressed in black trying to block the street. No matter what hour she arrived at Ethan and Selena's house, a gang congregated on both ends of the short block.

"Run 'em over if they get in your way," Dakota suggested, as if reading her mind. "They'll move quickly enough. Although they might damage the undercarriage of your car."

She was tempted. "Interesting theory. My favorite theory involves the questionable legality of mowing people down."

"I won't tell if you won't."

She couldn't stop the grin stealing across her face. Not only was Dakota a fabulous bedmate, he was funny. Dangerous combination.

"If you drove a bigger vehicle, mashing a few vagrants wouldn't be an issue."

There. He'd said something to annoy her. "What's wrong with my little car?"

"Small cars aren't safe."

Oh crap. He was a man who believed a night in her bed meant he acquired rights.

She gritted her teeth and pressed her foot on the gas pedal. Her car hitched a moment before lurching forward, drunk on an influx of fuel.

Dakota was right. Once she aimed, the men in the street scurried to the side. Ethan ought to report the thugs to the authorities. They'd blocked the street, twenty-four-seven, for weeks.

She parked at the curb, behind a massive black SUV. Gas hogs ought to be illegal. She couldn't imagine any of Ethan's acquaintances would drive such a monstrosity.

She stood on the sidewalk and waited while Dakota extracted himself from her car. The view, she had to admit, was nice. Very nice. For someone who allegedly drove a bus for a living, he was superbly put together. As he stood and stretched, something in her belly stirred. Okay. Maybe he wasn't a one-and-done, but rather the exception proving the rule.

The opening notes of "It's Five O'Clock Somewhere" bleated from her cross-body bag. She pulled out her phone to check the incoming text. And nearly dropped the phone to the sidewalk. Numbness depleted her strength, from the tips of her pedicured toes to her brain. Especially her brain.

"Are you okay?" Dakota's sharp tone pierced the fog.

She couldn't answer. All she could do was stare at the photo on her screen and try to not hyperventilate.

Judd Byrne was supposed to be out of her life. He was supposed to be in prison, thanks to her. How did he have access to a cell phone to text a picture to her? How did he get her cell phone number?

Yet there he was. On the screen. The orange jumpsuit he wore matched the color of his hair. New tattoos, the jailhouse version of graffiti, adorned his arms.

Hi, Britt, the accompanying text read. *Been thinking about you a lot.*

Maybe the breathing part wasn't going so well. The black spots dancing in her vision probably weren't insects.

Something grabbed her elbow. Dakota. She was shaking. He slid one arm around her waist, the only reason she remained upright.

"Britt?"

She blinked several times. He was several inches taller than she was but stooped until his face was practically in hers.

"Yeah?" Amazingly, her voice was steady. Her fingers cramped. She dropped the phone into her bag. She didn't want Dakota, didn't want anyone, seeing the text. "I must have stood too fast." Her excuse made no sense.

His dark gaze bore into her, as if using her eyes as a gateway to comprehension.

She forced a smile. "I'm okay. Really."

He didn't release her elbow or her waist. "You're the same color as the sidewalk."

She glanced down. Pale gray cement. Not a good color for the living. Her mother had lost her color shortly before she died. "I stood too fast."

She wasn't sure how she ended up in Dakota's arms. He carried her onto Ethan Calhoun's porch.

"I can walk," she complained.

"Ring the doorbell," he said. She complied.

A minute later, Ethan answered the door, his hair and clothes mussed, as if they'd wakened him. "Why are you carrying her?" He ended the question with a jaw-cracking yawn. He stood aside to let them enter.

"She's wobbly," Dakota replied.

Britt bit back a snarky comment. "I'm fine. I got slightly dizzy from standing too fast."

Ethan stared at her before saying, "Congratulations."

What the hell?

"Thanks," Dakota replied. "I have a problem, though." "Oh, you do." Selena wandered in, as tousled as Ethan.

Had she and Dakota interrupted a round of morning sex?

"You definitely do."

A fresh surge of resentment replaced Britt's reaction to Judd's text. Good. Focusing on the present instead of wallowing in the past was positive.

They were unquestionably discussing her. "I'm not a problem."

"No, you're not," Dakota agreed. "You are a delight."

"You can put delightful me down."

Dakota carried her to the living room, where the sole furnishing was a sofa. He sat, still cradling Britt in his arms.

She tried to climb off his lap.

He wouldn't release her.

"We have problems." Ethan opened a folding chair and sat. Backward. "Liam Peters' younger brother has been named interim congressman until a special election can be held."

Politics. Politics were boring. Before he vanished, Liam Peters had been named interim congressman after Bryant Peters' suicide. As far as Britt was concerned, they could all disappear.

"Why do you care?" she asked. Ethan hesitated.

"Ethan snuck behind my back and asked Bryant Peters for seed money for Night Shift." Selena sat cross-legged on the floor. "Then he talked to Liam."

Yay for Ethan. Britt clamped her mouth shut. She wished someone had warned her Ethan was getting more involved in Night Shift. He'd purchased a house with the perfect space in the basement for Night Shift's headquarters. He'd bought a computer for the business and helped them with all the government rules, regs, and assorted colored tapes. Learning he'd tried to procure funding irritated her.

Maybe his involvement was why Selena changed her mind.

Except Britt had put in way too many hours perfecting formulas for their products. She wanted Night Shift to be top-of-the-line. Abandoning her efforts after laying the groundwork was not an option. Who said she needed a partner?

Maybe she should call on the current Congressman Peters.

DAKOTA ENJOYED HAVING BRITT on his lap. She not only caused his hard-on, she hid the condition. While the situation could be a problem later, he currently had more pressing concerns. More pressing even than telling his sexy-as-life mate he was a werewolf.

Ethan's bombshell regarding yet another Congressman Peters in the House of Representatives took priority. The first interim congressman's fate was a secret. Ethan, Selena, and the surviving Varulv pack males had taken care of him. Liam Peters died shrieking for mercy between his agonized screams as the lycans...dismantled his body.

What scraps of physical matter left of Liam Peters existed in the droppings of the werewolves who'd...dismantled him. Searching wolf scat or the Warwick municipal sewer system would never occur to the authorities.

A Peters had held the congressional seat for generations. Ethan's grandfather was the first lycan to understand and hate the family and their politics. Hatch was also the first to identify the reign as a dynasty.

The Peters family dynasty was Ethan's problem, not Dakota's. Yes, Dakota assisted Ethan and Selena when they exacted revenge on Liam for helping his father rape a teenaged Selena, solely because honorable lycans always defended the pack females.

Other than revenge, Dakota had nothing to do with Ethan's mission.

The problem? The Peters family was so evil, they required a lot of revenge. Ethan couldn't progress with his task of convincing the Congressman Peters *d'jour* to vote to continue honoring the service for sanctuary treaties with the werewolves. The Peters dynasty secretly tried to annihilate all lycan packs, a legacy Ethan learned was more personal than he could have imagined.

Now Ethan had another Peters to persuade.

"What have you learned about the new one?" Dakota asked.

"Not much. Liam was the one being groomed for his father's seat. Connor is—"

"The spare," Britt offered.

"What?" Ethan was clearly confused.

"An heir and a spare. I read British aristocracy calls second sons the spare."

Britt read? Dakota never would have guessed.

"Makes sense," Ethan said. "Connor is the spare. Anyone know how many others there are?"

"A daughter," Selena replied. "Nola. Bryant had siblings, but I never met them."

Britt tried again to climb off Dakota's lap. Her squirming only made his situation worse. Neither Selena nor Ethan would be embarrassed by his erection, but until Britt was aware of the truth, he didn't want to risk offending her. "Stay put," he growled against her ear at the same time he gently thrust against her bottom.

He could tell the moment she realized his condition by the way her body stiffened.

"Are you going to visit the newest Congressman Peters?" Dakota asked as he tightened his arm around Britt's waist.

"Of course," Ethan replied.

"Maybe you should leave Night Shift to me and Selena." Britt sounded peeved.

She was clueless. Night Shift was Ethan's cover for why he wanted to see the congressman. Dakota couldn't tell Britt.

"I don't care," Selena said. "Let the guys talk to each other."

Britt's squirming increased as peeved morphed to pissed. "Don't I get a say?"

"Sure you do. Let's talk in the kitchen."

Dakota glowered at Selena as he released Britt, who jumped as if he'd jammed a needle in her butt. He crossed his legs, hoping to hide his condition.

Ethan snickered anyway. "You're going to have your hands full. Don't wait too long to tell her the truth. Remember Tokarz and Delilah."

No one who'd been present when Tokarz revealed his true nature to his new mate would ever forget Delilah's reaction.

"I will," Dakota snarled.

"She explains why you kept saying the house smelled funny."

"Yes." Was Ethan going to keep pointing out the obvious? "How are you going to handle the Peters Dynasty?"

"I'll meet with Connor the Spare," Ethan continued. "Tokarz believes I can negotiate support for the treaties. The sooner you talk to Britt—"

"I said I'd tell her. I mean, how long can I keep something like *you're my life mate* a secret?"

"Britt might not take the news well. She's her own female, and stubborn. Do you want me to see if Selena—"

"No." *Ancient Ones!* Did Ethan believe he couldn't handle his own mate? Ethan might be above him in the pack hierarchy, but Dakota wasn't a pushover. He was a male lycan. Even an omega male, lowest of the low, didn't need help with his mate.

"It was an idea." Ethan had the nerve to sound cranky. "Britt's a loose cannon. She might decide to go to Peters' office on her own to pitch for seed money for Night Shift.

I don't need anything—or anyone—else muddying the situation. You could help by containing your female."

"You let Dakota pick you up last night." Selena wet a sponge under the kitchen faucet.

"I didn't let anyone do anything. The attraction was mutual. I was pissed at you and needed to burn off my irritation." Britt leaned against the counter as Selena ran the damp sponge across the already clean sink. Britt didn't have time for her nonsense. "We need to move forward with Night Shift."

"Dakota isn't the same as other guys you drag home from Holsters."

"Tell me something new," Britt muttered. "How well do you know him?"

"I met him when he drove Ethan's father and grandfather from Colorado."

"So you've known him what? Three weeks?" Being married to a guy from Colorado didn't make Selena an expert on anything, especially men. Britt wouldn't be surprised if Selena was still a virgin, for all she'd hooked up with Ethan. She'd been the most chaste student on campus.

Except she now behaved like a well-laid woman.

Hmm. Maybe something in the Rocky Mountain air affected male performance. If she was the type to keep notes on her one-and-dones, Dakota would get five gold stars. And another chance. Or two. Or—

The muffled notes of "It's Five O'clock Somewhere" escaped her purse.

"You have the most obnoxious ring tone in town." Selena had made the claim ever since Britt added the song to her phone.

"I only keep it to annoy you." The banter was an old routine for them.

The signal repeated.

"Aren't you going to answer?"

"Work is probably wondering if I can come in early," Britt lied. Her employer's ring tone was "Take This Job and Shove It." When she'd had an employer.

"I need to get going." Britt's mind swirled in six different directions. "I need to move forward on Night Shift, so decide what you want to do. If you want out, tell me now. I'm not abandoning the project."

"Aren't you going to wait for Dakota?" Selena ignored Britt's request.

Britt stared at the woman who was supposed to be the only person who understood her. "No. I don't do repeats. So yes, before you lecture me, I admit hooking up with him last night was a mistake. And yes, the situation could get awkward, what with him staying with you and me working on Night Shift in the basement. Your other guests have gone. Right?"

Selena dropped the sponge into the sink. "You can't…Dakota isn't like the usual guys you sleep with. He's more of a one-and-only guy than a one-and-done."

"Life is full of disappointments. I'll call you later." Britt headed toward the door. She needed to get out of the house. The walls were closing in on her.

"Britt, I'm telling you—"

Britt ran out the front door and sprinted to her car. A quick peek in the side mirror confirmed it was safe to pull away from the curb.

She made the mistake of checking her rearview mirror. The bright blue door of the orange house opened to reveal Dakota.

Chapter 4

Dakota stood in the door of Ethan's house, deciding between being angry or amused as Britt drove away. He settled on humor for the time being. Britt's flight was his fault.

He loped after her car, past the thugs attempting to seal off Ethan's street, catching her at the stop sign. She yielded right of way to a car on her right. Dakota opened the passenger door and slid in beside her.

She shrieked.

Maybe he should have knocked first.

"You shouldn't drive around with your doors unlocked." He dumped her purse to the floor. Some of the contents spilled on the vinyl mat. "Don't you have auto locks on your doors?"

"You shouldn't go around climbing into other people's cars." Her voice quavered.

"You shouldn't have tried to ditch me without saying goodbye." He gathered her scattered belongings.

The driver behind her honked.

"You'd better move," Dakota advised.

"You can't come to work with me." She removed her foot from the brake.

"You're right. Except I don't believe you're going to work." He dropped her wallet into her bag. A hairbrush. An aerosol can.

Interesting stuff a female toted around. Some other items he vaguely recognized as female stuff. Her phone.

"What are you doing?"

"Picking up the stuff I spilled." He peered at the phone screen. "You have a new text."

She extended her right hand. "I'll take my phone, please."

"You shouldn't text and drive at the same time." He wanted to read the upsetting message. He resisted and placed the phone in her open palm. "Who's sending you dick pics?"

She slammed on the brakes. He hadn't fastened his seat belt. His chest hit the dash, his forehead met the windshield.

"Are you okay?" Her new concern was touching. She put the transmission in park.

Dakota considered playing up his non-injuries, but too many falsehoods clouded their relationship. He didn't need to go on as he had begun. "You weren't going fast enough to damage me." He rubbed his brow. "And I was kidding about the dick pic. I didn't look at your messages."

He'd been too busy memorizing her phone number.

"Not funny. Are you sure you're okay?"

She eyed him as if she had x-ray vision, weird considering he'd always heard a homo sapien's eyesight was worse than a blind homo lupus.

Her concern touched something in his heart. Yes, he recognized her as his life mate, but having a mate didn't mean a lobo had to *like* the female. He only needed to get her pregnant. Dakota had seen plenty of indifferent relationships while growing up. He wanted the other kind. A mating filled with friendship. Respect. Love.

"Yeah. I'm fine. Only a bump. You can kiss it and make it better." His lycan physiology meant he'd heal faster than a sapien.

Her expression changed from concern to exasperation.

So far, he'd made too many mistakes with Britt. He was so busy remembering and anticipating the sex part, he'd forgotten to respect her with the truth. He needed to correct his error and reveal himself.

"If you're not off to work in such a tearing hurry, where are you going?"

"I do have a life," she replied.

"Good. I'd hate to be having sex with a dead person."

"Um, about the sex." She faced the road instead of him.

"What about the sex?" His anxiety spiked. He was a beginner and not confident. "Did I hurt you? Weren't you happy?"

"The sex was good," she admitted. "And yeah, I stopped counting my orgasms because I had better things to do, such as enjoy them. Except good sex doesn't mean anything. I tried to explain this morning. We hooked up, we had great sex, we go our separate ways."

"No."

"Yes. Selena mentioned you might be more serious than I am. Let me explain again. I had a great time, but we're finished."

Dakota tilted his head and leaned toward her, as if to share a secret. "We're at the beginning of a relationship. Maybe we should have taken time to know each other before we fell into bed, but we are a couple." He left off the forever part. She clearly wasn't taking his news well, and the forever part might send her screaming into the ether.

"I need you to get out of my car. Immediately."

He hesitated. He didn't want to be mistaken for a creepy stalker guy, so he opened the door. A blast of wind blew into the car. "I'll meet you later." He inhaled deeply, imprinting her scent on his soul.

"What part of *no* don't you get?"

He startled her by leaning in for a goodbye kiss. "Later. Have a good day."

AFTER DITCHING DAKOTA, BRITT drove to a neighborhood park not too far from Ethan's house and checked her phone. At least Dakota told the truth about the dick pic. Not that she would recognize Judd's or anyone else's penis. Well, she'd encountered one guy who could have been a porn star—without enhancements. Another poor man cursed with a teeny peeny wouldn't be flashing around his stuff.

Nope. The newest alert requested thoughts and prayers for the Peters family while Liam remained missing.

She Googled the congressional office address. She could think of no reason she couldn't go directly to the congressman herself. Night Shift wasn't Ethan's affair. The idea had originated with her and Selena. They were the ones who needed to search for grant money to help get the business off the ground.

Not that she wasn't grateful for all Ethan had done by purchasing the house and computer and circumventing the tangle of paperwork.

No man was going to control her. She needed to be responsible for her life, including Night Shift.

Ethan had met with Congressman Bryant Peters, the one who'd blown off his head rather than be exposed as a pedophile who ran a Dark Web catalog of his conquests.

Maybe I should change my clothes. Yeah. She needed to wear something more professional than leggings.

She executed a U-turn with only one near miss and sped toward her apartment.

Britt met her roommate on the stairs. "Hi. You're home early."

"I was hoping to get out without running into you." Kathryn carried two bulging black trash bags. "I'm moving out."

Britt paused. "With no notice?"

"I wrote you a note last month," Kathryn said between clenched teeth. "You used the paper to wipe the kitchen counter."

Okay, maybe Britt wasn't Mrs. Clean, but unless the note was written on a paper towel or napkin, she wouldn't have used it to clean anything. "What about your share of the rent?"

"I paid you for this month. I don't owe you anything." Kathryn pushed her way past Britt.

Kathryn's departure was a disaster. The lease was in Britt's name, but she needed a roommate to help make the rent. Especially now.

"I guess I haven't seen you in a while," Britt called after Kathryn.

Who flipped her the bird after tossing the trash bags into the trunk of her car.

Britt blew off the gesture. She'd deal with the fiasco later. On the way to her bedroom, her foot caught in a discarded plastic shopping bag floating along the floor. She regained her balance before face-planting.

Her charcoal gray pantsuit with the chalk white pinstripe was still in a bag from the dry cleaners. Britt breathed a sigh of relief. The matching pearl-gray blouse hung nearby.

Ten minutes later, her clunky-heeled boots assaulted the wooden stairs as she descended to the street. She climbed into her car and pulled her phone from her purse, intending to access the directions to the congressman's office again.

Another text from a blocked number. She opened the message, expecting spam from Kathryn, who'd pulled similar crap on a couple of her exes.

Nope. Selena must have given Britt's number to Dakota, who sent a photo of himself dressed all in black, much as he'd been the previous evening. Jeans, denim jacket, T-shirt, boots. One shoulder leaned against a wood paneled wall. The sleeves on his jacket were rolled to mid-forearm. The tips of his fingers were tucked into his pockets.

He was hot. So hot.

She grinned all the way to the congressman's office.

Chapter 5

BRITT SAT ACROSS THE massive wooden desk from interim Congressman Connor Peters and plucked at the fabric covering her thighs. She wasn't sure how she'd gotten in to see him. In retrospect, she should have called to make an appointment. The man had to be inundated with stuff. What with his father's suicide and his brother's disappearance, Connor had to be buried. He didn't need her troubles snapping at his ass.

"I'm intrigued by your name." Connor Peters tried to blind her with his dazzling white teeth.

Britt narrowed her eyes. Something tugged at her, as if he was familiar in some way.

"Any relation to Pastor Paul Hauge?"

Damn it. She should have guessed the acting congressman spared a moment in his schedule for her due to a hidden agenda.

"He's my father," she admitted. She avoided acknowledging the connection whenever she could. She and Pastor Paul didn't see eye to eye. *If thy right eye offend thee, pluck it out and cast it from thee* might describe their current relationship. Just who had plucked and cast whom was a matter of opinion.

"Pastor Hauge and his congregation were devout supporters of my father," Connor continued. His smarmy smile never found his blue eyes. "What can I do for his daughter?"

With that offer on the table, she wasn't going to deny her father. Still, a nasty shiver skated along her spine. "I'm trying to launch a business," she explained. "My partner and I are hoping we can apply for a small business grant. I believe your father was investigating the matter."

Connor grimaced. "He worked on so many issues. I'll have someone on staff check for you."

"Thank you for your time." Britt stood. She pondered offering condolences for his father, then decided no one should mourn a pedophile.

He stuck out his hand. Not shaking would be churlish. Chills zinged into her arm, and not in a good way. He escorted her to the door.

"Thanks again." She hurried out of his office.

Ethan and Dakota were in the reception area. Of all the bad timing...

"Britt?" Surprise tainted Dakota's question.

She ignored him and crossed the room to the outer door. "I'll take care of her," Dakota told Ethan. "You do what you need to."

She quickened her pace, hoping to reach the elevator before Dakota caught her.

The man was fast. He grasped her arm as the elevator doors slid open. "Hold on, Britt. I didn't realize you worked for Congressman Peters. You did say you were going to work. Didn't you?"

"No." She'd only claimed he couldn't go to work with her. Which was true. Going to work wasn't an option. Yesterday, she'd been fired.

DAKOTA COULDN'T BELIEVE HIS eyes when the congressman's door opened and Britt emerged. She hadn't acknowledged him or Ethan. Instead, she'd blown past them and out of the office suite. Leaving Ethan to do damage control with Peters, he'd tried to subdue Britt.

"I'm having a crappy day, so don't start with me," she told him, as he dragged her onto the elevator.

"What are you doing here?"

"Trying to get seed money for Night Shift." She punched the button for the ground floor. "Why are you spying on me? Neither you nor Ethan are residents of this congressional district. You have no business talking to my representative."

She had a point.

"Ethan's grandfather is from the area, and Ethan's moving back."

"You forget. Night Shift isn't Ethan's business." Britt tapped her toe as the elevator descended. "I am sick and tired of the 'old boy' network interfering in my life."

"Who's interfering in your life? Ethan is trying to help you." Dakota doubted he'd ever untangle female logic.

"I'm capable of helping myself." The elevator jerked to a stop. The doors slid open, and Britt strode into the lobby. "Have a nice life, Dakota."

"Whoa." He rushed to keep up with her. "We're not done with this conversation."

"Yes, we are." She was out the door before he could stop her.

He hurried to the lobby receptionist and handed her the keys to his rented SUV with instructions that Ethan Calhoun would be collecting them, just as Britt drove past in her ridiculous car. He caught her at the end of the block, where she was stopped at a red light.

He knocked on the passenger window before he opened the door and climbed in. "You should lock your doors. If the car is equipped with child locks, I can set them for you."

She shrieked anyway. "You have to stop jumping into my car! Someone is going to see you and call the cops. I might call the cops. Maybe being locked up for a few hours will teach you to chill."

Him? Mellow out? He struggled not to laugh out loud. Britt was the only one in the relationship who needed calming.

He pulled out his cell phone and texted Ethan about the keys to the SUV.

"Is it lunchtime? I missed breakfast."

"Are you buying?" Britt asked after a long pause.

"Sure." Maybe he could get her to order strawberry shortcake or something. Once she'd eaten the berries, she'd be easier to handle.

"What are you in the mood for? Pizza? Chinese?" Britt listed the various fast-food franchises lining the street.

You. "I don't care."

"Do you eat sushi?"

He swallowed a groan. What was it with Minnesotans and fish? The Varulv pack behaved as if walleye was the greatest food in the world. They'd fed him so much fish he was surprised he hadn't developed gills and fins. "Only if I have to."

"I hate the stuff," she confided, as she left the avenue in favor of a side street. "I'm taking you to the best steakhouse in town."

If she weren't driving, he would have kissed her. "A female after my own heart."

"If you're staying with Selena, you're probably sick of fish. I roomed with her in college for four years. I got sick of smelling the walleye."

She entered the parking lot of a shack shingled in dark green. Cop cars occupied several spaces. Peeling paint on a warped board claimed the building was The Steak Out. Hole-in-the-wall restaurants were Dakota's favorite kinds of places to eat. A lobo could order a steak so rare the meat was barely warm, and no one whined about the health department. Ten minutes later, a perfect slab of beef sat on a chipped plate in front of him. Britt ordered a local brand of beer with her burger. Good. She'd given him a reason to confiscate her

keys and do the driving.

He cut into the meat. Red juice dribbled out. One bite soothed his taste buds. "Why are you so intense regarding Night Shift?"

She bit into her burger. Chewed. Chewed some more. Chewed long enough to make Dakota suspect she was avoiding answering him. She swallowed. Quaffed her beer as if to clear her palate. "Creating a line of healing creams and lotions is my dream," she finally confessed. "Haven't you ever had a dream?"

You. "Sure. But I don't go crazy."

"Tell me about your dream." She bit into her burger again. Her teeth gleamed in the dim lighting. Teeth were important. She had nice ones, which boded well for their future offspring.

"Driving. I love being a bus driver for Toke Lobo and the Pack. We don't tour much anymore, a mistake in my opinion. We need to tour to build the fan base." He shook his head. "Not my call. I've considered getting a job driving for the brewery."

"The brewery?"

"Moonsinger Beer. Brewed and bottled in Oak Moon, Colorado, a couple of miles from my hometown."

She tilted her bottle toward his glass of water. "Don't you indulge?"

"Nah." He'd have time later to explain how alcohol was poisonous to a werewolf's physiology.

"You have a career goal. I respect ambition. I have a goal, too." She raised her beer to her lips.

Again, he sensed she was prevaricating.

"Selena and I have a solid line ready to launch. All we need is help in the form of money. How much do you know about Night Shift?"

"Bits and pieces. Selena wanted to hire the females from Ulvskog to harvest the herbs and help concoct the potions."

Britt glared at him. "They're not potions. And Selena had some weird idea the women would harvest by the light of the moon, working the night shift. And *voila*. We created a brand."

"Night Shift is a good name, except for Ulvskog's recent problems."

"The mayor died." More than a hint of sarcasm tainted Britt's voice.

"He was murdered," Dakota corrected with as much gentleness as he could summon. "An unarmed old man, slaughtered in his own home. With an assault rifle. Ethan said he was splattered from one end of his house to the other."

Britt's eyes widened. She set her bottle on the table. Pushed away her partially eaten burger. "Selena never...I never saw anything on the news."

"There's an ongoing investigation." Dakota wasn't lying. The werewolves had taken care of Bryant and Liam Peters. They'd gotten one of the gunmen, a guy by the name of Curtis DiNardo. Others still needed to die for the Ulvskog Massacre. "Your visit to the congressman's office today could have blown..." He stopped abruptly.

"Congressman Peters had something to do with Selena's grandfather's death?" Britt whispered. "Can you prove his guilt? Why would my being in his office mean anything?"

She crossed her arms and leaned back in her chair. "Are you really a bus driver?"

Dakota merely cut deeper into his steak.

"I know for a fact Ethan plays steel guitar for Toke Lobo and the Pack."

"Yeah. He does." Dakota speared a piece of meat and raised his fork to his mouth.

"So he's a musician, not a cop or anything."

Dakota wouldn't tell her about the *anything* until she understood his relationship with the moon. He continued to chew.

"Except it is weird the first congressman killed himself before his son vanished," Britt pondered aloud.

Dakota let her ramble.

Service for sanctuary. Ethan was a part-time federal agent. In the past, lycans were the ultimate in spies, using their superior senses to help their adopted country in exchange for safety. Sometimes the tasks they were given were shady.

"What do the Peters have to do with Selena's grandfather?"

"Maybe nothing. But remember, Bryant was a pervert. And why did Liam disappear if he wasn't as guilty? You know what they say about smoke." Dakota ate another chunk of his steak.

"Liam's disappearance has nothing to do with me," Britt said. "If the current congressman can get me money to launch my business, I'm going to work him until I get the check."

"And where are you planning to conduct business? I doubt Selena will change her mind anytime soon. Weren't you going to work in Ethan's basement?"

Britt's scowl deepened, as did the color of her eyes. They'd been a pretty shade of blue at the congressman's office. They had since darkened to the color of thunderheads—gray and purple, bruises in the pale oval of her face.

"Are you done? I'm ready to go," she said.

He pointed at her plate with his fork. "You haven't finished your burger."

"Splattered bodies ruined my appetite."

"I was only trying to explain where Selena's head is currently at."

"That's fair. I have issues, too."

"Such as?" Dakota maintained the slow savor of his meal. He wasn't going to let her rush him through the best food he'd put in his mouth since leaving Colorado.

"Such as none of your business. The sooner we can market our products, the sooner I'm going to be a happier woman."

"You were happy last night," Dakota reminded her.

Pink filled her face as if the sun rose in her body. "I was drunk."

"No, you weren't." He wouldn't have gotten into the car with her otherwise. "You never finished your drink."

"I could have been on my third or fourth."

"I followed you from Ethan's house. You didn't have time for more than one drink. Eat your lunch. You're too skinny."

She blinked as if she hadn't heard him correctly. "Skinny?"

"Thin. You could use more meat on your bones." He speared the last bit of his steak. "This was great. Thanks for bringing me."

The server interrupted. Britt requested a doggy bag.

At least the food wasn't going to waste.

Dakota paid the bill. He waited until they were outside before commandeering Britt's car keys. "You drank a beer. Better let me drive."

"No. You're not insured."

"I'm a professional driver."

"You don't know your way around."

"I have an exceptional sense of direction." He stood in front of the driver's door with his palm extended. "Unless you want to make a scene."

Her purse began singing an old Alan Jackson song about it being five o'clock somewhere. She pulled out her phone along with her keys. She wasn't gracious about handing them to him.

Dakota didn't need grace. He needed the keys.

She checked her phone and all color left her face. Her hand, her whole body wobbled.

Dakota caught her around the waist before she hit the ground.

Her unsteadiness was becoming a routine. He unlocked the car with his free hand and sat her in the passenger seat. "You should have finished your burger." He snatched the phone from her.

She lunged, as if she believed she could wrestle the phone from him.

He scanned the screen. The message read, *Nice apartment you have on North George.* The photo was of an orange-haired man wearing an orange prison jumpsuit.

Whoever he was, he was going to have to die.

Chapter 6

Britt's hands twitched so badly she'd never be able to drive. Instead of digging in her purse for her keys, she handed the bag to Dakota. Other than the photos Judd texted to her phone, she had nothing to hide.

Dakota hadn't lied about his sense of direction. As near as she could tell—not that she paid close attention—he didn't make one accidental detour between The Steak Out and her apartment.

"Do you want me to carry you upstairs?"

She blinked. They were at her place so soon? Seeing Judd again, even in a photograph, converted her brain to a swamp. "No." She wasn't some weakling. She could make the trek to her second floor flat. The problem was she didn't want to go inside. If Judd knew her address, anything could lurk in her rooms.

A flicker of gratitude for Dakota's presence was extinguished by horrible suspicion. She shrank from his touch.

"What's wrong, babe?"

She hated being called babe, sweetheart, or any other term of affection deleting her as a person. She latched on to her irritation to pull her out of her funk.

"Who are you? Really?"

He could be the reason she was suddenly getting snapshots of Judd on her phone. The timing was right.

"I'm Dakota Towne, a friend of Ethan's."

Right. From Colorado. And she'd recognized Ethan before being introduced to him. Ethan was real. Therefore Dakota was real. A bus driver.

Judd was making her crazy again.

The past twenty-four hours had bombarded her with too much. The debris of her life tumbled around her head, bounced off the bone of her skull, only to career in another direction.

She focused on Dakota. His face. The way his dark beard framed a mouth so talented, it deserved its own Internet following. Concern shaded his dark eyes. Why should he give a damn about her? She'd let him pick her up in a bar last night. A seedy bar. For all he knew, she was a skank.

She was scared. Terrified. She needed to trust someone. Staying alone in her apartment when Judd knew the address was impossible. He might be in prison, but someone on the outside had resurrected his presence in her life. Someone who could get to her.

"Are Ethan and Selena driving you crazy yet?" she asked.

"Their house is safe."

What a weird response. Except safe was good. "My roommate moved out today," she told him.

The brown of his eyes gleamed like bronze. "You're all alone?"

"Yes."

"And the guy in the prison suit found out your address?" She couldn't suppress her shudder.

"You should move into Ethan's house with me."

"Not a good idea." She'd roomed with Selena for four years in college. They might be best friends, but live with her again? No way. Selena was too persnickety.

"You want me to move in with you?"

She considered the idea.

"I'd feel better if you weren't alone, and we should get better acquainted."

He was speaking code for sex. The sex with him was good, not something she'd have to be drunk for or endure. If sex with him meant she wouldn't be alone, she'd fuck his brains out. No hardship for her. Sex wasn't an offer she made to just anyone. As in no one else. Ever. At least, not since Judd. He'd been so many lessons learned.

The past two days had sucked. The only good thing had been sex with Dakota.

THE APARTMENT BRITT RENTED resembled a tornado disaster site. She opened a door to reveal an empty room. She sighed. "How did Kathryn move her furniture out?"

Britt's bones still shivered beneath her muscles and flesh. Dakota doubted she was aware of the quaking. Whoever the guy in the text was, he'd shaken her badly. Dakota was grateful he was around to protect her.

Britt's bedroom door was open. Dakota's feet tangled in dry cleaning plastic on the floor. The bag wrapped around his boot and his ankle like a living creature. He batted the plastic into submission. The clothes she had worn before her meeting were strewn across the bed.

"Amuse yourself while I change." She tossed something at him.

A television remote. He placed the unit on her bedside table, atop her alarm clock.

She dropped the striped jacket where she stood. Dakota scooped the jacket from the floor and retrieved a hanger threatening to fall from the bed. The suit pants slid from her slender hips once she unzipped them. "I'll take those."

Britt tossed the trousers to him. "You are so weird."

"No, only neater than you are."

She undid the pearly buttons on the front of her shirt. "Don't start on me. I'm not in the mood."

The silky gray fabric puddled on top of her feet.

"Don't bother getting dressed," he told her, as he crossed to her closet to hang the suit.

"Oh. Some afternoon delight?" She waggled her eyebrows.

Dakota figured her flippancy was an attempt to mask her true emotions. The racing of her heart betrayed her. She needed to sleep. They both did.

Dakota shed his clothes, laying his dress shirt and blazer atop a chair heaped with a significant portion of Britt's wardrobe. His boots fell next to her bed. His best pair of jeans, along with his boxers and socks, joined the rest of his clothes on the chair.

Britt stretched out on the mattress in a silent invitation. The linens were tousled from their antics the previous evening.

Except he didn't want Britt to believe their relationship was based on fucking. Although sex sealed their mating, sex would be only one part of their life together.

"Roll onto your stomach." His voice snagged on the walls of his throat and emerged husky. He hoped she wouldn't misconstrue the sound as sexy. His erection was enough of an undermining of his noble intentions.

She took her time, moving slowly as if to tease him. *Ancient Ones,* he didn't need teasing. A cold shower, maybe, but not teasing.

Once she settled herself, he straddled her hips. He leaned forward and placed his hands on her nape.

Her entire body vibrated, the way maximum volume reverberated an audio speaker. The underlying humming wasn't arousal. Her lust for him broadcasted a unique radio frequency, loud, intrusive, and flattering. The negative vibe was different. Bone-deep, seething, throbbing, roiling at Britt's core.

Yes, he'd been aware of her disquiet the previous evening. Something else had happened—not him—to amp the activity. His guess would be the upsetting text message.

He ran his knuckles along her spine, taking the time to press into each indentation, as if pushing a button could eliminate her agitation. Her moans, muffled by her pillow, betrayed how much she enjoyed his ministrations.

After a couple of passes along her vertebrae, Dakota switched his focus to the rest of her back. He rubbed her shoulders, digging his thumbs into the tense muscles.

"That hurts," she murmured.

"It's a miracle you can move without hurting." Her whole frame was rigid. He understood sapiens didn't have the pliancy of structure a werewolf had, but she held herself too tightly. He'd need the patience of water dripping on a rock to remold her. "Try to relax."

"I'd rather—"

"No, you wouldn't." Yes, his erection was pressed against the small of her back, and yes, his cock behaved independently of him. Dakota refused to surrender to lust. He made the decisions. As his hands tired from the effort of rubbing away her tension, a soft snore disrupted his concentration.

Even in sleep she was strung as taut as a tightrope.

Maybe her brain was relaxing.

He eased off the bed, trod on a discarded shoe, and barely bit back a curse. Several minutes later, he located her cell phone in the purse she'd dropped on the floor near the front door. He refused to feel guilty for keeping her safe. He'd snoop, pry, steal, and if necessary, kill for her.

He found two photos of the orange-haired man, both from that day. He forwarded them to his number, then erased the transactions from her phone's memory.

"Did Toke say you could use Luke if you needed to?" Dakota asked Ethan. Dakota was still at Britt's apartment, calling Ethan while Britt showered. He stood in the kitchen. Dirty dishes cascaded across the counter and into one half of the double sink.

"Yeah," Ethan admitted.

Ethan loathed Luke Thibodaux. Ethan and Luke were roomies on Toke Lobo and the Pack's tours. Luke, who was part sapien, surfed the Internet for porn, something full- blooded lycans found repugnant as well as bewildering. Eventually Luke took his expertise to the FBI, who hired him to surf the net for sex sites involved in illegal activities. He was the one to uncover Congressman Bryant Peters' hobby of underage girls.

"I'm hesitant to use him," Ethan continued. "I still haven't accomplished my mission. Did you find out why Britt was at the congressman's office?"

"You gave her the idea. Or Selena did. Seed money to get Night Shift into production. Rebuilding is going to take capital. Doesn't Selena's original idea have more merit now?" Dakota twisted the faucet. A bottle of dish detergent sat on the counter. "Did you get in to see The Spare?"

"Nope." Ethan sounded glum.

Maybe Dakota would be better off approaching Luke directly. All he wanted was a facial recognition program run on the orange-haired prison inmate who was harassing Britt. No one could fault him for protecting his mate. Still, he was only a tau lobo.

"Have you told Britt yet?" Ethan shifted the topic from his own failures to Dakota's.

"Not yet." He squirted dish soap into the sink. "I want to get some berries into her first." Yet another challenge. So far, Britt had shown no inclination toward plant-based foods. He'd scoped out her refrigerator. He approved of her meat-heavy diet, though the incarnation frustrated him: prefabricated frozen meals, ready to pop into the microwave for quick consumption. Her pantry habits, along with a host of others, were going to have to change.

"Is anyone aware you've mated?"

"How long did you wait before telling your family?" Dakota countered.

"I told them before I marked her."

Ethan's father and grandfather had arrived on Ethan's new doorstep uninvited. Difficult not to tell them to their faces. Dakota had driven them from Colorado, so he was aware of the awkwardness. Besides, Ethan had waited to claim Selena.

Dakota shut off the faucet. Unless he put Ethan on speaker, something he did not want to do, he didn't have enough hands to wash dishes.

"Besides, Selena is one of us," Ethan reminded him. And therein lay the problem. Britt was not a shifter.

According to Selena, Britt was blissfully unaware such beings existed.

"Why do you need Luke?"

Dakota had hoped Ethan wouldn't inquire. He piled the dirtiest dishes in the hot, soapy water. At least they could soak.

"Research I can't do on my own." Dakota could barely use his smart phone. He didn't own a regular computer.

"Related to my mission?"

Maybe Dakota's imagination worked overtime because Ethan sounded anxious.

"Nope. Something else."

"You're not going to do something stupid such as run a background check on Britt, are you?"

"I'm not that stupid." He and Britt would get around to having the *getting-to-know-you* conversations. Sometimes mating happened spontaneously. Life unfolded as it was lived.

"Selena claims Britt has a temper," Ethan said.

"She'll adjust." Dakota was confident he could rein in his volatile mate.

"No, she won't." Britt strode into the kitchen. A robe the color of summer lightning was tightly belted at her waist, and a gray towel hid her long yellow hair. "What are you doing? Who are you talking to?"

"Cleaning up and talking to Ethan." Dakota resumed his task. "Hey, thanks for the dinner invitation. We'll be there at seven."

"What?" Ethan sputtered. "I didn't invite you to dinner. What—"

Dakota disconnected the call and studied his mate's reflection in the window above the sink.

"I'm not going to Ethan and Selena's for dinner." Britt narrowed her eyes and tapped her foot. "I have other plans."

"Such as?"

"Such as none of your business." She stared at the dishes soaking in the sink. "What are you doing?"

"We don't want vermin."

"I've never had a problem."

Time to change the subject. "I need to go to Ethan's to get my car and my stuff."

The breeze in her brain shifted direction.

"I'm reconsidering my invitation for you to move in," she said, then dithered for a moment before blurting, "Would you be willing to pay rent?"

WHAT HAD SHE BEEN drinking when she asked Dakota to move in?

Yes, Britt needed a roommate to help pay the rent. She did not need a man.

Take washing the dishes. Yeah, he volunteered today. Tomorrow he'd complain because more would be in the sink. He'd probably whine because bras hung to dry from the shower rod. And he would expect bedroom privileges, despite not taking advantage of her earlier willingness.

On the plus side, he'd given her one amazing massage. She hadn't slept as well in the middle of the day since she stopped attending church.

He scared her. He was going to change everything. She'd fought long and hard to get to her current place. She was content with her life. Dakota Towne wasn't a one-and-done, but a disruptive force. She wasn't Selena, who was mostly placid and stubborn. Britt's emotions were laid out for anyone to abuse. People were so shocked by her superficial presence, they assumed she was shallow. Her preference.

Dakota scoured a coffee mug. "Sure. I'll pay the rent."

"Not all," she negotiated. "Half."

"Okay. What's my half?"

She named a figure closer to two-thirds.

"Fine."

Fine. She was going to have to let him move in. One day she was going to learn to keep her mouth shut.

"What plans can't you break to have dinner with your supposed best friend?"

His tone was too casual, as if she hadn't clearly told him her plans were none of his business. "My alleged best friend is disrupting my dream because

she's too busy fucking her cute new husband."

Dakota didn't flinch at her language. Maybe he blinked; his back was to her as he continued washing dishes. "You think Ethan is cute?"

"He's okay." He wasn't as fine as Dakota. She didn't want him aware of how attractive she found him. Men used such weaknesses against a girl.

"Define okay."

"He's...okay. What difference does my opinion make? He's married to Selena."

"Are you jealous?"

"No! Emphatically no." Where had Dakota gotten such a crazy idea? "I'm not into monogamy."

"What does monogamy have to do with your attraction to Ethan? Do you want to share him with Selena?"

Wait a minute. Was Dakota jealous? "Who said I was attracted to Ethan? He's too controlling." An understatement.

"Some females might be impressed because he's in a band."

As opposed to driving the bus for the same band. Okay. Dakota was insecure.

"I don't care for competition. When I'm with a guy, I want him focusing on me, not on who's next on his list."

"Not too focused." His tone was bland.

She wished she could see his face.

"I want him in the moment," she clarified. "Not planning the future."

Dakota turned, slowly, as if making her wait for something stupendous. "I plan for our future when I'm with you. You are my future."

Stalker talk. Stalker talk scared her. "That does it. You're gone."

Her bones rattled inside her skin as if they were being assaulted by an Alberta clipper. Clenching her jaw kept her teeth from chattering.

"We can't control facts or fate." He sounded calm and reasonable. "Mating is one of them."

Mating? What in blue blazes was he talking about? "Get. Out. Of. My. Apartment." She wanted to call 9-1-1,

except she couldn't remember where she'd left her cell phone. She backed away from the kitchen. From Dakota.

"You're going to make me walk to Ethan's?" He returned to the sink.

"You jogged to the bar last night. I live a lot closer to Ethan than he does to Holsters."

"I'll feel funny if I show up alone. Ethan invited both of us."

I'm not going to let him guilt me. "You shouldn't have accepted without consulting me. We are not a couple. We are not roommates. You are going to get out of my kitchen, out of my apartment, and out of my life."

"I can't." He used the spray nozzle to rinse the dishes he'd piled in the second sink. "I'll tell you why at Ethan's tonight."

She bolted. Her phone was in her purse, on the floor inside the front door. If she was dressed, she would have fled the apartment.

Deju vu, sickening and too familiar, created an undertow that threatened to suck her into a whirlpool from which she'd never escape.

Dakota followed her, drying his hands on a dishtowel. "Why don't you get dressed?" he suggested. "We'll head to Ethan's where I'll explain some things to you."

"I don't need any explanations from you." She hated the hysteria edging her voice.

"Yeah. You do. Explaining my...nature to you will be easier with Ethan and Selena to back me."

Selena was a traitor. She'd drunk deeply of whatever fruit punch Ethan was serving.

Britt fumbled in her bag, wishing for once she was one of those too-organized people who owned compartmented purses—a place for everything and everything in place. Her fingers closed around the hard rubber case. "I'm calling the cops," she said, as she drew the phone from the bag. "Don't say I didn't warn you."

He took a step back. Held up his hands. "Okay. I get the message. I scared you."

"Get out."

"You're blocking the door."

How could he sound so reasonable?

Right. She sidled to her left.

Dakota opened the door. "See you later." He hung the dishtowel on the knob.

The door closed quietly behind him.

Britt's legs barely supported her as she stumbled to the door. She slid the chain into place. Made sure the lock was engaged. Neither flimsy barrier would stop anyone determined to get in.

For a crazy, insane moment, she considered calling him back and offering to drive him to Ethan's house. Self- destructive behavior.

There was only one solution when this kind of mood hit her.

Chapter 7

Dakota debated his next move. He could jog to Ethan's house and retrieve his SUV and the duffel containing his meager belongings, or he could wait to see what Britt was going to do next. The female's brain was as chaotic as her apartment.

If he understood his mate at all, she'd panicked. His fault.

He settled in the shadows. Within ten minutes, she appeared on her porch. The peachy light of the late afternoon sun stained her as she emerged from the house. She glowed. He recognized how she was dressed and what her clothes meant. Jeans so tight only a miracle kept the seams from splitting. She'd donned a pair of dark blue cowboy boots, adding a couple of inches to her height. The glittery fabric of her tank top clung to her breasts. *Scat.* She wasn't wearing a bra. Maybe he wasn't a breast man, but she shouldn't be flaunting her goodies to anyone except him. A pale purple vest finished the outfit. She carried a gray cowboy hat in her hand.

Britt planned to hookup.

Selena had told him about Holsters, Britt's usual stomping grounds. He was more than familiar with the type of venue. Toke Lobo and the Pack spent years bouncing from one version to another.

Fortunately, the kind of action Britt believed she wanted didn't start for hours yet.

He'd have to follow her.

BRITT CLIMBED INTO HER car and locked all the doors. If nothing else, Dakota had reminded her she wasn't always careful enough. She couldn't stay another minute in the apartment. Maybe she'd drive to Ash Street and try to talk some sense into Selena.

Maybe check if Dakota arrived at Ethan's safely.

No. She didn't care if Dakota was safe or not.

Except the action at Holsters—or anywhere else— wouldn't begin for hours yet. She needed to dance. She needed to fuck someone else so she could forget Dakota.

She pulled her cell phone from her bag. Maybe she could find someone else to waste time with until the night got ready for her. Scrolling through her contacts list was pitiful. Selena. Other women with whom she and Selena experimented creating bath bombs. She wasn't especially friendly with anyone. No former co-workers.

Her father's phone number mocked her. She kept the number in her phone as an early warning system in case he tried to contact her. In case Bart or Susie needed her.

Judd Byrne. How in the name of anything holy did Judd's name get in her contacts? At least no number accompanied his name. Was Mercury in retro or something?

She deleted the entry.

She jammed the car key into the ignition and twisted. The engine coughed to life. Judd was why she'd invited Dakota to live with her. How had she forgotten? Judd had her cell phone number. He had her address.

Maybe she could catch Dakota as she drove to Ethan's house. She could apologize. He was a fine specimen of a man. Strong. Lots of muscles. Nice muscles. Smart, too. Being smarter than Judd wouldn't take much, but Judd had a criminal savvy, a street-smart frame of reference prison probably honed into a murderous weapon.

She put the car in gear. Her foot hit the gas pedal too enthusiastically, and her car jerked away from the curb.

Rubber tires shrieked on asphalt. A blaring horn sent her foot to the brake pedal.

"Are you okay?"

She shook her head to resettle her brain. Dakota pounded on the window as if to get her attention. When she didn't respond, his fist smashed through the safety glass. The window spiderwebbed around the hole, breaking into small, precise cubes, some of which fell into the car. On her.

"What are you doing?" she shrieked, as he unlocked her door. She flung pebbles of broken glass at him. "Get away from me!"

"Are you crazy or stupid?" a strange male voice shouted. "You should check before you pull into traffic."

"Are you okay?" Dakota repeated, his voice hoarse. He seized the door handle. Metal screamed as he ripped the door off its hinges.

She scooped another fistful of broken safety glass from her lap and hurled it at him, then kicked out. Her booted toes met nothing but air. Where the fuck was her phone? "I'm calling the cops! You're a crazy man!"

"You could have been t-boned by a pickup." Dakota tore the seatbelt from its moorings.

"Don't touch me." She kicked again and found his shin. He didn't even wince, but pain shot up her foot.

"Is she okay?" the strange male voice asked.

"Yes," Dakota replied, as he lifted Britt from the car, completely unhindered by her struggles. "You were able to keep from hitting her. Good driving."

Good driving? The guy nearly caused an accident and Dakota was dismissing him with compliments?

She punched his shoulder. "Put me down, you jerk!"

"Do we need the cops?"

"No accident, so no need for a report." Dakota tossed her over his shoulder and smacked her ass. "Behave."

Her blood rushed to her head, making her dizzy and sick. It would serve him right if she barfed on him.

"Shit. You did a number on her car."

"Yeah. She'll recover."

"No, she won't." Britt bit Dakota's waist. He yelped.

"Okay," the stranger said. "You got this?"

"It's under control," Dakota replied.

The stranger laughed. "Yeah. Good luck with that."

She glimpsed the back of a guy, wearing jeans and a white T-shirt, scurrying to a black pickup sprawled diagonally in the street. He gunned his engine as Dakota set her on her feet.

"Behave," he warned her again.

Instead of launching herself at him and clawing out his eyes—her first instinct—she swung around to examine the damage to her car. Broken glass, jagged metal edges where the door belonged, and a flapping seatbelt. Yeah. Dakota was strong. Scary strong.

Adrenaline. Fear could cause a rush of adrenaline, gifting incredible strength to the person whose glands responded.

Dakota had been afraid for her.

Something warm and squishy snuggled deep in her gut, offsetting the sudden stinging in her hands and the thudding pain the rush of blood rage trapped in her skull. The pickup drove away, leaving Britt alone with Dakota. Now she could kill him without witnesses.

"Are you out of your mind?" Britt turned on him. The roaring in her ears deafened her. As soon as she located her phone, she was calling the cops. No more threats. Action. "Look what you did to my car!"

He might as well have crushed beer cans against his forehead.

She tried to pummel his chest, but he grabbed her wrists. "You're bleeding."

He gripped her too tightly to wrench free. She hated him. Truly hated him. Her week had already gone to shit and now this.

"You're a crazy stalker." She panted as she struggled.

He studied her palms. "You must have cut yourself on the safety glass when you threw it at me. A couple of nicks. Not as serious as it could have been had he hit you. You'd have a lot more damage to you and your car, and you would have been at fault for damage to his truck, too."

Why was he being so damn reasonable?

He released her wrists. She wiped her palms on his shirt, smearing her blood down the sleeves.

"He stopped. No accident. You did all the damage," she pointed out. In her outdoor voice. Her very outdoor voice. "What were you doing hanging around? Stalking me? I am calling the police."

The near accident had spilled the contents of her bag, including her phone, to the floor of the car.

"Do you want to get them involved? You could get ticketed for reckless endangerment."

She climbed into the driver's side to gather the contents of her bag. "Not hardly. There wasn't a wreck."

"Cute," he said.

She leaned across the console, presenting her back to him, bending as she stretched to snag her wallet.

"You really shouldn't pose with your butt hanging out." His voice was throaty.

She peered at him over her shoulder. He stood too close to the gaping hole in the side of her VW Bug, staring at her. Not her eyes. Lower. His Adam's apple bobbed several times as he swallowed. His chest rose unevenly, too.

"Especially in those jeans." He curled his fingers. Did he want to spank her bottom again?

As if she'd ever let him get that close to her again. *Ha*!

She resumed collecting the strewn contents of her purse without answering him. Her brain was still shaken from being tossed over Dakota's shoulder. Her conscience screamed she'd scared him, so he'd overreacted. Fortunately, she'd had lots of practice ignoring her conscience. The bitch.

Equally as unhelpful was the worry. How in the name of all that was unholy was she going to get her car fixed? Without personal transportation, employment options plummeted.

What she needed was to go dancing, work off the explosion she could feel building inside her. If she didn't release some pressure soon, the result would not be pretty.

She also needed a new place to dance. New partners. The problem was the lack of country music bars in Warwick. She couldn't stand any other genre of music. Not in the mood she was in. She needed to work off frustration, and that meant dancing. Country was the only music worth dancing to.

"Hi, Ethan?"

What was Dakota doing? She sat up, brushed a few strands of hair off her sweaty cheek, and narrowed her eyes at Dakota.

He'd placed a few feet between her car and his body. He was on his cell phone, still watching her. "Britt had a mishap with her car."

"You trashed my car!" Britt shouted.

"Can you and Selena bring my SUV to Britt's place?" He listened for a moment while Britt tried to ignore him.

She restarted the engine and pulled the car as tight to the curb as she could. The dangling door screeched as the steel scraped across the pavement. The tang of hot metal filled the air.

She was going to have to call her insurance company. Explaining the damage would be a challenge. *A continuation of the shit my life has become.* She killed the motor. Too bad insurance policies never covered Mercury-in-retro or shitstorms.

"I'm aware Selena can't leave the house after dark, but it's still daylight, and Britt's apartment is only a few miles."

Ethan was keeping Selena a prisoner?

DAKOTA WASN'T SURE HOW he was going to manage to keep Britt from running upstairs and barricading herself in her apartment. All he needed was ten minutes for Ethan to arrive with his SUV. Otherwise, anything the neighbors might see could be misconstrued as an abduction.

Mating was a lot harder than Dakota anticipated. If Britt was lycan, he could avoid accusations of stalking and being labeled a kidnapper.

The only way to keep her on the street until Ethan arrived was to block her exit from her car. She finished gathering the contents of her spilled purse. He closed the gap.

"Get out of my way." The blue of her eyes darkened to gray.

"I'm making sure you're okay. Maybe you bumped your head when you slammed the brakes," he improvised. "Do I see a lump on your forehead?"

She cringed and inched away from him.

She was too tall to scoot across the console and exit the passenger door. "All these years," she muttered, "and I finally pick up a psychopath."

"I'm not a psychopath." The label hurt. Maybe he wasn't something spectacular like Ethan or Toke Lobo, but he wasn't a nut job, either.

"Okay, a sociopath." The accusation whipped out of her mouth.

His fraying temper snapped another thread. He managed to hold himself together. "No. I told you what I am. You didn't believe me."

Her lower lip wobbled.

"We're going to be okay, Britt." The words echoed hollowly as he spoke them.

"I'll bet Ted Bundy said the same thing to his victims."

Okay. She didn't need to insult him. He reminded his pride she didn't comprehend their fundamental differences. She would need time to accept she was the mate of a werewolf. He'd experienced the varied reactions of several sapien females mated to males. Some were public embarrassments. Others were private.

He wanted private. No problem with Ethan and Selena witnessing the disclosure. He planned to reveal himself as soon as they were safely ensconced at Ethan's.

Ethan's bright red truck pulled to the curb behind her Beetle. He was alone.

"Where's Selena and my SUV?" were the first words out of Dakota's mouth.

"I told you. I don't want her leaving the house. Not until the circumstances change."

"You're keeping her prisoner," Britt muttered.

"No, he isn't." Dakota knew he wasn't supposed to hear Britt's comment. "He's keeping her safe."

Chapter 8

Dakota's steady gaze remained on Britt. She wondered if he was hypnotizing her. Folklore claimed a hypnotized subject couldn't be made to do anything against her will, but Britt had doubts as she climbed into the cab of Ethan's red truck.

"Dakota will explain," Selena had assured her on the phone. "You're safe. You've never been safer."

"Yes, I will tell her at your house," Dakota repeated when Britt handed Ethan's phone to him.

Now he stared at Britt as Ethan maneuvered his way toward Ash Street and stopped in front of the house. Dakota exited the truck and offered his hand to her. Britt hesitated before accepting his assistance. Each time he touched her, weird stuff happened in her body. After several heartbeats, she gave him her fingers. He helped her from the truck cab. Britt found Selena sliding a baking pan into the oven.

"What are you making?"

"A hot dish. Helga shared her favorite recipe."

Britt was familiar with hot dishes. Dinner out when she was a kid meant going to a covered dish supper at church, a.k.a. hot dish central. "You're kidding. The woman across the street in the sparkling purple house?"

"She's teaching me to cook," Selena admitted, as she set the timer on the microwave. "Ethan doesn't care for fish. I'm not doing very well. Helga says when a recipe calls for a clove of garlic, one should use three and add a flake of dried red pepper. What does that mean?"

Britt didn't blame Ethan. Even a hot dish was preferable to a steady diet of fish.

"I know less than you about cooking. What's going on?" she asked Selena.

"Dakota needs to explain something to you. Want something to drink?"

Whatever beverage Selena served would be nonalcoholic.

Britt could have used a hurricane. "Water is good."

Selena pulled a glass from the cupboard and ran the faucet.

"How well do you know Dakota?" Britt studied the nicks on her palms. She should probably clean them.

Selena filled the glass. "Well enough, I guess." She shut off the water.

"Want to explain?" Britt took the proffered glass from Selina but didn't drink. The cool glass soothed her stinging palms.

Selina dried her hands on the thighs of her jeans. "You always told me I was weird back in college."

"You *were* weird. As far as I can tell, you still are."

"My culture isn't the same as yours."

"Hey, I'm from a don't-drink-dance-or-fuck world myself."

Selena's smile was tight. "Not the same. I could never rebel to the extent you did. Ethan is from the same culture. That's why we...why we're together."

"Dakota is from the same culture?"

"Yes."

Dakota interrupted them. A battered black duffel swung from his shoulder. His nose wrinkled. "What do I smell?"

"A hot dish," Selena replied. "I'm learning to cook."

"Great. I'm going to toss my bag into my SUV. I'll be right back."

"I changed the sheets on the bed in the guest room," Selena said. "You two could stay here tonight."

"Britt's roommate moved out, so I'm moving in with her." Dakota's expression dared Britt to contradict him.

"Why don't you wait?" Selena suggested.

"Britt is going out tonight," Britt announced. "I'll have to call Uber because some guy tried to demolish my car, but I'm not staying in, doing the domesticated couples boogie." The glance Dakota and Selena exchanged bothered Britt. She swallowed the—what, foreboding? Ridiculous.

She'd known Selena for years.

Dakota left the kitchen.

"What's going on?" Britt asked.

"Dakota needs to tell you something," was all she could get out of Selena. "Why don't you go with him?"

"I'm going out," Britt repeated. "Dancing. Hooking up with someone who's not a crazy stalker."

"I need to see you for a few minutes before you go," Dakota called from somewhere deeper in the house.

"Give him a few minutes," Selena advised. "Life will be easier after Dakota explains."

"Not in this lifetime." Dakota was going to corrupt her into the same mindless drone Selena had become since Ethan arrived. Some kind of Colorado kink. While Britt wasn't averse to kink, brainwashing wasn't on her list of activities requiring a safe word. "I'm history."

Except Ethan blocked the door. "Not until Dakota talks to you. Five minutes. You can leave after you listen to what he has to say."

Britt didn't care for the expressions on their faces. Solemn. Expectant. Weirdness practically shimmered in the air. Dakota was a worse mess than Judd.

They're not going to let me leave. Ever.

She headed toward Dakota's voice, her chin raised and shoulders squared. *Battle stations.*

"Second door on the left," Selena called after her.

Britt fumbled in her purse as she strode toward the room where Dakota waited. Her fingers wrapped around the smooth metal can of pepper spray. The top snapped off with an audible click. She poised her finger above the spray button and opened the door to find Dakota sitting on the edge of the bed, a sheet draped across his lap. His clothing formed a lump in the center of the mattress. His boots stood on the floor next to the bedside table.

"Oh, no. Not again." She tried to leave but someone had closed the door. The knob wouldn't budge.

"Wait." Dakota's voice sounded different. Hoarser. He tossed aside the sheet and stood.

He was one fine man. Everywhere.

The room grew warm. Pressure built in her head until she thought her sinuses would explode. Everything in the room shimmered. Dakota himself wavered, as if the growing heat was deconstructing him. Her ears popped with the continuing barometric weirdness.

She swallowed. Hard. The compression in her head didn't equalize. Her vision clouded. Sound should have punctuated what she was seeing. The grinding of bones, cracks and pops of muscles and tendons rearranging themselves. And the heat. The heat should have generated the stink of sweat, of singed hair and burning flesh. Should have scorched her lungs as she continued, miraculously, to breathe. But the metamorphosis was silent. Odorless.

Dakota, the very fine masculine specimen vanished, leaving in his place...something with four legs. A tail. Black fur. Deep brown eyes.

A beast. A wolf.

Britt slid to the floor, the solid, wonderful floor; her back pressed against the unyielding door, unable to speak. Unable to process what her eyes had seen. The heat faded. The pressure lessened, quickly returning to normal.

The wolf stared at her with the same brooding quality she'd sensed from Dakota only twenty-four hours earlier at Holsters.

She tried to swallow again, except her mouth was dry. Arid. Her saliva had evaporated in the heat of what she'd seen.

Her brain swirled with her father's voice thundering about wolves in sheep's clothing, roaring lions, and devious demons. All the lore she'd rejected, when she settled on science as her religion, sat on its haunches before her. The creature with whom she'd shared her bed.

Her head hurt. Maybe Selina had slipped something in the water. Except Britt hadn't drunk from the glass. All she'd done was enter a room where naked Dakota waited for her.

The heat, the pressure, the messed-up vision returned, but the full sensory hallucination didn't last as long the second time.

Naked Dakota was back.

He sauntered to her side and squatted next to her. "Britt?"

She huddled away from him. She would have crept further away, except his...transformation sapped her strength. The can of pepper spray fell from her numb fingers and rolled beneath the bed.

"I told you," he murmured. "I'm a werewolf."

She vaguely recalled a joking response to her accusation of him being a vampire.

"Another werewolf fact for you," Dakota added in a low voice, "we're monogamous. The only female a male lycan can be with is his life mate. I've been going crazy, smelling your presence here for weeks."

Crazy. She seized on the word.

"You *are* crazy." Her voice was slightly more than a croak.

He continued as if she hadn't spoken. "Selena and Ethan are also lycans. Werewolves."

Britt shook her head. Impossible. She'd lived with Selena for four long college years. Yeah, Selena was weird, but she was human weird. Britt would have noticed anything odd about her.

Odd like never going out drinking.

Odd like subsisting on raw fish.

Odd like never dating. Not only a celibate life, but she never once had gone out with a guy, one on one.

None of which made Selena a werewolf.

"In sapien terms, you're my wife."

"No!" Britt scrambled to her feet.

Dakota stood. "Yeah. We're mated. In lycan culture, I'm head of our household. Lucky for you I'm not in the least alpha."

"No." Maybe if she denied his words often enough, Dakota's fantasy would go away. Maybe he would go away. Back to Colorado. Back to anywhere not near her.

Dakota stretched his arm in her direction, his palm open as if to caress her cheek.

She ducked away from the touch. Noticed again he was naked. "Ulvskog means wolf wood," she babbled. "Selena is from Ulvskog."

"Is that what the name means? Makes sense. Her pack—"

"Stop." She hated the betraying vibrato in her voice.

"Welcome to your new reality. I can't stop."

"Werewolves do not exist." *There.* She found her voice. The voice of her god science, who alternated between sounding like Bill Nye and Neil deGrasse Tyson.

"I'm standing next to you," Dakota replied. "Should I shift again?"

"No!" She couldn't bear to have her senses assaulted by his trickery again.

"We're not the first mixed mating." Dakota's tone was somewhere between a singsong and a drone. "Tokarz—Toke Lobo to you—is mated to a sapien."

"Toke Lobo is not a werewolf!" Britt shouted. Except Toke Lobo and the Pack sounded suspiciously animalistic. Oh, the coincidences were too much. Dakota had taken random facts and woven them together in a tale to drive her mad.

Dakota went on to name every member of the band whose greatest hit to date was "Full Moon Lady," and the genus of their spouses.

"Ethan is the only one of us with a lycan mate. Mixed matings are becoming more common. Luke's grandfather was busted to omega for mating with a sapien. Tokarz eventually reversed his grandfather's ruling." Dakota...chuckled. He actually chuckled after accusing her favorite band of being beasts born of Satan.

No. The label was what her delusional, close-minded father would call them.

Science meant being receptive to new theories. She had chosen open-mindedness over religion.

My life is no longer random.

Chapter 9

"Where's my say?" Britt's voice warbled.

"You don't have one." Dakota was blunt. He had to be.

"Wrong. My life. I make the decisions. I never decided to . . . be monogamous with a werewolf."

Dakota kept his eyes on Britt. The quiet, her stillness, was alien to the woman she'd been to date. "You must have questions. Comments."

He remembered Delilah's shrieks at Tokarz once he'd revealed his dual nature and tried to anticipate Britt's questions. "No, you will not change into a werewolf. Silver bullets aren't deadlier than any other type. Garlic is a stinking plant sapiens use too much of in their food, not a werewolf repellent. Moviemakers and storytellers invented myths to thrill people."

She didn't speak. Her eyes were wide, fixed on him with wary intensity.

"Our offspring will be half homo sapien and half homo lupus. When adolescence sets in—the time when lycans attain the ability to shift—our offspring will shift only on the full moon."

She might have shuddered. Too much, he supposed he could call it *data*, coming off her scrambled his senses. He couldn't process everything. And her stillness; the awful calm...

"Plenty of sapien females live in Loup Garou. You won't be lonely."

"Damn right I won't." She produced a lycan-worthy snarl. Her leap for the open window caught him off-guard.

The screen shredded as Britt lunged out the window.

"Scat," he muttered as he followed her. If she cut herself on the mesh, the vampires at the end of the block might react like sharks when they scented her blood. He needed to stop her.

"Britt!" Selena screamed from the back porch. "Don't!"

Grateful for Selena's help, Dakota shifted, to better defend the females against the menace lurking beyond the perimeter of Ethan's property.

The only problem with his strategy was how Britt might react if he tackled her while in wolf form. She needed to get used to the idea a big bad wolf was a permanent part of her life.

He caught her as she attempted to breach the backyard hedge. Poor choice of escape route. Ethan's hawthorn hedge was part of his security system. Long, spiky barbs caught at Britt's clothes. Her skin.

Dakota tried to place his body between hers and the shrubbery. He was only partly successful.

Sharp thorns pierced his pelt like teeth tearing into his fur and flesh. He focused on Britt, protecting her from the fangs of both hawthorn and vampires.

Limbs tangled—Britt's, Dakota's, the bushes. She whimpered as she struggled to free herself. He needed to choose between shifting again to reassure her or using his wolf form as a barrier. He opted to remain wolf for the moment.

"Let's get you up," Ethan said.

Britt's scent so distracted Dakota, he'd missed Ethan's approach. Not good. What if instead of Ethan, the newcomer had been a vampire? Ethan and Selena could swear their house was charmed against vamps and other evil creatures all they wanted. Vampires staying at the ends of the block didn't mean scat.

Ethan helped Britt stand.

"You said I could leave." Britt's voice cracked.

"I did," Ethan admitted.

Why? Dakota wanted to shout.

"I meant using the front door," Ethan said, as if searching for an out. "The hedges are to keep the vampires at bay. Breeching them isn't easy."

"*Vampires?*" Britt screeched. "There is no such thing!"

The starkness of the silence immediately following her outburst was broken by snickers drifting on the air from the corners of Ash, Oak, and Hawthorn Streets.

The vampires are mocking my mate. Dakota wanted to rip a few dead hearts from their corpses.

Britt stomped toward the house, leaving a vapor trail of blood scent in her wake. What if the aroma lured the vampires past their self-imposed barrier? Dakota didn't trust Ethan's mutterings about a sacred triad of trees forming a magical fairy ring. Maybe Ethan was willing to trust his mate's safety to myth; Dakota was not.

Britt limped as Ethan escorted her to the house. Dakota should be the one offering support, except he wasn't prepared to shift to human again. Shifting consumed a lot of energy. He wanted to make sure human form was the safest. He wasn't taking any chances with Britt's safety. Ignoring his own injuries—those thorns *hurt*—he patrolled the perimeter of Ethan's enclosed yard. Satisfied the space was secure, he bounded into the house, intending to check the front sidewalk and empty lot next door.

Ethan stopped him in the entry. "I've checked the front. See to your mate."

Moments later, human-shaped again and wearing sweatpants, Dakota joined Britt and Selena in the basement where the females planned to manufacture their products.

Britt perched on one of the work tables. Selena was treating the myriad of cuts and scrapes on his mate's face, hands, and arms. Blood stained her shirt.

Dakota wanted to howl. The annoying itch of healing irritated his wounds. Britt needed additional help. Her injuries were his fault. He should have explained his true nature in a gentler manner. He shouldn't have tackled her in the hawthorn hedge.

"I'm sorry," he whispered.

Britt averted her face to stare at the giant whiteboard hanging on the opposite wall, waiting for Night Shift, but not before he witnessed her wince as Selena applied one of her herbal concoctions to a nasty gash.

"What are you using?" he asked, as if whatever Selena replied would make sense to him.

"Comfrey. It speeds healing."

"Lucky you had some." Lycans wouldn't need such an herb.

"Not much. I was experimenting with a night creme."

"Human testing," Britt muttered.

"Not a test. The stuff works," Selena retorted.

"Then why isn't comfrey part of the Night Shift line?"

"I TOLD YOU." SELENA was less than gentle as she daubed her potion on another abrasion on Britt's arm. "My grandfather died. Night Shift was supposed to help support him and my hometown."

"Dakota told me your grandfather was murdered." The liquid stung.

Selena stopped her ministrations to glare at Dakota.

Britt planned to ignore the lying man for the rest of her life.

"Why hasn't the story been in the news?" she pressed Selena. Murder was always the top story. A journalist one- and-done once told her *if it bleeds, it leads.*

"Werewolf murders aren't news. Genocide is a nasty secret. The authorities don't investigate." Selena's hands were unsteady as she set the bottle containing her tincture on the table next to Britt. "No one investigates. No one cares."

"You are not a werewolf. I lived with you for four years. I would have known if I was sharing a bathroom with an animal."

"Werewolves aren't animals. We're homo lupus, as opposed to you, a homo sapien. We're housebroken, too."

"You never tried to kill me in my sleep." The argument was a weak one. Her head still reeled from Dakota's magic show.

"We don't kill people in their sleep. If we kill people at all, they deserve death, and we want them aware of exactly why they're having their throats ripped out. If we're feeling magnanimous, we let them pray for forgiveness from their god before we pounce. By the gods of our elders, we are not vampires who kill for blood or sport."

"Vampires don't exist."

"Tell the creatures at both ends of the block," Dakota interjected, "not us."

Ignore him. If I ignore him long enough, strong enough, he will go away. I need him to go away.

"Tell the vampires who assaulted me," Selena said. "Of course, I destroyed the second one, so he'd be hard to reach. Maybe it was the same one who attacked me the first time."

Britt wanted to run. Again. Except Dakota was too fast for her. She was a prisoner in Ethan's house. She had no doubt if she tried to leave by the front door, Ethan or Selena would find an excuse to detain her.

She should try anyway.

She hopped off the table. "I'm going to call Uber. I'm going home."

She couldn't go hunting for a new one-and-done in ruined clothes. The prickers on the hedge had done a number on her shirt. Her favorite sparkling navy blue tank top was in tatters, and her lavender vest was smeared with grass stains. The seams of her jeans might have split. Her purse was still in the bedroom where Dakota...exposed himself. She needed her phone, her keys, her wallet. Maybe her pepper spray.

She merely needed to climb the stairs, find the bedroom where Dakota tricked her, gather her belongings, and leave by the front door. Simple.

Except she hurt. Physically. When the dog—it couldn't be a wolf, couldn't be Dakota—brought her down, she'd landed awkwardly. Any landing would have been awkward.

He tried to cushion your fall.

Ridiculous. The entire situation was beyond ridiculous.

She sensed Selena and Dakota trailing her as she mounted the stairs. The handrail was sturdy. No wobble. Good, since her legs were unsteady.

She had no problem finding the bedroom where she'd left her purse. She'd be damned if she'd crawl under the bed to retrieve the pepper spray. She hurt too much. Even scooping her bag from the floor required energy she could barely spare.

She checked her phone. No missed calls. One text message.

See you soon. We have unfinished business.

The phone fell from her fingers. Her shaking fingers.

Judd. Judd was coming for her.

DAKOTA HATED BRITT'S CONTINUED passivity. Her behavior was out of character. The unnatural calm made him uneasy. "Should I check on her?"

"Give her time," Selena advised. "I would imagine learning about the reality of werewolves and vampires rocked her foundations."

Sixty more seconds ticked by.

"I should check on her. What if she jumped out the window again?"

"We would have heard her."

"I don't hear anything." Except her heart. He would always hear her heart. The muscle worked overtime, fueled by a whiff of fear. Maybe mating fever sharpened his senses, but her heart thudded more heavily than usual.

Something was wrong.

"I'm going to check on her."

"Dakota, she needs space."

He ignored Selena and hurried to the bedroom, where Britt hid behind a closed door. He knocked. "Britt?"

No response. He counted to two before opening the door. She sat on the edge of the mattress, her face so pale he could see the blue-purple trails of her veins beneath her skin.

She stared at her feet, her beautiful eyes unblinking. Her chest hitched, as if breathing were a chore.

"Britt?" He approached the bed. His foot sent something skittering across the floor.

Her lack of reaction escalated his concern to fear.

He perched next to her and lifted her hand from her lap. Icicle fingers. Her lips, her whole body shivered.

Maybe she was going into shock. "Let's get you beneath the covers." He wished Parker was around. Parker might be a werewolf EMT, but some conditions were universal.

Her body was stiff; breakable if he manhandled her.

Brittle. He tucked a blanket around her.

He longed to curl next to her and share his body heat. Every one of his instincts howled against his plan. Until she accepted the reality of him, he was going to have to quash his mating urges. He'd marked her. For the time being, claiming her had to suffice.

The familiar music of Britt's ring tone shattered the stillness.

Dakota followed the sound across the room, to where her phone rested against the wall. He picked up the phone and checked the screen. Another text message, from the same orange-haired man. An ominous message.

He didn't want to leave her alone, but he needed to text the photo to Luke for facial recognition information.

He forwarded the latest photo to his phone and again erased the transaction from hers.

He padded across the room, opened the door, and softly called for Selena. "Hey. Can you lend Britt something to wear?"

"Sure."

"And can you sit with her while I take care of a couple errands?" He didn't want to spill Britt's secrets, even to her best friend.

He returned to the basement, seeking privacy for his call to Luke.

"How are Abby and the twins?" he asked, when Luke answered.

"Fine. Did you call to check on my family?"

"Nope," Dakota admitted. "Can you run facial recognition on a text if I send the photo to you?"

"Does your request have anything to do with Ethan's mission? If so, why are you involved?"

"My mate has a problem."

"You found your mate in Minnesota, too?" Luke's amusement annoyed Dakota.

"Yeah." Dakota tamped his temper. He wasn't going hostile on someone from whom he needed a favor.

"And you don't recognize her?" The hint of sarcasm relaxed Dakota. Luke was giving him guy scat.

"Something like that," Dakota agreed. Luke wouldn't get into trouble for doing something wrong when Dakota left him in the dark.

"Depends on the photo."

"My guess is the picture is a selfie taken with a cell phone. I have more than one."

"Send them along."

"How long will it take?"

"Depends," Luke repeated.

"The person in the photo," Dakota said, "might be in prison, except how would an inmate get his hands on a cell phone to send texts?"

Yeah. He felt stupid. He never should have shared his ideas.

"If prisoners can get drugs, why not a cell phone?"

Good point. "Okay, I'm going to disconnect and forward the pictures to you. Oh, and Luke?"

"Yeah?"

"Can we keep my request between us?"

GET AWAY. I HAVE to get away.

Britt huddled into the flannel shirt Selena placed on the bed next to her. Her body heat would warm the garment soon enough. In the meantime, she clutched the comforter closer. Her brain was trapped in a centrifuge, her thoughts whirling and separating into a gooey mess. She needed to get away. Hide. Judd was coming.

The stinging of her cuts and scrapes increased.

"Did Dakota leave?" she asked Selena, who hovered.

"He's taking care of some business." Selena closed the window. "How are you?"

Britt lifted her chin. "Dazed. Pissed." *Terrified.*

As much as the whole werewolf nonsense upended her, the idea of Judd coming for her was worse. Dakota was a delusion; Judd was real.

Judd knew her address. Judd was getting out of prison.

Maybe being fired from her job was a blessing. He wouldn't be able to track her through employment.

Dakota might exhibit stalker behavior, but he hadn't hurt her. He was crazy, yeah, but not sociopathic, despite her flinging the word at him. The label didn't stick.

Focus on saving your own hide, not Dakota's derangement.

"Time to face facts." Selena perched on the end of the bed.

"I'm not in the mood for fantasy hour," Britt retorted. "I've got other stuff on my mind besides your husband's friend's fetish."

"Being homo lupus isn't any more a fetish than being homo sapien," Selena snapped. "I don't have time to coddle you into understanding or believing."

"Coddle me?" Britt was offended by the idea. "I don't need coddling."

"Yeah, you do, and Dakota is going to do his best to pamper you. You need to be aware of a couple realities he won't tell you."

"His drug use?"

"If you weren't a puny sapien brat, I'd bitch-slap you through a wall. Shut up and listen to me." Selena pounded her fisted hands on her knees. "Our culture has aspects Dakota's not going to tell you because he takes them for granted. The big one is that you're the most important thing in his life. Everything else stems from that."

Britt stifled a snigger.

"I'm serious. He will do anything to protect you. He'll try to keep you safe from everything. He will give his life guarding you."

The snigger morphed into a full-fledged laugh. "Please," Britt said between gasps. At least Selena distracted her from worrying about Judd.

"He will die for you," Selena repeated. "Consider that."

Britt had pondered the premise her whole life. Her father's religion was based on the same principle.

"So yeah," Selena continued, "he hurt you by tackling you, but he tackled you to keep you safe from the vampires at the end of the block."

Now they were back to vampires and werewolves. Better than felons getting out of prison and coming after her. "Did you say protect me?"

"Yes."

Protection. She could use some protection. She needed to hide. Maybe Dakota could help her.

Wait. Hadn't Dakota muttered something about protection when she'd mentioned birth control? Her memories of their first night were murky.

She had to make some decisions, and fast. The whole werewolf story was weirding her out. The idea of Judd was worse. Far worse.

She could trust Selena. Maybe. The werewolf tale was farfetched, but Selena had been in her life longer than anyone since her mother died. Selena would hide her.

"Can I stay with you?"

"Yeah," Selena said. "You can't leave tonight, anyway. The vampires are out."

Vampires were as good an excuse as anything.

A soft tapping on the door distracted Britt. Everything distracted her.

Dakota stuck his head in the room. "How are you doing?"

Britt reminded herself: the lesser of two evils.

"Should I leave you two alone?" Selena asked.

"Please." Dakota stared at Britt.

Selena hopped from the bed and left, closing the door behind her. Britt huddled deeper into the blanket. Despite wearing Selena's shirt, she was cold.

Dakota sat on the edge of the mattress. "Are you okay? I threw a lot at you tonight."

"No kidding."

He ignored her interruption. "I'm learning a lot of bothersome stuff about you, too."

Her? Her life was an open book.

"Who is Judd Byrne, and why is he texting you?"

Chapter 10

Dakota waited.

Britt's eyes grew wide, and a surge of rank fear filled the room. She fisted her hands.

"None of your business." Her voice quavered before her defenses snapped into place, and she squared her shoulders. "Wait a minute. I should be asking why you believe I know someone named Judd Byrne."

He opted for truth. "I almost stepped on your phone, so I checked to see what was upsetting you."

"And you randomly found the name Judd Byrne? On my phone? No way, Bus Boy."

Her bravado didn't hide her terror.

He dialed back his swell of fury. "I need to tell you some other stuff."

Such as werewolf pacts and spying for the government; knowing guys who know guys.

"Oh, you've told me enough."

"I haven't told you everything. I admit I screwed up, but you need to tell me about Judd Byrne, and why he's coming after you."

"We attended the same high school." Her tone was sullen.

"Why is he in prison?"

"Why he's getting out is more important." Her voice fractured; panic clung to the jagged edges.

"I can find out." Luke should have included the information in his report.

Something blazed in her eyes. "You can?"

"Yes. People convicted of aggravated robbery in Minnesota are eligible for parole."

"If you read his texts, you'd realize he's not getting out for good behavior."

"The threat is implied." As if he dealt with stalkers regularly. "I can't keep you safe if you won't tell me what's going on."

She hesitated. "He was my boyfriend. In high school. You might say he's the personification of my rebellion."

How did her rebellion land a guy in prison? Dakota couldn't ask her. She was already so terrified even sapiens could read her distress signals.

"And he wants you back after eight years?"

Her translucent complexion grayed. The sunken arcs beneath her eyes darkened. "They're supposed to tell me when he's getting out."

"He's not out yet." Dakota wanted to pull her into his arms and reassure her. Comforting her was a responsibility he longed to claim. "You're safe with me."

"Selena said I could stay."

One less item on his worry list. "Great idea." He could better protect her in Ethan's weird house. Plus Ethan and Selena could back him up.

His brain raced. Britt was obviously terrified. He accepted responsibility for part of her panic. He could have handled his revelation in a gentler manner. Her reaction had been of the fight-or-flight category. He understood her crashing out the window to escape. Her reactions were part of her charm.

The recent text from her ex had her cowering. Britt was too strong, too much of a force of nature to be squelched by a mere selfie unless a hidden subtext only she understood threatened her.

"I can't protect you unless I know what you fear."

"I fear demons," she said. "I fear you. What you did, morphing into—"

"Stop making your irrational behavior my fault. The being you say you fear is who will protect you. Why are you afraid of this Judd guy?"

"Isn't the fact he's currently in prison enough?" Color returned to her face. Strength seeped into her words.

"You don't believe in demons."

Her chin jerked. "You don't know anything about me. I believe science can tame demons."

"You believe in science?"

"Damn right I do."

"Isn't science based on evidence?"

"Science relies on evidence. Stop trying to distract me." Her color improved with every word. "I'm not afraid of Judd."

"Liar. I can smell changes in your physical body, the same way a lie detector measures anxiety. If you lie to me, if you're afraid of something, I can smell your emotions on you. You're afraid of Judd Byrne."

"He's in prison for a reason. He's a criminal. He does bad stuff."

"He's in prison for aggravated robbery. I was told he used a weapon while robbing someone."

"He did."

"I can have my FBI contact get me the details." *Wouldn't Luke love being called an FBI contact.*

"You have an FBI contact?" Britt considered him for a moment. "I guess you do still need to tell me stuff."

"We're both keeping secrets."

"Yours was bigger. A werewolf." The wind toyed with the shredded screen; the mesh tapped at the window and Britt flinched before visibly regrouping. "You, Selena—maybe I'm trapped in a nightmare."

"Not a nightmare."

"Tell me about your FBI contacts." She huddled deeper into the blankets.

Dakota took a chance and sprawled next to her, albeit outside the covers. When she didn't protest or try to escape, he stretched out until he was comfortable. "I hope history doesn't bore you."

"I'm not going anywhere." She shivered. Her expression told him she wanted to flee yet understood the futility of escape.

He wanted to kiss a long scratch marring the side of her face. Guilt for having hurt her warred with his need to protect her. He jammed his hands behind his head to keep from touching her.

"Lycans—werewolves—have been around as long as your kind. Sapiens persecuted the lycan in our European homelands. My family is originally from France. Selena's family immigrated from Scandinavia. You'll have to get the specifics from her. Ethan recently found out he is Limmikin—a native American shifter. That's his story to tell."

Britt's eyes drifted shut. "Go on."

"During the American Revolution, one of the pack leaders, a guy named Garnier, approached Thomas Jefferson, who was ambassador to France, about striking a deal. Service for sanctuary. We would act as spies for the Americans if we could immigrate and be left alone. Service for sanctuary."

"Spies?"

"Sure. We can shift and sneak around as wolves. Our hearing is supposedly better than sapiens, as is our eyesight. I can't compare my senses to yours. I only know how I hear and see."

"And smell?"

His right eyebrow rose. "And smell. Plus we're fast. We're a breed of secret weapon. Except as technology has advanced, the government requires our services less. In my pack—and Tokarz de Lobo Garnier is a direct descendant of the Garnier who cut the deal with Jefferson—we've handled a couple of missions. I wasn't directly involved. My status in the pack is on the low side."

"Low?"

Lycan life was filled with subtleties. Britt was ignorant of them all. "You've heard of alpha males?" "Yeah."

"Tokarz de Lobo Garnier is my alpha. Toke Lobo. You've met Restin?" Tokarz's cousin was in Minnesota on the alpha's orders.

Britt nodded. "He's an ass."

"That's the guy. He's the pack beta. I'm way below him."

"A serf?"

"You familiar with the Greek alphabet?"

"Not especially."

"I'm a tau. My surname is Towne. Anyway, the new federal administration wants to break the treaties. Not only with my pack, but all the packs. Each pack has a treaty with the government, but the possible elimination of the treaties has a lot of lobos anxious. Tokarz sent Ethan to Minnesota to negotiate with Congressman Peters. The congressman availed himself of Varulv services. He knew the value of having lycans work for him."

"You make everything sound...real," Britt said. "You make werewolves and treaties sound plausible."

She still believed he was telling tall tales. "Would you believe me if I shifted again?"

Britt shuddered. "No. I—I believe you. I do. You're presenting a logical sequence of a world, a culture, a secret society living among the rest of us."

"The world is ours, too. Where else would we live?" He resented the implication of her kind's superiority. "Who's to say you're not living in the world with us?"

"It boggles the mind how much we have yet to learn."

Maybe she did believe him.

"Thomas Jefferson, huh?"

"So the story goes."

"And Ethan is in Minnesota on a secret mission to deal with Congressman Peters."

"Yeah. His coming to Warwick was good. Otherwise, he might never have met Selena, and they'd both be single for the rest of their lives."

"You make being single sound like a bad thing."

"Compared to being with your soul mate? Yeah. Single sucks. We don't have to worry. I found you."

"No."

"Yes."

"No." She twisted until she faced him. "I'm willing to concede maybe werewolves exist. Either that, or you've constructed an elaborate hoax. Congratulations. I still refuse to be bound to any one man. Ever."

"Our mating isn't a choice." Her statement irritated him. If she assumed he was going to tolerate other males in her life, of her having sex with others, she was going to have a difficult learning curve.

"I can't make the situation any clearer to you. You're a one and done. We're finished."

"You're my one and only, and we've just started our lives together," he corrected. "You contradict yourself by saying you and I have no future, yet you want my protection."

"Judd scares me, and I'm not stupid. You and Ethan offered protection."

"Tell me about Judd."

"WHAT MORE CAN I tell you? He was my bad boy period. My rebellion."

Dakota spilling his guts with his tales of the American Revolution, spies, and the supernatural didn't mean Britt had to bare her soul.

Besides, the story of Judd Byrne wasn't as romantic. Not that she believed a word of Dakota's story. Okay, maybe a few words, but werewolves in service to the government? Seriously?

Then again, he was discussing the government, where truth and fantasy mingled without repercussion. His fable was much nicer than hers. Hers was teenage rebellion, squalor, death, and an everlasting hatred for the man who'd fathered her.

"How old were you?"

"Seventeen." She hadn't meant to tell him anything. "A very young, very naive, and very angry seventeen."

No mention of the heartbreak, the suffocating sense of loss. She could justify everything she'd done by claiming she was driven to desperation by her circumstances.

"We were in high school. How many high schoolers haven't done something stupid?"

"I grew up in a different culture, so I don't know."

"Me, too." She hated sharing her childhood. Hated even remembering the claustrophobia of being a preacher's kid. "You at least grew up in the mainstream of your community. Right?"

"Yeah." He sounded puzzled.

"My father is a pastor. He's fairly well-known in northern Minnesota."

Dakota's brown eyes fixed on her face, as if she were one of those three-dimensional drawings where one needed to defocus one's eyes to see a hidden picture.

"He has his own mega church," she continued. "He wants to be more famous than he is. He has a lot of local influence. A syndicated TV show that started on cable access, the local religious radio station, and last I heard, he has a podcast. He's even interfered in elections."

"Interfered?"

"Okay, donated a lot of money and had his flock support his chosen candidates. He's going to hate you. You, according to his belief system, are a demon."

She bounced from topic to topic, seemingly unrelated, yet each bit of information she tossed in Dakota's direction was a link of the chain binding her. She would never rid her head of her father's voice. And Dakota's earlier revelation still disturbed her equilibrium. "Anyway, we were home schooled until I was sixteen."

"We?"

"My brother and sister and me."

"You have siblings? Older or younger?"

"Younger. Why?"

"Lycans tend to have small families. Especially nowadays. Having siblings is something rare. The best we can do is cousins."

"Oh. I have Bartholomew and Susannah." She waited for Dakota to comment on how Bart and Susie had biblical names, unlike her own. He didn't.

"Are werewolves Christian?" She didn't see how they could be.

"No," he admitted.

"Do you believe in God?"

"We believe in the Ancient Ones. The Varulv call them the gods of their elders. Ethan's grandfather refers to the Creator."

A lot of words, dancing around her question. "And you? What do you believe in?"

"Science." Her response was prompt. Firm. Rooted in experience. Bred from defiance. "Logic is why—one of the reasons why—I'm having such a difficult time reconciling what I saw with reality."

"What you saw *is* reality."

So he claimed. The scientist in her wanted to refute her experience. The hallucination hadn't been only visual.

Waves of heat had enveloped the room. Searing, oxygen- stealing heat. The change in air pressure played havoc with her sinuses and inner ears. Her innate curiosity demanded further research.

Her innate skeptic reminded her of the "miracles" she'd seen her father perform.

And the frustrated teenager she'd once been snickered at her latest rebellion: fucking a demon in order to pay back her father for his zeal.

"How does what you've told me make Judd Byrne a current threat to you?"

"As I mentioned, I was home schooled. I didn't attend public school until I was seventeen. I was unfamiliar with the secular kids. Cliques and mean girls. Judd hit on me. I was flattered. He was cute, had a lot of friends, and I was unbelievably naive." She glided over the reason she was in public school. "He paid attention to me when I was starved for attention."

"He seduced you." Dakota's voice teetered on an edge of anger.

"He listened to me. He believed me. I was tired of being the good girl. I was tired of virtue and meekness and my father's brand of woo-woo." Why was she defending her actions? She owed Dakota nothing.

"What woo-woo?"

"Religion. Hocus pocus. Abracadabra. The supernatural. Don't all charlatans and practitioners of other-worldly arts claim theirs is the one true way? You've presented more evidence to me of your lycanthropy than my father's faith ever summoned." She couldn't keep the bitterness out of her tone.

"Okay," Dakota replied, his tone hesitant.

Even she recognized the contradictions in her words.

"I was vulnerable." She muddled on. "Judd figured out how to play me. His survival tool is zeroing in on a person's susceptibility, then twisting their weaknesses to his advantage. He used me, he used Curtis, he used every one of his satellites."

"Curtis?" Dakota's intense mien sharpened. "Who's Curtis?"

"Judd's best friend. His shadow. Curtis isn't the brightest bulb in the chandelier. He went to prison, too, with a lighter sentence than Judd's. Wow, I haven't thought of Curtis in years."

"Curtis isn't the one threatening you. Could he be the source of Judd's cell phone?"

Her patience was rapidly shrinking. In a minute she was going to shriek. "Does the source matter? The fact Judd claims he's getting out and is threatening me is the problem."

"The cops will say he hasn't threatened you."

"They don't know Judd."

"Oh, I'm sure the guards in prison have gotten familiar with him."

"If they have, they wouldn't be letting him out."

"You don't know he's getting out."

"You read the messages." She couldn't keep the snark out of her tone. She was still pissed he'd snooped. "What's your interpretation?"

"He's horny?"

If Dakota meant his answer as a joke, she didn't care for his sense of humor.

"Anyway, I've decided I'm going to stay with Selena. Judd won't be able to find me. Me staying doesn't mean you and I—well, we're not involved."

"If you're going to stay in Ethan's house, you'll need to honor Ethan's code of conduct, and he's a werewolf who believes in one mate."

"You're getting your buddy to pimp for you?" She'd ridden this road in the past. "Forget me. I'm out. Find some other sucker."

"I can't forget you. I will never forget you. I'm incapable of forgetting. I've found you. I've marked you. Nothing you can do or say will change what happened between us. The Ancient Ones meant for us to find each other. Otherwise, Tokarz would have sent the other driver with Restin and Ethan's family."

A minuscule part of her wanted to believe him. Wanted to be important in someone's world.

She tamped the emotion like an itch she refused to scratch.

"Aren't you warm?" Dakota's forehead glistened. "Too bad the screen is ripped, or else I'd open the window."

"Go ahead." She had blankets.

"We'll be bombarded with insects."

"Insects bother you?" How odd, considering he spent part of his life as a wolf.

"Mosquitoes. Ticks. Fleas." He studied her with hooded eyes. "My inherent immunities only include diseases like mumps and chicken pox."

"Interesting." After mulling his revelation, questions barraged her brain. His nature intrigued her. Not enough to shackle her to him for the rest of their lives, but enough to distract her from her current influx of problems.

Current influx? Who was she trying to kid? Her life had been one disaster after another from the day she was born. The only calm, the only wedge of sanity were the four years she'd lived with Selena.

Even then, she'd peered over her shoulder, waiting for Judd's retribution.

Chapter 11

BRITT SAT AT SELENA'S kitchen table and cursed herself for forgetting Selena didn't drink coffee. Morning sun smeared everything with sticky butterscotch light.

She hated butterscotch. She hated morning. Mornings without coffee ought to be illegal. Lack of a car prevented her from hitting the nearest Caribou for her morning fix. Nor could she borrow a vehicle. Everyone else in the house was asleep. Dakota had explained werewolves were nocturnal creatures. Britt was, too.

Nocturnal or not, she was awake now. Too much going on. Dreams of being chased by wolves kept waking her.

She buried her face in her hands, her elbows propped on the table. How much of the previous evening had been real and how much a hallucination?

She'd been under a lot of stress, what with losing her job, Selena's reluctance to move forward with Night Shift, her roommate moving out, and Judd appearing on her phone, if not in her life. Dreaming Dakota had shifted from human to animal was logical in the cold morning light. Logic insisted her memory was nothing more than a vivid dream.

Except the cuts and scrapes decorating her body were real enough. Painful enough. So, yeah. She'd jumped out the window last night. Witnessing Dakota morph into a wolf hadn't been a dream.

Damn, she needed coffee. Maybe she could find a Caribou or Dunkin' or even a Starbucks within walking distance. At this point, she'd settle for gas station coffee.

And if Dakota or Selena hadn't been joking about vampires at the ends of the block—vampires, for crying out loud—she'd be safe enough in daylight. Unless the sun being deadly to vampires was one of the tropes Dakota claimed writers and moviemakers invented to scare people.

She could use a toothbrush, too. The one she usually carried in her bag had vanished. Her mouth tasted as if a pack of werewolves used it as a toilet.

Standing, she wrapped Selena's shirt tighter around her and made her way to the bathroom. What makeup she hadn't left on the pillowcase in the guest room collected in the hollows of her face, most noticeably around her eyes. She washed her face, using a Night Shift sample Selena kept in the medicine cabinet.

Why did werewolves need medicine cabinets? Or bathrooms? Wouldn't doing their business in animal form be easier? She splashed water on her face.

According to her reflection, she appeared normal. She'd slept with Dakota two nights ago. As near as she could tell, nothing changed inside her. She was still restless. Still determined to never let a male of any species control her with sex. And not only sex. Ever. She'd witnessed how her father had manipulated her mother. She'd let Judd victimize her in high school.

Now she was the one in control. Her sex life was on her terms.

Still, Dakota's claim they were meant for each other wouldn't leave her alone. The sex was better with him than with anyone, even in the early days with Judd. But married to Dakota? Maybe as a *fuck-you* to her father. Probably not. He wasn't worth destroying her self-reliance. She was never getting married.

She rummaged in her bag until she found her hairbrush. A few minutes later, she decided she'd primped enough to go in search of coffee. She plugged the street address into her phone and sure enough, a diner a few blocks north of Ethan's house popped up.

The thugs—for lack of a better word—at the end of the block allowed her to pass with only their usual annoying catcalls.

The diner was further than Britt realized. Ethan's house wasn't in the best neighborhood, and Mooney's Diner reflected the general rundown atmosphere.

Britt perched on a stool at the counter. The waitress took one look at her and dropped a mug littered with advertising in front of her, followed by coffee to the brim. "Cream?"

Britt shook her head as she wrapped her chilled hands around the warm mug. She took a tentative sip, fragrant steam bathing her face. Bitter and hot, like her mood.

"Need a menu?"

Britt shook her head again. She'd be able to speak after a few ounces of caffeine.

The diner was full. Britt had taken the last stool. She propped her elbows on the counter, not caring if Selena's shirt got dirty from whatever coated the Formica. She registered the clink of forks against plates, the chatter of morning people at breakfast.

She loved diners in the middle of the night, after the bars closed. Sometimes she and her one-and-done, pre- done, of course, stopped for breakfast before concluding their transaction. More often, though, she stopped for coffee, alone, after leaving the 'done.' Sitting on the stool in Mooney's was almost as good as being home.

Her brain was so preoccupied with musing, she missed her phone ringing. She didn't recognize the number. Not a text. Judd wasn't cyberstalking her again.

"Hello?" Her voice cracked from disuse. "Brittany Hague?"

She didn't recognize the female voice. "Speaking." "Please hold for Congressman Peters."

Congressman Peters? Which one? The missing heir or the acting representative with whom she'd met regarding Night Shift?

"Brittany? Connor Peters."

"Hello, Congressman." She squinted at the clock hanging above the door. Nine-fifteen. She waited, hoping he bore good news regarding small business funding for Night Shift.

"Did I catch you at a bad time?"

Due to Connor's newness to the political life, he didn't grasp his was the time with value.

"Having a cup of coffee and planning my day," she admitted. "Can I help you with something?"

"I'd like to meet with you to continue our discussion." He oozed charm across the cell frequencies.

Don't be too eager. Don't be a fool. Her head and her instincts bickered like siblings. "Did you have a time in mind?" *There.* Her question made her sound as if she had value, too.

"I'm free for lunch today."

Her stomach lurched. "One o'clock would be good for me." She'd have enough time to go home, shower, and change her clothes. What else did she have in her closet besides her pinstripe suit? Something less formal. Formal had been fine when she initiated the contact; the situation was reversed.

"Great. I'll pick you up."

Her insides stilled. Dove headlong into paralysis. "I'm going to be running errands all morning," she lied. "Why don't I meet you somewhere?" Not that she had a car, thank- you-Dakota-Towne. Selena used public transportation all the time. How difficult could finding her way around be?

"Are you sure?"

"Yes." She didn't hesitate. Running errands meant she could dress casually. She wouldn't be dependent on him. Nor did she want him to have her address. She'd made that mistake with Dakota. Never again.

"I'll make reservations at Eclipse." Brusque. Businesslike. "Unless you prefer something else?"

"No, Eclipse is fine." She'd never heard of the place, but her phone came equipped with GPS. "See you at one." She disconnected the call before he could detain her.

"See who?"

Britt nearly fell to the floor. "How did you find me?" she demanded of Dakota, who claimed the stool next to her. What happened to the patron who'd occupied the seat when she'd arrived?

"Followed your scent." He acted as if he didn't have a care in the world. The waitress arrived. "Two scrambled eggs and a side of bacon, not crispy. No coffee for me, but could you refill her cup?"

"Bless you," Britt murmured, as the waitress topped off her mug. Britt waited until the waitress worked the length of the counter before she asked, "Why did you follow me?"

"You sneaked out. I was worried."

"I wish you wouldn't."

"My DNA isn't hardwired to do otherwise."

She curled her fingers around the newly heated mug. She didn't want or need a lovesick werewolf dodging her steps. "Let me put it another way. Don't."

He grinned. "After your initial reaction, I have to admit you're adapting to your new reality. You have a few areas needing improvement, especially involving the aspects I can't control. They're part of my DNA, for lack of a better description. One is needing to affirm you're safe."

Maybe she could use him to her advantage. "You trashed my car," she reminded him. "I need to deal with repairs. And I have an appointment. As you are aware." She tried to glare at him. "You owe me."

"Okay. I'll help you with the insurance stuff and finding a body shop. And I'll drive you to your appointment." He waggled his eyebrows. "You're in luck. I am a professional driver."

Good thing she hadn't called her meeting with Connor a date.

"So you've mentioned. I need to go to my apartment and grab some clothes and stuff. I'll be staying at Selena's indefinitely."

"Makes sense." He eyed her as though he didn't trust her acquiescence. "And you have an appointment."

"Yes, I do." She raised her mug to her mouth and drank, her eyes never leaving Dakota.

~ ~ ~

Although she would never tell him, Britt was glad Dakota accompanied her to her apartment. Yes, she was annoyed with him, but she believed his claim her safety was his top priority. She'd argue with him later, once the whole Judd situation straightened itself out.

Dakota arranged for her car to be fixed. He called her insurance company while she showered.

The hot water stung her cuts. One on her arm continued to ooze blood. She'd have to wear something with long sleeves.

And trowel on the makeup, she decided a few minutes later as she wiped the steam from the bathroom mirror. If she didn't know better, she'd swear she'd gone a couple of rounds with another woman in a barroom cat fight. If she'd known how badly she cleaned up, she never would have gone out for coffee.

She blessed the lousy lighting in Selena's bathroom for hiding the truth. She'd needed caffeine. She also made note to never put on her makeup at Selena's. And another note to purchase better lighting for their basement workshop.

Since Dakota had outed Selena as a werewolf, her fondness for dim light made more sense. Not that Britt preferred bright lights. She didn't. Except in a lab. Lighting was everything in a lab, and Selena's basement was supposed to be their lab.

Britt settled on a long navy tank dress paired with a lavender linen jacket for her lunch with Connor Peters. Lavender sandals completed the ensemble.

"You look nice." Dakota narrowed his eyes as he conducted a full-body scan.

"Thanks."

"For your appointment."

"Yes."

"Where are we going?" he asked nonchalantly, as if his attendance were a given.

"I have a meeting. Make your own plans. Although you do owe me a ride." Her statement was clear. Her meeting with Connor Peters had nothing to do with Dakota Towne. Except for chauffeuring her to the meeting site. Any time she didn't have to call Uber would help her budget.

Her stomach knotted. *No.* She couldn't think about her personal finances. Not the negative aspects. Positive vibes. She was going to charm the pants off Connor Peters and procure federal money so she could launch Night Shift with or without Selena. Her own line of creams and lotions had been her goal since her college days. She was going to make her dream a reality. She didn't care what she had to do.

"Where's your meeting?" Dakota's question pulled her out of her pity party.

"Someplace called Eclipse. I'll Google it."

"Sounds trendy."

"Yeah." She pawed through a basket containing her jewelry. Where was her amethyst amulet?

"Sounds like tiny portions of highly priced organic food no one ever heard of," Dakota continued.

She found the necklace. The silver chain had knotted. She picked at the links.

"The person I'm meeting with suggested the venue." The tangle in the chain fell free. Britt slipped the chain over her head.

"And who are you meeting with?"

Britt straightened and faced him. "Connor Peters."

His face betrayed nothing. "The acting congressman. You called him again."

"No. He contacted me."

"Really?" Dakota's soft voice chilled her. "Any idea what he wants?"

"Hopefully he wants to give me money." Maybe Selena would regain her motivation if funding was available. "Can we get going? The congressman's time is valuable, and I don't want to keep him waiting."

WHAT ABOUT MY TIME? Dakota wanted to howl. *I've waited for you all my life. Don't I have value?*

He swallowed his frustration and focused on what was right. Trashing Britt's car yielded some unexpected side benefits, such as her dependency on him for transportation. All the better to keep an eye on her.

She was beautiful. He resented her primping for Connor Peters.

Dakota had learned secrets regarding the congressman's family, secrets in addition to the public scandal smearing his father, who'd committed suicide rather than face exposure of his sexual perversions. Secrets he couldn't share. Connor's older brother, Liam met justice face to face, too; Dakota had participated.

Britt wasn't going anywhere near Connor Peters unless Dakota was present to protect her. She'd argue, so he wouldn't tell her. Besides, Selena's secrets were hers to share, not his.

He didn't know if Selena remembered he'd been present on retribution day. The memory made Dakota want to wince and cover his privates. Something else he wasn't going to get into with Britt.

He searched for the restaurant on his phone. "Aren't you in a hurry to leave?" He punched the address into his map app.

"How far is the restaurant?" Britt asked, as she brushed her long yellow hair.

"I want to check the place out before you meet with Peters," Dakota admitted.

"You're more paranoid than I am." She dropped her brush to the top of her bureau.

"You're aware of his father's secret life?"

"Everyone knows about his father. Everyone knows Selena and Ethan were with him right before he blew his brains out. What does Bryant Peters have to do with anything?"

"His older son is missing," Dakota reminded her. "Connor wanting to meet with you could mean something. It might not. Let's err on the side of caution instead of taking chances with your safety. I'll check the restaurant before texting you."

"You don't have my number."

"Don't I?"

She changed the subject. "You believe Connor Peters is dangerous?"

"Do you have reason to believe otherwise?"

She scrunched her face. "He struck me as...overwhelmed the other day. Trying to find his footing. I'm guessing he never considered himself the heir, so he never bothered with the protocols of being a politician."

"Interesting take."

Britt opened her mouth, closed it, opened it again. "You're right. We should get going."

"You do realize I'm going in with you."

Her toe tapped against the wood floor. She crossed her arms. "I never agreed you could accompany me."

"You don't have a say." He winced. His words were more bullying than he'd meant. "That came out wrong. I'm not going to join you. Peters won't know I'm around."

Her disbelief showed in every line of her body. "Someday," he said in a soft voice, "you're going to

appreciate how I consider you my everything. I have good reasons to fear for your safety. Don't mock them."

"I'm not mocking them. I don't mock. I learned tolerance through religion. You believe what you believe, and I have my own creed."

She still didn't grasp her new status. "Aren't you a scientist?"

She squared her shoulders. "I am."

"My lycanthropy isn't a creed or a belief. It *is*. Nothing more. Nothing less. What other evidence do I need to give you? Could Connor have yanked the door off your car last night?"

"He wouldn't dare." She was visibly amused. "The Peters family doesn't need more bad publicity. Are you ready to leave?"

Chapter 12

BRITT SAUNTERED INTO THE restaurant after Dakota texted her an all-clear. A low-level throb behind her eyes edged up a notch. A peek around the brightly lit dining room as the hostess led her to the table where Connor Peters waited revealed Dakota seated in a far corner, his back to the wall. Her heels striking the tile floor added a loud clack to the clamor in the room.

Connor rose and pulled out her chair. Being treated with old-fashioned manners was new to her. "Thank you."

"No, thank you for meeting me on such short notice. Would you care for something to drink?"

A glass of amber liquid over a few ice cubes sat in front of him. He hadn't waited for her to order his iced tea. Except the drink didn't smell like tea. Funny. Usually her sense of smell wasn't keen enough to pick up on alcoholic beverages unless she was close enough to kiss the consumer. Or the guy had consumed too much. Weird how she could smell the contents of Connor's glass from across the table.

"Water with lemon." She needed to keep her head.

Connor flashed an *aw-shucks* expression at her. She figured he had luck melting female hearts and panties whenever he grinned. He had a boyish air going for him. She was nauseated. Something about him was...off.

"How are you settling in?" she asked to break the ice.

"I'm not. My brother is the acting congressman. I'm only running the local office until he returns."

"Any word from him?"

Connor raised his glass. Ice cubes clinked against the side as he sipped. The server arrived to take their order before he answered her question. After the server left, he swallowed another mouthful of his drink and grinned at her again, flashing his dimples. Deep dimples.

The interruption couldn't have been better timed for him.

"We've caught up on my family. How's yours?"

"I haven't spoken to them lately." She kept her tone as light as she could. "No news is good news."

"Your father is a committed supporter of my brother."

The server returned with Britt's ice water. A wedge of lemon clung to the rim of the glass. "Your meals will be out in a minute."

"Thank you." Connor acknowledged the young man.

Britt didn't contradict Connor's erroneous belief about her father. The only agenda Pastor Paul committed to was his own.

She waited for Connor to speak. He sipped his beverage and stared at her. Nothing else. For a man who should have been busy, he was awfully lackadaisical. He slumped in his chair. Something about him—

"So?" She gave the word a jaunty spin. A sunbeam leaked through a skylight and spilled across the tabletop.

He tipped his glass toward her, as if saluting her. "You wanted to meet with me," she reminded him.

"I like sharing a meal with a pretty girl."

Her spine stiffened. She sipped her water. "We're not discussing business?"

"You want to launch a business. You need seed money."

"Yes."

"Pretty girls shouldn't need to go into business. You should find someone to take care of you."

"I'm perfectly capable of taking care of myself. I have been for years." Keeping the anger out of her voice wasn't easy.

"Can you pass a background check?"

Her lungs seized. She hadn't considered how her foolish, youthful errors would come back to bite her butt. "Of course." *Maybe.*

"Anyone who lends you money is going to want a guaranty you're a good risk."

"I'd prefer grant money." She kept her tone cool. In control. "We are trying to create an industry and intend to employ people. We have a business plan."

"Selena Wolfe is your partner? Can she pass a background check?"

"I have no idea. Wasn't her father one of your father's friends?"

"I wouldn't call him a friend. He did some odd jobs for my father. Lots of people do odd jobs for my family. Odd is a good word to describe Erik Wolfe."

"You met Selena's father?"

"Never had the pleasure." He sipped again. "I've heard stories."

"So have I." Selena's father was one of the casualties at the Pentagon on September eleventh.

"If she's anything like her old man, you could have problems getting funding."

Britt set her glass on the table so gently, not even an ice cube dared betray her action. Something in Connor's conversation, a hidden subtext, bothered her. Instinct told her she ought to understand what he meant without being told. "I beg your pardon?"

"The government doesn't give money to subversives."

She bit her tongue to keep from pointing out the lie with *what about* questions. Classic political deflection. She refused to play his game. "You're accusing Selena and me of being subversives? Her father?"

"No. I'm not. A background check might find problems."

"Are you telling me you consider me less than what I seem?" Anger seethed in her veins.

"Aren't you?"

High school shenanigans hadn't kept a man off the Supreme Court. How could they prevent her from getting a business loan or grant? "I'm not old enough to have a notorious past."

Except for Judd, who was in prison.

Connor chuckled. "If you say so." He tipped his glass at her again.

The server arrived with Britt's salad and Connor's wrap. His potato chips smelled wonderful.

Britt raised her fork and plunged it into the ragged-edged greens. She didn't lift the food to her mouth. Her throat closed. She could chew; swallowing was another story.

"The past never goes away," Connor mused. "The news is full of stories exposing past transgressions."

She made no secret of being a honkytonk angel. "My sex life is no one's business."

"Some might argue you're wrong."

He knew. Somehow he'd learned about Judd and her notorious high school years. But how? He'd attended boarding school while she slummed an education at Warwick High.

"You're saying no one is innocent?"

"I guess they aren't. Boys will be boys." He drank again.

"And girls will be victims."

"Or sluts. Mostly sluts."

She wanted to fling her water in his face. Instead, she laid her fork across her plate. "I see why you're not the politician in the family."

"What? I've offended you?" Disbelief colored his words. She lashed out, forgetting she needed his help. "Nor does the apple fall far from the tree. In this instance, maybe there isn't a good apple in the whole bunch."

She pushed away from the table, her chair scraping loudly against the tile floor. "Our meeting is finished. Thanks for your time."

DAKOTA DROPPED A COUPLE of twenties on the table and hurried out of the restaurant in Britt's wake. He didn't care if Peters noticed him.

Too much ambient noise in the tile-floored eatery prevented Dakota from easily eavesdropping on Britt and Peters' conversation. He caught the general tone. Britt deserved a medal for not killing Peters.

She waited for Dakota by his SUV. He used the remote to unlock the doors. She was inside before he could give her a boost, exposing way too much leg as she hoisted her narrow skirt above her knees. Heat poured from the vehicle. Her melting makeup slithered down the side of her face.

"I assume the meeting didn't go well," he said, as he climbed in next to her.

"He's as much of a pig as his father."

"Ouch." What had The Spare said to her? "Do I need to kill him?"

"Please." She believed he was kidding. "Can I help?"

"You don't have the right physiology." He twisted the key in the ignition and checked the restaurant door. "I hope you weren't keeping me a secret from Peters because I believe I have been outed."

Britt didn't bother to check. "He's a waste of space."

"He's watching us. He must have followed me out."

"I'd flip him off, except I don't want to waste the energy."

Her tone was brittle.

Dakota wished he could wrap her in his arms and take care of her, but Britt wasn't fragile. *Correction*, she didn't want to be treated as if she were fragile, yet she was nowhere near as strong as she portrayed herself.

"Good call." He exited the parking lot. "Where to next?"

"My place. I want to pack a bag to take to Selena's."

Good. She was taking her safety seriously.

"I want a drink. Selena doesn't drink, so we need to go someplace where I can order a buzz."

"Lycans are allergic to alcohol."

"You probably get enough of a buzz when you..." Britt waggled her fingers. "You know. Change into a wolf."

Several blocks passed before she spoke again. "What's it like? Shifting into a wolf."

A week ago, he wouldn't have been able to answer. "Sex. Orgasm."

Britt twisted in her seat. "You're kidding."

"Nope. Maybe that's why we aren't promiscuous." Besides the fact male physiology prevented sex with random partners.

"So if you get horny, you do whatever it is you do to initiate your change, and bam. You climax?"

He couldn't prevent his chuckle. "I never claimed shifting was as good as sex. The sensation is similar."

"And I'm not going to change into a werewolf, even though you bit me."

Was disappointment or his wishful thinking coloring her words? "Nope. You will always be as you were born. You were born just right."

"Flattery isn't going to get you laid."

Dakota choked. "I'm not talking about sex."

"Sure you are. Everything is about sex." She sounded bitter. "In the end, we're all searching for the ultimate orgasm. Some people use their genitals. Others don't."

"Whoa. That's pretty bleak." What happened to make her so cynical? She lacked joy in her life. He'd have to find ways to introduce happiness to her.

She twisted in her seat to face him. Bleak described her expression, too. "Maybe life is all fun and games for werewolves, but we sapiens don't have strict guidelines the way you do. At least, the way I interpret what you've tried to tell me. We have no guidelines except the ones some people invent and call religion, and everyone has been changing dogma to suit their own personal vision since religion was invented."

There was more to her reaction than the visible. Britt had depths, for all her one-and-done bluster. How much longer could he wait before discovering the true woman at the center of the storm? In the meantime, he'd have to take extra special care of her.

"Did you get a chance to eat your lunch?" Dakota asked. "Nope. Did you?"

"Not a bite. Wanna go to the Steak Out?"

DAKOTA'S SUGGESTION WAS MORE than welcome. Britt had done the girly thing and ordered a salad for her lunch with Connor, whose behavior negated the urge to be an acceptable female. She might as well be who she was. That woman wanted a burger. Rare. Something she could sink her teeth into and tear apart with great pleasure. A substitute for the substitute congressman.

Besides, choices at Selena's house consisted of hot dishes or walleye.

Something about Connor niggled at her. He sounded way too familiar with her history. Either someone had done some serious digging into her life since the time she'd left her father's house, making a government business grant impossible, or—

No. Too coincidental that she started receiving texts from Judd in prison around the same time her name showed up in front of the congressman. The idea a connection existed between Judd Byrne and Connor Peters was too absurd to consider. Judd was from so far past the wrong side of the tracks, he might as well have been on Mars, whereas preppy Connor Peters probably hired a servant to wipe his ass after he used the bathroom.

Connor hadn't grown up in Warwick. He wouldn't have been around for the debacle of her public high school sojourn. Still, people talked. Warwick natives never left. Plenty of people could tell tales. Generic tales. The specifics were known only by Judd and his best buddy Curtis.

Dakota parked his SUV between two police cruisers.

A couple of officers greeted her as the hostess led her and Dakota to a booth in the rear of the dining room. "Mickey. Tom," she acknowledged. Knowing the cops had her back reassured her. Some days she was a swirling mass of contradictions. Take today. Her barroom antics could be dangerous, yet she continued to pick up guys at Holsters. Tom Anderson and Mickey Clerkin were married to their high school girlfriends, who snubbed Britt whenever their paths crossed. Judd Byrne's leftover. Daughter of the crazy preacher Paul Hauge.

"You're too quiet," Dakota observed, once they'd placed their orders.

"Quiet is bad?" She clenched her teeth as she debated how much to share with Dakota.

He waited.

"Connor said a lot of upsetting stuff," she blurted. "He acted as if we'd met back in my wild woman days."

"Last week?"

She glared at him. "Funny. You probably won't believe me, but compared to my high school days, I am the model of decorum."

Dakota quirked an eyebrow.

"Don't be rude." Remembering her Judd-phase always made her queasy.

"Do you know those cops?" Dakota jerked his head toward the entrance where Mickey and Tom sat.

"Yeah. We went to high school together."

"They questioned Selena and Ethan about Congressman Peters' suicide."

"Doing their job. Ethan and Selena were the last ones to speak to the congressman."

"I'm not disputing their responsibility. If you were such a wild woman in high school, how did you get to be friendly with two of Warwick's finest?"

"Warwick is a small city. Where's our food? I'm starving."

"What did The Spare say to you?"

"Ah. Changing the topic. Good strategy." She was fond of the tactic herself.

"My gut tells me the two are related."

"Mine, too."

"Someone like Connor Peters could arrange for an inmate to get a cell phone," Dakota said.

"How would Connor Peters know Judd?"

"Ask the cops."

"What?"

"Your buddies by the door." Dakota sent an additional nod that way. "You said you all attended the same high school. Maybe they remember something you don't."

Drat. She couldn't face their censure. The past belonged in the past. She'd lived with the motto since college. She'd reinvented herself twice—three times, if she counted transitioning from being home schooled to the private religious school. The Brittany who had been expelled from Faith Ministries was an audition for the aching girl who found herself in the culture shock of public school.

Freedom. No less than a prisoner newly released after seventeen years of incarceration, she'd wanted everything hitherto denied her. She wanted her own life, not one based on someone else's idea of who she should be.

"All we have to do is—"

"We?" she interrupted. "There is no *we.*"

"Okay, you." He sounded impatient. "Tell them you've been getting texts from Byrne and you're worried."

Worried? She was terrified.

Dakota had a point. Mickey and Tom knew the role she'd played in Judd's arrest and conviction. Judd shouldn't be contacting her. Not from prison. Not from anywhere.

"Okay." She plucked her napkin from her lap and stood.

She did a lot of napkin tossing today.

"I didn't mean this minute."

"I'm only going to tell them I need to talk to them. After I eat. Otherwise, I'll pass out from hunger."

Unlike the cold white tile in the upscale restaurant Connor chose, the worn wooden floors of The Steak Out didn't announce her passage. Mickey and Tom watched her approach. She pasted on a smile and tried to cloak herself in a casual air.

"Hi. I'm sorry to interrupt your break. Can I talk to you before you leave? Or, better yet, can we meet later this afternoon?" The plates on their table were empty except for the ruffled green leaf garnish.

"Is something wrong?" Tom had played center on the basketball team.

"I hope not," Britt replied. "We'll talk later. I need to get back to my table."

"Wait." Tom and Mickey exchanged a glance. Mickey cleared his throat. "The guy you're with."

"Yeah?"

"How well do you know him?" Her brain blanked. "I'm sorry?"

"Your date. How well do you know him?"

"He's not my date." The words were automatic. "He's a friend of my college roommate's husband."

"He's not some guy you trolled in a bar?"

Her reputation preceded her. She gave Mickey what she hoped was a withering glare. "Anyone I troll is a one-time encounter."

"You attended college with Selena Wolfe?" Tom asked.

Okay. Something was going on she didn't get. Unless the two cops were still suspicious Selena and Ethan had done something to prompt Congressman Peters' suicide. "She's one of my closest friends. Look, I'm starving, Dakota's buying me lunch, and he's waiting for me." She drew a blank on possible locations to rendezvous. "Can we meet at Holsters, say around three?"

Few patrons would be at Holsters late in the afternoon. "Okay," Mickey agreed, after another glance at Tom. "Thanks."

Their behavior made her uneasy.

"That was quick." Dakota stood to pull out her chair.

"I told you I wasn't going to get into stuff with them before I ate." She draped her napkin across her lap. "They, on the other hand, wanted to discuss you."

"Me?" Dakota took his seat.

"They got more interested after I mentioned you're a friend of Ethan. Do they know about his secret mission?"

"Shh." Dakota scanned the room. "If they did, his mission wouldn't be much of a secret."

"Why would they be interested in you? What else aren't you telling me?"

Dakota refocused on her. "What?"

She narrowed her eyes. He didn't deny the possibility the authorities had reasons to question her involvement with one of Ethan's friends. "You still have a lot of stuff to tell me." She wasn't asking.

He squirmed. The grown-ass man actually squirmed in his chair in a public place.

"I don't see how you can top being a werewolf."

"I ordered you a burger and beer." He was just as good at changing the subject. "Medium rare, right?"

Her stomach growled. "Thanks," she echoed. "I'm going to assume the rest of your confession can't be made in public."

His grin was all the reply she needed.

Their food arrived. Britt busied herself eating the burger but ignored the beer. She wanted no question of her sobriety when she met with Mickey and Tom.

Britt and Dakota dawdled over their meal. They'd missed the worst of the lunch rush at the Steak Out, so their table wasn't needed. Britt brooded, the blue of her eyes clouded with her secrets.

"Where are we meeting the cops?"

Britt worked the label on the beer bottle with her thumbnail. She wouldn't meet his eyes. "Holsters. The place you and I hooked up. It's safe. Three o'clock, before happy hour."

"I don't have a problem with bars. I spend a lot of time in them myself. Won't a police cruiser parked outside keep people away from happy hour?"

"The meeting will be private." One strip of the foil label fell to the table. Britt retrieved the scrap and worked the paper between her thumb and index finger, creating tiny balls to scatter across the dark wood like giant grains of colorful salt.

Her statement warmed him. Maybe she was coming around if she trusted him to be at the meeting with the cops.

She returned her thumb to the still-full bottle of beer.

"What's wrong?" He expected her to lie.

She didn't speak for a long time, long enough for him to assume she wasn't going to answer at all. "High school was not my best moment. You're young, you're stupid, you're the victim of raging hormones."

The only part of her litany he could relate to was the raging hormones, and in his case, they were lycan hormones. Random shifting, not being able to shift at will. Werewolf adolescence was a hideous time.

"I regret some of my decisions," she continued.

"Judd?"

"Judd. And Judd was the poster boy for dysfunctional relationships." She stopped talking.

He got the impression she wanted to say more. Instead, she pushed away from the table. "Let's go. We can hang out at Holsters as easily as we can here."

Dakota scanned the dining room. They were the only patrons.

She stood, her toe tapping. He could swear the barometric pressure in the room was plummeting.

"Good plan," he muttered, as he followed her out of the building.

He boosted her into his SUV. A moment later he was seated next to her.

"Do you need directions?" she asked.

"You insult me." He had the best sense of direction ever gifted to a werewolf, and he was proud of his gift.

He made the trip with half an hour to spare. Britt appropriated the back booth, a place hidden deep in the shadows. Dakota had no doubt her cop friends would zero in on the dark corner. He slid in next to her.

"What do you want to drink?" he asked Britt, who hadn't uttered a word since the parking lot of The Steak Out.

"I suppose we have to order something." She sounded distracted.

"If we're renting booth space." Maybe he could offer her the traditional mating gift of berries. He'd done his homework. "Let me order you a virgin strawberry daiquiri."

The waitress guffawed. "Virgin and Britt Hauge in the same sentence? Whoa. That's deep."

Britt ignored her. "No, water's fine. In the bottle. I need to keep my head straight. No one's going to accuse me of being impaired."

Scat. He didn't mind her not drinking. He approved of abstinence. He simply didn't know how to get her to accept berries from him.

The waitress returned only a moment later with two bottles of water.

Britt ran her thumbnail along the label on hers, peeling the paper from the plastic.

"What's wrong?"

She buried her face in her palms. "My life is falling apart."

Chapter 13

Britt's cop friends were fifteen minutes late.

"What's up?" the taller one asked, as he waited for his partner to slide across the booth.

"Why wasn't I told Judd is being paroled?" Britt cut to the root. "Notification was part of my deal, Tom. Judd stays in prison, and I am to be given notice should he be paroled."

"Who says he's getting out?" Tom folded himself into the booth, his legs in the aisle.

She pulled out her cell phone, found the most recent text from Judd, and handed the phone to Tom.

He read the message, before passing her phone to his partner. Neither face betrayed any reaction.

"He has contraband. Not unusual." The second officer placed the phone on the table.

"He's not supposed to contact me, even if he gets out."

"Do you have an order of protection?" Tom asked.

"No! He's supposed to be in prison. Can you find out when he's getting out?" Britt sounded desperate.

Her request irked Dakota. He had Luke researching Byrne's status. Maybe her nerves erased the fact from her brain.

"He's threatening me. He needs to stay put." She spoke as if saying words could make her desires happen.

"Can you forward the texts to me?" the second guy asked.

"Sure. What's your phone number?"

The cop lifted the phone again and pressed a bunch of keys. He handed the phone to Britt.

"Thanks, Mickey." Tom stood.

"Where are you going?" Britt demanded. "I'm not done."

Mickey and Tom refrained from physically exchanging a look, but Dakota sensed a mental one as clearly as if he were a mind reader: *Humor her.*

Tom sat.

Didn't they see the slight tremor in her hands, hear the quaver in her voice? Were sapien senses so much weaker that her agitation didn't exist for them?

"What do you guys remember about Connor Peters from our high school days?"

Distaste flitted across Tom's face. "Nothing. He didn't go to school with us."

"He didn't live in-state," Mickey added.

"I remember." Britt worked the label of her water again. "But was he ever around?"

"You know who might know something? Curtis DiNardo." Slyness curved Mickey's lips. "You remember Curtis."

Britt's water bottle tipped. The contents splashed across the table, in an echo to what Dakota's gut did.

"Wasn't Curtis Judd's sidekick?"

Dakota didn't believe Tom's innocent tone for a second. If he wasn't so stunned by the question, he would have ripped off Tom's face, followed by Mickey's.

He knew Curtis DiNardo. Remembering the taste of DiNardo's blood rekindled the desire for revenge.

Numbness paralyzed Britt. She couldn't even grab a napkin to mop up the spilled water.

Asking if she remembered Curtis DiNardo was cruel. She didn't deserve the insult.

"Why would a lowlife like Curtis have anything to do with Connor Peters?" she managed to rasp out of her too-tight throat. Cool water dripped from the table onto her lap.

"I'm surprised you don't remember. Curtis bragged about the connection constantly. His Uncle Tony works for Connor's grandfather. His claim to fame."

She longed to lunge across the table and slap the sanctimonious smirk off Tom's face. Her paralysis faded enough to sense something going on with Dakota, whom she'd forgotten for a few moments. His body was rigid. She might have imagined a subsonic growl.

"Good luck finding him, though," Mickey added. "He disappeared around the same time Liam Peters vanished."

Maybe the low rumble wasn't her imagination.

"What does Curtis DiNardo have to do with anything?"

"Connor used to slum around with Curtis when he was home from prep school. Allegedly, the elder Peters focused on grooming Liam and the sister and ignored Connor."

She was going to puke. Then faint. Or maybe the other way around. She snatched a napkin from the dispenser and dabbed at the spilled water.

"Curtis has gone to ground, making him a person of interest in the disappearance of Liam Peters."

Dakota coughed.

"Curtis has to be flattered. Being of interest to anyone has to be a new experience for him," she quipped. At least, she hoped she quipped.

Tom guffawed, so she must have succeeded. "I'm sure there were some guys in the pen who were interested."

"Maybe Curtis learned some interpersonal skills," she continued.

Dakota grabbed her thigh.

"He did his time," Tom said. "He was working for his uncle before he pulled his Houdini act."

"I'm surprised the Peters family would allow a convicted felon in their presence."

"Servants," Tom explained. "All Tony DiNardo does is odd jobs for the old man."

"Odd jobs," Britt echoed. Puke or faint? Fuck that. She was going to scream until her throat collapsed.

Dakota tightened his grip. His body heat seeped past the fabric of her dress, radiated along her skin, and thawed parts where she didn't realized panic had frozen. Strength emanated from his touch. She seized his energy, greedy for calm and composure.

"Curtis is a follower. He hasn't had an original thought in his life," Mickey continued. "If Uncle Tony tells him to jump in the lake, Curtis asks what one."

She forced a laugh. A titter. "Precisely how he ended up in jail. He was the same way with Judd."

"At least he was smart enough not to have a gun the night they robbed the church."

Dakota's grip on her leg tightened even more. Yeah. She had some explaining to do.

"Back to Connor." She never wanted to lay eyes on Curtis DiNardo again.

"Curtis is the only townie who had anything to do with him," Tom repeated. "If you can find Curtis, ask him. And if you do find him, have him check in with the police, okay?"

DAKOTA MANAGED TO KEEP his mouth shut during Britt's police moment. He didn't utter a word after Mickey and Tom left and he was alone with Britt in her favorite bar.

He was tempted to order a strawberry daiquiri for her, but she didn't summon a waitress. She didn't tap her foot or jiggle her leg to the danceable tune blasting from the speakers. Instead, her fingers worked the soggy napkin into tiny balls.

Britt knew Curtis DiNardo, and Dakota knew his fate. Dakota had assisted meting out a fit end to the stupid lowlife.

He and Britt needed to talk. Their whole relationship consisted of secrets. Yes, they were still in the getting-to-know-each- other stage, but for them, the process delved much deeper than favorite colors, Coke, or Pepsi.

He tugged on her hand, signaling her time to leave. She'd mentioned stopping at her apartment to pack a bag, so he headed to North George Street.

"I'm afraid to go in," she confessed as he parked at the curb in front of her building.

"We're not staying," he replied, his voice rusty from disuse. "You wanted to pack a bag."

"Right." She didn't move.

Dakota climbed out of the vehicle, hurried to the passenger side, and opened the door. "Come on, Britt. The sooner you start, the sooner we can leave."

Her fingers fumbled with her shoulder harness. He covered her hand with his and released the latch.

"Aren't you going to ask me? Judge me?"

When she decided to talk, she never prevaricated.

"Have I ever judged you?"

"Maybe." She rubbed her forehead like a fretful child.

"Let's get you packed for a lengthy stay at Selena and Ethan's house. We'll talk later."

Where you'll be safer. Where ancient magic—the stuff Britt didn't believe in—protected Ethan's property.

He helped Britt from the SUV. He wanted her badly. He hoped he would be able to maintain control of his urge to mate long enough to convince her of the reality of their bond. If she'd given him the slightest inclination she wanted his touch, he would have held her hand as they approached her porch. She was more remote than she'd ever been. He took her key from her and led the way.

The door at the top of the stairs was slightly ajar.

Dakota pressed his index finger against Britt's lips. Had she been in such a hurry to meet with Connor Peters, she forgot to lock the door?

Her wide eyes and the fear he read in them pierced his heart. Part of him wanted to find an intruder he could deal with to prove to Britt he would protect her always.

Another part was still shaken by what he'd learned about Curtis DiNardo. He took comfort in knowing DiNardo was not responsible for the open door.

Dakota gestured for Britt to stay where she was. He didn't move until she nodded.

The hinges creaked as he nudged open the door. His initial reaction was wondering how he could tell if someone had tossed the place. Britt was a slob. He lifted his head to better sniff the air. According to his nose, only he and Britt had been in the apartment recently. He closed his eyes to enhance his hearing. Only the rapid thunder of Britt's heart echoed in the rooms. They were alone.

"We must have forgotten to lock the door." He gestured for Britt to join him.

"How do you figure?" She held back.

"They say a werewolf's senses are sharper than homo sapien senses. I don't detect any heartbeats or breathing except ours, and the only lingering scents belong to you and me."

"You're chock full of surprises." She pushed past him. "My own personal burglar alarm."

"You don't need to be snarky. You asked. I explained. The first of many explanations we're going to share today," he said as she headed toward her bedroom.

Her back stiffened. Her pace lost rhythm, as her steps stuttered. She recovered and continued toward the rear of the apartment. "Whatever," she muttered.

"I heard that. Along with your breathing and your heart beating."

"But you can't read my mind."

"Nope."

"Small favors rock." She vanished into her room.

Dakota decided to give her some privacy. He put away the dishes he'd washed the previous day, while he listened to her knock around her bedroom. Dishes stowed, he found her broom and swept the floor. Kitchen clean, he headed toward the living room to see what he could do to make the room livable.

"You're handy to have around," she observed, as he hung a coat in the closet near the door.

"You're a slob. Why do I picture spending the rest of my life picking up after you? Don't scientists need to be organized? Structured."

"I am. In my work." She propped a pale purple rolling suitcase against the door. "I want to relax at home."

"Babe, there's a difference between chilling after a long day and—" He gestured at the mess. "Your apartment resembles the relaxation of a body after it's been dead for a while. The bowels let go, and—"

"Are you calling my apartment a shitstorm?"

"Your words, not mine. You ready to go?"

"Yeah."

"Give me your house key. I'll lock up."

She handed him the key without an argument. He also took her suitcase from her.

A shaft of sunlight pierced the dusty air and highlighted Britt's face. Dark circles she couldn't mask with cosmetics betrayed her sleepless night.

She trailed him down the stairs. No one lingered, nothing lurked at the bottom. He tossed her suitcase into the backseat of his vehicle, before assisting her into the front. Her narrow-skirted dress was pretty, but if she ever needed to run, she was a dead woman.

"So you have enhanced senses," she said after he climbed in next to her.

"I don't know. My senses are mine. They're normal to me." "Okay. That makes sense. You can hear my heartbeat?" "Yeah." He pulled away from the curb.

"What happens when you're in a room full of people?

All those heartbeats in your head aren't distracting?"

He wasn't sure where she was going with her line of questioning. "I was born with all my senses, and I learned to focus the same way, I guess, as I learned to walk. By instinct."

"You can smell people, too? Anyone, not only someone who hasn't showered or who marinated in cologne?"

"Yeah. Mostly scent is based on emotion. Take fear. If someone is afraid, I can detect a specific...marker, I guess. I've never tried to describe my senses before. I don't have the words to explain them. Being what I am is my normal," he repeated. "I don't know how you experience the world."

"I'm trying to put your normal into perspective. I mean, did you pick up anything from Connor at the restaurant?"

He frowned at her instead of paying attention to the road. "What?"

"Watch where you're going," she warned after he swerved too close to a parked car. "Did you happen to focus on Connor at all while we were at that pretentious restaurant?"

"No." He sailed through a yellow light. Tires and brakes squealed a discordant duet somewhere to his left.

"Will you please pay attention to your driving?" Britt yelled.

"Why would I want to read Connor Peters?" he shouted in return. *Ancient Ones,* he should have tried to get a read on the congressman. He'd been so intent on Britt, focusing on Peters never occurred to him.

He'd handled everything all wrong.

"Because he was with me." Britt sounded smug. "I remember you telling me I'm your whole life."

He was positive he hadn't said quite those words; she clearly understood the gist.

"Yeah. You distract me. And yeah, I should have tried to get a sense of him. You have me in knots, female."

"Don't blame me if you can't control yourself."

"I lost a good chance," he admitted. He'd be kicking himself for a long time.

"He was drunk."

"Huh?"

"He'd been drinking. He was still drinking. Of course, I don't have your sense of smell, so I could be wrong."

He ignored her sarcasm. "I'm not familiar with sapien drinking habits, but isn't it early in the day for hard liquor?"

"That's why I mentioned the booze. The guy is supposed to be representing the family we elected to Washington, and he was inebriated before noon."

She lowered her voice. "Maybe the alcohol confused him, but he acted as if we'd met. Which is impossible. My private school experience in no way mirrors his."

"Private school?"

"I lasted six months at an evangelical school before I was expelled."

"Why were you expelled?"

"According to their pious asses, I was incorrigible."

He could see why narrow-minded people might suppose she was hopeless. He believed her irreverence added to her charm.

"What happened next?"

"Public high school. Friendships and cliques were set years earlier. Being a newbie, especially one with no social skills, was brutal. I was desperate. I had no friends, no allies."

"No pack," he muttered. "What?"

"No pack," Dakota repeated. "The people who accept you and always have your back, no matter what."

The heat of her stare burned him. He didn't dare take his eyes from the road. Only a few more minutes until they arrived at Ethan's house.

"Like wild animals?"

"No." That wasn't at all what he meant.

"Pack is a good description. The only pack open to me was as rebellious as I was. The wild ones. The feral."

She'd mentioned rebellion before. One way or another, Dakota was going to get to the truth about Byrne. He needed to understand how DiNardo fit into the picture and if Britt had any fondness for him.

Not a discussion he wanted to have while driving. He wanted to be able to give Britt one hundred percent of his attention.

She had a lot of talking ahead of her, whether she wanted to or not, before the moon rose again.

Chapter 14

Britt found Selena in the kitchen, staring at a piece of paper on the counter. "Thank you for letting me stay. I hate imposing."

"No problem," Selena replied. "Do you ever cook?"

"No."

"But you understand recipes. Helga across the street sent me a recipe that sounds good, but the instructions make no sense."

"Why would I know anything about recipes?" Britt pulled a glass from the cupboard. She was getting too familiar with Selena's kitchen.

"They're the same as formulas," Selena reasoned. "The only difference is the list of ingredients."

"Yeah?" Selena had a point. "Trust me. Even with your herbs added, you don't want to eat my concoctions. And speaking of concoctions—what did you put on my cuts last night? They're practically all healed."

"An herb my pack healer suggested."

There was that word again. *Pack.* Selena tossed out the word as if Britt was supposed to accept a whole new reality.

"How are you doing mentally? Emotionally?"

Britt opened the freezer door and helped herself to a couple of ice cubes. "How am I supposed to be doing? Everything I believe in as a scientist denies what Dakota claims. Yet, as a scientist, I'm supposed to keep an open mind. I'm not even going to go into how he's shown me more evidence to validate his claim than my father ever showed me supporting his religion."

Wow. She hadn't meant to spew all her doubts. Dakota and her father had nothing to do with each other, except for her father's insistence anything unfamiliar was spawned from the devil.

Selena pulled several short bottles from a cupboard. "I don't understand the cooking properties of these herbs."

"And whoever invented the recipe probably doesn't appreciate the medicinal properties." Britt turned to the sink and twisted the faucet.

"I'll figure out this cooking stuff eventually," Selena muttered. "Having Helga across the street has been a blessing."

The ice cubes bobbed in Britt's glass, chinking against the sides like an off-the-beat musician.

She had no other place to hide, or else she'd leave. Besides, these accommodations were free. Without a job, she needed to massage the most out of every cent.

"What do you know about folklore?" Selena abandoned the recipe and stared at Britt.

"Not a lot," Britt admitted. "Why the change in subject?"

"I'm trying to deepen your acceptance of your relationship with Dakota."

"You guys are werewolves." *There.* She'd acknowledged the aberration aloud.

Selena's expression remained intense. "Being lycan is only part of what's happening. The reason Ethan bought this house is for the location within the sacred triad of Oak, Ash, and Hawthorn. The three trees are an ancient safety charm."

Britt reminded herself ancient practices were often rooted in scientific realities. "Explain."

"The address is Ash Street. The cross streets forming this block are Oak and Hawthorn."

"So?"

"So forty-two Ash is a safe place, allegedly filled with fairy magic."

"And you believe in magic?"

"I believe in the healing properties of plants," Selena replied. "Trees are plants. Hawthorn is also the preferred wood for staking vampires."

"Vampires don't exist."

"Try to convince the undead guarding the end of the block every night. I've fought them. They're as real as you."

Since she was trapped in a nightmare, how real could Britt be? Yet, she was at forty-two Ash Street, believing she was safe. Did the source of safety matter if the house was a fortress?

"Fine. You live in a house protected by the Tooth Fairy."

"There's a lot going on you don't understand."

"I have my own issues," Britt retorted. *No job, no roommate, an ex-lover threatening me from prison, my damaged car, an ex-lover threatening me from prison.* Yeah, Judd counted twice.

"So I've gathered. Dakota is waiting for you on the back porch."

Britt gripped her glass and shuffled toward the kitchen door. Ethan's property included a nice backyard, fully enclosed by a thorny hedge, as she'd discovered last night. To keep out vampires, Selena claimed not two minutes earlier. Britt was willing to concede the existence of werewolves. She'd seen Dakota change into one. A living, breathing creature. Vampires, on the other hand, couldn't possibly exist because they were, by definition, dead.

Maybe she could distract Dakota with a lively debate on the possibility of vampires, zombies, and other dead threats.

Anything to avoid a discussion of Judd.

Dakota still wore his jeans. He'd exchanged his golf shirt for a T-shirt that clung to his muscles. Scuffed black boots finished the bad boy disguise. He leaned against the porch railing with his arms banded over his chest. His feet were crossed at the ankles.

Sexy. The man was too sexy for his own good. How did a bus driver develop those muscles?

"You're looking at me as if you want to tear off my clothes." His words shattered her mood. "Wanna go to the bedroom?"

At least he hadn't been crude with his suggestion.

"No. I don't get outside often enough." She eyed a grouping of Adirondack chairs beneath the huge tree in the back corner of the yard. "Let's sit under the tree."

"You don't want to sit there," Dakota said. "Why not?"

"Mulberry trees are bird magnets."

"So?"

"They crap on everything in the general vicinity. A lot."

"Okay." She lowered herself to the step.

Dakota towered above her.

She swallowed hard. "What do you want to know?"

"Everything about your involvement with Judd Byrne."

As if she would ever tell anyone everything.

"Okay. Brace yourself. I told you I was home schooled until my mother got too sick to teach us."

"I remember."

"And I told you we were sent to a private evangelical school, where I was expelled, despite who my father is."

"He's one of those famous rich guys with the big churches on TV?"

"He's working on being number one," Britt agreed.

"The root of your rebellion."

"Not quite. I hate my father because he killed my mother."

DAKOTA STUCK HIS PINKY in his ear to clear it. He couldn't have heard Britt correctly. A religious guy killing his mate? Maybe the traffic a couple of blocks west interfered with his ears.

He was no expert on sapien religions, but Toke Lobo's road manager liked to view TV Bible thumpers while the band was on the road. He claimed he was getting an inside scoop on the enemy. Televangelists didn't act as if they had the balls to murder someone.

A lot of them, though, acted smarmy enough to hire someone else to do the dirty work.

"I need you to explain," he told Britt.

"Mom was diagnosed with breast cancer when I was thirteen. Pastor Paul decided faith and prayer alone would heal her." Britt's tone was flat, void of any emotion. "No medical doctors. No treatments of any kind, including herbal or New Age. Only his prayers. His congregation's prayers. His children's tears."

Dakota gripped the railing so tightly, the wood splintered into his hand. His senses narrowed until all he could see was Britt; only her heartbeat thrummed against his eardrums, the simmer of her undiluted rage assaulted his nose.

"He begged scholarships for us at Faith Ministries Academy by claiming the death sentence he slapped on Mom was a hardship."

Dakota could not imagine watching his mother die and standing by, unable to do anything. No wonder Britt wrestled with anger issues. A male werewolf always honored and protected his mate. Glimpsing into her childhood explained a great deal.

"He expected me to be supportive. He expected me to be a model child. My mother was dying of something doctors might have stopped with treatment. He chose to anoint her with holy oil. My younger brother and sister didn't understand what was going on. Every day, the school headmaster would embarrass us by calling us up front during morning assembly to pray for our mother. Our private grief was horribly public." Her voice cracked on a couple of words, but for the most part, she maintained a control she'd honed with years of practice.

Britt's gaze fixed on the mulberry tree. Dakota figured she wasn't seeing the birds steal the fruit or the wind prancing on the leaves.

"Science might have saved my mother's life. Surgery. Chemo. Radiation. Maybe not, but she would have had a better chance than my father's ambition gave her. After she died, and we went back to school, I had to go into what they called science class and listen to fantasies disguised as fact. The class wasn't science at all, but rather another religion class patched together to meet the state's curriculum requirements."

Oh yeah. Lots of baggage. He forced himself to keep his arms crossed. If he touched her, he might dam the flow of words, and he needed her to expel the poison before they could move forward.

"The administration didn't care for what I had to say about their alleged faith-based voodoo woo-woo."

"They expelled you."

"You betcha." The corners of her mouth lifted but her expression was void of emotion. "My father wanted me to stay home and keep house for him. Substitute mother for Bart and Susie. I wanted to go to a school where they taught real science. Pastor Paul fought me, so I reported him to the state."

His lips twitched, despite his need to keep a straight face. *Ancient Ones*, his female had strong defenses. He admired her determination.

"He had to enroll me in public school." "Where you met Judd."

"Where I met Judd," she echoed.

She stood. Stretched. Her dress was wrinkled. The cuts and scratches on her face and arms were mending quickly. Selena had a gift for herbal healing.

Britt perched on the railing opposite Dakota. She stared at him across the rim of her glass as she sipped her water. Ice cubes clinked against the glass. After she drained her drink, she set the glass on the railing next to her. "Heard enough? Are my dirty secrets filthy enough for you?"

"What aren't you telling me?"

"Details." She tried to blow him off.

"Judd Byrne. According to your cop friends, you were involved with his arrest."

Her lips quivered. If he hadn't watched her so closely, he might have missed the tell.

"Yeah. Judd decided to rob my father's church. I didn't care. My father deserved to be robbed. At gunpoint, too. No problem."

He believed her. "What happened?"

"My younger brother had a lot of crap going on, what with Mom's death and all. He's afraid of the dark. Pastor Paul bellowed for the darkness to leave Mom's body, so Bart believed darkness is cancer."

She averted her face. "Judd told me to lock Bart and Susie in the closet where the choir robes hang. He's my baby brother. Maybe my father is an asshole, but my brother was only a kid. He wasn't supposed to be at the church that night. I never would have gone along with Judd if I'd known Bart and Susie would be involved. I'm not a monster."

"No, you're not a monster." How could he fault her for protecting her younger siblings? He wished he had siblings to protect. He found her actions endearing.

"Judd backhanded me. Knocked me off my feet. That set the kids off even more. Curtis finally locked them in the closet. Judd pistol whipped my father, who deserved worse. Seven-hundred-fifty-two dollars." Her lips formed a thin line. "Judd's big score."

"Your father knew you were part of the robbery."

"Yeah, I called the cops before the pastor managed to free himself. I got immunity, Judd and Curtis got jail time."

"What happened to DiNardo?"

"He did his time. His sentence wasn't as harsh as Judd's. Judd had the gun and was clearly the leader. After that, I'm as clueless as you are."

"DiNardo is out of prison?"

How many lowlifes named Curtis DiNardo could there be?

"So Tom and Mickey said. Curtis doesn't worry me. He's not the brightest bulb in the chandelier."

Dakota's exact assessment. Killing DiNardo hadn't deprived the world of anything worthwhile.

"DiNardo is the link between Byrne and Peters," Dakota reminded her in a soft voice. "According to your cop friends."

Britt choked on an audible dreg of hysteria. "You have no idea what a stretch that is. Connor Peters is a prep school prick, and Curtis is nothing more than rat shit in a gutter."

Strong words. "Tell me how you really feel."

"There is no way Connor Peters has anything to do with the gutter."

"Didn't you say he was drinking early in the day?"

"Alcoholism doesn't mean he associates with sewer flotsam."

She unquestionably loathed DiNardo, and Dakota was glad.

"I don't care how many odd jobs Curtis's uncle did for the old congressman, a sow's ear is still from a pig, no matter how many silk purses you try to make. Why are you determined to find a link between Connor and Judd?"

"You're the one who believes Peters was hinting around about you and Byrne."

"Sluts will be sluts," Britt murmured, almost as an afterthought.

"What?" Dakota didn't bother swallowing his outrage.

"Connor claimed I might not pass a background check to get a government grant because sluts will be sluts. I assumed he meant high school. I mean, yeah, I'm a honkytonk angel with a different man in my bed every weekend, but I have good credit, and I'm not...irresponsible. High school was different."

"And the only way he would know about your high school years is if someone told him. He was in prep school while you were in public school. He has a link to DiNardo, who was Byrne's sidekick. Someone smuggled a cell phone to Byrne and is trying to get him sprung early. Who wields that kind of power and influence?"

"The Peters family."

"The Peters family isn't the group of grand patriots everyone assumes they are," Dakota continued. "They've double-crossed Selena's pack, and they tried to wipe out Ethan's pack."

"There's more than one pack?" Her voice was faint.

"Hundreds of packs live in the States. I'm from the Loup Garou. We immigrated from France. Selena is from the Varulv, Scandinavian immigrants. Ethan grew up with the Loup Garou, although he recently learned he's Limmikin, at least on his father's side. Limmikin are indigenous packs."

"I'm Scandinavian. Norwegian."

"Like Selena."

"I'm not a werewolf."

"She's not a blond."

"Having different color hair isn't the same," Britt protested.

"Okay, she's not the same religion as your father." "Still not the same."

"You're both mated to werewolves," Dakota pointed out. "Yeah, Ethan and I are from different backgrounds, and although we're from the same pack, we're not the same person. We're both homo lupus. As is Selena. You're not. Neither is Toke Lobo's mate."

"Toke Lobo is not a werewolf." Her voice warbled.

Dakota arched an eyebrow. "Wanna bet?"

Britt brought her hands to her face.

Dakota winced when she touched a particularly nasty scab, but Britt didn't react. He crossed the deck and lightly grasped her wrists. "Don't."

"They itch." Her protest was muffled.

"Itching means they're healing."

"So I've heard. Doesn't stop the itching, though."

Her eyes wouldn't meet his, confirming his suspicion she hid something about Byrne.

"How is your brother these days?"

"Okay, I guess. My father took out a restraining order on me. I can't contact Bart or Susie."

He still clasped her wrists, so he separated her arms and stepped into the opening he'd created. Her body heat brushed against his. "Your life sucked."

"I survived."

"Your father's a pile of vampire scat."

"You're too kind."

He leaned closer. "I am your champion." His voice clogged roughly in his throat. "I'm the best thing that will ever happen to you. Once you accept me, once you believe in me, you'll never have to worry again."

"I wouldn't believe that," Selena interrupted from the door, as Dakota leaned in to kiss Britt.

Dakota groaned. "Go away, Selena."

"You're feeding her a line of scat."

Dakota experienced his first ever urge to throttle a female.

Selena wouldn't stop. "Yeah, you're the best thing that will ever happen to her."

"Thanks."

"Do I need to listen to more propaganda?" Britt's voice was husky. She'd been in the moment, too.

"Never having to worry about anything ever again is a line," Selena admitted. "Take me, for instance. The vampires at the end of the street worry me. I've got Ethan, the best thing that will ever happen to me, but blood sucking murderers scare the scat out of me."

He returned Selena's glare. "The blood suckers are your problem. They're a side effect of Ethan's mission. I'm only the guy who drove the extra hands Ethan requested."

"You didn't mind helping with—"

"Ethan asked," Dakota interrupted. He didn't want her blurting out DiNardo's death yet, or how he'd taken the lead. "I didn't have a lot of choice."

Selena's smile was unpleasant. "We all have to do what we have to do."

Britt made a sound, as if she were choking. Dakota abandoned his death glare at Selena to tend to his mate.

"I guess I'm not the only one with secrets," Britt managed.

"You have no idea." Selena paused. "So what's this scat about you meeting with Connor Peters today?"

BRITT TRIED TO SQUEEZE past Dakota, angry with herself for nearly submitting to a kiss from him. He wasn't letting her pass. She figured her compulsion to kiss him was hypnotism or a vampire spell, not unlike what she'd read in vampire fiction back in college. While she didn't read a lot of fiction, she'd absorbed enough myth to figure maybe the ability also belonged to werewolves.

The theory was the only sensible explanation she could formulate. She didn't want Dakota to kiss her. All common sense fled when he kissed her, and she needed her wits.

She owed Selena.

"Go away," Dakota told Selena over his shoulder.

"This is my house," Selena replied.

"Were you eavesdropping?"

Britt resented how Dakota had a way of making her discuss stuff she hated. What magic did he use to breech her defenses? If she asked, he'd blame being a werewolf.

She was still torn about believing in their existence. His existence. She'd witnessed him transform. She'd endured the heat, the severe shift in air pressure battering the empty places in her skull.

He stared at her with obsidian colored eyes; black holes sucking her willpower, her strength, her sense of identity right out of her brain. Only the memory of him in her bed the night they'd hooked up remained. The memory erased her early days of being sexually active.

Active, but never fulfilled. Not the way Dakota fulfilled her. No man ever satisfied her the way he did.

He brushed a bruise on her cheekbone. She winced. "Are you with us?"

"Yeah. Sorry."

"Connor Peters," Selena repeated. "He called me. Not my idea."

"You met with him the other day." Selena's voice held anger, impatience, and a shopping list of other negative emotions.

"Yeah. I want to move forward with Night Shift. Guess what? He informed me neither of us could pass a background check to qualify for a government grant."

"What?" Selena's fists clenched at her sides. Her face was as pale as the clouds drifting overhead. "What scat are you talking? Did you tell him who my father was?"

Yeah. Dissing Erik Wolfe nailed Selena right in her pride.

"He hinted your father might have been subversive."

Selena's nostrils flared, and her voice quavered. "Connor is a vile vamp scat eater. My father was a patriot."

"He sure was," Dakota said. "He's a legend. Every werewolf in the United States honors Erik Wolfe."

"Connor Peters isn't a werewolf," Britt pointed out. "Unless you forgot to add him to your list."

"He's not one of us." Selena sneered. "He's your breed."

For some reason, Selena's words sounded nastier than if she'd called Connor a motherfucking-cock-sucking-whatever.

Britt wished she had the knack to destroy with only tone of voice. "Maybe the vampires should claim him."

Not that she believed in vampires.

Dakota snickered.

"Why would anyone want to?" Selena asked. "Take his father and brother, for instance."

"Brother?" Congressman Bryant Peters had been exposed as a secret perv. But the brother? Liam Peters vanished. The massive manhunt underway continued to dominate local news headlines.

Selena and Ethan were the last ones to see Bryant before he blew out his brains. They'd phoned in the suicide. "Surprisingly un-messy," Selena had claimed.

Until the ugly stuff surfaced. Raping minors. Snuff films. An active presence on the Deep Web.

Nasty whispers didn't touch the oldest son, who had been named interim congressman until a new election could be held.

Selena and Ethan were among the last to see him alive, too. He'd visited their house. Others had seen him leave, had watched Ethan and Selena wave goodbye from the well-lit front door.

He hadn't been seen since. His vehicle was parked in his driveway. Only his fingerprints were on the door or steering wheel. No surveillance footage existed. The security company hadn't yet scheduled the appointment to install the system the acting congressman had ordered for his house shortly after his father's suicide.

No wonder Connor drank.

Selena's comment made no sense.

Selena and Dakota exchanged a secret-betraying glance.

Time to change the subject.

"Mickey and Tom asked how well I know you," Britt told Dakota.

"Did you tell them 'not as well as you're going to?'"

"I doubt they'd appreciate your humor."

"They didn't have a problem with me at Holsters."

"Maybe they ran a background check on you."

"I'm a bus driver from Loup Garou, Colorado, working for Toke Lobo and the Pack. What you see is what you get."

Yeah. She'd seen.

"What happened to Liam Peters?"

"He vanished," Dakota replied.

Britt caught the smirk on Selena's face.

"Okay." She changed tacks. "Let's discuss Curtis DiNardo."

Selena flinched. "How did he get into the mix?"

"You know Curtis?"

"Yeah. His uncle owned the house I was renting on Pine Street. Curtis was supposed to replace the windows after the vampire broke in. How do you know him?"

"I went to high school with him."

"We're a small town." Selena shrugged.

"I found out today he's missing, too."

"No loss," Selena muttered.

Britt couldn't disagree. "Odd how both he and Liam Peters disappeared at the same time."

"Who says?"

"Mickey and Tom, a couple of other guys I went to high school with—they're cops."

"Mickey and Tom? As in officers Clerkin and Anderson?"

"Those are the guys."

"Yeah." Selena acted as if cops were nothing. "They've been around a bunch."

"Were you aware Curtis's uncle—your former landlord, I guess—does odd jobs for the Peters family?"

"No. Should I be?"

Okay. Selena wasn't aware of Judd. The texts. Britt's notorious past. Yet Selena's reaction bothered Britt. Selena was hiding something regarding the disappearances of Liam Peters and Curtis DiNardo.

Meaning Dakota might have been involved.

"Tell me again how Ethan wound up in Warwick."

"Didn't Dakota fill you in on the treaties?"

"Service for sanctuary?"

"Yeah. The Varulv kept their end of the bargain. The treaty is why my father was at the Pentagon on September eleventh. Doing something for Congressman Peters. Peters has betrayed us and the treaties. The current administration wants to abandon the treaties. The lycan world fears a lack of guaranteed sanctuary could recreate the same scenarios we fled in Europe."

"What do treaties have to do with Ethan?"

"Ethan was sent to Warwick to convince Congressman Peters to vote to maintain the treaties."

"He used Night Shift as an excuse to get in to see the congressman?"

Selena sighed. "That's my guess. And no, I didn't know."

"Was Liam aware of the treaties?" Britt purposely used the past tense.

"Yes." Selena lifted her chin.

"You're sure?"

"Yes." No further explanation.

"He helped." Dakota reinforced Selena's claim.

"Aren't you merely the driver?" Britt taunted.

"Driving doesn't make me deaf or blind. Liam Peters helped his father whenever he could."

Nausea roiled into Britt's throat. She'd voted for Bryant Peters. The scandal of his pastimes angered her. To learn his oldest son...

"Right, wrong or even legal doesn't matter. Something Dakota might have neglected to tell you about our makeup—not our culture, but our DNA is we take care of our own. If someone hurts one of us, we take our revenge. Retribution isn't optional. Revenge is our way of life. So be careful. Dakota will torture and kill anyone who hurts you."

And I'll smile the whole time," Dakota added. "Should your father be first?"

Britt didn't care. She had bigger problems than her father. "Seeing him flip out and scream biblical invectives against you if you shifted in front of him would be hysterical, except he's not worth the energy."

"What about Judd?"

"Who's Judd?" Selena asked.

"My high school boyfriend," Britt replied. "Dakota promised to really hurt him. Bad. Make him suffer."

"Laughing the whole time," Dakota added. "And I'll make his pain last a long, long time."

"Can I be a witness?" She'd dissected frogs and other animals as part of her training. Gore didn't bother her. She'd nursed her mother as breast cancer ate her alive. Britt would be the first to admit to the rage she couldn't exorcise.

For the first time, she wished...no, she envied Selena. If Selena could shift the way Dakota did, from woman to wolf, she was what Britt longed to be. If she were a wolf, she could maul Judd the way he deserved to be savaged.

"What's it like, killing an enemy?" she asked.

Dakota's jaw dropped, while Selena laughed.

Britt's face warmed. She genuinely wanted to know.

"Bliss." Selena spoke matter-of-factly. "The saying, 'revenge is a dish best served cold' is okay for sapiens, I suppose. Nothing compares to the sweet, hot, surge of blood in your mouth as your fangs rip into vulnerable flesh, and the music of your enemy's screams fills your ears."

"You're giving her the wrong idea," Dakota muttered. "We're not vampires. The Ancient Ones would never condone killing for killing's sake."

"She said enemy," Selena retorted.

Dakota frowned at Britt. "If you need enemies dealt with, use me."

"Don't worry my pretty little head?" She couldn't keep the snide tone from her voice.

"Right."

She expected anger from him, not worry. She didn't want his concern.

She possessed a secret weapon against Judd. And Curtis, if he was still content being Judd's sidekick. Maybe Curtis learned something in prison, although Britt doubted he was capable. He wasn't bright enough to see beyond the current moment.

Dakota. Dakota would protect her. Judd could have learned prison yard tactics and honed his fighting technique, but what chance would he stand against a werewolf?

She regarded Dakota with a new perspective. Being with him provided perks she hadn't considered.

"You're burning too many brain cells," Dakota warned her.

"I'm putting pieces of a puzzle together, trying to see the whole picture. I'm getting more focused. You should be grateful. The outcome is all in your favor."

He narrowed his eyes.

She cupped the curves of his shoulders with her palms and pulled him closer. Like any other male with the possibility of sex involved, he responded.

Something stirred inside her. Not the usual *gosh-I've-got-an-itch-let's-hook-up-and-scratch-it* horniness she often confused with frustration, but honest-to-goodness desire. For Dakota.

Britt couldn't remember the last time she'd experienced anything similar.

"Selena, go away." Her voice came out raspy. Husky. Hopefully something Dakota would find sexy.

"Okay."

"Why did you say okay to her, but not me?" Dakota asked.

"She's my friend, and she's sapien, not operating off DNA. Cheer up, Dakota. It's all good."

Dakota rested his forehead against Britt's. Her nipples tingled from the heat of his body. "Is she right?"

"Yeah."

Dakota tilted his head, as if searching for the perfect angle. His rough, callused hands clasped her bare upper arms as he closed in for a kiss. The tips of her breasts brushed his chest. Her body sparked.

Her lips parted as Dakota brought his mouth to hers. The sparks ignited her senses. His tongue rubbed hers as he pressed his lower body closer. She shifted enough for his more interesting parts to land where she wanted.

She thought she heard a low rumble in his throat.

His unique scent filled her head. She wanted more from him. Needed more from him.

He sucked her lower lip into his mouth in the most erotic foreplay she'd ever experienced. He took his time, as if inching toward the main event was something important. She'd always wanted the fucking finished, wanted her climax as quickly as possible so she could move on with the rest of her life. Sex was the same as using the bathroom.

She needed an orgasm, got one, washed her hands, and proceeded with her life.

Dakota had other ideas, and shockingly she was open to a new experience. He removed his hands from the railing behind her and rested them on her hips.

"Are you aroused by the idea of me killing Jed?" he murmured in a break between kisses.

"It satisfies me."

"What? You don't believe I can satisfy you?"

"Who says I'm going to let you stop until you do?" Turnabout was fair play. She nibbled on his bottom lip.

His hands slid to her bottom. Her butt cheeks filled his palms as he pulled her closer to him. His erection rested in the notch where her thighs met her groin.

He broke the kiss. "Sounds fair. Why don't we go to the bedroom before we forget others are hanging around. Unless you want to put on a show?"

She stiffened.

"Okay, what did I say wrong this time?"

DAKOTA WASN'T SO FAR lost in lust he didn't realize he'd dumped cold water on her. But he didn't let go of her.

Every time he believed he was making progress with Britt, something happened, and he was back at square one, no different than a child's board game.

He didn't wait for an answer but carried her into the house. They could talk in the bedroom as easily as they could converse on the back porch, and if they could move past whatever was bothering her, sex would be easier. He wanted to have sex again. Keeping his libido in check all day was fraying his nerves. Sitting with cops who'd eyed her chest, being around Connor Peters who rubbed him wrong by existing...he was past ready to howl at the moon.

Britt was as rigid as the porch railing when he tossed her over his shoulder. Somewhere between the back door and the bedroom she'd become more pliant. Maybe not as fluid as she'd been when he'd kissed her, before he opened his big mouth and said something to irritate her. Someplace between. He'd simply have to kiss her fluid again. No hardship.

"I apologize for whatever I said or did to upset you." He dropped her onto the bed.

The tips of her fingers grazed his cheek as he leaned above her.

"I have baggage," she admitted. "Sometimes I'm too paranoid. I have triggers."

He needed to learn those triggers. He dropped next to her on the mattress, rolling to his side to face her. "Don't shut me out."

"I get scared. When I get scared, I get stupid. Before I get scared, I get mad, and I get really stupid."

"You could never be stupid. Careless, maybe. But not stupid. If you were stupid, you'd still be arguing with me about staying in your apartment."

"I know Judd. I can't imagine prison reformed him. He's the kind who'd use the opportunity to learn new methods of torture."

Dakota hated the way her voice dripped bitterness. "Did he torture you?"

"Mental cruelty." She must have sensed how much she was giving away; her tone changed to a mocking mode.

"In addition to your father?"

"I'm a poor, put upon female." She continued her self-derision. "First world problems."

"They're yours. And mine by default."

"My baggage is mine. I'm the one who needs to get rid of my past."

"I can help."

"Your FBI friend?"

"Yeah. Tom and Jerry—"

"Tom and Mickey," she corrected.

"Your cop friends aren't taking the threat seriously. Byrne is in prison, yet he has a cell phone and has been texting you."

"Yeah. How did he get my number?"

"You don't have the same number you had in high school?"

Her disdain could have evaporated Niagara Falls. "My family had no money for worldly trappings such as cell phones. Pastor Paul hauls the cash in now. We were poor during my school years."

"Someone had to give Byrne your number."

"I don't share my number on social media or hookups. I never gave my number to you."

He grinned. "Your number is in my phone."

"You stole the number, something Judd can't do."

"Is it on the paperwork you filed for Night Shift?"

She stared at him. "Yeah. I had to provide a phone number. How would Judd have access to business filings?"

"Your applications could be public record." He'd have Luke check.

"They are. If he learned basic computer skills in prison, he could keep track of me online." Her pale complexion turned translucent.

"Don't stress." He ran his thumb across her cheek. "You've got me. You've got the whole werewolf community backing you."

Not many lycans remained in Minnesota.

She rolled from him and stared at the ceiling. "Criminals shouldn't be allowed Internet access in prison." Her voice warbled. "Yeah, teaching computer skills to inmates is rehab, but he's stalking me."

"Or someone is feeding him info." When Dakota found out who, he was going to kill the vamp-scat-eating creature slowly and painfully.

"Maybe Curtis," Britt ventured.

If a person believed in ghosts.

"Except I don't want to find out where Curtis is." She shuddered.

He wanted to tell her DiNardo would never bother her again. He couldn't. DiNardo's fate was a lycan secret carried to the graves of the ones who had torn the sniveling fool apart. DiNardo was much better off dead than he would have been had Dakota known what he'd done to Britt. Yeah, he'd died in agony but only because he was stupid. Dakota regretted not having prolonged his suffering. He could have...

"And I'm still trying to figure out how Connor Peters fits in to what's going on."

Something in her tone alerted him. Except he didn't want to bother with any of this scat. He was in bed with his mate and only moments ago she'd been receptive to his kiss. She hadn't fought him while he swept her into the bedroom. He merely needed to figure out what he'd done to switch her mind to high school from enjoying how wonderful they were together.

"When did you get the first text from Byrne?"

"The morning after you and I first met."

Coincidence was always suspect. DiNardo couldn't possibly have been the person to alert Byrne when Britt hooked up with a werewolf.

Dakota needed to talk to Ethan. Ethan had visited Congressman Peters' office before the first one committed suicide. He'd talked to Liam a couple of times before he helped kill him for raping Selena.

DiNardo was a link to Byrne. Connor Peters had a tenuous connection to DiNardo. Shaky, but linked.

"I was a happy male the morning after you and I first met," he reminded her. He pressed his freshly burgeoning erection against her hip.

"I was worried. You weren't supposed to be so happy you wanted to stick around."

"Sticking around is genetic."

"So you claim."

"Someday you'll learn to appreciate my devotion to you. Someday, you're going to wonder how you ever existed without me making you happy."

"Someday, maybe I'll believe one of your lines."

"You look nice in that dress. I'd hate to damage it while I tried to get closer to you." He propped himself on his elbow, blocking her view of the ceiling.

"You're always trying to get me out of my clothes."

"We can make love with your clothes on if you want." He was willing to try anything.

"Don't." Her voice grew strangled.

"Don't what?"

"Call our fucking making love."

Those crude words stabbed at him.

"Don't change sex into something romantic."

"Oh, Britt." His tone was as gentle as he could manage. "When I'm touching you, tasting you, deep inside you, I'm making love to you. Nothing you can say or do will change my emotion. Whether you accept my love or not doesn't matter. My heart, my soul, my very being is making love to you."

"Are you going to get all mushy on me?"

"Mushy? Babe, it's hard." He nudged her with his erection.

"And I'm flashing back to my father's rants," she admitted.

Now what was she talking about?

"I don't mean the premarital sex rant." She grew solemn. Introspective. Britt wasn't prone to deep contemplation and her pensiveness bothered him. "I abandoned the faith and beliefs of my father years ago."

"When he let your mother die."

"Yes. Some habits—"

"Indoctrinations," Dakota corrected.

She nodded. "According to my father, you're a demon."

Everything in him stilled. He waited. Blood drained from his cock.

"You're a beast. Not human."

"I'm as human as you," he whispered. "Just a different genus within the same species."

"I don't change forms, except for gaining or losing weight."

"A sapien trait. My shifter ability is a lupus trait. Our two species can intermingle, unlike dogs and cats. Or homo lupus and wolves. Luke, Toke Lobo's drummer is proof. Toke Lobo himself mated with a sapien, and they have a son. If we weren't meant to be together, the Ancient Ones would have created us to be different. You are the only living, breathing being with whom I can be a sexual creature. Doesn't my devotion count for something?"

"I find your story difficult to believe. You're too skilled to be a beginner."

He preened at the compliment. "Not skill. Instinct. My instincts, my very being are in tune with you."

Many times in Dakota's life he'd wished he'd been born something other than lycan. The longing sliced into him with ax-like destruction. Britt wouldn't be denying him his rights if she didn't retain her father's teachings. Why did the demon indoctrination have to be the one sticking with her? "Demons, according to your culture, are evil. Do you believe I'm evil?"

Her blue-gray eyes stared at him. "I don't—we've known each other only a couple of days."

"Do you believe I'm as evil as Judd?"

"Oh, no!"

"Congressman Peters? Any of them?"

"Of course not." Indignation colored every syllable.

"Who's the real demon?"

She turned away, as if she couldn't bear to look at him. "Me."

Chapter 15

Saved by the bell. Or in this case, the buzzer.

Britt extracted herself from Dakota's weight as he dug into his pocket for his vibrating phone. She rolled into a sitting position. "Answer that."

She swiped at a few annoying strands of hair sticking to her cheek. Her hand trembled, and she was glad Dakota was paying more attention to his caller than to her.

She'd shared more of her crappy life with him than with anyone else. Ever. Who she'd been before college didn't matter.

"What do you mean he's out?" Dakota growled. His glower could have shattered the window.

Britt froze. Not only couldn't she move, his question raised goose bumps on her arms. The hairs on her nape stood at attention.

"Britt was supposed to be notified of his release," Dakota snapped. "Find out why she wasn't." He disconnected his call.

She was going to be sick. Where was the bathroom? She leapt from the bed and hurried to the door, cursing how the narrowness of her skirt prevented her from running. She barely found the commode on time. The distinct sound of fabric tearing accompanied her retching.

"Get out," she rasped at Dakota between bouts of nausea as he squatted next to her and held her hair away from her face.

"You'll be okay," he crooned. The tone of his voice was strange. "I'm not going to let Judd Byrne—or anyone—get to you. You're safe with me."

"Go away." *Couldn't a girl puke in private?*

Someone rapped on the door. "Britt? Are you okay?" Selena, who knew what to do.

"Make him leave." Britt barely managed coherence.

"She wants some privacy, Dakota."

At least Selena understood.

"It's a female thing."

"Female thing? You mean pregnant?" He sounded appalled.

"No, not pregnant. Unless you've been careless. Females don't want to be around others when we're sick."

"I'm not other." He sounded as if his teeth were clenched.

Britt rested her hot face against the cool porcelain. The faint odor of urine lingered under the stench of her vomit. What did he mean? He was more *other* than anyone she'd ever met before. Except Selena. She still couldn't wrap her head around the fact she'd roomed with a werewolf in college. If anyone in the room was other, it was her.

"Let me get you a glass of hot water," Selena offered.

"I'm good." Britt's voice was raspy.

"Or tea. Tea will settle your stomach." Selena flushed for her. "Or should I get you some grass to chew on?"

"Not funny," Dakota muttered.

"She doesn't get the joke. Sapiens are ridiculously fond of dogs."

Whatever they were yammering about drifted above her head. Who chewed grass? Everyone Britt knew smoked theirs.

At least the knots in her stomach might prevent her from barfing again, if there was anything remaining to purge. Her limbs twitched, echoing the erratic beat of her heart.

"I'm not leaving her side," Dakota declared.

"Don't be ridiculous," Selena said. "You'll settle into your sex life."

"Our sex life isn't the problem. Britt's safety is."

"Her safety?" Selena sounded confused.

"Never mind," Britt croaked. She lifted her head. Her mouth tasted vile. "Is your offer of hot water still good?"

"Sure."

After Selena left, Britt focused on Dakota. "Judd is out."

Dakota's mouth formed a grim line. He dropped from his squatting position to sit next to her on the tile floor. "My FBI contact put a flag on Byrne's file to keep track of what was happening."

"Why wasn't I notified?"

"Luke's checking into why the system failed." He brushed at her hair again, annoying her with the gesture. "Whoever neglected his job is a dead man."

Britt wished his posturing was true. Heck, she wanted to help.

"I will protect you with my life." His dark eyes made promises he couldn't possibly keep.

Selena didn't bother to knock when she returned. She handed Britt a mug of hot water. Britt sipped, and surprisingly, the water calmed her stomach.

"Why didn't you ever give me hot water in college?"

Selena rolled her eyes. "I hoped you'd learn not to overindulge. Besides, you created enough hot water on your own."

"Some friend you were." Britt stretched her legs.

Dakota snaked an arm around her and helped her to her feet. "Steady, there."

She didn't want to lean on him. She wanted to stand on her own legs. Walk her own walk. Shaky as she was, Dakota released her once she was upright. She appreciated his reading her mind.

"Are werewolves psychic?"

"What?"

"Can you read my mind?"

"No. I read your physiology and make deductions from your physical responses. I know you want to make love with me again, but you're listening to echoes of your father's rants programmed in your brain."

"You're not a demon."

"Not even close. I'm just an average guy, low pack status, mostly content with my life."

He hovered as they returned to the bedroom. She noticed the window screen had been replaced. She ought to offer to reimburse Ethan for the repair, even if she had lost her job and couldn't afford to pay for the damage.

"Only mostly content?" Anything, including inane questions, to avoid discussing Judd.

"A lot more content, since I found you."

"I was never lost. Why mostly?"

He hesitated so long, Britt wasn't sure he was going to answer her question.

"Sometimes living in a culture where some mandates are strictly adhered to can be restrictive if you're not part of the upper echelon."

A nice and vague answer.

"One of the reasons I enjoy driving the tour bus for Toke Lobo is because I'm in control of everyone while we're traveling."

"You're a control freak." Yeah. Not a big surprise.

"I have no control." He spoke softly. "Now you know my darkest secret."

"Seriously?" Maybe she was comparing lightning to eclipses, but his secret didn't feel nearly as dark as hers. She would never tell him—or anyone—her darkest secret. She had enough lighter ones to distract anyone who wanted to dig around in her past.

Such as Connor Peters.

The mere thought brought the shakes back. Connor Peters, tied to Curtis DiNardo, tied to Judd Byrne. Her stomach wasn't the only part of her body knotted up.

Her phone buzzed. She checked the screen. "Mickey Clerkin says Warwick police were notified Judd was up for parole."

"He's out," Dakota corrected.

"According the what Mickey texted, he's not."

"Are you willing to take the risk?"

No. She wasn't willing to risk anything as far as Judd was concerned. He'd used her, abused her, taken advantage of her naivety.

Her phone buzzed again. "Mickey and Tom want to stop by to talk to me again."

"Have you told them where you're staying?"

"Do my whereabouts matter?"

"Yeah. Some people can't enter the block of Ash between Oak and Hawthorn."

"Vampires?" She texted her location to Mickey.

"So Ethan claims."

"Trust me, Tom and Mickey aren't vampires or any other kind of supernatural beings. Maybe they're going to offer protection."

"Cops are too understaffed and underfunded to offer anything. They may sincerely want to, but lack of money and manpower will prevail."

"Oh, right. You're a secret agent man."

"I'm a bus driver for some government special agents. I'm inconsequential except for the fact I know some guys who know some guys."

She would have laughed at his joke except she sensed real pain behind the playful words.

"Why don't you change out of your dress. The skirt doesn't give you a lot of freedom of movement."

"In case I need to run?"

"Can you think of a better reason?"

DAKOTA KEPT HIS BACK to Britt while she stripped off her blue dress.

"Jeans will do," he suggested. "Nothing fancy."

He didn't want her trying to be attractive to any male except him. Not even cops she'd known in high school. Especially guys from high school who still sniggered about her history with Judd Byrne. Except she was the most beautiful creature Dakota had ever seen. Other males were naturally attracted to her.

A moment later she announced, "I'm decent."

She'd pulled on a pair of loose-fitting pants made from a fabric the same gray color as the pre-dawn sky. The garment elongated her legs. Her textured sweater molded to her breasts, making them appear bigger than they were. At least, how he remembered them. He hadn't seen them in too long. The outfit emphasized her sexiness.

He wondered, only for a moment, if he was male enough to handle her.

Of course I am. He was lycan, the ultimate definition of male. Her beauty and her background, her one-and-dones, were minor obstacles all.

"I'm not hiding in the bedroom," she stated firmly.

He agreed. "Let's join Selena and Ethan."

"Let me freshen my face."

Her beauty routine fascinated him. She didn't need the cosmetic enhancements. He preferred her without them. He also understood she needed to face acquaintances in full battle gear, and the painted-on mask was part of her armor.

Their gazes met in the mirror. "You're making me nervous with your hovering."

"You'll get used to my fascination with you." Dakota willed his words to be true.

She swiped something clear and shiny across her lips, giving him inappropriate ideas. "I don't suppose you'd let me kiss you."

She stared at him as if he requested something outrageous.

"You're so gorgeous, I want to kiss you. Everywhere," he continued. "And I do mean everywhere, if you get my drift. Your lips are all nice and wet and parted and—"

He broke off when she blushed redder than a stop sign as she grasped his meaning.

He hoped.

She merely shook her head, leaving him to interpret the motion however he wished. "Later," she whispered.

Ethan slammed into the house as Britt and Dakota joined Selena in the kitchen. "Scat sucking politicians," he muttered.

"What's wrong?" Selena switched off the oven. Whatever sapien concoction she was cooking smelled good for a change.

"I had an appointment with the current Congressman Peters this afternoon, and he stood me up. I was prepared to argue our case. And his snotty receptionist wouldn't reschedule me. Says he's off to Washington in a couple of days."

"He was drunk," Dakota said.

"What?"

"Connor had been drinking when I tried to have lunch with him today," Britt put in.

"You had lunch with him today?" Ethan's scowl deepened.

"He called me. He was drinking when I arrived at the restaurant and from the smell of him, he'd been drinking all morning."

"And you know drunks," Selena muttered.

"You bet I do." Britt jabbed a finger at Selena. "And he made damned good and sure the place was public enough for witnesses to see me walk out on him."

"Your desertion reflects badly on him," Dakota said.

She stared at him as if he were dumber than a box of bones. "Losing my cool makes me look like a temperamental bimbo."

"Yeah," Selena echoed. "What did he say to make you mad enough to leave?"

"Besides dissing your father?"

"Yeah."

"He was a pig. I don't want to discuss him." She started opening overhead cupboards, as if searching for something. "A real oinker."

"As bad as his father with the Sexorcist stuff?" Selena asked.

"Yeah." Britt slammed a door.

"I'm going to kill him, too."

Everyone in the room stilled. The oven ticked as the metal cooled. Outside, birds continued their conference.

Sometimes Selena talked too much.

Several awkward moments passed before Britt turned to Selena.

"*Too*? You did have something to do with Bryant Peters' suicide."

Dakota held his breath. This was Selena's mess. She could fix it.

Selena lifted her chin and met Britt's gaze straight on. "Congressman Peters committed suicide. He made the decision to take his own life. I had nothing to do with his decision process."

Britt's gaze never left Selena's face. "You were aware of the Sexorcist."

Selena didn't blink. "The Deep Web stuff surfaced after."

Dakota hoped Britt wouldn't connect random dots.

"From the FBI. Dakota's friend Luke is with the FBI. Luke the drummer from Toke Lobo and the Pack."

Dakota winced as Britt turned to Ethan. They could all pretend Britt was shooting in the dark, when in fact, she was shooting fish in a barrel.

"What prompted you to investigate the congressman's background?" she asked.

"I came to Minnesota to persuade the congressman to continue supporting the treaties between the government and the werewolf packs. Background checks are standard operating procedure." Ethan sounded bored.

"Maybe the cops are buying your line of crap. I'm not. They're unaware of the werewolf angle. You can lie all you want, claiming to talk to him about funding for Night Shift, but if he was aware of your true nature...did he threaten to expose your existence to the world?"

"He's been aware of our existence for years." Selena punctuated her statement with a snicker. She grabbed a couple of potholders and opened the oven door. "I got this recipe from Helga. It's supposed to taste like chicken."

Dakota admired the way Selena danced around the truth.

"Congressman Peters used us," Ethan said. "He's the one who sent Selena's father to the Pentagon. His father is the one who ordered

Selena's pack to massacre mine." He opened an overhead cupboard and pulled out a short stack of plates. "What's in your hot dish?"

"Chicken," Selena replied.

"Speaking of chicken, why are you afraid to tell me the truth?" Britt demanded.

"You can't be forced to tell what you don't know." Dakota sighed at having to explain. Again.

"Dakota." Selena's tone held a warning.

He didn't care. "We don't need Britt being careless with her guessing games in front of the wrong people. Such as her buddies the cops. Who are on their way."

"What?" in stereo from Selena and Ethan.

"We?" Britt added a backbeat.

"A couple of guys from Britt's high school are stopping by to talk to her." Dakota expanded on his statement. "They're cops. Familiar cops." He'd been around a couple of times when the authorities dropped in unannounced. Selena and Ethan weren't free from suspicion.

"Who?" Ethan opened a drawer and pulled out a fistful of forks.

"Mickey Clerkin and Tom Anderson."

"They've questioned us before," Selena said. "After Liam disappeared."

Dakota hoped Britt missed the eye-flicker Selena exchanged with Ethan.

She didn't. "Oh, shit. You guys are hiding something about the Congressman's suicide and Liam's disappearance."

"Relax." Dakota stood between Britt and Selena. "You're misreading the situation."

Ethan and Selena didn't know something. They knew everything. Dakota had driven the SUV carrying Liam to Ulvskog, where he'd met the fate he'd earned.

"The cops are dropping by for something totally unrelated." Dakota continued to spin. "Something involving Britt."

"What's going on?" Selena demanded.

"My ex." Britt's lips barely fluttered.

"You stayed with someone long enough to designate him as an ex?" Selena didn't bother to hide her snark.

"The first one, wise-ass. High school. Before you met me. The reason you never approved of my relationships with the opposite sex."

"What relationships?" Selena countered. "Labeling what you do in a relationship is like saying you have a relationship with toilet paper. I'm not wired to understand casual sex. I have one mate. Ethan. Dakota has one mate. You. Or haven't you accepted your new reality yet?"

"That's enough, Selena." Dakota's sharp tone sliced through the nonsense like a knife slashed tissue. "You don't have all the facts, so back off."

"Why doesn't someone provide us with some facts?" Ethan interjected, as he stared at the half-assed job he'd done setting the table for their meal.

"Fine. I haven't puked enough today." Britt paced from one end of the kitchen to the other. She recited the bare facts about Judd and why he was in prison.

Britt grabbed the sponge from the sink and wiped the counter. "He's been sending me stalker texts from prison. And I'm afraid of him. I'm the one who reported him for robbing my father's church, and my testimony sealed his conviction."

Selena and Ethan stared at her. Dakota couldn't stand not touching her. He massaged her nape, which was as tight and rigid as the wooden cupboards at her back. At first, her tension increased. Slowly she accepted his comfort. His support. Maybe she believed someone, for the first time since her mother's death, was on her side.

"Wow," Selena said. "Okay. That's intense."

"I'm so grateful for your stamp of approval." Ever the snarky tone.

"Do you have a restraining order?" Ethan asked.

"He's supposed to be in jail! Why do I need an order of protection against someone who's incarcerated?" Britt whirled on Dakota. "Why doesn't anyone get that? A piece of paper isn't going to stop Judd from coming after me."

Fear cracked her voice; he hated her control was shattering. His beautiful and brave Britt.

"An order of protection is a legality." Ethan rearranged the flatware on the table. "Criminals aren't bothered by laws, except if he violates a law, he's committed another crime."

"Has he texted you again?" Dakota's fingers dug deeply into the tense muscles in her nape.

Britt checked her phone. "Nope. Nothing since he sent the picture."

"The cops will want your phone." Ethan shoved his hands in his pockets and glared at the table.

"No problem." She shuddered.

Selena had been studying the pan she'd pulled from the oven. "Is anyone hungry?"

Britt collapsed in the corner of the sofa and told herself she'd held her crap together. She could have said plenty to Selena-The-Pure. Her tongue was sore from biting it. Selena was kind enough to give her sanctuary when she needed a place to hide. Britt retained some fragments of her mother's teaching. *Don't bite the hand that feeds you* was right at the top.

She focused on her phone, the screen swimming in the tears filming her eyes. She wasn't going to cry. Not in front of everyone, especially these everyones, and not before she spoke to Tom and Mickey again.

She didn't have a lot of contacts stored. Most of the people on her list were former colleagues and she currently didn't care if she ever contacted them again. On the other hand, she might need them for networking purposes should she get around to finding another job. Kathryn, her former roommate, could go to hell. Selena, of course. Tom and Mickey. *And looky there.* Dakota must have programmed his number when he filched hers for his phone.

Her life was as pathetic as her contact list was skimpy. The take-out restaurants wouldn't care if she got a new phone number. Same with her mechanic. Her landlord would believe she skipped town. Doctor and dentist were easy enough to change. No one else. No sorority sisters, no generic buddies, no family.

Especially no family. Except of course, "Speaking of the Devil" Daddy. She missed Bart and Susannah. They weren't kids any more. Maybe she could find a way to contact them. Her father couldn't control them forever.

Others broke the law with impunity. Why shouldn't she?

Notifying everyone who mattered by text took two minutes.

Dakota leaned on the door frame. "All set," she said.

"We're going to take care of you. Byrne isn't going to get to you."

"I wish I could be as confident as you."

"Ethan is lighting a fire under Luke's ass to find out what happened."

"I don't see how my situation is related to Ethan's secret mission. Will you get into trouble?"

His gaze slid away. "No."

He was lying. "How much trouble?"

"None. You're my mate. Mates supersede even Tokarz de Lobo Garnier." He brightened for a moment. "Only the Ancient Ones control mating or what a male has to do to protect his female."

If Britt were an eye-rolling female, she might have indulged in the habit.

The doorbell rang. Selena greeted someone.

"Mickey and Tom." Dakota showed off his allegedly superior hearing. "Only the truth, Britt."

"Okay." As if she had lies to tell them. Lies of omission didn't count.

"Britt. Towne." Mickey nodded at them, apparently the good cop tonight.

"I didn't realize you were staying with Selena Wolfe and Ethan Calhoun."

Yup. Tom's belligerent tone pegged him as the bad cop. They weren't on her side.

"Have a seat." Dakota gestured toward the folding chairs comprising most of the furniture in Ethan's living room.

"Selena was my roommate in college, and Dakota and Ethan are old friends." Britt's lips were stiff, her throat tight. "I'm scared to stay at my place ever since Judd texted me with my address. He should not have been able to find out where my apartment is, nor should he have gotten my cell phone number. I'm staying where I'm safe." The words whirled out of her in a tornado of emotion.

Mickey cleared his throat. "About Judd Byrne—"

"Tell me he's back in jail."

"He's out on parole." No emotion in Mickey's voice.

"He's not supposed to be eligible for parole. I'm supposed to be notified. I wasn't notified. Isn't that enough to send him back?" She hated the notes of hysteria in her voice.

"No."

"Isn't contacting me harassment or something? I plan on getting an order of protection tomorrow, for all the good a piece of paper will do Dakota when Judd kills me."

Next to her, Dakota started.

She hadn't meant to commit to Dakota; her words could be interpreted no other way.

"He's texting her," Dakota reminded the duo. "He's threatening her, and the best you can say is what? Nothing?"

"We're delivering your official notification." Mickey sounded gentle.

"After the fact." Her bitter tone had no effect.

"I'm sorry, Britt." Stoic. By the book.

"No, you're not. You're thinking Britt Hauge is finally getting what she deserves for getting involved with Judd Byrne in the first place."

Dakota placed a hand on her knee. She ignored him.

"I lived a sheltered life. I'd lost my mother and was expelled from the religious school my father insisted I attend. Did anyone at Warwick High try to befriend me? Spare me a second of kindness? Yeah. Judd Byrne did."

All the anger she'd ignored for years kept spewing from her mouth. She couldn't stop the outpour. She wasn't sure she wanted to stop.

"Who the fuck are you to judge me yet again?" Her throat hurt from screaming. She didn't remember climbing to her feet, but she was practically on top of Mickey. Only Dakota's one-handed grip on her wrists kept her from clawing the stunned expression off Mickey's face. "I paid. You have no idea how much I've paid. And now you're telling me I have to pay again? I won't. Are you listening? If he comes near me, I will kill him."

"Britt." Dakota's deep voice was almost subsonic. He released her wrists and grabbed her around the waist.

She kept raging. "You and the rest of the Warwick PD better make damn good and sure he doesn't get anywhere near me. If he does, you're accessories."

"This was a courtesy call." Tom sounded more annoyed than anything. "You don't need to be rude."

"Wanna bet?" Dakota snarled. He didn't loosen his hold on Britt's waist. "How would you react if someone you arrested and helped convict texted your wife? Stalked her?"

Neither cop spoke.

"He used her, and when she retaliated, she risked everything to do the right thing. She came to you guys. What have you done for her?"

"There are laws." Tom sounded stiff, as if reading from a script.

"If he comes near her, I'm going to help her kill him. Consider yourselves warned. As she said, you'll be accessories."

"We're witnesses." Ethan spoke from the doorway.

Britt was surprised to see Ethan and Selena had joined them.

"You two seem to be everywhere." Tom scowled at them.

"It's my house," Ethan replied. "I live here."

"The last place Liam Peters was seen." Mickey's face remained impassive.

"Seen leaving," Selena corrected. "Brittany and I are old friends, as are Ethan and Dakota. Of course, they're staying with us until it's safe for Britt to return to her apartment."

Since there was nothing more to say, Tom and Mickey left. A few minutes later, Ethan confirmed they were gone.

"Are you sure?" Britt paced the living room, circling the sofa. How had the focus of Tom and Mickey's visit shifted from her troubles to the damned Peters family?

"I heard their car leave," Ethan assured her. "Are you okay?"

"No, I'm not okay. I'm fucking furious." She kicked the arm of the sofa. Pain blossomed in her toes.

"I meant besides being ignored."

"I'm serious. I will kill Judd." Tears threatened to spill, and she hated the sign of girly helplessness when her rage gave her strength and courage.

Dakota massaged her nape again. His thumb dug deep into a sinew or something. "I said I would help you, and I will."

"I'll help, too," Selena offered. "So will Ethan. You're not alone. We're not going to tolerate any scat from anyone."

"The cops didn't take my phone." Britt's anger flared again. Tom and Mickey should have confiscated her phone in order to trace Judd's text messages. The authorities didn't care for her safety. She'd testified for them, received a pat on the head, and was sent on her way.

Dakota stretched out his hand. "I'll deal with them." She gave him her phone.

"You guys should have taken Britt's cell phone," he said, after punching in a number.

He was silent for a moment. "Listen, I hate to interrupt your litany of excuses, but I'm taking your indifference as permission to mail the phone to my contact at the FBI."

Even Britt, with her inferior sapien ears, heard the explosion on the other end of the connection.

"You wasted your chance." Dakota's tone was as cool as the fiery reaction of Tom or Mickey wasn't.

Ethan pulled out his cell phone and made a call. "You're going to get us into trouble," he muttered at Dakota.

Dakota showed Ethan his back and strode from the living room, still sniping at either Tom or Mickey. "FBI. Federal Bureau of Investigation."

"He's blowing our cover." Ethan's agitation grew.

"He has mating fever," Selena retorted. "He's being a good lobo."

"I know what he's going through better than you do," Ethan snapped.

"Maybe we need to get out of town for a bit," Selena suggested. "We need a road trip."

Chapter 16

Britt was native to northern Minnesota, but this part of the state was as foreign to her as New York City or Los Angeles would be. Tall trees blocked out most of the sun. Deep shadows camouflaged the road as the crumbling pavement snaked through the forest and slithered around the mountains.

Creepy. How could anyone find comfort in the dank darkness?

She sat next to Dakota, who handled his SUV effortlessly on roads she'd avoid, had she been driving her VW bug. Ethan and Selena were in the back seat.

"We're wasting a day," Ethan said for the umpteenth time. "The Peters clan know about Ulvskog."

"They don't know we're rebuilding." Selena spoke with a serenity Britt had never heard from her. "Nor are we aware what Connor knows."

Funny how they never mentioned the missing Liam Peters. Britt couldn't shake the notion Selena and Ethan had something to do with his disappearance.

They were right. Ignorance was bliss.

"Did you mean it when you asked your cop friends what would comfort me if you were dead?" Dakota's hand rested lightly on her knee, and he spoke in an intimate tone.

She hoped Ethan and Selena couldn't hear him.

Her emotions were out of control when she'd flung the statement at the cops. She hadn't been as crazy since right before Judd's trial. If not for Dakota's attempts to keep her grounded, she might have done something really stupid, such as go after Tom or Mickey.

Dakota found a better way to contain her fury. He'd stripped her naked and proceeded to caress every millimeter of her body with his fingers and mouth. *Every* millimeter. And after, he'd crawled between her splayed thighs and fucked her the way she'd always dreamed of being fucked. She could get used to him far too easily.

"Wouldn't you be upset if something happened to me?"

"Inconsolable. What if something happened to me?"

"I'd be bothered," she admitted. "Upset. Maybe even cry."

He withdrew his hand; she missed his touch.

"I'm getting closer." She meant every word. "Do you want me to lie?"

He gave a barely perceptible shake of his head.

"Last night was...the best. Ever," she told him, hoping to inflate his ego to compensate for wounding his heart.

"We're soul mates," he grumbled. "Sex would be good with anyone who was your soul mate."

"Not anyone is my alleged soul mate."

He replaced his hand and squeezed her leg above the knee.

She was glad he did. "Have you been to Selena's hometown before?"

She never had. Although she and Selena were roommates and friends, neither of them included their families in their lives.

"Yes." Dakota didn't elaborate.

"Is it a nice town?"

"I never saw it inhabited. It burned to the ground after her grandfather was murdered. Restin, Parker, and Ethan's family have been helping rebuild."

Britt made a conscious effort to close her mouth. She couldn't wrap her brain around murder, much less arson. "Isn't anyone doing anything to catch the people who did this?"

"Congressman Peters ordered the massacre of Selena's pack. They arrived with automatic weapons and wiped out almost everyone. There were so many corpses to deal with, the easiest way was to cremate them."

"I don't understand why the congressman would order a massacre." If the congressman was taking advantage of the werewolves' services, why would he cripple his secret army?

"Prominent people might be embarrassed if we ever told what we've done for them in the name of patriotism. The stench would be as bad as Ulvskog before we burned it."

"You were there?"

"The reason I'm in Warwick is because I drove the others to help deal with the aftermath of the slaughter. Yes, I witnessed the results of the attack. I saw the decaying bodies. I helped set the fire when we cremated the remains. The smell alone..." He broke off, as if remembering.

She placed her hand atop his and squeezed, expecting him to acknowledge her. He stared straight ahead, his profile sharply etched against the fading light.

He was handsome. Stunningly easy on the eyes. His obsession with her continued to amaze her.

"One pregnant female, Addy, escaped with her mate. Selena tried to keep her in Warwick, at Ethan's safe house, but she wanted to come home. To give birth in the place of her ancestors. To be the first to increase the Varulv pack. That's patriotism, not some scat the politicos would have us do."

Britt withdrew her hand.

"They slaughtered the babies and the grannies first,"

Selena said.

So much for privacy.

Selena continued. "On the afternoon before the full moon, the post-gestational women and pre-adolescent children— including babies—gather in a full moon lodge. Everyone else shifts while the grannies tend the children. Except they're all together in one spot. What's the expression? Shooting fish in a barrel? Simply open fire on the helpless."

Britt had never heard Selena's voice clogged with tears before. Never. The words were barely discernible.

"How many escaped?"

"Around two dozen."

"There's nothing you can do?" Britt refused to believe—

Oh. Wait. Congressman Peters blew out his brains. Liam vanished.

"What happened to Liam Peters?"

No one spoke.

"He's not coming back, is he?"

No answer.

Britt swallowed hard. "Okay. If I don't know, I can't be forced to tell."

"No one ever accused you of being stupid." Dakota lifted his hand from her leg and gripped the steering wheel.

A world of difference separated stupid and foolish; she was queen of the fools.

She was in a car with three probable murderers heading to the middle of the north woods. What had she been drinking? She'd needed to get out of Warwick. Judd would never find her in the forest, Selena assured her. What if she disappeared like Liam Peters? Had they brought Liam to Ulvskog on some pretext and—

"Chill," Dakota said. "I can practically taste your paranoia. Nothing is going to happen to you. I'll die before I let anyone harm you."

THE TALL TREES HOVERED, mimicking something out of a nightmare. Leaves rustled in alien communication.

Dakota hated Ulvskog. He loathed the forest of northern Minnesota. He longed for the open spaces of Colorado, where a lobo could see more than ragged-edged patches of sky, where a lobo could breathe because the air had space to circulate. He was homesick and wanted nothing more than to grab Britt and head to Loup Garou.

He drove into a clearing where a few haphazard shelters huddled and parked in front of the largest. Though the place appeared deserted, his ears confirmed activity.

Selena was out of the SUV before the vehicle fully stopped. Ethan followed. The stench of wet ashes crept into the cab.

Poor Ethan, stuck with a mate who wanted to live in a chilly, damp place. Maybe Ethan carried enough Limmikin DNA to tolerate the same milieu.

Restin strode out of the big structure. He carried a hammer, although Dakota figured the tool was for show. Most members of Toke Lobo and the Pack hated Restin, who was their fiddle player and the pack beta. Dakota didn't mind Restin. He was so low in the stratum of the pack, Restin didn't bother trying to impress or bully him.

"This is Selena's hometown?" Britt's eyes were wide. Her fingers clutched her shoulder harness as if to make sure it kept her belted in the SUV. "The place is appalling."

"This will be the new Ulvskog," Dakota responded. "Selena's—and Ethan's—home sweet home."

"Lucifer's stepchild."

Maybe she believed she was speaking under her breath, but Dakota heard the invocation.

"Ulvskog is no Loup Garou," he agreed.

"They want to come back to a hovel?"

"They've marked their territory." He understood the Varulv's logic. *Let them have these creepy woods. All the more Colorado for me.* "I'm glad we're in agreement. I could never be happy living in Ulvskog."

She hesitated, giving him hope. Pausing before answering meant she was no longer rejecting him outright.

"Are you saying if I go along with your mating scheme, you would live in Minnesota if I asked you to?"

His first response was to say no, loudly and clearly. Instead, he jerked his head. "I hope we could reach consensus."

"Define consensus. With my father, consensus meant my mother did what he wanted and shut up about it."

Ouch. "I want to return to Colorado. Have you ever been?"

"No."

"Would you come home with me to see if you would want to live in Loup Garou? If you hate Colorado, we'll talk again."

"Okay," she said. "I've always wanted to see more of the world. I've never had the means. I'm not saying travelling is a lifelong dream, but I'm not adverse to going to Colorado with you. Can we leave tonight?"

~ ~ ~

"What did you just say?"

Funny. She'd been using one-syllable words.

"Can we leave tonight? Can Restin or somebody drive Selena and Ethan back to Warwick after they're finished with whatever they're doing?"

"We're trying to hide you from Judd."

Britt wanted to stomp her feet and howl. She wanted to curl into a ball and hide in a corner, beneath a bed. "You said Connor Peters is aware of Ulvskog."

"I said his father ordered the inhabitants murdered. I don't know how the Spare fits into the picture."

"I'm scared. I want to go to Colorado."

"Connor is aware I'm from Colorado," he reminded her, his tone dripping with exaggerated patience. "He is aware Ethan is from Loup Garou. His father and brother knew it, too."

"Don't you have a whole town of werewolves in Colorado? Wouldn't I be safer in Loup Garou?"

"Ulvskog is a town of werewolves, too. Didn't do them any good against Congressman Peters' vigilantes." His dark eyes gleamed as if harboring unshed tears. "They had no idea what was coming. Selena's posted sentries now. Everyone's awareness is heightened."

"You couldn't prove security by me. We passed no checkpoints. Maybe they recognized you, but no one questioned my presence."

"You're with their alpha."

"What?"

"Selena is the Varulv pack alpha."

Britt was confused. "I thought alphas were guys."

"Alpha means being in charge. Pack leadership is familial. Selena's father should have inherited from her grandfather. After he was killed, only Selena remained. While female pack alphas are rare, they're not unknown. Selena's a levelheaded individual. She's taken charge despite her grief."

Dakota's explanation clarified Selena's reasons for losing interest in Night Shift. She had a lot on her plate, more than Britt had comprehended.

"How does Ethan feel about having such a powerful woman?"

"Ethan's grandfather was the son of the Limmikin pack alpha, giving Ethan an alpha heritage. He's cool. They'll manage. They're a solid couple."

"You're not alpha, are you?" He acted awfully bossy sometimes.

"No. I'm barely in the alphabet. A generic pack member."

She remembered him telling her. The verification relieved her. "You're autonomous, right?"

"Not really. Except relating to you. I have rights as a mated male, but if I'm ordered to stay in Warwick, if I'm ordered to be in Ulvskog, I have to obey." His expression and the tone of his voice betrayed nothing. He shifted his focus from her to somewhere outside the SUV's windshield.

"You told me you'd keep me safe. Does my protection fall into your rights as a mated male?"

"Yes."

"I'm scared," she repeated. "I'm depending on you to keep me safe. Do you believe I'm safe at the site of a recent massacre?"

He swung to face her, his eyes narrowed. "Are you trying to give me a reason to leave?"

"Yes."

He sat back in his seat, relaxing behind the steering wheel. "You really want to go to Colorado?"

"I said so, didn't I?"

"You change your mind like a weathervane in a tornado," he told her.

She ignored his insult. "I'm serious."

"Cell service in the forest is spotty. Byrne can't text you."

"He could still track me by cell phone GPS."

Another reason Mickey and Tom should have confiscated her phone.

"Okay, you have a point. Colorado, huh?"

"Or Connecticut, or California. Florida. New York. New Mexico. I want out of state. If Judd's on parole, he can't leave Minnesota. Right? Isn't that how parole works?"

"All of a sudden he's going to pay attention to laws?"

"Let's go. Tomorrow." Ulvskog scared her more than her apartment did.

The deepening shadows, where trees loomed and offered hiding places to anyone planning an ambush, were enough to give nightmares to any sane person.

"I can't go rogue," he argued. "I need to check in with my alpha. Cell reception sucks with all the trees and mountains."

"Don't you have a secret agent satellite phone or something?" She couldn't believe they were being hindered by something as ordinary as bad cell reception.

"I told you. I'm not a secret agent or a spy or anything exciting. I'm the guy who drives the tour bus for a country band. Nothing more. I don't live a fancy life. I'm a plain guy. My life is calm. I let others bask in the glory and glamour."

She'd offended him, and she wasn't sure how. "Fine. Maybe I should have blocked Judd's number. Maybe I should—"

"Relax. Take a deep breath."

If he told her to calm down, she was going to bolt. As soon as they got back to civilization.

"I'm too afraid to relax." She was being as truthful with him as she could be. What part of her terror didn't he get? "You're not listening to me or taking me seriously."

He frowned. "What do you expect from me?"

The problem, she discovered, was she didn't expect anything from him. "Nothing." He was no different than her father, Judd, or the bartender at Holsters.

He was just another guy, unable to leave his dick out of any decision.

Chapter 17

BRITT WAS IRRITATED AGAIN.

Dakota couldn't figure out why she aimed it at him. He was only trying to protect her. He understood why she believed Ulvskog might not be safe. *Ancient Ones,* he had reservations.

He couldn't recall the slaughter of Varulv children without wanting to hurl. The site wasn't so much haunted by ghosts of the ones who'd died as by his memories of the bodies and the stench, not only of rotting flesh, but also of the fire they'd used to cremate the dead and destroy the village. Punishing and executing Liam Peters on site couldn't reverse the desecration.

Okay, Dakota was putting a spiritual meaning on Liam's demise he didn't deserve. He was a rapist who'd violated a young lycan female. The pack's retaliation was not severe enough.

Yes, Ulvskog was secure after the Peters family paid for their atrocities.

"I need to tell Restin we're heading home."

"Why do you have to tell him anything? He's a jerk."

Rumors concerning Britt and Restin clashing had reached Dakota. Britt resented anyone telling her what to do, and Restin didn't use another method to communicate.

"He's my pack beta, meaning he's second in charge after Tokarz, and I brought him to Minnesota. I'm part of his team."

"Convincing Congressman Peters to vote in favor of keeping your treaties?"

"Treaty stuff is Ethan's mission. The rest of us were sent to help the Varulv, Selena's pack, recover from the massacre."

"Why were you in Warwick instead of Ulvskog?"

"Restin sent me to town to discuss aspects with Ethan and Selena."

"Bad cell service."

"Exactly."

Restin approached the SUV during the conversation and rapped on the window. Britt jumped.

Dakota unrolled the window. "What?"

"Are you two going to stay in the car all day?"

"Maybe," Dakota replied. "Have you met my mate, Brittany Hauge?"

Restin's nostrils flared. "Your mate?"

"Yeah." Dakota stuck out his chin. "As you can tell, I've marked her."

"Congratulations." Restin's sarcasm was potent.

"Thanks. I'm taking Britt home to meet my parents."

Restin's crazy blue eyes—Delilah Garnier called them berserker eyes—widened. "When?"

"Now." Britt sounded calm, but Dakota smelled her worry.

Restin ignored her. "We could use another pair of hands. The rebuilding is going slower than we estimated."

"I don't have carpentry skills," Dakota said. "I'm a bus driver. My mate's safety is my priority. We're returning to Colorado."

"Her safety?" Restin scoffed. He finally spared her a glance, filled with contempt for no other reason than she was a sapien female.

"Her ex has been paroled from prison, and he has reason to want revenge. She's the one who called the cops."

"She betrayed him?"

Only Dakota's need for control kept him from leaping through the window and tearing out Restin's throat. "That's a scat thing to say, even for a beta."

Restin recognized the insult.

"She had a choice to betray her family or betray someone who lied and abused her." *There*. Restin ought to appreciate family loyalty. The packs revered family above all else.

"Don't judge me." Britt's voice quavered.

Dakota hoped the quaver was from rage, not fear or hurt. Anger was stronger. Anger in the correct dose was a survival tool.

"I'm not judging you." Restin acknowledged her presence. "I'm stating a fact. Your ex, whatever that means, did something you found repugnant, so you ratted him out to the authorities. Am I wrong?"

"You forgot to add I also testified against him."

"You betrayed his trust in you."

Nausea churned Dakota's stomach. Restin was warning him to be cautious about what he shared with a female who betrayed her previous male.

Dakota could be her next victim.

Currently, she believed he'd keep her safe, so she was docile...for Britt. Once the danger passed, who could predict what she would do? Britt was wilier than he'd anticipated. She possessed survival skills he never would have predicted.

Dakota understood the warning.

DiNardo deserved killing. As did Liam Peters. Given Britt's background, the way the voice of her father randomly intruded, Britt could decide Dakota, Ethan, Selena, and the other Varulv didn't have the right to judge much less mete out a punishment. Retribution. Revenge.

She knew cops. Knew them well enough to discuss Byrne, to mock Connor Peters.

Getting her away from the scene of his crimes was a good idea. Colorado was a great idea.

"My first priority is to my mate," Dakota reminded Restin.

But Restin had planted the doubt, a skill at which he excelled. Dakota witnessed him undermine Tokarz, Stoker— every member of the band who was mated—with misgivings.

"Have a safe journey," Restin said.

"Can you make sure Ethan and Selena get back to Warwick?"

"You're the only transportation."

Ethan should have driven his truck.

"I doubt Ethan is going to want to leave Selena by herself," Restin continued. "Why don't I send Parker back to Warwick with you? He can drive Ethan's truck."

Dakota glanced at his mate. "We have to stop in Warwick anyway to pack our bags."

Britt nodded, the movement as jagged as a bolt of lightning.

"Fetch Parker so we can leave," Dakota told Restin.

He wasn't getting out of the vehicle, not even to piss. He didn't want more of his scent anywhere near this place.

BRITT'S BRAIN WAS NUMB. *Colorado. Judd will never find me in the Rocky Mountains.*

A felon without a conscience wouldn't obey any law trying to keep him in Minnesota if he wanted out. At least Dakota was listening to her.

No, her brain wasn't numb. Gray matter whirled in circles, tossing out ideas and priorities like debris in a tornado. She needed to pack her belongings. Figure out what to do with her apartment. What clothes should she bring?

Parker sat in the front seat with Dakota. She'd met him once or twice at Ethan's house. He was quiet.

She was grateful for the relative solitude of the second seat.

She pulled out her phone to make a list. "It's Five O'Clock Somewhere" intruded on her plan. She hesitated. She never should have listened to Dakota. She should have blocked Judd's number after the first text.

The alert wasn't for a text and wasn't from the same number Judd had used.

She answered with caution. "Hello?"

"Brittany?" The voice was familiar. "Yeah. Who's calling?"

"Connor. Connor Peters."

She raised her eyes to discover Dakota watching her in the rearview mirror. She averted her face.

"Connor? What do you want?" She should have disconnected the call instead of asking. Her question gave him power.

"I want to apologize for lunch yesterday." He sounded contrite. "I should have realized the past might upset you."

"Why would I be upset?" Her voice was tight; she worried she might squeak, betraying her state of mind. *You were drunk.*

"I'd like another chance." He glossed over her question.

"Another chance at what? Helping me find money to launch my business?" Her brain settled enough to prioritize what she wanted from Connor.

She checked the rearview mirror. Dakota was scowling. She wanted to tell him to pay attention to the narrow, tortuous pavement before he killed them all. Instead, she kicked the back of his seat and gestured toward the windshield.

"Maybe." Connor's charm oozed across the airwaves. "My sister is having an intimate gathering tomorrow for some out-of-town colleagues of my father."

"What does your sister's party have to do with me?"

"I'm offering a chance for you to mingle with power brokers. Network with them."

The preacher's kid, mingling with power brokers? What would Pastor Paul say about her now?

"I'm expected at seven. Why don't I pick you up at six- thirty?"

"I never said yes," she pointed out. "In fact, you've ignored me the entire conversation."

"I'm nervous."

She couldn't tell if he made a confession or an excuse.

Dakota was shaking his head. His wanting her not to go out with Connor Peters was a huge shock. *Not.*

He didn't understand *she* didn't want to go out with Connor. Connor rubbed her the wrong way. A business event was not the same thing as a hookup. Connor would never be a one-and-done.

"Six-thirty. Tomorrow night."

"I have one condition, Connor. My business partner, Selena Wolfe, is married to the steel guitar player for Toke Lobo and the Pack. You must have heard of the band. They're a hot country group. Anyway, Ethan—he's Selena's husband—is nervous. Too many coincidences of your father, your brother, and even Selena's grandfather's murder, worry him. He stuck me with a bodyguard-slash-driver. I can't go anywhere without him." She was proud of her brilliance.

Parker guffawed. The rearview mirror once more reflected Dakota's eyes on her.

She kicked the back of his seat again.

"The guy you were with after lunch, in the black SUV?"

"Yes. I don't go anywhere without him. I guess Selena was attacked on the street after your father…" She couldn't say *suicide* or *killed himself*.

"I wasn't aware she'd been attacked." Connor's tone remained neutral.

"Your father had loyal constituents."

"By vampires," Dakota muttered.

Maybe she wasn't kicking the seat back hard enough.

"He did a lot of good for the people he represented." Connor spoke as an indoctrinated one. "Selena and her husband were present when my father died. I'm surprised she hasn't encountered more angry people."

"My point is, I go nowhere without my bodyguard- slash-driver."

"Doesn't that get awkward?" Connor's tone softened. "When you want to be alone with someone?"

"Nope. In fact, he's so hot, I tend to stay in." *There. That ought to keep Dakota from summoning his inner wolf.*

"Nice touch," Parker murmured, as if he'd read her mind.

"I'll call you back at this number," Britt continued, "to confirm whether or not I can attend."

"Need to check in with your bodyguard?

"Goodbye, Connor." She disconnected.

"I heard all of your conversation."

She couldn't tell if Dakota was angry or pouting.

"I figured," she replied, as she tucked her phone into her pocket.

"I'm not your bodyguard-slash-driver."

"You will be tomorrow night." Britt stretched her legs across the backseat.

She'd never been one for long car trips. Maybe she could convince Dakota to fly to Colorado. If she couldn't do a round trip from Warwick to Ulvskog without bursting apart at the seams, she'd never survive a car ride to Colorado.

"You're my secret weapon." She studied his reflection in the mirror and hoped she hid her fear. "I have no intention of going anywhere alone with Connor Peters. With anyone. Not until Judd is back in prison where he belongs."

"Who's Judd?" Parker asked.

Britt waited for Dakota's explanation. Nothing.

"Someone I attended high school with," she replied after a mile of nothing. "He recently got out of prison, and he's after me."

"I take it his release is not good."

"Britt is my mate." Dakota's tone was flat. "Of course his release is not good."

"Kill him if he bothers her."

"I plan to."

Britt swallowed a snarky comment. If only getting rid of Judd was as uncomplicated as killing him. Dakota couldn't murder the memories of how Judd abused her. Of how careless he'd been with her loyalty.

Her lunch meeting with Connor released memories from the trap where she'd banished them. Or maybe the flashes haunting her all day were from a nightmare instead of a genuine memory. Regardless, Connor was responsible.

Maybe she needed to find Curtis DiNardo.

"I DON'T REMEMBER THIS many vampires before I was exiled," Parker observed, as Dakota turned onto Ash Street. "Where are they all coming from?"

"The Peters family has unlimited resources."

Dakota didn't want to have this discussion around Britt. Yeah, she slept, sprawled across the backseat. He was positive the soft, snuffling snores were genuine, but why take chances?

"Not surprising." Parker waited until Dakota pulled to the curb in front of Ethan's house. "I don't trust them, not after the congressman killed himself, and they tried to pin his death on Ethan and Selena."

"He was scared. He knew Ethan had uncovered his sex crimes and was prepared to go public. He couldn't face a scandal. And believe me, what Luke found on the Deep Web would have put him away for life—if he managed to get to trial with his balls intact."

"Tough to be a pervert without your parts."

Dakota snorted. "Tough to be anything worth being without your parts."

"I'm going to crash here tonight." Parker yawned. "I'm tired, and I don't want to drive back to the woods. In fact, I may put off going back for a couple of days."

"Don't blame you. Why the Varulv want to return is a mystery." Dakota put the SUV in park and shut off the engine.

"I did my time. I'm more than ready to leave. If Restin wasn't adamant I stay, I'd be in Colorado so fast, you'd mistake me for a greyhound."

"Britt and I are going back. Maybe tomorrow. Want to hitch a ride?"

"Restin's never going to let me go. I'm stuck until he says I can leave. Unless my mate shows up, too." He laughed. "Right."

Dakota climbed out of the front seat and opened the rear door. Britt sprawled in an unladylike fashion. Luckily he didn't love her for her ladylike qualities. He didn't want to admit he might not love her. She was his mate. The Ancient Ones bonded them. Love would come later. First, they needed acceptance.

Her face was pale in the strange orange glow of the streetlamps. He so seldom observed her at rest that when he did, her beauty amazed him. The rest of the time, her animation amused or annoyed him.

He didn't want to wake her. She expended too much energy while awake and needed the downtime to recharge. Otherwise she would burn out. Her energy belonged only to him. Selfish lobo, but he wasn't going to deny his nature to make her comfortable. He couldn't change his DNA.

Yeah. Acceptance.

He gathered her into his arms.

She roused. "I can walk," she mumbled.

"Yes, you can. But you don't have to. I've got you. Can you kick the door shut?"

She complied, the slam reverberating in the quiet neighborhood. She snuggled closer to him. "I'm cold," she murmured.

Parker unlocked and opened the front door.

"Gee, I feel like a bride," Britt said, as he carried her inside.

"Huh?" Sometimes he questioned if he'd ever grasp the way her brain worked.

"Never mind," she grumbled. "Human joke."

"I'm human. I'm homo lupus, whereas you're homo sapien. So your joke would be a sapien joke." She still didn't believe he was her equal.

He carried her to the sofa, where he sat, still holding her.

Her stomach rumbled. "Hungry?"

"Starving."

"We could order in wings."

"And pizza," Britt added. She was fully awake now.

Dakota didn't need carbs. He wanted flesh. "Any idea where to order takeout?"

Britt pulled out her phone. "Takeout is a single woman's best friend."

"Single male," Parker corrected. "Females are more apt to cook for themselves."

"Don't stereotype me," Britt warned. She peered at the screen on her phone. "I know a pizza and wing place that delivers. What do we want?"

"Plain wings, not overcooked." Dakota never could figure out why sapiens mucked up their food.

"If vampires barricade the end of the block, maybe we should order garlic parmesan wings."

Dakota couldn't tell if Britt was being serious or sarcastic.

"Couldn't hurt," Parker said.

"Oh, come on. Garlic probably isn't any more poisonous to them than silver is to us."

What was wrong with Parker, encouraging Britt to believe in myths?

"Like I say, couldn't hurt. I'm all for doing anything to stay safe."

"The delivery person might not be able to get past the blockade," Dakota said. "Even if we order garlic parmesan wings."

"The blockade is specifically aimed at Selena." Parker propped himself at the far end of the sofa, as far away from Britt as he could get, while still sharing the sole seating with her.

Dakota appreciated Parker's sensitivity.

"Selena stays inside after the sun sets," Parker continued. "The rest of us aren't on their hit list."

Britt dialed the phone. "I hope one of you has cash."

Dakota hoped the three dozen wings and two large meat-covered pizzas she ordered would be enough. He was starving and Parker's sojourn in Ulvskog had cost him some weight. Dakota had seen Parker put away a couple dozen chicken wings on his own. Wings were a bar staple in the places Toke Lobo performed before he hit the big time.

"Twenty to thirty minutes," Britt announced after she disconnected.

Parker dumped a couple of wilted bills on the arm of the sofa. "My treat for bringing me back to civilization."

"Great. Thanks. Now explain the vampires to me.

"Fairy woo-woo allegedly protects the block," Parker said. "The triad of trees keeps the vampires away. And before you tell me vampires don't exist, you need to talk to Ethan and Selena. They've fought them twice."

"Selena told me. I still don't follow."

"No one does," Dakota said. "Most of what you believe concerning werewolves is wrong. I'll bet the same is true with the bloodsuckers." Pacing the length of the living room, his skin prickled, as if a heavy dose of energy was saturating the atmosphere.

"Big problem," Parker interjected. "We have no experience fighting an unnatural enemy."

"Luke did some Internet research for Ethan. Stakes to the heart. Decapitation. Fire. You'll find all kinds of wooden stakes lying around the house. Selina tore the heart from the last one's chest. Something exploded inside of Ethan's truck. The detail place needed to clean the interior twice."

Skepticism painted Britt's face. "How did Selena tear a heart from anyone's chest?"

"The same way she'd kill any prey, except she ripped open its chest instead of throat. She doesn't remember. She was deathly ill from the vampire cooties she accidentally ingested."

Britt heaved an exaggerated sigh, as if Dakota said something ridiculously stupid. "Vampire cooties? Really?"

"Have you ever encountered a vampire?" He kept his tone polite.

"No. Have you?"

"Maybe. At the end of the block. Some guy flashed fang at me, so I showed him a couple back. I'd say we were evenly matched. And they patrol only at night. During daylight hours, the minions aren't as… luminous."

"They don't reflect the moon as nicely as the night vamps," Parker added.

"Another reason not to believe in vampires." Britt's forehead wrinkled in concentration. "The moon doesn't generate light. It reflects the sun. Aren't vampires allergic to the sun?"

"Clearly direct sunlight gives them problems. And don't pick on the moon. You're going to learn to love her."

"I'm not picking on the moon. I've always been fond of the moon. It's so romantic."

Her sarcasm annoyed him. "We'll see how romantic you think she is after you're living with a pack of shifters on the night of the full moon."

Britt's complexion paled.

"Not good," Parker muttered.

Britt squared her shoulders. Her throat rippled as she swallowed. "Are all paranormal types ruled by the moon?"

"We can only speak for ourselves," Parker said.

Dakota wanted to smack Parker for his irreverence.

"Define paranormal."

"What's eating you?" Britt demanded. "You've been cantankerous ever since we got back."

He was miserable. And taking his wretchedness out on the others. She was the reason.

"You need to call Connor Peters and decline his invitation. You're a mated female. You don't go on dates with other males."

"I don't care for Connor," she admitted. "However, he's offering too good an opportunity to ignore."

"Opportunity for what?" What could she possibly need that Dakota couldn't provide?

"To network with some movers and shakers to knock loose some funding in order to move forward with Night Shift."

Night Shift again. Dakota was sick of Night Shift. "You said you wanted to move to Colorado."

"Relocating is not going to stop me from launching my company. *My* company," she repeated. "If Selena wants out, I'll buy her shares."

"Why do you need a company? You don't need to earn a living anymore." His ego was insulted, he decided. She wasn't treating him with the respect and delight he needed from her.

"The world needs the lotions and creams I've crafted. Night Shift is my calling. My mission."

BRITT WATCHED AS DAKOTA circuited the room, his restlessness betraying his usually calm demeanor.

"My mother died of breast cancer," she reminded him. "Her illness is how I first considered creating concoctions to soothe her. Her skin...deteriorated. Death does that." She paused, her throat closing.

She spent all her willpower in not burying her face in her hands, and stated, "Night Shift might be Selena's name for the company, but my mother's memory is in every formula. Maybe I should rename the company after I strike out on my own. Grace. I could call the product line State of Grace."

Her voice didn't crack. She didn't crack.

"I can make my wares anywhere, including Colorado."

"The brewery has a distribution network in place." Parker sprawled on the sofa, his eyes half-closed.

Britt needed to explain why she didn't want Moonsinger's help. "I owe Selena enough to make sure her...pack is the pack of record, not your pack."

"Your pack, too." Dakota sounded like a broken record.

"I'm an independent contractor."

The front doorbell rang before Dakota could respond. She didn't want to hear what he had to say. He was more focused on his agenda than hers.

Britt grabbed Parker's money from the arm of the sofa. "Did you include a tip?"

"Yes."

She hurried to the front door.

Tom and Mickey, standing outside, were not bearing pizza. "Can we come in for a few minutes?" Tom asked.

Britt stood aside. "Company, guys," she called.

"We stopped by earlier. No one was home," Tom continued.

"Errands." Dakota joined Britt at the door. "Did you have any problem getting past the vigilantes?"

"Vigilantes?" Mickey seemed perplexed. "What vigilantes?"

"The guys at the end of the block. Both ends." Dakota pointed. "They limit access twenty-four-seven. Have been, for weeks."

"We didn't see anyone," Mickey said. "Never have, other than a few pedestrians out for a stroll."

Britt peered toward Oak Street as she closed the door. The horde had shrunk, yet shadows shuffled, like storm clouds converging to wreak havoc. Maybe the cops dispersed the gang. Or maybe the gang patrolled only to intimidate Selena, and since Selena was no longer in residence...but Britt *had* observed those shadows.

"You should always check who's at the door. Especially now."

Oh, Tom's words did not bode well.

"Want to explain?" Dakota's question was closer to a growl than a voice.

"Judd Byrne is out." Tom's mouth formed a grim line.

The skin on Britt's face tightened as her scalp tingled and the room undulated before her eyes. She grabbed Dakota's oak-sturdy arm to steady herself. "Where is he?"

"We're headed out of town tomorrow," Dakota said at the same time.

"Leaving might be for the best." Mickey spoke from the shadows. "Byrne took off his tracking bracelet."

"You're a fed." Britt's voice, her whole body, vibrated as she paced the length of their bedroom. She'd been silent while they ate, barely acknowledging Dakota or Parker. "Put me in witness protection."

"Witness security," Dakota corrected. Food hadn't improved his mood. "Judd's crime wasn't federal, so you don't qualify. And I'm not a fed. I transport some guys who freelance for the government."

"He's going to hurt me." Her eyes were wide and wild, like thunderheads he'd once seen while driving in Montana. "Did we tell too many people about Colorado? I can change my name, cut my hair, and dye it brown—"

He gripped her shoulders, stopping her mid-circuit. "Slow down. Take it easy."

"He's going to hurt me!"

"First of all, you'll use my name. We're mated. You're now Brittany Towne. We won't do any of the legal paperwork stuff until Byrne is permanently out of commission."

He waited for her to blast him with some sapien feminist logic.

"Judd doesn't know about you." She sounded hopeful. "What does permanently out of commission mean?"

"Back in prison for good." He didn't hesitate with the lie. He planned to kill Byrne. Britt needed to remain ignorant.

"You're a werewolf. Can't you do better than sending him back to jail so another crooked politician can get him out again?"

"We do things our own way." More lies. Truth needed to follow. "My sacred duty, responsibility, obligation, and delight, my utter delight, is to protect you no matter what happens."

"I'm no one's sacred duty." She bristled, as if she were a she-wolf defending her litter.

She was wearing him out.

"I don't need your permission or your approval. I don't need your cooperation." *Ancient Ones*, he hated when he had to pull rank on her.

"Oh, really?" Her soft question held the hint of a dare.

"Put aside your ego for a few days and let me do what I have to do," Dakota bit out. "You can get all radical bra- burner on me later."

"Radical bra-burner?" He recognized the tone. The next few minutes would be tricky. He should have used a more tactful phrase.

"Wanting to have a say in my own life makes me a negative stereotype?"

He counted to five. Were all females as difficult as Britt? He tried another route. "Okay, maybe I don't grasp the nuances of sapien idioms, and I apologize if I insulted you. And yes, you should have a say in your life. Except Byrne is out of prison, you weren't notified, and you're scared. I take every one of those factors seriously. I *believe* you when you say he's going to hurt you. The thought is intolerable to me. I may be merely a tau in my pack, but I'm going full-mode alpha on Byrne."

She paused. Inhaled deeply. Her shoulders relaxed beneath his hands. "I'm sorry. Being scared is making me crazy."

He nodded. "You can pack for Loup Garou in the morning."

"Okay." She leaned into him before drawing back. "The party."

"What?" Sometimes following her logic required a GPS.

"Connor's party."

"Don't go." As far as Dakota was concerned, Connor Peters wasn't worth the effort to scat on.

"I can't be rude. What if I need his help later? Besides, you told me the whole reason Ethan is in Minnesota is to convince the congressman from this district to do something about some old treaties. Until a special election is held, Connor is the guy."

"What's your point?"

She stepped back. "The gathering is important."

"More important than your safety?"

She opened her mouth, and he expected her to concur. She didn't. Instead, she narrowed her eyes and plopped onto the bed.

"Don't tell me you want to go to his sister's party."

"Judd wouldn't dare crash a fancy soiree."

"Are you out of your mind? No. You can't go. You begged me to take you to Colorado, we're going to Colorado. In the morning. You're scared, remember?"

She nodded, but Dakota read the hesitation in her body language. Her eyebrows met above the bridge of her nose. The index and middle fingers of her left hand covered her lips. Her shoulders hunched.

She was fickler than a hurricane deciding where to make landfall.

"You can't be that scared." Every instinct he owned roared.

She peered up at him. "I'm safe with you. You'll be with me as my driver-slash-bodyguard."

Heat flushed through his body. "I'm your mate. Husband, in sapien terms."

"The only way I get in to meet these people is if Connor escorts me."

"You're not a single female." His jaw ached from clenching his teeth.

"I won't go without you."

Good. He'd refuse to go.

"Night Shift is important to me. I might not have another chance to pitch my dream to this caliber of audience. I need to put on my big girl panties and be a professional." She lowered her hand from her mouth. Her lips formed a crooked smile. "I trust you."

She couldn't have said anything else to twist his guts into knots. *Zing.* Right for his weak spot.

"I trust you to keep me safe." Her voice quavered, as if admitting their relationship bothered her. "I won't go without you."

"Am I supposed to be grateful for scraps from you?"

"What? Why would I expect your gratitude for anything?"

"You haven't been a cooperative mate."

"Are you trying to lay a guilt trip on me? I'm immune. You're the one who should be guilty. You staked your claim without telling me you're a werewolf."

She had a point.

"I'm doing okay considering I never believed in werewolves, and if such creatures do exist, they're demons. Part of the time I want to hold a silver cross in front of me while chanting a prayer to keep you away."

"What a rotten thing to say."

"And what you did wasn't?"

"That's the way lycan culture works!"

"In case you've forgotten, I am not lycan."

"Oh, I haven't forgotten. A lycan female wouldn't consider going out on a date with another male before she was mated, much less after."

"I'm not going on a date. Connor will be introducing me to people who might be able to help me with financing for Night Shift, and you are coming with me."

"What happened to *take me to Colorado*? I want to go right away?" Dakota mimicked her frantic tone.

"I still want to go to Colorado. I'm still scared. Except I have to be an adult. Responsible. For one night. I'll be careful all day tomorrow.

You'll be with me. I'll be safe. After the reception tomorrow night, we can leave."

"You're making me crazy. I don't get you at all," he muttered. "How am I supposed to handle a problem you continue to ignore unless someone rubs your face in scat?"

She bristled. "I've had a lot on my mind. You know, such as staying the hell away from my ex? Coping with you being a werewolf—a huge ick factor for me. I'm trying to come to terms with my world being upended by a beast."

"I am not a beast!" Dakota bellowed. He wanted to punch something. "Homo sapien and homo lupus have co- mingled since the beginning of time. Our offspring will not be abominations. Lycan and sapien is no different than you having blue eyes and me having brown."

"Except I don't change into something else on the full moon."

He gulped in air. Someone needed to be grounded in reality, and he preferred to be that someone.

"I don't change into something else, either." Okay, his teeth were clenched, and the words strained, but he was no longer shouting. "I manifest another facet of what I am, no different than your monthly female changes."

"Are you comparing being a werewolf to having a period?" Britt's eyes were wide. Her voice squeaked. She jumped from the bed and closed in on him.

"Why not?" He wouldn't retreat.

"Don't female werewolves menstruate?" Each word was punctuated by a poke of her forefinger to his chest.

Ancient ones, he wished he'd never made the comparison. "I've never known one well enough to inquire," he snarled. "Yet you made the comparison of changing into an animal."

He grabbed her hand before she punctured his chest. "And how would you know what happens?" she continued.

"Sapien females talk."

"And where do you hang with sapien females who do all this talking?"

Okay. Easy answer. "I've spent more than my fair share of time in honkytonks."

"Next to the women's room?"

"Who said their conversations were limited to the bathroom? Besides, males discuss cranky females all the time. On the rag, ragging on me, PMS-ing." He tightened his grip on her hand.

"I wouldn't believe mansplainers about something they've never experienced."

"You've never experienced shifting. I was merely trying to point out you can't appreciate something you have no experience in."

He closed his eyes and begged the Ancient Ones for patience. "All I want to do is love you. My instinct is to toss you on that bed and—"

"Force me?"

"Do you really believe I would rape you?" Anger and hurt battled.

"I don't know you at all."

"You say you trust me to keep you safe. Choose, Britt. Either you trust me, or you don't trust me."

Her throat muscles worked as she swallowed. Her lips twitched. Her gaze flitted away from his. "Selena told me I'm the most important thing in your life."

"I'm the one who told you that, but if you want to credit Selena, hey, my feelings won't be hurt."

"I trust you. I have to."

"Thanks a lot."

Her face crumpled, and he wished he hadn't spoken so harshly. He longed to pull her into his arms and comfort her. He feared being rebuffed. The misery etching her features had him tugging on her hand. He tried to maintain a respectful distance, but she was breaking his heart.

She didn't resist.

She fit perfectly against him. The way she laid her head against his shoulder, right above his heart, nearly did him in. She smelled faintly of one of Selena's herbal concoctions.

"Unless you had my father thundering his hellfire and damnation in your head for sixteen years, you can't possibly appreciate the shades of fuck-up-ed-ness in my psyche." Her voice vibrated against his chest.

He didn't understand why her father would have traumatized her the way she claimed. After one's mate, one's offspring were the most precious, beloved, cherished things in a lobo's life. The unmated were to be pitied.

He knew no wisdom or cheap pop psychology to offer her. All he had was himself, and everything that encompassed.

Chapter 18

Britt stared at herself in the mirror as she blended gray and lavender eyeshadow on her lids. Dakota, more snappish as the day matured, was now unbearable as she prepared for Connor's party.

Most women would be dressed in black. Britt didn't own a stitch of black clothing. Instead, she'd found a long grayish-lavender dress in the back of her closet. The narrow skirt, topped by a close-fitting bodice, was made from a fabric with a slight sheen, revealing a subtle glimmer as she moved. She slipped her feet into pewter-colored stiletto heels. Amethyst cabochons set in silver graced her earlobes. She needed an understated, professional presentation.

Connor didn't have to share this opportunity with her. The package had to be perfect. No flash, no glitter, but disguising her inner honkytonk angel.

"You clean up nice." Dakota sprawled across her bed, taking in her every twitch.

"Thanks. You do, too."

He'd done the head-to-toe black look, giving him an air of bad-boy invincibility.

A real bodyguard in this situation would resemble a secret service agent in a suit and tie. She preferred Dakota's interpretation. Letting others see his strength wasn't a bad idea. Judd would appreciate toughness, might even respect brute strength.

Her dress was conservative, for all the close fit. Her collarbone was covered and no slit in the skirt meant she wouldn't reveal too much leg. Only her arms were bared.

She draped a pewter lace shawl, the dull metallic thread adding shimmer, across her shoulders. Shimmer was okay.

"Not too gaudy?" She twirled for Dakota.

"You look great. Classy. The opposite of cowgirl you."

"Is that good?"

"I have a weakness for cowgirl you," he admitted.

"Good thing I'm not high-maintenance. I don't even remember why I bought this dress." She'd found the whole ensemble while packing for Colorado.

He arched an eyebrow. "I guess we have different definitions of high maintenance, because sweetheart, you're not easy."

"Why should I be?" Her temper surged. "I've endured a lot of crap to get to where I am today."

She was nothing. But she wasn't going to mope over her lousy week. She'd endured worse and survived.

"Where is the Spare meeting us?" Dakota asked, as if they hadn't discussed the itinerary a dozen times.

"Here. I had to give him an address. Six-thirty. Nothing has changed since I talked to him last night."

Dakota overheard every word Connor exchanged with her on the phone. She'd declined a post-party dinner for two. He should have sensed how much Connor Peters disturbed her.

"You're going to be only feet away from me. Right?"

"Right," Dakota confirmed.

She blew hot and cold between canceling and attending.

"I'll support your final decision," Dakota had declared.

How refreshing. She couldn't remember a time she'd had anyone's support for anything.

At six twenty-eight, her doorbell rang. She swiped gloss across her lips.

"Wipe it off," Dakota growled. "Too suggestive."

She glowered. "You have sex on the brain."

"So does Peters."

She tucked the gloss into her minuscule pewter-colored bag along with a few tissues, a twenty-dollar bill and her house key. Her phone and pepper spray didn't fit.

"Are you going to answer the door?"

"Are you ready?"

"As I'll ever be." Big difference between prepared and ready.

Dakota lumbered down the stairs, more resembling a bear than a wolf, and she pondered the existence of bear shifters. If one species could shift, why not another? The world was probably filled with secret creatures.

Counting the instances her father labeled demonic in nature was better than brooding because she'd be stuck with Connor in the close confines of a car.

Too bad her pepper spray didn't fit in her evening bag.

"Change of plan," Connor announced. He was dressed in a charcoal gray suit. A blue tie matched his eyes. "I couldn't get clearance for your vehicle or driver."

"I'll drive your vehicle," Dakota said.

The early evening sun cast unflattering shadows on Connor's face. "I have my own driver."

"Then I can't go." Britt tried to sound sorry. "My bodyguard accompanies me at all times. You agreed."

"Brittany, many important people are at the event. Senator Richard Tuttle from Tennessee is attending. Trust me. Security isn't a problem."

"I don't trust you, and I don't move without my bodyguard."

"I'll drive your car," Dakota repeated. "I have a Colorado CDL Class C license. I can drive anything."

"I have my own driver."

"Fine. I'll sit with him. Britt doesn't leave my sight. You agreed to her conditions. If you're going to renege on your promise, you should wait until you're sworn in as your father's replacement."

"Funny." If Connor was amused, he hid his reaction well.

"That's Dakota. A laugh a minute. Thanks for the invite, Connor. I have to pass." Britt tried to close the door.

"You look amazing." Connor ramped up the charm as he slid his foot between the door and the jamb. "I'd hate to waste your efforts."

"Are you saying I'm usually not presentable?"

"No. Of course not. I don't see why only the two of us can't go to my sister's party. Nola is a practical woman. Her sole agenda tonight is showing off for Richard Tuttle. Senator Tuttle has built a strong base but has also created enemies. He goes nowhere without security."

Dakota stepped between Britt and Connor. He crossed his arms and spread his legs. "Neither does Britt."

Connor snorted. He actually snorted. "Brittany is an unemployed chemist."

How did Connor learn she'd lost her job? She hadn't told anyone she'd been fired.

He was spying on her.

Squaring her shoulders, she fought back. "Maybe I can get Toke Lobo to back Night Shift. After all, Ethan's married to one of the partners. Right, Dakota?"

Dakota's dark eyes glittered. He remained planted.

"Didn't you tell me Toke Lobo has something to do with Moonsinger Beer?" she continued babbling, wanting Connor aware she had options besides what he might be able to do for her business. "Maybe they'd be interested in diversifying."

The outer corner of Connor's left eye twitched. "Fine," he snapped. Not as masterfully as Dakota snapped, but a snap nonetheless. "Ride in front with my driver." Connor offered his arm to Britt.

Dakota narrowed his eyes. He didn't budge.

How much of his behavior was for Connor's benefit and how much was the real Dakota? He claimed he wasn't an alpha male, yet he was ahead in this pissing match.

"Bodyguards are supposed to be discreet," Connor said.

"Unless their client is threatened." Dakota's calm tone still conveyed control. Mastery. Alpha male cliché.

"Let's get this show on the road," Britt said, tired of the posturing. "Dakota?"

She didn't take Connor's arm. The idea of touching him repulsed her.

Dakota strolled to the dark limo at the curb and opened the back door. She scurried past Connor and into the back seat.

Dakota's gaze caught with hers. She must have imagined simmering fury. No living being could contain that much rage and not combust. Flames ought to be shooting out his ears and nostrils. Until she remembered his shift to wolf form, how the heat seared her lungs and evaporated her saliva. He could handle incandescence.

All she could hope was he would stay focused and not let his fury distract him.

Connor's expensive cologne slipped into the back seat before he did. He rapped on the glass separating the driver from the occupants before sitting back as the limo shot forward.

Leaving Dakota behind.

"You asshole," Britt spat. If the car hadn't been speeding, she would have jumped out. Where was her pepper spray when she needed to spritz someone? "Dakota warned me you were bad news."

Connor's chuckle was cut short when the door beside Britt opened and Dakota climbed in.

"What the—" Connor sputtered, like an engine running out of fuel.

Oh yeah. Dakota was good at jumping into moving vehicles. A werewolf of many talents.

"You didn't tell your driver to wait for me," Dakota said in a mild tone.

Even Britt was wary of Dakota, and he wasn't upset with her.

"I guess I'm a passenger, then." Dakota crossed his arms and closed his eyes.

As the car plummeted forward, the early evening sunlight mutated by the tinted windows painted Connor's face a shade of ugly.

He found his voice. "What the hell are you doing?"

"What we agreed to." Dakota didn't bother to open his eyes, as if Connor wasn't worth the effort. "You might be comfortable breaking your word on a whim. I am not. You were told in no uncertain terms Britt goes nowhere without me. Luckily, I'm smarter than you are."

Britt leaned against the luxurious leather seat back and stretched her legs toward Dakota, feigning relaxation. "I don't care for being messed with," she explained in a low voice. "And you're trying to play me."

"You have good instincts," Dakota replied, although she hadn't been addressing him. He was barely mussed from his sprint to catch the limo. "Why are you fucking with Britt?"

Connor raised his arm, as if to rap on the window again. Dakota caught his hand before Connor's knuckles could graze the glass.

Even with his eyes closed, he could read Connor like a comic book.

"You didn't answer our questions," Dakota chided. His eyes opened, and he pinned Connor with a glare that should have had him wetting himself. "Are we headed to your sister's party or do you have other plans for Britt?"

"Or all of the above?" Britt crossed her ankles. Dakota's knuckles whitened.

Connor winced. "Let go of me," he ordered in an authoritative voice. He must have been channeling his pervert father.

Dakota flung the wrist away. "Going to have me charged with assault?"

"Hardly." Connor acted as if Dakota's grip meant nothing.

And Britt realized Dakota could have shattered the bone without blinking.

His treatment of Connor was evidence of the things Dakota had told her. How his senses were sharper than hers. She tried to make her body smaller. Stiller. She didn't want anything to interfere with whatever Dakota planned.

"I don't sue people like you." Connor sounded bored. "I use them." Contempt colored every syllable.

Dakota's teeth flashed. "I'd like to see you try to use me. Or Britt."

"You don't scare me."

"Breathing slower might help regulate your heartbeat," Dakota suggested.

Connor's only reaction was a widening of his eyes.

Britt tried to follow Dakota's advice to Connor. "Who will be at the reception beside your sister and Senator Tuttle?"

Connor cleared his throat. Threw out the names of a few local politicians; the mayor of Warwick, the state senator, the county executive.

"Why isn't Tuttle in Minneapolis?" Britt asked. "Warwick isn't the heart of the state."

"My father and the Senator had a special relationship."

"Yeah, the whole country suffers from what your father and Rich Tuttle have…accomplished," Dakota muttered. Connor ignored Dakota, even though Dakota was right.

Between Peters and Tuttle, a lot of legislation in Washington hadn't happened. Important agenda items had gone undone.

In many ways, Senator Richard Tuttle was more powerful than the president.

"He's in Warwick to pay his respects to the family. He's also concerned about what happened to Liam. People don't just vanish."

"Maybe Liam was abducted by aliens," Britt offered.

"Aliens? Are you suggesting an undocumented immigrant sneaked across the border from Canada and took my brother hostage in order to get him to vote in their favor?"

"Clearly you've considered the idea," Britt replied. "I was referring to Martians. Or the ghosts of his victims."

"Or werewolves," Dakota added.

"Or werewolves," Britt agreed, surprised Dakota would mention himself. "Why did you try to ditch my bodyguard?"

"You can't blame a guy for trying to be alone with an attractive woman." Although Connor imbued his words with smarmy charm, Britt wasn't fooled.

"Pissing off my body guard isn't how you impress me. Pissing him off only annoys me."

"I can't believe you were serious about the bodyguard. What could possibly happen to you while you're with me?"

Again, that hidden note in his tone...

Britt lowered her chin and stared at Connor. "Anything could happen. You used to hang out with Curtis DiNardo. I do know Curtis. Or I did. We don't move in the same circles anymore."

Connor sat back, training his laser-like blue stare on her. "Curtis? I would hardly describe my interactions with him as hanging out. He's the nephew of my grandfather's handyman. Besides, nobody's seen him or heard from him in a couple of weeks."

"How would you know unless you're keeping tabs on him?" Dakota pointed out.

"Are you saying he disappeared at the same time your brother did?" Britt asked. "Weird coincidence."

"Ever visit Elysian Estates?" Connor wasn't as adept as Dakota at changing the subject. He named the gated community located outside of Warwick. Figured his sister would be isolated from the rest of the world. Where else would a political dynasty headquarter?

Britt didn't bother to answer.

The limo slowed. Stopped. The driver murmured something to a sentry. The car resumed traveling along a smoothly paved road. Didn't the roadbeds in exclusive residential areas warp the way the ones in the real world did?

Britt stared out the window, trying to take in the neighborhood. She assumed tonight would be the only time she'd be in such an exclusive enclave.

Carefully constructed landscaping gave the impression of being naturally wild. Buildings peered at the road, shrouded by branches and shrubbery. A bland sameness shuttered everything. No personalities were present.

She preferred Ethan's shabby neighborhood to this example of people who were afraid of life.

Fear brought them together behind their fences and walls; fear kept them from being individuals. Safety in numbers. Werewolves travelled in packs. Maybe her problem was being a loner.

No businesses operated in Elysian Estates. No corner markets or neighborhood taverns existed where people could gather. Maybe they had no individual ideas to share. A clubhouse might cater to the golf and tennis crowds, but no music prompted them to dance until sweat gushed from every pore and the back beat replaced one's heart pumping the blood. Everything was bland. Flavorless. Colorless. No garlic or red pepper flakes.

She found herself seeking Dakota's hand where Connor couldn't see. The connection reinforced her sense of self. She didn't fit in. She had too much personality. Too much life.

No wonder ghosts were always depicted as translucent white. The residents of Elysian Estates weren't among the living. Instead, they were tasteful shadows of everything they were missing.

She wanted to live. Being a honkytonk angel meant she was alive.

DAKOTA'S BOILING RAGE SLOWED to a simmer when Britt's hand crept into his. All the trappings of wealth must have scared her. He was glad she sought him. Maybe her action was conscious, maybe a reflex, but by the Ancient Ones, she'd reached for him. He welcomed any progress with joy.

The limo slowed to turn into a circular driveway guarded by green shrubbery. Nothing as functional as Ethan's hawthorn hedge, more decorative than useful, unless you were a thief. A thief might find the cover handy.

As soon as the vehicle stopped, Dakota darted out the door.

Britt slid across the leather seat. The fabric of her skirt clung to her legs and crackled with static electricity. Her long, unbound hair sparked with her energy. Dakota helped her out of the limo, steadying her when she wobbled on the thin heels of her silly shoes. She rearranged the shawl across her shoulders.

He stepped back as Connor joined them. Connor might be Britt's official escort for the evening, but Britt had clutched Dakota's hand.

She'd reached for him. The small gesture meant...everything.

The limo pulled away, and Dakota thought he caught a flash of...No. Not possible.

Again, Britt ignored Connor's proffered arm. She lifted her chin, straightened her shoulders, and ascended the steps to the massive front door beside Connor.

Why did anyone need big phony columns, or a porch the size of a dance hall? Dakota didn't spy rocking chairs or lounges. No one used the space to relax and enjoy the view. The door opened, as if someone had been watching for them. If the mansion was Connor's childhood home, why didn't he let himself in?

The snoot who'd opened the door tried to stop Dakota. "I'm with them," Dakota explained.

"You're not on the guest list," Snoot replied.

"I'm not a guest." Dakota jerked his head toward Britt. "I'm with them."

Snoot must have decided Dakota wasn't going to surrender and let him pass.

Extraordinary security.

Connor relieved a wandering waiter of two flutes of straw-colored liquid. He handed one to Britt.

Unlike Dakota, Britt didn't abstain from alcohol, but she impressed him when she didn't sip from the glass.

Again, Connor tried to grasp her elbow. She evaded his touch.

Dakota attracted stares from the other guests, making him uneasy. He wasn't all duded up in a suit and tie. Men eyed him with hostility, while the females responded with either distaste or lascivious interest. These women might be dripping with real jewels and expensive clothes, but their nasty minds occupied the same gutter as any honkytonk angel.

He hung back as Connor herded Britt toward a tall woman standing next to a chinless, neckless man who was all too familiar. A younger, faded version of the male stood next to him. The woman resembled Liam Peters more than she did Connor. Dakota figured she was the sister. Nola Peters.

"Senator, may I present my younger brother, Connor, who's filling in for Liam." Her voice was low and melodic. "And this is?"

"Brittany Hauge," Connor filled in. "One of our local entrepreneurs."

Britt offered her hand and murmured, "Pleased to meet you."

Nola glared at Connor before she continued the introductions. "The Senator's son, Rick Tuttle."

Why was Nola Peters irked at her brother?

"And what type of business do you have?" the Senator inquired.

"Organic, healing beauty products. Body lotions, face creams...no animal testing, using locally grown herbs."

The Senator guffawed as if she'd told a wonderful joke. "Dozens of natural products clutter the shelves of every drugstore in the country."

"Not," Britt spoke with a hint of arrogance, ignoring the insult, "with the herbal components harvested by the light of the moon. Night Shift. We plan to hire indigenous women who live in the forests north of here to harvest."

"Doesn't sound productive," one of the local pols interjected.

"Of course not." Britt lowered her voice. "Our products are high-end and exclusive."

"Where are you planning to manufacture?"

"Mayor Kinsey." At least Britt recognized the speaker. "We want to stay local. If not in Warwick, we'll relocate production closer to where the plants are harvested. Our business plans currently call for us to be in Warwick. Easier to distribute."

She turned, as if she sensed her time with the bigwigs had ended. "On the other hand, the brewers of Moonsinger Beer have expressed interest. I hope to meet with them later this week. They have experience with major distribution. Too bad my product has a different demographic. Nice meeting you. Thank you for having me." Britt walked away from Nola Peters, her spine as straight as an aspen on a still day.

Connor scurried in her wake, as if he were no longer the facilitator. He'd become rabbit scat someone brought in on the sole of their shoe.

Dakota tried to remain unobtrusive as he trailed Britt and Connor. He occasionally helped himself to finger food— why were the barely-a-bite morsels called finger foods?—as servers passed him. The stuff wasn't anywhere near as tasty as a finger.

Connor periodically stopped to introduce Britt to someone. Dakota caught the words *exclusive spa line*. He finally understood why Britt insisted on attending the event. Only Connor could get her in.

Only Connor could provide her the opportunity. Dakota could give her merely a threat to move the business elsewhere, and politicians never supported industry—and jobs—leaving their area.

Still, something wasn't right. The hair on Dakota's nape prickled, and not from static electricity. Danger lurked nearby. Connor had more in store for Britt. Connor was using the party to get Britt to drop her guard. He'd proven his evil intent when he tried to ditch Dakota.

Dakota snagged another bacon-wrapped something or other. When he looked up again, Britt and Connor had vanished.

He popped the appetizer in his mouth and scanned the room. Britt's distinctive long yellow hair and pale purple dress weren't anywhere.

His heart surged; his throat sealed as if filled with tarmac. He strode to where he'd last seen Britt, bumping into anyone foolish enough to stand in his path.

No visual. His olfactory kicked in. The room was a cauldron of scents. His fear distracted him for a few crucial seconds before he trapped a thread of Connor's aftershave. Britt was more difficult; she didn't wear perfume, and the delicate fragrances of her soap and shampoo were so subtle, they couldn't compete against the wall of stink in the room. Then he grasped a sharp spike in Britt's natural scent. *Fear.*

Connor Peters had sealed his death warrant.

An older female with dagger-like red claws tried to stop him. He ignored the hand on his forearm as he rushed past her.

Britt's terror led him to one of the floor-to-ceiling windows overlooking an elaborate, too-fussy garden. The lower pane was slightly ajar. Cool evening air crept into the room. The sunlight waned toward sunset, casting sharp shadows.

Dakota scanned the garden, and noted broken branches on a flowering shrub. Caught a whiff of the sap, betraying how new the breaks were. He opened the sash and climbed outside. Tracking was much easier in the open. All he needed to do was follow Connor's cologne, the muskiness foreign in the natural setting.

A third foreign scent joined Connor and Britt at the edge of the garden. Unfamiliar. Dakota increased his pace.

How could Connor have whisked Britt away so quickly? Who owned the third scent?

BRITT WINCED AS CONNOR pressed something into her side. Not a knife. Otherwise, she'd be cut and bleeding. His weapon might be a gun. Guns scared her.

"Slow down," she panted, stumbling in her stupid stiletto heels. "Or at least let me take off my shoes."

"No traces," Connor snarled. "Get moving."

Connor was so stupid he didn't realize her heels were leaving deep gouges in the earth.

Hopefully Dakota would spot them.

"What is your problem?" She struggled to speak. She was woefully out of shape and her narrow skirt wasn't designed for running, not to mention her shoes with their four-inch spikes.

Connor didn't answer. He tightened his grip on her wrist, pressed his weapon deeper into her ribs, and pushed her along.

They followed someone in a hat and dark suit. His way of moving bothered her. A clump of dread settled in her stomach.

The cluster of trees behind the Peters' property did a good impression of a forest. The sun was quickly fading by the time they emerged from the grove. The long, low silhouette of a parked limo hulked next to a ditch.

"Get in the car." Connor opened the rear door and shoved on her shoulder.

"No." Britt knew the stats. Women who got into the car ended up dead. She had no intention of dying due to Connor Peters.

The other man removed his hat, the brim no longer shadowing his face. Or hiding his red hair.

"Judd," she whispered, as she stumbled.

"Here. I got her for you. We're done," Connor said.

Judd grabbed her other arm. "We're done when I say we're done."

Judd. Connor Peters was giving her to Judd.

"She's still cute." Connor eyed her in a way that made her want to puke. "I wouldn't mind another go at her. I recall—"

The nightmare hadn't been a dream. Her subconscious had recognized Connor's voice. He'd been present the night Judd…

"You don't know where her mouth has been the past ten years," Judd sneered.

"I didn't mean a blow job."

"We don't have time for you to ream her ass. I need to get going before her bodyguard finds me."

"Too late." Dakota crouched on the hood of the car. Connor and Judd released her arms.

Britt wanted to sag with relief. She didn't know how easily Dakota could handle two jerks, so she surreptitiously slipped out of her shoes, praying Judd and Connor wouldn't notice she'd lost several inches in height. If she needed to run, she would, despite the constriction of her skirt.

Connor swore.

"Judd Byrne, I presume?" Dakota growled. "I thought I spied red hair after you dropped us off. I'd hoped I was wrong."

Judd rocked on the balls of his feet. "You've been fucking my leftovers."

Dakota didn't take the bait.

"Normally, I'd say okay, except I'm not done with the bitch yet."

This was Dakota, she reminded herself. He was a werewolf. He could tear Judd apart.

"Yes, you are done with her," Dakota replied. "Who wants to die first?"

"Careful what you say and do in front of the bitch. She'd just as soon blow your cover to the cops as blow you." Judd giggled at his joke.

She would never forget the sound of his giggle, so incongruous with his innate evil. Woe to anyone who mocked Judd.

"Thanks for the warning."

Britt wanted to die. Judd was trash talking, trying to rile Dakota. She hoped Dakota was smart enough not to fall for his patter.

"Britt, get in the car while I take care of this piece of shit," Judd ordered.

"No." Her voice rang clear and strong in the fading light. "You're going back to prison, and I'm going to help the process. What does Judd have on you, Connor?"

Why isn't Dakota bursting into a wolf and taking care of this mess?

Judd's fingers closed around her upper arm.

She lifted her feet, dragging him with her as she fell to the ground.

Dakota! Do your thing! What kind of bodyguard are you? She grabbed one of her shoes and slammed the heel into the back of Judd's hand.

He yelped and released her.

"Peters, you'd better run," Dakota warned. "You're next."

Heat flashed. Agony pierced her sinuses.

Connor shrieked.

"What the fuck?" Judd scrambled to his feet, blood dripping from his hand.

The beautiful black wolf bared its fangs. Judd backed away.

"He has a gun!" Britt shrieked as Connor waved his weapon.

Connor fired.

"Watch it, you moron!" Judd yelled, as he ducked.

Britt followed, still wielding her shoe. Maybe she could drive a heel into his eyeball.

Dakota lunged at Connor.

"You stupid bitch!" Judd grabbed for Britt.

"I'm not stupid, you asshole. And speaking of assholes, what's been in yours while in prison?" She used her stiletto as a hammer against the side of his head. He tried to snatch the shoe. She swapped hands.

Connor screamed.

Sirens wailed. Oh damn, someone must have called the cops.

The back door of the limo gaped open, where Connor had tried to force her inside. Britt heard fabric rip when she dove headfirst into the car and slammed the door. The locks clicked as she pressed the button.

Judd, bleeding from the wounds she'd inflicted, plastered himself against the window.

Britt ignored him, opened the partition between the front and back of the limo, and crawled into the driver's seat. The key dangled from the ignition.

Judd hadn't gotten smarter in prison.

She twisted the key. The engine purred. She worried she couldn't handle a stretch limo, being used to driving her little Bug, but she'd never learn until she tried. If only she could get Dakota's attention before the authorities arrived.

She spotted her chance when Judd jumped to the opposite side. She found a panel on the door giving the driver control of the doors and windows. She unrolled the window in the door closest to Dakota and screamed his name.

The wolf bounded into the back seat. She punched the control and prayed the glass finished ascending before Connor or Judd reacted.

She shifted out of park and slammed her bare foot to the floor. The back end of the limo fishtailed. Judd's body splayed across the windshield. "I wish you'd shift back and take control of driving this yacht," she told Dakota.

Dakota bared his teeth at Judd and growled.

Britt tried cutting the wheel; Judd stuck like a splattered insect. She couldn't see around him. Blood smeared across the glass. She'd inflicted serious damage with her shoes, although she had missed his eye.

She eased off the gas. Sirens grew louder.

Chapter 19

Dakota tried to scare Byrne into letting go of Peters' limo; Byrne was as determined to stick as Britt was to shake him.

The vehicle careened along the narrow road. Not ending up crumpled against a tree would take a miracle. Dakota needed to shift to human form and take the wheel from Britt. He owed Britt. Big time. He couldn't decide who to go after first: Byrne for stalking Britt or Peters for betraying her.

The moon peered over the horizon. She'd be full in a few more days, and she quickened in Dakota's blood.

Speaking of blood, The Spare's tasted sweet, sweeter than his scat-sucking brother's. Dakota had left him alive. Alive and hurting. Hopefully in excruciating pain. Peters would be hard pressed to explain his injuries.

Dakota couldn't wait to finish him off—maybe after he'd healed a bit.

He shifted. Byrne's bellows spoiled what was usually a sensual experience. Dakota's tattered clothes were in the ditch with Peters, possible evidence proving whatever Peters blubbered might be true. Shifting and leaving a witness was a mistake. He should have killed Byrne and maimed Peters before retrieving the scraps of his clothes, leaving behind no evidence. And he would have, except for Peters' gun.

Dakota stretched his arm past Britt and pressed the wiper control. Washer fluid squirted onto the glass. Byrne screamed as the alcohol sprayed into his wounds. How had he gotten those round holes in his face? Dakota gave the fluid release another jiggle, and more blue liquid landed in Byrne's open wounds. He let go of the car and fell from the hood to the ground.

Too bad they couldn't run him over.

"Pull into the next driveway," Dakota instructed, his voice still thick from shifting. "I'll drive."

"About time." An underlying tremor in Britt's voice betrayed her true state. "What took you so long?"

"You did fine. I didn't want to disrupt your glory."

"My glory? Are you out of your dog-breath brain?"

"Don't compare me to a dog." *Ancient Ones*, he hated canine comparisons.

"Where are your clothes?" She slowed the limo to prepare for the turn.

"One of the pitfalls of shifting is ruining your clothes. They're back with Peters. In shreds."

"Oh, hell," she said.

He figured she wasn't praying.

"Maybe you can find a blanket or something to cover yourself. How are we going to explain your lack of clothes to the cops?"

"Why do we have to explain anything?"

"You don't believe Judd and Connor aren't going to tell the authorities what happened?"

"Byrne removed his ankle bracelet. He's in violation of his parole. My guess is he's going to go to ground until he can recoup. And Connor Peters has a whole lot of explaining to do. No, I'm not worried at all."

"Why didn't you kill them? I wanted you to kill them." Her voice caught on a sob.

How could he explain his hesitation without sounding as if he didn't trust her? *Because you don't.* Her testimony put Byrne in prison. She wasn't a reliable keeper of secrets. "And I will," he snapped. "But not on Connor Peters' turf."

"Judd was trying to kidnap me."

"You know, I picked up on that." He wasn't stupid and resented her attitude.

"Connor helped him. Apparently, Judd has something on Connor. Why am I not surprised?"

"Can we rehash later? I want to get us out of here."

Britt's hands trembled so badly she could barely steer the car. Dakota shifted the transmission to park.

"Switch places," he growled.

Britt opened the driver's door. "Where's my shawl?" Her voice trembled as badly as her hands. She peered into the back seat. "I don't see my shawl."

"I'll buy you another one."

"I wanted the shawl to cover your..." She waved her hand.

Dakota wanted to howl. "Don't get all modest on me. You like my..." He mimicked her gesture.

"I didn't say I didn't. What if we get stopped?"

"We won't," he said with more conviction than the situation warranted. "You need to trust me. I'm a professional."

Britt's brain raced faster than she could grasp her thoughts. Foremost was Dakota's lack of clothing. If they were stopped, the authorities would question why he was bare-ass naked. They'd want an explanation for his shredded clothes in a bloodstained ditch next to a seriously wounded Connor Peters. The Peters family had dominated the news far too much lately to let slide the discovery of an injured one.

Dakota's DNA was on Connor, on his tattered clothes.

Oh shit.

"Put your head between your knees," Dakota ordered.

"What?" The car interior wobbled like a stop sign in a hurricane.

"You're hyperventilating and are going to pass out if you don't breathe normally. Stick your head between your knees."

"Of course I'm hyperventilating!" She would have continued with a wonderful tirade, except Dakota put his hand on her nape and shoved her head toward her lap.

"Breathe slowly," he directed.

"Pay attention to your driving." Her voice was muffled against the fabric of her skirt. Although the garment was torn, she still couldn't get her legs far enough apart to do as Dakota instructed. She was going to get rid of every narrow skirt she owned. They were misogynistic traps to keep women from running away from bad situations.

"I am."

Except he wasn't driving.

She gulped in oxygen.

"Stop. Calm down."

"Never in the history of the world has anyone calmed down because some arrogant macho werewolf told them to."

"Remind me to laugh later."

The car inched forward, much more smoothly than when she'd driven. Dakota had control.

She sat up.

"Don't distract me," Dakota warned.

"I didn't plan to." She needed to process the situation.

Make sense of the senseless.

Judd had something on Connor. If only she could remember. She'd spent too many years trying to forget her time as Judd's woman. Some parts were easy to erase. Judd smoked a lot of weed and sometimes forced her participation. The first couple of times she'd enjoyed the floating, the peace. Except Judd's mean streak surfaced, his overbearing demand to be obeyed couldn't be ignored, the humiliations...

Connor could have been a part of the ongoing nightmare.

Maybe the night Curtis...

She wanted to puke. No, she wanted to smash something. A lot of somethings. She wanted to destroy the barriers of the past still blocking her way to a normal life. Bad stuff happened to other people who still managed to move forward and be successful.

Tears welled. She blinked them away. Dakota didn't need to deal with a sniveling female while he tried to get them out of Elysian Estates. She was stronger than she was behaving.

Why hadn't Dakota killed Connor? Or Judd? Or both? He'd promised. He'd told *them* he was going to kill them. Why hadn't he?

"Careful what you say and do in front of my bitch," Judd told Dakota. *"She'd just as soon blow your cover to the cops as blow you."*

Did Dakota believe him?

She trusted Dakota with her life. Even now, as they were trying to escape from the weird events of the night, she trusted him.

What if he didn't trust her the same way?

The idea numbed her. She would never betray him for keeping her safe, for dealing with her enemies or the people who'd hurt her. Judd hurt her brother. Judd hurt her. Judd betrayed her. Dakota would never do to her what Judd had, not after what he'd shared with her concerning werewolf mating habits. She'd never have to worry he'd barter her for favors.

She battled the swell of nausea rising in her throat. The shaking in her arms and legs, in her soul, resumed.

Dakota focused on his driving. "There must be a service entrance somewhere," he muttered.

"Won't the police have all the exits covered?"

"Gated communities usually have private security forces. They may not be versed in everyday crime scene procedures."

"Private security?"

"Right." He scowled at her. "Later. Stop distracting me."

She told herself he was only depersonalizing her to keep his attention on finding a way out of Elysian Estates.

"Let me out," she suggested. "I'll limp back to the Peters' place, tell them I escaped the crazy chauffeur. You can crash the limo, shift and meet me back at Ethan and Selena's."

"I'm not leaving you."

"Okay, stick around, naked as the day you were born."

He didn't speak for quarter of a mile. "If we get separated, can you manage to act dazed and confused?"

"I *am* dazed and confused. No acting required."

"I don't want to leave you," he repeated.

She placed her hand on his knee. His bare knee. Dark hair textured his skin. "I don't see how else we're getting out unless you do leave me."

"I could go back and retrieve what's left of my clothes, if they haven't been taken for evidence."

"Judd and Connor saw you shift." Disaster. Total disaster.

"No one will believe them." Dakota projected confidence. "I doubt they'll say anything. Especially Byrne. He's long gone."

"He can't get out any more than we can."

"On foot? Yeah. He could."

"Then why can't we?" Britt swallowed her irritation. Dakota was supposed to hang out with secret agent types. Apparently, he hadn't learned much.

Trust him.

She didn't have a choice. If she did, she'd still trust him. Even though he hadn't killed Judd. Even though he hadn't protected her the way he'd promised. He had her back, the same way she had his. His presence alone was more than she'd had from anyone since her mother's death.

"We need to wipe the limo," Dakota pointed out.

"With what? Your bare butt's going to do a thorough job."

"Your dress. Unless there's a blanket or something hidden in the back seat. Napkins from a mini bar?"

"Oh goodie." Britt's sarcasm increased with each degree of her temper. "I'm glad you're not sending me to forage for leaves big enough to handle the limo. Harvesting is Selena's job, not mine."

"We don't need to wipe the whole limo, only the interior."

"I've got news for you, Bus Boy. You were on the hood."

"I'm not worried about the exterior." He tried to sound confident. "The feds have my fingerprints on file, remember? Any search would trigger a flag."

His statement might have been true before the movement to abolish the treaties gained momentum. Now? A mystery.

"Then why wipe it down?"

"You were driving. I was driving. We don't want anyone to know how we escaped. As I mentioned, I'm betting Byrne has a hidey hole someplace where he's going to lie low for a bit."

"Until he sees another chance to grab me, you mean."

"Maybe. Or maybe we don't want anyone to know we drove away unscathed from the scene of Peters and Byrne's injuries."

"Oh." Selena was silent as he searched for a place to stash the limo.

He located a spot away from residences or gates and pulled off the road into a grove of evergreens.

"What about using only the bottom of my skirt? The dress is ruined, but I don't have anything else to wear for my getaway. You can shift so your stuff isn't waving in the wind. I'm more modest than you are. Besides," Britt's tone turned sly, "you don't want me running around naked in front of the cops should we run into them."

The female was learning how to play him.

"I figured you could take off the dress, let me clean the interior, then you could put it back on."

She considered his suggestion. "If we cut the skirt off at the knees, I'll be able to travel faster."

"Good point."

"I'll need your brute strength to help me."

"Brute strength?"

"Compared to me. The seam is torn, so ripping will be easy."

He grasped the thick, slippery fabric with both hands and yanked. The material separated in a jagged tear. Minuscule particles of cloth drifted into his nostrils.

Britt contorted suggestively as Dakota freed the entire bottom of the skirt from the knees down. The action revealed her bare feet.

"Where are your shoes?"

"Near your clothes. Ruined, too. One has Judd's blood on the heel."

"Good for you."

"Yeah. Too bad I missed his eyes." She was serious.

He loved her for her courage. "Too bad," he agreed, as he rubbed the steering wheel with the hem of her dress. Britt climbed out of the car and waited for him.

He wished he had a way to leave Byrne's prints on the wheel while eliminating everyone else's. He made sure he got the shift and the wiper fluid release. The door handles. The window between the driver and passenger areas. His inherent lycan speed helped him be thorough without wasting time.

He did what he could to erase his and Britt's presence from the front seat of the car. He tied the strip of cloth to his forearm and joined Britt on a moss-covered boulder. Her knees were drawn to her chest.

"Should we wait until full dark?" She plucked at the moss.

"The moon is waxing toward full," he replied. "She could betray us with shadows. Hush!"

He laid a finger across her lips and cocked his head. A vehicle approached their position, tires humming on the well-maintained road surface. Dakota scooped her against his chest and carried her behind the boulder. "Someone's coming," he whispered against her ear.

She nodded, and he relaxed a bit. He wrapped his arms around her and settled her against his chest. Her bottom rested on his groin and the inevitable happened.

Silver light from the moon sneaked into gaps in the trees. The boulder cast a big enough shadow to hide them from her revealing light.

The vehicle continued toward them, slowly, steadily. Dakota caught glimpses of a spotlight flickering into the landscaping. They'd find the car, no problem. He'd hoped he'd have more time. His luck had run out.

Placing a finger against Britt's lips to warn her to keep quiet, he stood. He flung her across his shoulders and traveled on silent feet deeper into the trees. Unfortunately, every bit of cover in the expensive enclave of the wealthy was as shallow as the inhabitants. There was barely enough to hide them from the road.

He placed Britt on the ground. Squatting next to her, he tore the fabric from the bottom of her dress into two parts. Britt's heart thundered. She stayed silent as he wrapped her feet in makeshift shoes. The cloth would protect her soles.

Something fluttered against his cheek. Her hand. Chilly from the night and her fear. He read the gesture as a *thank you*.

He stood and summoned his shift.

Britt's image blurred, but he glimpsed her face raised to the heat his morphing energy created. A moment later, he stood before her in wolf form. Her hand hovered above his head, the first time she'd ever indicated she wanted to touch him when he showed her his lycan side.

Her touch was hesitant, and maybe she was afraid—hard to tell given their situation—but she touched him. Willingly.

"There's the limo," someone said. A radio crackled.

Britt blanched. She'd heard the speaker, too. Her heart rate increased.

Dakota jerked his head away from where they'd left the car. Britt nodded. He hoped she understood.

DAKOTA IN WOLF FORM was blacker than the shadows surrounding them. Britt studied the sky. The moon was as bright as Dakota predicted.

She climbed to her feet as quietly as she could. Very little bracken covered the ground, so nothing rustled. She imagined the homeowners' association paid people to rake the ground in the common areas. The cloth Dakota tied around her feet offered only minimal protection.

Dakota headed deeper into the grove. She followed. He blended with the shadows, whereas she, with her blond hair and pale dress, stood out like a ghost.

She hoped he hadn't lied when he boasted of his sense of direction.

If not for her, he could have made his way out of Elysian Estates.

He should have killed Byrne when he had the chance.

Sharp objects—stones, sticks, and an untallied inventory of bits and pieces—jabbed at her feet. She didn't make a sound. The conversation at the limo faded with each step she took. Periodically Dakota would step into a puddle of spilled moonlight, reassuring her she still followed him.

Eventually they found a clearing. A tall hedge grew in front of them, a natural barrier to keep the riffraff out of Elysian Estates. Lightning bugs flickered like malfunctioning fairy lights. If the wall was only a hedge, they'd be able to squeeze between the shrubs.

Dakota must have had the same idea and tested the theory. He sniffed around the base of the hedge before settling on a spot in the shadows. He began to burrow. Hopefully he'd make the passage deep enough to accommodate her.

He stopped pawing at the dirt. A burst of heat she was coming to recognize along with the pressure in her sinuses and behind her eardrums warned her he was shifting. Why? He needed to keep digging so they could crawl out of this elaborate version of a prison.

"Do you have your phone on you?" he asked as soon as the morph was complete. His voice was thick and heavy, as if his vocal chords hadn't fully transitioned. He steered her away from the hedge, into the grove.

"No." Even if she'd crammed the phone in her purse, she'd lost the bag at the same time she'd lost her shawl and shoes. Damn. Her house key, much-needed cash, and her favorite lip gloss were in that bag. "Where's yours?"

"With my clothes. I'm going to have to go back."

Her too-tight chest was going to snap apart; her heart would burst. "Why?" She didn't want to be alone.

"Wait here. I need my phone." He tramped around the clearing until he found what he wanted. He returned with a long, sharp tree limb. He studied the sky and muttered something she didn't catch.

"Stay out of the moon. You shine like a beacon. You probably won't need the stake—stick. In case you do..."

He handed her the heavy limb. She nodded and was rewarded with another blast of heat as he changed yet again.

THANK YOU, ANCIENT ONES, for letting the moon be waxing when I need her strength.

Shifting sapped energy. Dakota never, not even as a teenager learning the changes in his body, shifted as many times as he would this night. Thank the Ancient Ones the waxing moon would share her energy with him.

His ability to shift was the only tool, the only weapon they possessed. He needed his cell phone to report what he'd found in the hedge to Britt's cop friends.

Who he'd found.

Racing in the night was easier alone and in his lycan form. The shadows were his friends. Shadows and moonlight were his tools. The moon for strength, shadows for stealth.

He only hoped the private security force wasn't as thorough as sanctioned law enforcement and hadn't yet discovered his clothes.

No crime scene tape marked the spot, even though Connor Peters no longer sprawled on the berm. Another cesspool of scents clumped together. Many people had congregated. Dakota had problems figuring out what had gone down. He wished Stoker was around. Stoker could tell—by smell alone—the make and model of a car twelve hours after it had driven past. But Stoker was in Colorado, composing more hit songs for Toke Lobo and snuggling with his mate.

Dakota hopped into the ditch. A trickle of water in the bottom wet the pads of his paws.

His clothes were soaked tatters of fabric. He shifted again and grabbed the rags before running into the shrubbery. His phone was in what remained of a pocket. He'd taken Tom Anderson's number from Britt's phone. Anderson was his first call.

Life would be much easier if he could howl the news to the ones who needed to know.

"I'm calling in an anonymous tip."

Anderson hesitated.

"Anonymous, or I disconnect."

Anderson sighed. "Go ahead."

"Are you aware of anything happening in Elysian Estates?" Dakota spoke as quietly as he could, but he was losing control of lesser functions.

"Why?"

"Brittany Hague and...her bodyguard were present— well, they were there as witnesses."

Anderson's tone sharpened. "Where is Britt?"

Dakota ignored the question. "You need to get to the north wall of Elysian Estates STAT. Or send someone you trust. Stuff is going on I don't get. I'll be in touch when I can."

Dakota disconnected, muttering, "Hope I did the right thing."

The phone vibrated. Anderson. Dakota disconnected the call. The phone had to go. After he made one more phone call.

A moment later, Dakota pried a good-sized rock from the earth. He crushed the phone in his hand before dropping the fragments into the indentation the rock made in the dirt. He replaced the rock. Hard. More breakage.

He searched for a patch of moonlight. Lunar power would lend him the strength to shift again. He needed to get back to Britt.

She shouldn't be alone with Judd Byrne's corpse.

Chapter 20

THE WIND MADE ALL kinds of weird sounds. Britt imagined a variety of scenarios. She huddled closer to the rough bark of the tree where Dakota left her, clutching the stick as a security blanket. Her brain wouldn't settle. What was he doing? Why did he abandon her? Okay, he wanted his phone. She understood. What did people do before cell phones?

Something rustled from the direction where Dakota had dug. She held her breath. *Please be Dakota.*

The crackling stopped after a few moments, replaced by a moan.

Her upper teeth sank into her bottom lip. The taste of her blood tingled on her tongue. She wrapped an arm around her torso and tried to shrink. The night grew chilly.

Dakota had been gone an awfully long time. She was scared. Her feet hurt. Her legs ached from running. She wasn't an athletic person. Dancing and sex were the only times she sweated.

Don't think about sex. Sex gained a new face. Dakota's face. He had miraculously replaced Judd as her definition.

If she ever got out of this mess alive, she was going to jump Dakota's bones—*no, wait.* He hadn't killed Judd. He'd threatened. He'd promised. But Judd was still at large, proving her fears hadn't been baseless.

She needed to exorcise her father's voice, louder since meeting Dakota, thundering in her head and smashing against her conscience. She should ask Selena if eating sage or drinking sage tea would have the same cleansing effect on her brain as burning the herb did to banish bad vibes in other spaces. Pastor Paul was unquestionably a bad spirit.

I've paid you back. Delivered the goods. What did Connor mean?

No, she couldn't be distracted by what he'd meant.

Where was Dakota? She wanted to bounce ideas off him. Wanted the comfort of his presence. She'd never felt so alone. Loneliness invited the past in. She wasn't in the mood for memories. Banish her father. Banish Judd. Banish the way Connor's voice haunted her. She couldn't angst about Judd and the others. Not now. Not ever. Especially not tonight, huddled beneath a tree in Peters' territory.

Senator Tuttle. Safe topic. Everyone hated Rich Tuttle.

Yet his constituency continued to reelect him.

Britt wasn't a political woman, but some topics were difficult to avoid. Tuttle was a powerful man.

Maybe she could wrangle an invitation for Ethan to meet him. Ethan could work on his precious treaties with Tuttle.

Another moan sliced into the jumble occupying her brain. The sound was louder than before. Snuffling and heavy breathing followed. Drew closer. She tightened her grip on the splintery bark of her weapon. A puff of icy air skittered along her bare arms.

Rustling accompanied the harsh respiration, as if someone was shuffling through the brush toward her. Her blood drumming against her ears prevented her from pinpointing a direction.

She spotted him. Not Dakota, who, logic told her, would approach her as a wolf. Someone else. Someone less graceful. Whose stride was less purposeful. Someone shorter. Less bulky. Someone who used his arm to shield his eyes from the moon.

Dakota worshiped the moon.

A stray beam glinted off a...fang.

Dakota, Ethan, and Selena all spoke of vampires. Britt had scoffed. Even now, she told herself she was hallucinating. Her imagination had gone wild.

She wasn't imagining the increasing chill of the night.

Whatever, whoever, was lurching toward her with a lack of grace that convinced her the creature couldn't be a vampire. Vampires were smooth. Fluid. Or so they were portrayed in popular media.

At least Dakota left her with a weapon. He called the limb a stake. What hadn't he told her?

How the hell did one stake a vampire?

A low growl behind her distracted her. The maybe- vampire continued to stumble toward her. The cold intensified. Bone snapping cold. Her breath crystallized in front of her face. Too frigid to move. To defend herself.

A wolf lunged past her, knocking the maybe-vampire to the ground. Something hissed. Something else snarled. The darkness hid the tussle, intensifying the sounds of battle.

Lightning bolted from the ground to the sky.

She'd never seen such a thing and stared in awe as a second bolt forked toward the moon.

The wolf stared at the phenomena for a few precious seconds, giving an advantage to the other thing.

Britt hefted the branch in her hand. Bigger than a stick. What if the wolf wasn't Dakota? What if the beast turned on her and attacked?

But what if the wolf *was* Dakota?

Who decided the creature's heart needed to be accessed from the front? Lore taught people to stake vampires in the heart. Their bones would be either soft or brittle from lack of vitamin D.

Britt inched closer to the fray. The two bodies rolled on the ground. She raised her weapon. "Move!"

The wolf leapt away. She ran to the body awkwardly trying to rise, raised the limb above her head, and plunged.

The creature rolled and glared at her. The wolf distracted the thing as Britt pulled her weapon from the dirt. She whirled and struck again, piercing the creature's ribs. The impact vibrated and traveled the length of the wood to tingle her palms as bones shattered. The creature snarled and hissed again. Another wave of arctic air attacked her. She shivered so violently she fumbled her weapon. The wolf lunged again, distracting attention from Britt.

Third time was a charm. Her aim was true. The end of the branch sank into the creature's back. Her entire body numbed as the thing exploded. The remnants drifted around her like snow or fiery ash, searing her exposed skin.

Frostbite.

The wolf—it had to be Dakota—lay on the ground, panting. White flakes scattered on black fur.

"Is that you?" she whispered.

The wolf whimpered. She took that as a yes. "Are you all right?"

Its—his—eyes were closed. The panting didn't slow.

The panting meant he was alive. "Are you okay?"

Dakota didn't respond.

What if he wasn't? Someone was bound to find them inside the compound, and because they were behind the fence, Britt was convinced a rescue wouldn't be friendly.

And what if whatever she'd staked had allies who would search for it?

She dropped to the ground next to Dakota. Her feet throbbed. She kept her stake on her lap.

Activity in the distance increased. She couldn't make out much. Something else approached her hiding spot, striding with more confidence than its predecessor.

"Dakota? Britt?"

The call of their names was soft, barely more than a breeze ruffling the night. Waves of frigid air did not accompany whatever crept toward her. "Britt? It's Ethan."

She wanted to melt into a puddle. Instead, she blinked back her tears and sniffled.

Ethan, wearing only a pair of dark drawstring shorts, strode into a nearby splash of moonlight.

"Here," she managed to croak. She could trust Ethan.

"Are you okay?" He knelt next to her. "I smell vampire."

"Vampire? There's no such—" She stopped.

Ethan ran his hands over Dakota's pelt.

"Are vampires cold? I mean sub-zero freezer cold."

"Cold? No. They stink so bad you believe the stench will never leave your nostrils."

"Whatever the thing was, it was cold. Even after it exploded, the dust was more like snowflakes than ash. But colder. I'm a native Minnesotan. I'm familiar with cold. This was...colder."

"I believe you, but a vampires' defining characteristic is their reek."

"Are you saying I staked a zombie?" She was only half joking.

"Zombies don't exist," Ethan replied.

"There isn't a union of paranormal creatures or epic battles between the species or anything? I don't have to worry a dragon will swoop down and set my hair on fire?" The warble in her voice meant she was going to lose control and the time for a meltdown was later.

Ethan ignored her banter. "You staked a vampire?"

"Limbed it? Branched it? Dakota gave me a big branch before he shifted. I jabbed the stake into the creature a couple of times before I found the heart. Do vampires have hearts? Why?"

"You staked a vampire with a tree branch and came out unscathed?"

He sounded as if he didn't believe her.

"I staked something, and I never would have been able to succeed without Dakota doing what he did."

"Scat. Vampire cooties."

A giggle escaped. She was self-destructing.

"He's in the condition Selena was after she fought off and killed a vampire. We theorized she ingested vampire cooties when she chewed into its chest to get to its heart."

"I have a theory. I don't think Dakota bit the creature. Based on the amount of heat he generates by shifting, could he have depleted his energy? He shifted an awful lot tonight."

Ethan studied the area around them. "Good theory. Shifting does consume a lot of energy, although the closer to the full moon, the less energy required. I'm worried he's unresponsive. I need to get the two of you home. The dead body on the other side of the hedge has the cops swarming everywhere."

Dead body? "How did you find us?"

"Dakota called me."

Dakota had taken time to help her when he could have escaped. He'd come back and battled an unknown being to keep her safe. Now she needed to protect him.

"What do we need to do?"

Ethan studied her, his eyes black as the shadows. "Parker is with me. He's an EMT. We can use the commotion caused by the dead body to escape through the service entrance."

Ethan shifted to a squat next to Dakota's still form. "He'll be okay. Selena said the sleepiness sapped her focus."

"You told me she fought a vampire. Whatever I fought—"

"I smell vampire," Ethan interrupted. He wrapped his arms around Dakota and lifted.

Britt didn't see him strain. He hoisted Dakota over his shoulder. "Follow me," he instructed.

DAKOTA WAS VAGUELY AWARE help had arrived. Vampire stink clogged his sinuses so thoroughly, he couldn't identify the newcomer by scent. Britt's calm acceptance assured him Ethan was on the scene.

His next bout of awareness included vertigo or wooziness or maybe being on a boat, except he'd never been on a boat in his life, so seasickness was foreign to him. If he had more energy, he would hurl.

Judd Byrne. Britt needed to know Byrne was dead. She was safe.

Dakota heard her soft conversation with Ethan. "Can we sneak out the service entrance?"

"The police are otherwise occupied. We couldn't plan a better diversion."

Yeah, Ethan was acting like the alpha wolf he should have been, had the Peters family not attempted to annihilate the Limmikin.

Hands not belonging to his mate groped his body.

"You're right." Parker's voice. "He has the same condition Selena contracted. Could be an allergy to vampires."

"You don't know?" Britt sounded concerned.

He was glad. A mate should be concerned. Worried.

Judd. He needed to tell them...

"Let's go," Ethan said. "Before we attract attention."

Chapter 21

"Britt, Parker, you remember Helga, right?" Selena acted as if she'd mainlined too much coffee, except Selena didn't drink the stuff.

They'd arrived at Ethan's house on Ash Street without incident, although the vigilantes at each end of the block were more in Britt's awareness than before, especially the cold they emanated.

Parker ignored everyone and carried Dakota, still a comatose wolf, into the guest room.

"Purple house across the street," Britt guessed. "She's teaching you to cook. Hi, Helga."

Helga acknowledged Britt and the others. She claimed to be a witch, something Britt did believe in. Although she'd thrown off the shackles of her father's preaching, Helga's presence always caused queasiness.

"You need to get a radio if you won't get a television," Helga declared.

"You keep saying," Selena replied.

"You." Helga pointed at Britt. "According to the cute news reader on the local cable news, you've been kidnapped by your old boyfriend, an escaped convict. Connor Peters— Congressman Peters' youngest son—was critically injured trying to protect you."

Britt blinked. The room whirled before settling to a waver. "What?" She turned to Ethan. "What?"

"You're missing. Kidnapped by your old boyfriend." Helga peered at Britt. "You don't look very kidnapped to me."

Britt limped to the sofa. Her feet hurt crazy bad. The strips of cloth protecting her soles were bloodstained tatters.

"You're injured," Selena exclaimed. "Get Parker."

"Let Parker tend to Dakota. He needs Parker more than I do."

Ethan had told her Parker was a lycan EMT. A human—a sapien—doctor wouldn't be much use to Dakota.

The scientist in her was fascinated. The woman hurt.

"Selena knows her herbal cures." Ethan emerged from his bedroom, dressed in jeans and a pine green Henley shirt. "She can tend to Britt's feet."

Britt's legs were scratched, too, barely recovered from her foray into Ethan's hawthorn hedge.

"Britt needs to share her version." Ethan leaned against the doorframe, arms crossed. Secret agent mode.

Britt relaxed against the sofa back and closed her eyes. For the first time in hours, she could inhale without tightness in her chest.

Selena removed the rags from her feet, gently pulling the fabric away from cuts and punctures. Britt winced.

"I need a basin of water," Selena muttered.

"I'll get one," Helga offered.

Britt didn't want to talk. She wanted to remain missing, at least until Dakota regained his senses. She kept her eyes closed.

Selena and Helga did things with hot water and Selena's miracle plants that smelled nice. Soaking her feet in the herbal tea was heavenly. Her wounds stung. Once the water loosened the dried blood, Selena finished removing the fabric.

"Smart to protect your feet," Helga said.

"Dakota wrapped them." Britt finally opened her eyes. "Judd would have kidnapped me if not for Dakota. But Connor wasn't hurt trying to protect me. Dakota attacked him as he tried to give me to Judd."

"Scat," Ethan whispered. He sat next to her on the sofa, as if he wanted to hear her heart beating as she shared the events. "Quickly. Anything else? Dakota told me to call your cop friends once I had you safe. They'll be by any minute."

Tears leaked from the corners of her eyes and trickled onto her cheeks. She swallowed hard. "I should have listened to Dakota. Should have gone with my first instinct to run away to Colorado."

She focused on the friend kneeling at her feet. "I wanted to network with some rich people, to try to get them interested in Night Shift."

"Night Shift is dead." Selena's soft voice barely disturbed the air. "At least my interest in continuing. I wanted to use my share of profits to help sustain my pack. I have only remnants of a pack remaining. The man we solicited for money is the one behind my grandfather's murder."

"Night Shift is my gift to my mother," Britt replied. "She died when I was a teenager. Breast cancer. I wish I'd had Night Shift products to massage her with. She's my motivation."

Maybe she was being selfish. Definitely foolish. If anyone knew how resourceful Judd could be, she did. Dakota—

No. She couldn't ask him for anything. Couldn't expect additional assistance from him. Ethan said Dakota's state was similar to Selena's after she'd fought a vampire. Britt needed to believe. Needed to have faith Dakota would recover as Selena had. If he didn't, she would have another cross to bear. He never would have gotten hurt if she hadn't insisted on networking with Connor.

"I'm sorry about your mother."

Roommates for four long years of college, and yet their pasts remained unshared.

"Yeah. I don't talk about my family." For a lot of good reasons.

The doorbell rang.

"I don't want to talk to the cops, not while Dakota is..." Britt fluttered her hand toward the guest room as she struggled to maintain a calm façade.

"I understand." Ethan stood and resumed his pose against the doorjamb. "But you don't have a choice. We can't have the authorities running around searching for you when you're safe."

Such a shame his point was valid.

"I'll answer the door," Helga offered.

"Keep your feet in the water," Selena ordered. "I'll add the comfrey later."

"You left by the service entrance," Ethan instructed her.

"What about Dakota?"

Helga led Tom and Mickey into the living room.

Tom stopped short when he saw Britt. "You're alive."

"I'm tough," Britt bragged. "Do you have my purse? I dropped it when Connor tried to give me to Judd."

Tom and Mickey exchanged a glance.

"According to Peters, Judd Byrne kidnapped you. According to an anonymous tip"—Tom cleared his throat— "Byrne was murdered. His body was left outside Elysian Estates. Except we can't locate a body. Plenty of blood, but no body. Any idea why?"

Britt tried to ignore the tightening in her chest. Judd had not been the creature coming after her. The one she'd staked. His red hair would have been visible in the moonlight.

"Connor jammed a gun in my ribs. He forced me out of the party and tried to give me to Judd. He said something like he'd grabbed me for Judd." The memory wasn't clear; a potent cocktail of terror and rage tainted the moments. "Do you have my evening bag? I need my house key."

She was still shaking inside. Jangling and jittery, ready to burst from her skin. "I should have suspected something when Connor ordered his driver to take off without my bodyguard."

"Bodyguard?" At least Mickey was listening to her.

"Yeah. I refused to attend a party at the Peters estate unless I took my bodyguard. Dakota. You met him yesterday afternoon."

Mickey narrowed his eyes. "He's a bodyguard?"

"He's my bodyguard. And driver." She lifted her chin. "What else was I supposed to do with Judd out of prison?"

"What did Peters say to Byrne?" Tom asked.

"I don't remember. I was scared. Believe it or not, I'm not used to people sticking guns in my ribs."

"Where's your bodyguard now?"

Mickey and Tom had individual focuses. Was that to trip her up?

Her throat closed. She couldn't answer even if she wanted to. If she didn't speak, she couldn't be accused of lying.

"She's upset," Ethan interjected. He dropped his arms to his side.

"She's got some explaining to do," Tom countered. "We have a BOLO out on her. How did she get from Elysian Estates to Ash Street? Are you going to tell me she walked?" Britt lifted her battered feet from the pan of pink-stained water. The pile of bloody rags from her feet lay crumpled on the floor next to the basin.

"I need to change the water," Selena murmured.

"She's safe. Isn't that what matters?" Ethan widened his stance. The shadows behind him shifted.

"Britt's safety is the only thing that matters." Dakota clutched the doorjamb next to Ethan.

He'd pulled on a pair of jeans but left the fly unzipped. He was bleary-eyed and pale. Too pale. No visible bruises marred the perfection of his body. He'd been fighting. She'd seen him punched. Except for the way he propped his body against the door frame as if he couldn't remain upright without support, he exhibited no signs of the fight.

If she recognized his weariness, so would Tom and Mickey.

"How did the two of you get to Ash Street?"

"I'm a bodyguard. I can't divulge my methods of protecting my client."

"Can you divulge how you called me and told me the location of a body that doesn't exist?"

"Anonymously."

"All right. *Anonymously.*" Tom sounded peeved.

"With a cell phone. What do you mean, a body that doesn't exist? I found a dead someone matching Byrne's photo outside the fenced hedge on the north side of Elysian Estates."

Tom's lips tightened. "Are you sure he was dead? There was no body when we arrived. Plenty of blood, but no body. Could he have been injured? Did you kill him or merely wound him?"

If Dakota wasn't so sick, he'd be pissed at Anderson's accusation. But he was barely upright, only due to the strong oak frames in Ethan's house supporting him. "If I had killed him, I would have reduced him to DNA level."

Anderson never blinked. His glare encompassed Britt and Dakota. "All we have is a puddle of DNA. You threatened to kill him. You called us and told us he was dead."

"I didn't kill him. Someone beat me to it." Dakota had listened for a heartbeat against Byrne's chest. Had listened for respiration. Dakota knew dead. Byrne was dead.

"Maybe the murderer snatched the body," Britt suggested.

Dakota forced himself to focus on anything besides Britt. Otherwise, he might start howling.

Byrne had not been the vampire who'd attacked them. Byrne was still at large.

"I called you, trying to be a good citizen while also trying to protect Britt. Whatever Connor Peters told you is a lie. He tried to ditch me when he picked up Britt, he forced her out of the party at gunpoint and tried to give her to Byrne. I will claim any damage done to him. But I left him alive."

For the moment.

The room undulated. The weakness trying to bite into his bones clenched tighter. Only Britt's safety had drawn him from his bed.

"You don't look good," Clerkin—or maybe Anderson— said.

Dakota was having problems focusing. The taste in his mouth was as foul as anything he'd ever experienced. Agony battered the inside of his skull. His eyes burned.

Vampire cooties.

As long as Britt didn't mention the vampire she'd staked, they could get out of tonight relatively unscathed. As long as she didn't volunteer anything other than the barest answers to the cops' questions.

"How did you get from Elysian Estates to Ash Street? Not exactly the same neighborhood," Clerkin pressed.

"He called me after he called you," Ethan admitted. "I met them a few blocks from the service entrance."

Dakota wished Ethan hadn't spoken. The less the cops were involved, the better.

"Didn't you think we'd want to talk to you?"

"You've found me," Dakota managed. Barely.

"And you knew where to find us. Otherwise you wouldn't have called." Anderson spoke as if he had the right to be pissy.

"I called."

"You want a medal for reporting a dead body? We ought to arrest you for leaving the scene of a crime."

"I called you. You agreed to anonymity. Why would you want gawkers at the scene of a crime?"

"I'd say you were more of a witness than a gawker. You found the body."

"I've told you everything I can. I was searching for a way out of Elysian Estates, located what I believed to be a gap in the hedge, and found Byrne's body on the other side. His red hair is hard to miss. Without a body, how can you be sure a crime was committed?"

"Byrne took off his ankle bracelet, meaning he's in violation of his parole," Anderson reminded him.

"Will you be posting guards around my house?" Ethan asked.

"Not enough money in the budget."

"Do you have a safe house?" Britt's voice broke. "Since my house key is missing, I can't go home."

If what Dakota suspected was true, she'd be safer at Ethan's than her apartment. "Nothing has changed. Your apartment isn't safe."

Maybe he spoke in a harsher tone than he'd intended; her complexion paled, her lips thinned, and she huddled deeper into the corner of the sofa.

"Why did you guys bother to show up?" he asked the cops. "Wasting budget money when there's no body and no crime."

"Besides your threat against Byrne? Attempted kidnapping. An attack on Connor Peters." Clerkin recited his list. "A Judd Byrne sighting."

"Connor Peters tried to kidnap Britt. Tried to hand her to Byrne. I prevented her abduction." Dakota nearly choked on his next sentence. "As Britt's bodyguard, I performed my job."

The cops did a couple more minutes of nasty double- edged questioning—exactly what they were supposed to do given the circumstances. If Dakota wasn't so sick, he might not have minded. They probed for answers he couldn't give. Thank the Ancient Ones Britt was clueless.

But not calm. "Hey," she snapped. "We approached you. I trusted you. Okay? Remember? Judd was texting me from prison, so I came to you. We have come to you every step of the way. Why are you treating us like suspects? I'm the victim here."

"Survivor," Ethan muttered.

"Whatever. Why aren't you going after Connor Peters? He held a gun on me. He tried to give me to Judd. Why aren't you bothering him? *Where is my evening bag?*"

Clearly irritated, Clerkin snapped, "We're handling Connor Peters. Anything found at the crime scene has been tagged and taken into evidence."

Eventually Clerkin and Anderson left, along with Helga. Dakota sank to the floor, his back still against the door frame. Britt struggled to rise, as if to come to him. As much as he wanted her, he didn't want her to discover the extent of his weakness.

Selena beat her to him. She squatted next to him. "You okay?"

She was the only one who could relate to his symptoms. "I'm getting okay. Vampire cooties?"

"You recouped fast."

"I didn't ingest as many as you did."

Ethan chimed in. "Parker ought to be documenting everything for the archives."

Selena bristled. "Whose archives?"

Dakota did not want to get in the middle of a territory war. "Britt? Are you okay?" He should have been the one to rescue her. Not Ethan. He never should have called Ethan.

Scattin' vampire cooties.

"You changed into a wolf in front of Connor," Britt pointed out. "He knows your secret."

"Connor has always known I'm lycan. Frankly, I'm more concerned about why Byrne's body vanished."

THE ROOM SWAM AROUND Britt. Or maybe she was scuba diving without an oxygen tank. "What do you mean?"

Dakota switched his focus to her. "Byrne is dead. I found his body. Someone else lost him."

"Bodies don't vanish."

"That's the problem."

How could Dakota be so laid back when Judd clearly wasn't dead?

"Does he have someone who would care for him?" Ethan asked, after exchanging a long glance with Dakota.

"Curtis DiNardo was his best friend," Britt offered.

"They say he's disappeared. Maybe he's helping Judd."

Maybe she was crazy, but tension in the room hummed louder.

"Anyone else?" Ethan asked.

"Nope. Judd's mother abandoned him when he was a kid. His dad is a junkie. No siblings. He had his gang, his pack. Curtis. Me. A couple of others. Curtis and I were his mainstays. I purposely lost touch with everyone after Judd went to prison."

"So much for that theory," Ethan muttered.

"A lobo can hope," Dakota added.

"Curtis could be helping Judd. I can't imagine who else would be," Britt insisted.

"You were attacked by a vampire tonight," Dakota stated flatly. "Not Byrne."

She couldn't swallow. Swallow? She couldn't breathe. She could barely speak. "What are you saying?"

"Vampires were lurking, maybe drawn by the scent of Byrne's blood. The ground around him was soaked. They could have...rescued him."

"Rescued?"

Selena broke in. "Changed him. Into one of them." "But—"

"His status depends on who killed him," Dakota said. "I couldn't smell anything around the body except his blood and vampire stink. Vampires could have killed him, infected him. His body wasn't necessarily retrieved."

"He got up and walked away?" The words left Britt's throat on a squeal and shattered as they hit the air.

"Maybe." Selena clearly wouldn't commit to anything.

"*Maybe*? Well, maybe I'm being dense. Will someone please tell me what is going on?"

"All we have is theory." Dakota's hands dangled between his splayed legs, an attitude of defeat Britt hated. "Lack of knowledge is part of the problem. Vampire culture is alien to us. Despite what monster movies and popular fiction portray, werewolves and other non-sapien beings don't mingle. They have their ways, we have ours."

"You're saying Judd has been turned into a vampire." "Not necessarily," Selena insisted at the same time Ethan said, "Probably."

Britt sat. Sitting was good. Otherwise, she would have fallen. Judd as a teenager was mean. *Scratch that*. He'd been vicious. If he'd been given powers, another set of skills to hurt people, he would gleefully accept the gift and test his new ability to see how far he could go.

"Your house is vampire proof?" She whispered the question.

"So far," Ethan replied.

She was never going to leave again.

Except to move to Colorado with Dakota. In the daylight.

They could leave while the sun shone.

Britt focused on her breathing. Slowly in. Slowly out. "I've got bad news for you. If Judd Byrne is a vampire, we're in big trouble. The world is in big trouble. Unless his master can control him. Don't vampires have to obey the one who changed them?"

"According to popular fiction. But according to popular fiction, only silver bullets can kill a werewolf. Not true. Any bullet can kill us. Popular fiction isn't a good source for facts."

"Then let's hope Curtis rescued him."

"Oh." Dakota's eyes widened and his voice rumbled. "That would not be good."

"Really bad," Selena added.

Okay, the day had been long and stressful, especially the past several hours. Maybe Britt's synapses weren't sparking or something. Dakota and Selena acted as if they knew Curtis.

"Curtis isn't the brightest bulb in the chandelier, but—"

"DiNardo is out of the picture." Ethan stuffed his hands into his pockets. "Leave him out of the equation."

"I forgot to tell you," Dakota muttered. He sagged against the frame, his eyelids half shut. "Connor Peters used to go slumming with Curtis DiNardo. Curtis DiNardo was Judd Byrne's best friend."

Every eye in the room focused on Britt. The problem was, she couldn't remember.

The tightness in her chest compressed, squeezing her heart and lungs, crushing the organs she needed to survive.

Dakota tried to stand. Either her vision was wonky or he was still weak from vampire cooties. "You're wheezing," he said.

White spots drifted like snow, except snow didn't fall in June, not even in northern Minnesota. Especially indoors. Snow never fell inside. Maybe not snow. Maybe ash, like after she'd rammed the stake into the back of the creature in the grove and it exploded into a blizzard.

"Shove her head between her knees," Parker suggested. Britt hadn't noticed him.

He crossed the room and put his hand on her nape.

Dakota roared, "Get your paw off her."

Maybe Dakota wasn't roaring. Even the air was loud. Parker pushed her head until she faced her bare thighs.

"She's going to faint."

Chapter 22

"Wʜᴀᴛ ᴅɪᴅ Cᴏɴɴᴏʀ ᴍᴇᴀɴ when he told Judd he wouldn't mind another go at you?"

Britt swallowed, and straightened the sheet over Dakota. She'd finally gotten him back into bed. "You're supposed to be resting."

Of all the things Dakota remembered about his initial encounter with Judd, he would have to latch onto that.

Judd shotgunned a toke of weed into Britt's mouth. She loathed smoking dope, but Judd liked her better stoned, claiming she wasn't such a tight ass.

"I'm not the one who fainted." Dakota sounded irritated.

"I didn't have a chance to eat at the party. You have vampire cooties. Rest."

He loosely caught her wrist. "I thought we were through with secrets."

Britt perched on the edge of the mattress. She didn't try to free herself from Dakota's grasp. If she could transfer her strength to him, she would. Maybe Helga knew a spell...

"I already don't feel guilty enough because you're infected?" She tried for a light tone, but her words clunked.

Judd slipped his hand under her T-shirt and cupped a breast. "You have real nice tits."

Why wouldn't he leave her alone? Dope always made her sleepy.

"You're sidestepping my question," Dakota accused.

"Are you always this cranky when you're sick?" She slipped her wrist from his grasp, then twined her fingers with his.

"No. I don't get sick."

Great. Even more guilt.

Maybe she could distract him. "I should have listened to you. You were right. About the party. About Connor. About everything."

"Stop trying to placate me." He tightened his fingers on hers as he turned onto his side.

"I'm not." He wasn't the only one who could be fractious.

"You like having your tits sucked," Judd said.

She nodded.

"Man, I wish I could suck both of them at the same time. Wouldn't you go crazy for that?"

"You know Connor Peters from the old days," Dakota accused.

Britt shook her head. She forced herself to look him in the eye. Her throat was so tight she was amazed she could speak at all. "I might have met him once. I don't remember." How could she explain something she didn't understand?

"You don't remember meeting a congressman's son?"

"No. I don't. Not exactly."

"I'm so lucky," Judd said in an unfamiliar tone. "I gotta pretty girlfriend with pretty tits. I feel sorry for Curtis."

What did Curtis DiNardo have to do with anything?

"Curtis is a jackass," Britt muttered. She hated Curtis even if he was Judd's best friend. Curtis was loud, boorish, and usually unwashed, or at least smelled nasty.

"He doesn't have a girlfriend." As if lack of a woman explained all of Curtis's defects. "He's never even seen tits in real life."

"Get him a blow-up doll," Britt suggested. *Judd rolled away from her and lit another joint.*

"What does 'not exactly' mean?" Dakota pulled her down to lie next to him. Either you remember or you don't."

"Judd smoked a lot of pot and insisted I partake."

Judd pinned her to the mattress and forced second-hand smoke into her mouth and nose again. She tried not to inhale. Judd wanted her completely wasted.

The room spun when he finally raised himself. He smirked. Flicked a nipple.

"Where was I? Oh. Yeah. Curtis has never seen much less touched real tits."

Dread built in her stomach. She did not like the direction Judd steered the conversation.

"I need Curtis to do a big favor for me. I told him he could play with your tits for a little while."

Britt tried to raise her arms to cover her breasts. Her muscles turned to rocks. Or maybe spaghetti. She shook her head, but the world was underwater. Like Atlantis.

"Curtis can suck your tits while I suck your clit. Can you imagine how fantastic that will feel?"

She rolled her head and found a straining zipper at the crotch of a pair of grimy jeans. At eye-level.

Dakota's gaze never left her face. "Are you saying Connor was Judd's dealer?"

"Oh, I wish it was that simple." What she really wished was the ability to lose the flashbacks haunting her since meeting with Connor in the congressional office.

"Hey Curtis," Judd said. *"Suit up and you can fuck her when I'm done. The rubbers are on the table."*

"I didn't handle drugs well. I don't handle alcohol well, either," she confessed to Dakota. "I kept drinking through college, with too many hungover mornings. So yeah, I do drink, but believe me, I don't overindulge the way I did when I was a kid." She plucked at the sheet covering him. "Mostly I drink to take the edge off."

"Sex?"

Dakota was reading her mind. At least she didn't have to get explicit.

"I've noticed you don't drink when you need to keep your wits. Like tonight," he said.

Curtis took Judd's place when he finished.

"Get off me," she whined and pushed at his bony shoulders. The dope made her weak. Ineffectual. She squeezed her eyes shut, wringing tears onto her cheeks.

"You're someplace else," Dakota said when she fell silent.

"I keep having...impressions. Maybe they're flashbacks. The last night Judd and I were together. I don't have any clear memories, only blurs." Her voice broke. The room shimmered through her tears.

Dakota wrapped her in his arms. "You can tell me anything."

So she did.

"What's going on?"

Britt opened her eyes to find a stranger in the room. A blue-eyed stranger.

"Who the hell are you?" Judd demanded.

"A friend of Curtis. He texted me to stop by."

"He's cool," Curtis added.

"Mind if I join in?"

"Why not?" Judd snickered. "She can suck you off. She's getting better at blow jobs."

The stranger quickly undid his pants and exposed his penis. He placed two fingers under Britt's chin to raise her head. "If you bite, you'll rue the day you were born."

"Blow him, or you'll be sorry," Judd warned. "Open up." Judd never made idle threats.

As Britt spoke, she struggled to keep her shame hidden. The mortification of what she'd let Judd do to her ruled her every breath since that night. She'd gotten good at diversion. No inflection in her voice was allowed. No emotion of any sort permitted. No one could ever know the depth of her humiliation.

"When the stranger complained to Judd because I wasn't very good, Judd told him who my father was. The stranger laughed and suggested Judd rent me out. He could make a fortune having Pastor Paul's daughter give blow jobs." A lone tear crawled out the corner of her eye.

Dakota didn't move. Her story probably paralyzed him with revulsion.

She had to tell him the rest. If she'd gotten as far as she had, she ought to be able to speak one more sentence. Make one more confession.

"I'm ninety-nine percent certain the stranger was Connor Peters."

Chapter 23

Britt curled next to Dakota on the bed in Selena's guest room, dry-eyed, and stared at the window blinds. Not that she could see anything in the dark. Hopefully Dakota couldn't read her face. She lay on her side, and he was behind her, but who knew what a werewolf could do?

He'd puked after she told him about the flashbacks.

She wanted to vomit, too. She couldn't tell Dakota for certain how much was reality, how much was the dope, how much was nightmare.

Now she understood why Connor's voice bothered her from the very first.

Dry eyes? Her lids were the texture of sandpaper.

She never should have told Dakota the story. Her twisted memories had no bearing on what Ethan was doing. She didn't rate even a footnote in the Peters Dynasty saga.

"I'm going to kill him," Dakota told the shadows above the bed.

"Who? Judd? He's already dead."

"He's undead. After I get done with him, he's going to be *un.* Period. Both of them."

"Both?"

He didn't answer.

"What do you mean, both?" Her tale included three men. "I wish I had DiNardo to do over." Dakota whispered the confession. His words echoed in the corners, disturbing the cobwebs.

Her mouth was as arid as her eyes. "Do over?"

"Curtis DiNardo will never bother you again. I can guarantee—with a clear conscience—you're safe from him."

"You can't be sure."

He hesitated. "We dealt with him a few weeks back."

Her stomach clenched. "Define 'dealt with.'" She asked because his hint was the same as driving past an auto accident. A person couldn't help but gawk.

AFRAID TO JOSTLE BRITT, Dakota lay as still as a lycan could while seething inside. She hadn't betrayed Byrne by going to the cops or testifying against him.

He'd betrayed her, and she sought vengeance. The knowledge changed everything Dakota believed concerning Britt. Reassured him of her trustworthiness. He hated that trusting her was based on her having been so horribly abused. The moment DiNardo sealed his fate in the forest outside Ulvskog, Dakota had yet to meet Britt. DiNardo died for betraying Selena to the vampires, for doing Peters' family dirty work. He'd been caught. Punished.

Dakota wished he could dismantle DiNardo's still-living body again. Multiple times. But Byrne? Byrne was going to pay. With his life. With his afterlife. If he was now a vampire, his death ashes would be salted. Quick limed. Submerged in a cesspool of pig scat.

And if he wasn't a vampire? Toke Lobo would have to compose lyrics to the melody of Byrne's death shrieks, his pleas for mercy. Stoker Smith could orchestrate the dirge.

Dakota could tell Britt what happened to DiNardo. He could trust her with a portion of his secrets.

"DiNardo is dead," he finally confessed. "He signed his death warrant when he threatened Selena. We do not take threats toward our females lightly or kindly."

Britt's tense body relaxed. Slightly. Only enough to register with his heightened senses.

"Did you hurt him?" she whispered.

"As much as we could. His screams silenced the birds and insects for hours afterward."

"Will you do the same to Judd?"

"No."

"No? Why not?"

"DiNardo's death was easy. Even if Byrne is a vampire, he will wish for his easy death again. And again. And again."

"I want to help." If only she could. "I don't have fangs or claws or any of your weapons, but I staked something tonight. I stopped a creature by using a tree branch. I have killed, too."

She was so innocent.

"Yes, you've killed, too."

Dakota wasn't fond of killing. He could count on one hand the number of times he'd helped end a life. Each time the life hadn't been worth the carbon dioxide it exhaled. After learning Britt's story, he was glad he'd helped kill DiNardo. He only wished he'd acted alone and with more savagery.

"I need to hurt them," she confessed.

He understood. His need to protect her warred with wanting to satisfy her blood lust. Britt was not some weak, sniveling female. She was a force. She understood her power. She was a survivor, not a victim. She'd made sure Byrne went to prison. Maybe not for what he'd done to her, but he'd been incarcerated. The system failed her; she had not failed herself.

"I don't want to go to Colorado tomorrow."

"Okay." Made sense. He didn't want to go, either. A lobo didn't run away from his problems. He faced them head on and defeated them. Britt was becoming an ideal lycan mate.

"I'm never going to be free until Judd and Connor pay."

Revenge. His sweet, sweet Britt was talking revenge. He loved her a bit more.

"Why didn't you kill Connor or Judd tonight?"

"Connor held a gun on you." His logic was self-evident. "I am not faster than a speeding bullet. Bullets don't have to be silver to kill me. Or you. I didn't know if Byrne was armed."

"Right. The gun. I forgot."

Had she been upset he'd left Peters alive and let Byrne escape?

"Thank you for what you did. Shifting so many times must have exhausted you."

He didn't need her thanks. He'd done what any lobo would have done to protect his mate. Her gratitude meant nothing without love.

Whoa. Where had *that* come from?

He was lying in bed with his mate, who presented her back to him, as if he'd done something wrong, and yet she was thanking him for what he'd done right. Mixed messages. What if he touched her? Placed his hand on her shoulder?

She needed comforting. She needed reassurance her sordid tale didn't repulse him.

On her terms. The realization broadsided him. Maybe she wasn't aware how her behavior was based in what Byrne had done to her. He'd used sex to control her. To demean her. Her nights at Holsters and her hookups were her efforts to control her sex life on her terms. Her say-so. The storm wasn't random, but subconsciously targeted.

He rolled onto his side and rested his palm on the curve of her shoulder. Her flinch barely registered, as if she were surprised he wanted to touch her as opposed to not wanting to be touched.

"You weren't harmed. That's what matters."

"I might have a bruise on my ribs where Connor jammed the gun into them."

He slid his hand down her arm, a steady inch by inch. "Right or left side?"

Britt's slower metabolism wouldn't heal as quickly as a lycan female.

"Left." The exposed side.

"Can I touch you?" He needed her permission to continue caressing her. After the story she'd told him, he would need her permission every day for the rest of their lives. If she said no, if she *ever* said no, he needed to honor her decision. He would have, anyway. Her tale magnified the need.

"You already are."

She shifted her arm away from her torso. He cautiously placed his hand on her ribs. Each one was clearly defined under his fingers through the soft fabric of her sleep shirt. She was thin.

"Where?"

"Lower."

She inhaled sharply through her teeth when he located the spot. A bruise thickened beneath her skin. Swollen and roughly circular in shape, the contusion was somewhere between the size of a nickel and a quarter.

"Parker should examine you."

"I've had worse. My feet, for example. Thank you for trying to protect them."

"Your pains hurt me."

"You're an empath as well as a werewolf?"

"I'm not being literal." He shaped his fingers to the contours of her torso.

"Selena mentioned male werewolves are protective of their wives."

"Mate. Soul mate. Maybe you don't currently feel the connection, but you will. We can't hide from or deny our destiny."

"Blind acceptance of my fate? Sounds similar to my father's version of the Bible."

"All I know of your Bible is the story of Joshua and the Battle of Jericho." Stoker's mate had convinced Restin to emulate the strategy with wolves howling outside the stockade fence at the New Sinai cult compound. The strategy ended in disaster.

"People, mostly men like my father, warp the words to match their version of reality."

The Ancient Ones had left no writings. They'd merely endowed their creatures with knowledge. No one argued the basic tenets of being lycan. No one fought the mating instinct. Sometimes, misunderstanding strained things for a while, but everything eventually worked out.

"That's what killed my mother, you know. Not breast cancer. My father's distorted sense of importance."

Distorted was a good word. "I will never distort you," Dakota promised.

Weariness battered Britt's brain. Dakota's hand on her side aroused her, something she hadn't believed possible, not after sharing her nightmare with him.

She believed him when he claimed he hadn't killed Judd because he was protecting her from Connor's gun. Everything he did was to protect her.

The idea couldn't take root in her head. Somewhere, deeper than her heart, maybe her soul, the facts were burrowing, clamping.

Maybe there was a basis to this mate stuff. Something good. Maybe telling someone what happened had been cathartic and made her appreciate Dakota's attention.

No matter the reason, logical or not, Dakota's hand on her rib gave her ideas.

She wiggled backward to get closer to him. He spooned his body around hers. He emitted an enveloping heat. As long as she remained in his forcefield, she was safe. Safe from harm, but not safe from him. She was no longer certain she wanted to be safe from Dakota.

His erection pressed against her bottom before he inched away.

"I won't pop like a bubble." She squirmed closer again.

"I'm not one of your saints, with endless patience and control," he growled.

Good. She could attack him with the fierceness filling her. He exercised solicitude, when she craved reassurance she was still desirable to him.

"Thank your Ancient Ones. I don't want a saint. Saints are boring. Pious. Wracked with guilt because they're not perfect. I want someone who admits he's not perfect and doesn't give a damn."

Dakota made a sound she couldn't describe or define.

"I didn't let what happened deform my attitude. Shape my standards? Yeah. On my terms."

"I figured out that part."

"Okay. Follow the rest to the logical conclusion." She rubbed her butt against his erection.

"You want to have sex?"

Really? "Yes."

"Why?"

I like you. A lot. You make me feel safe. I trust you. I need to prove you still want me even though you know my shameful secret.

"If I'd come on to you before I told you about Judd, would you question my motive?"

When Dakota didn't answer, she added, "Nothing has changed."

If her feet weren't hurting so badly, she would have leapt from the bed, torn off her sleep shirt, and opened the blinds to invite in the moon. But Parker had ordered her to stay off her feet as much as she could to give Selena's comfrey time to work.

Instead, she whipped her shirt over her head. "I shouldn't be wearing clothes in your bed, at least according to what you've told me. Since this is Ethan's house, I assume werewolf culture rules."

His breathing became audible and uneven. "Ancient Ones, you're beautiful, even if you are crazy."

"You can see me?" The room was darker than black.

"Not as well as I'd like to."

"Is the moon still out?"

The bedding rustled, the bedsprings creaked. His body heat hovered around her as he made his way to the window, where he opened the blinds.

Silver stripes blared into the room like neon signage proclaiming, *Here I am*. One illuminated his face. Glittered in his dark eyes. The tips of his fingers brushed her side. "You do have a bruise."

She peered at the spot where another moonbeam revealed a shadow on her ribs.

He knelt at the side of the bed. Pressed his lips against the wound. His mouth was hot, contrasting with the chills rampaging her body. He licked the spot, as if his tongue could mend the broken capillaries.

She wasn't prepared for him to kiss his way to her waist, for him to slide his massive hands to cup her butt cheeks and hold her steady. She suspected his motive when he licked his way across her abdomen. A swathe of moonlight gleamed in his dark hair, tinting some strands a deep cobalt blue.

She rested her ankles on his broad shoulders as he buried his face between her splayed thighs. For someone who claimed he'd never been with anyone except her, he'd certainly learned the basics quickly. He used the right amount of pressure to apply each lick, suck, and nibble.

She forgot her aching feet. The humiliation of revealing an assault she wasn't sure happened. Every extraneous thought fled as he loved her with his mouth until she shattered. And after the pieces of her merged together again, he slid up her body, rearranged her legs to accommodate his presence, and was pressing into her with his massive erection. He felt good. So very, very good.

She tried to sink her fingers into his back. His muscles didn't yield. *Oh, this. This.*

He released her butt once she found his rhythm. He was making her crazy with want, with having, yet she wasn't sure how to touch him.

He deserved something, too. Making love was a mutual act. Shredding the skin on his back wasn't an act of love.

She'd never given a rat's ass whether or not her partner was enjoying himself. He was a guy, getting off. Ejaculation was enough for any of them. Except Dakota. He deserved more. She couldn't ask him what he wanted. She was the extent of his experience. She wanted tonight to be special. He'd been too weak after fighting the creature. Worn out. He'd barely regained his strength when he thrust into her.

She reached between their bodies. Stretched her arm, her hand, her fingers as far as they would go. She couldn't grasp her target. She readjusted her shoulders.

"What are you doing?" He never paused his thrusting rhythm.

Her fingers grazed his balls.

His breath hitched.

A tad further, and she was able to curl her fingers gently around him.

He groaned.

Her shoulder ached with the effort of stretching, but she managed to rest his testicles in her palm.

He shuddered as she lightly squeezed. His balls tightened. He thrust into her as deeply as he could go and stopped moving. His tense body quaked as he climaxed. Every nerve in her body was aware of him inside her.

"What was *that*?" He struggled to catch his breath. At least he hadn't fallen asleep.

She couldn't answer. Maybe a one and done from the past begged her to touch him like that, or maybe she'd read somewhere men liked their balls squeezed during their climax. Or maybe instinct, finely tuned to Dakota, led her to touch him.

"Did you like me touching you?" Her voice was throaty.

"Probably."

"Probably?"

"We'll have to try it again to make sure," he murmured before nuzzling her neck. His words rumbled in his chest and vibrated against her breasts. He didn't move.

He should have been heavy atop her. He wasn't. If only they could stay entwined forever. No notions or words of love. No worries about the outside world, her past, or his culture. Only the two of them, in bed. Sex didn't have to play a role. Being together, like this—

They'd survived kidnapping. Vampire cooties. Judd was still at large, stalking her. She shouldn't feel safe. She shouldn't feel like forever was within her grasp—

Or was holding her.

Chapter 24

He shouldn't have jumped her bones.

Britt was fragile; hurting physically, emotionally devastated. He'd still let his cock make his decisions. When she grasped his balls, Dakota feared she was going to try to rip them off, and she'd be justified. Instead, whatever she'd done magnified something so intense, the top of his head should have blown off.

The morning light slanted across their naked bodies, giving him a better view of her injuries. She was a mess since meeting him. Someday he'd make the pain up to her. He would do anything, including pay Helga to call down the moon, to make this up to her.

Byrne wouldn't be bugging her if Ethan hadn't come to Minnesota to work on Congressman Peters. Everything linked back to that scat-sucking vampire-loving coward.

The Peters dynasty needed to be destroyed.

He'd seen them last night, sucking up to the senator from Tennessee. Sucking, like mosquitoes that needed swatting. If Ethan hadn't come to Minnesota—

He wouldn't be in Warwick either. He never would have found Britt. Ethan wouldn't have found Selena.

He rolled away from Britt, not wanting to disturb her sleep. She needed rest to heal.

Everyone in the house still slept except him. His conscience wouldn't let him sleep.

Britt grabbed his thigh before he could slip from the bed. "Where are you going?"

"For an early morning run," he replied.

"Don't be ridiculous." Her voice was raspy with sleep. "Stay in bed with me."

"I was on you all night. You need your sleep."

"I need you more than I need sleep."

Dakota's heart fluttered. "We need each other healthy," he said. "Neither of us is going to recover from yesterday without rest."

"So come back and rest," she grumbled, as her hand crept along his thigh toward his decidedly sore private parts. If he was sore, she had to be hurting, too. His cock twitched, a dying gasp rather than an acceptance of her invitation. "Really rest."

"My brain is going off in a billion directions." He couldn't handle not having a steady course. If he didn't get his act together soon, he would be howling at the moon without bothering to shift.

She stilled her hand, as if she sensed he was depleted for the moment. "I need you to stay with me so I can sleep." He exhaled slowly. She was saying she felt safe with him. He didn't have the words to tell her how much her faith in him meant. They were building a basis for a good future together.

"As much as I want to stay with you, I have errands to do in daylight, without the threat of vampires."

She released his thigh and sat up. "Right." She scrubbed her face with her palms as she swung her feet to the floor.

"You're not going anywhere."

"Yeah. I am."

He grabbed one of her scabbed and bruised feet.

"You're supposed to stay off your feet." *Thank the Ancient Ones.* He didn't need another excuse to leave her behind, where she would be safe.

"I need to get my phone."

"We'll send the cops to your apartment. Someone could have broken in. Even if your purse was recovered at the scene and tagged as evidence, that doesn't mean the contents were intact."

She stared at him with parted lips. "Someone stole my key? I didn't think—"

"Our ongoing problem. We aren't seeing the whole picture of anything. None of us."

"I agree. We're missing something important."

"We need to trace events back." He didn't mean as far back as Ethan's grandfather's claim of how a former Congressman Peters ordered the annihilation of the Limmikin werewolves. "Nothing happened until Ethan arrived from Loup Garou."

"Who else besides us knows why he's in Warwick?"

"I have no idea." Dakota wasn't in the loop. Which had been fine until whatever was going on threatened his mate. Now he wanted answers.

"We need to meet. Confer. Every lycan in the area, including the ones trying to rebuild Ulvskog. Byrne threatening you from prison, immediately after you and your business partner go to the Peters family for their support, is too coincidental. Coincidence doesn't exist."

"And once we figure out what we're dealing with, we can deal with it?" Britt sounded skeptical.

"Not you. You don't have the inherent traits needed to protect yourself. You got lucky with your tree branch last night. I don't want to trust our wellbeing to luck. I want you locked away where I am the only one who can get to you."

He read the conflict in her eyes and softened his tone. "I need you safe more than I need anything else."

"I know. And in your world, Ethan's house is safe from vampires. At least, as safe as you can be sure."

The tension in his body fled. Britt was going to cooperate.

BRITT STAYED IN THE bedroom until noon. She wasn't used to an idle life. She'd worked her way through college. She'd worked after college, even if a job wasn't in her chosen field. She wasn't lazy, and playing the sloth only increased her jitters. She couldn't even properly pace the too-small room. Her feet hurt. By noon, she was going out of her mind.

The others in the house stayed in bed until after noon. She limped from the guest room as if she'd been imprisoned. "Werewolves are nocturnal," Selena explained with a yawn. "Have you ever known me to rise with the sun?"

"I guess not."

Ethan pulled a carton of eggs and a package of bacon from the refrigerator. "Want some breakfast?"

Her stomach growled. She was surprised at the food choices. Selena always wanted fish.

"What can I do to help?"

"Set the table," Selena suggested, as she unearthed a cast iron frying pan from a cupboard. "Ethan and I have a routine. Is Dakota awake yet?"

"He's out for a run," she admitted. She needed coffee. Badly. If she was going to be staying with Selena indefinitely, she needed to lay in a supply. "He believes I'm safer here."

"Ah. You're a prisoner with me." Selena remained intent on peeling slices of bacon from the greasy slab and laying them in the frying pan. She spoke without rancor, without inflection.

"Your curfew is temporary," Ethan reminded her.

"Being housebound doesn't feel temporary. I feel as if my whole life has been spent behind orange walls except for our trips to Ulvskog."

"Dakota says we're not seeing the big picture," Britt shared. He didn't tell her she couldn't discuss his theories. "He says we need to trace back to Ethan's arrival in Warwick to convince Congressman Peters to honor some treaty or something."

"Something," Selena echoed. "Except Ethan is not what kickstarted a long-running feud between the Peters Dynasty and the lycan communities. Arriving the way he did on the day he did was purely coincidental."

"Go ahead. Steal my thunder." Ethan cracked an egg into his frying pan. The gelatinous mass sizzled as it hit the hot iron.

The frying egg smelled delicious. Britt's stomach rumbled.

"Your thunder?" Selena asked. "Ha! I triggered everything. I met with Congressman Bryant about the treaties. My grandfather sent me, even though I argued with him because I didn't want to go. You see, the congressman and his oldest son, Liam, the missing one, raped me. I was fifteen."

Selena's toneless voice gave Britt no way to gauge her mood.

The meaning of the words sank in. "They raped you?"

"Yes."

Strange how two damaged women should be thrown together in college, become friends, and not be aware of the other's wounds.

Britt fumbled with a chair and sat at the kitchen table. Her feet ached in relief.

"Ethan happened to arrive as I was threatening Liam with exposure if he didn't convince his father to support the treaties."

"I know, I know. Service for sanctuary." Britt's impatience was palpable. "Great spies. What do your precious treaties have to do with what happened to your grandfather?"

"Give me a minute." Selena flipped the bacon before continuing. "Later that night, the night I threatened Liam, the same night Ethan arrived, a vampire broke into my apartment and tried to kill me. My first encounter with a vampire."

She shuddered. "I will never forget the smell as long as I live."

"The stench was awful," Ethan agreed.

"Dakota claims a vampire attacked us last night, but I didn't smell anything," Britt said. "I experienced cold. I mean frigid cold. Middle of Lake Superior in January cold."

"The one I killed the night Congressman Peters committed suicide was cold on the inside, but its heart wasn't frozen."

The rumor was true.

"The vamp exploded in the cab of Ethan's truck. Two weeks for the detailing place to get the truck clean."

"A big pouf, then stuff, not heavy, but light like snow, falling?"

"Yes."

"Whatever I rammed a tree branch into last night did the same thing."

"I smelled vampire everywhere." Ethan lifted the edge of an egg with his spatula.

Selena used tongs to flip the bacon. "Did Dakota tell you what happened in Ulvskog?"

"He told me some stuff," Britt admitted.

"I didn't tell her everything," Dakota said as he entered the kitchen. He dropped a large to-go coffee on the table in front of Britt.

"Why not?" Selena asked.

"I love you," Britt muttered, as she raised the cup to her mouth.

"Not everything is mine to share," Dakota replied after a long pause.

"Okay, here's the Cliff Notes version," Selena said. "The Peters men didn't care for this victim coming back to bite them in the ass. The congressman hired a couple of thugs with automatic rifles to wipe out the pack at Ulvskog. My grandfather was probably the first victim."

How could Selena sound so calm?

"Long story short, we knew who'd ordered the hit. We uncovered information Congressman Peters never expected would be exposed. Luke Thibodaux has a side gig with the FBI doing undercover computer work on sex crimes, and he uncovered the Congressman's...hobby. When we confronted the congressman with our evidence, rather than face the scandal, he blew off half his face. We didn't see him fire the gun, but we heard the shot. Saw the immediate aftermath before we called the cops."

Britt's gorge rose. The aroma of bacon and eggs usually soothed. Not today.

"How do you want your eggs?" Ethan asked, as if massacres, blown off faces, and slaughtered babies were everyday fare.

"I'm not sure I can eat."

"Sure you can. You need your strength. Today isn't going to be easy for you. For any of us. Why don't I cook them till the yolk is hard. Don't sapiens prefer hard yolks?"

She didn't argue. She couldn't. Ethan and Selena's tale had grown more and more bizarre. "Where did Curtis fit in?"

Selena lifted the bacon from the skillet and draped it on a paper-towel lined platter.

"Curtis was spying on me for the Peters family. Curtis was the gunman who murdered my grandfather. Did I mention Gramps' body was in pieces? Chunks. How many rounds from an automatic weapon will cut a man in half?"

Before Britt could react, Selena muttered, "Yeah. I don't know either."

"Dakota killed Curtis." Britt stared at a grease spot on the table.

"We *all* killed Curtis. Curtis had only one life we could snatch as payback for what he'd done to my pack. We didn't kill him until after we'd finished dismantling Liam Peters."

"You killed Liam Peters?" Britt turned to Dakota. "You guys really killed Liam Peters?"

"I would kill him again if his death could undo the damage he caused." Dakota showed no remorse.

"The world is searching for him. What happens if they find him?"

"They won't." Selena sounded sure. "We didn't leave enough of him to find, except maybe in random piles of wolf scat."

"You ate him?"

Selena slipped a plate of bacon and eggs in front of her. "We're not cannibals."

Britt shoved the plate to the side.

Dakota picked up a fork and helped himself to Selena's breakfast.

Britt was going to be sick. She'd kissed Dakota's mouth last night. Had thoroughly explored the recesses with her tongue. And he'd been eating politicians and their flunkies. She might have whimpered, because Ethan, Selena, and Dakota all gave her strange looks.

"Your reaction is part of why I didn't tell you everything," Dakota said. "If you had a chance to destroy Byrne, would you?"

Britt stared at him. "You killed a congressman and ate him."

"Dig deep into your psyche, Britt. Into the darkest part of your soul. Are you sorry DiNardo is dead?"

"No."

"And if you had a chance to obliterate Judd from the face of the earth, would you?"

Selena sat across from Britt, her own plate heaped with food.

Dakota didn't drop his gaze. Britt could no longer ignore the intensity.

The memories she'd tried to quash for years echoed like thunder in a canyon. Judd was supposed to still be in prison. Someone arranged for him to get out. Someone wanted to hurt her. Why her? Other women must know Connor was as much of a pervert as his father. Why focus on her?

Dakota's fork clattered to his plate, startling her out of her reverie. He watched her. Waiting.

Would she wish a werewolf vengeance on Judd?

Yeah, especially if retribution is served with a healthy dose of humiliation. Obliterate Judd from the face of the earth.

Better than obliterating him from her memory.

Her throat burned. *I told Curtis he could play with you.* That part of the memory was real. That part of the nightmare was true, making the incident as bad as she remembered.

The scrape of Selena and Ethan's forks on their plates as they calmly consumed bacon and eggs—while Dakota waited for a response from her—brought her out of the tunnel of her stressing.

Dakota might claim a culture difference.

"Britt?"

She swallowed the persistent nausea. Opened her mouth to answer. Couldn't.

Her father's stentorian tones bellowed between her ears.

Sin! Sinner!

She'd survived Judd's sin against her. Curtis's sin against her. Connor's sin against her. She'd survived, damn it. She'd put Judd in prison, put Curtis in prison where both belonged, yet they roamed the streets anew.

Judge not! Pastor Paul bellowed. Yet he judged her when she was barely more than a child.

If she could destroy Judd Byrne, help obliterate him from the face of the earth, even if his destruction meant letting werewolves savage him, she would.

She couldn't speak her desire. She could only nod.

Dakota sat back in his chair and picked up his fork. "I hate cold eggs."

"I NEED TO GO back to Ulvskog," Dakota announced.

Britt washed dishes while Selena dried and put away.

Dakota and Ethan remained at the table. Observing Britt's domestic side was discombobulating. He never would have guessed she could wash dishes.

"Why?" Parker entered the kitchen. "Ulvskog is creepy. Any breakfast left?"

Selena's spine stiffened.

"We need the others," Dakota explained.

"Why?" Ethan asked.

"The full moon is in a couple of nights. They need to be in Warwick, not Ulvskog."

"Are you out of your mind?" Selena slammed the cupboard door.

"You haven't arrived at a solution to deal with the vamps at the end of the block." He tried not to sound accusatory. After all, Selena and Ethan were both alpha.

He failed.

"You *are* out of your mind." Selena dropped a frying pan onto a burner and lit the flame. "Has mating with a sapien driven you mad? Or maybe Vampire Cootie Coma is better than a sapien mate."

"Stop." Dakota didn't care if Selena was an alpha female and leader of her own pack. She was being dense and ridiculous. She had no right to insult Britt; he should be at Ethan's throat for not keeping his female in line.

"Excuse me?" Selena snapped.

"We can't anticipate how the cooties will affect us in full moon mode."

"Exactly." Her tone was low and dangerous. "We don't know. I won't risk anyone else in my pack."

"She's right." Ethan rose and stood next to Selena, as if Dakota needed a visual of a united front. "You have no right to ask."

"Yes, I do. Her pack isn't the only one in Ulvskog. Restin hasn't returned to Loup Garou."

Ethan's father and grandfather were also in Ulvskog. They were still technically part of the Loup Garou pack, although Hatch Calhoun recently revealed he was secretly the alpha of the Limmikin, believed to be extinct.

"No one can defeat a pack of werewolves on the full moon." Why couldn't the others grasp the idea?

"You surmise," Ethan corrected. "We're dealing with vampires. Vampires smell bad to us and sapiens can't smell them. A single vamp will buffer our sense of smell so badly we might as well not have a nose. That's the extent of our knowledge."

Dakota couldn't argue Ethan's point. He was mostly recovered from his run-in with the vampire at Elysian Estates, except his nose still wasn't up to snuff.

"Do you have another idea, or are Selena and Britt supposed to stay entombed for the rest of their lives?"

"They aren't entombed." Ethan sound exasperated.

"What would you call their inability to leave your house at night? Safe?"

"Imprisoned," Britt muttered. "Maybe Selena is used to strictures on her movements. I am not."

"The world isn't ready for the first vampire-werewolf war," Selena argued.

"Says who?" Dakota asked. "You?"

"Careful." Ethan's warning came with a growl.

"I'm not questioning her leadership because she's female." The waxing moon was making everyone shorter- tempered than usual. "I'm concerned she lacks experience."

"She doesn't have any," Britt offered. "She's my age. We roomed together in college. Since we graduated, we've been working on perfecting the Night Shift line."

"What do you know about lycan life?" Selena wasn't any more cordial with her alleged best friend than she was with Dakota.

"Nothing," Britt admitted. "I never claimed I did. But you're not the only one who's fought a vampire. You're not the only one who's killed one."

"Goody for you, Buffy."

"Go fuck yourself," Britt retorted. "I may not know what all this alpha female leadership crap is, but I know the smell of bullshit."

Dakota lifted his chin. He didn't have enough status to counter Selena's nonsense, but Britt wasn't bound by the strictures of lycan hierarchy.

"If Dakota believes a pack of werewolves can take on the vampires, I'm all for trying. I want to be warm again. I'm surprised I can't see my breath at night, and I'm telling you the cold is coming from whatever congregates on the corner. I know you, Selena. You never like anyone else's ideas." Britt tossed her sponge into the sink. "Come on, Dakota. I need some fresh air." She stalked from the kitchen and out the front door.

He followed.

He found her standing by his SUV.

"I want to go back to my place. I need my regular purse, even if I can't take my phone."

"We're meeting Anderson and Clerkin at your apartment in an hour."

"You couldn't have told me sooner?" She was as snappish as any lycan spellbound by the full moon.

"We had a couple of other conversations going."

"When did you talk to them?"

"While I was running. You're surrendering your current phone to the authorities."

Chapter 25

Britt sat back in her seat and mentally kicked herself. She couldn't believe she'd let Dakota persuade her to return to Ulvskog. He'd presented his case on the drive to her apartment. Mickey and Tom confiscated her cell phone after she'd checked for messages. Nothing new from Judd.

Once they were finished with the cops, Dakota replaced their cell phones at the mall. The first call she made was to her landlord to tell him her key was stolen, and he should change the locks.

"Now what?" she'd asked after disconnecting. "Ulvskog."

"Creepy Town."

"You don't need to get out of the car. I'm going to see if I can get Restin, Hatch, and Rand to come back with us."

"Who? I remember Restin. Crazy eyes. Who are the others?"

"Ethan's father and grandfather."

"Isn't Ethan's grandfather too old to be fighting vampires?" Britt thought maybe Selena had a point.

"His choice. He's an alpha male. He's aware of his limitations."

Britt had her doubts. Old people could be senile. She wouldn't want his blood on her head. She'd been baptized in enough blood lately.

"I can't believe you're kidnapping me," she grumbled.

"I bribed you," he corrected. "Hey little girl. Want some candy?"

She laughed. She hadn't wanted to laugh in a long time. One didn't realize how oppressing the house on Ash Street was until one escaped. Guilt pinged. She ought to be grateful to Ethan and Selena for giving her a place to stay. And she was.

The summer sun was high and bright, the sky as blue as a sky could be. The trees were fully leafed, lush and green. The ride to the north woods was scenic and peaceful. So why did her stomach knot? Wasn't this outing a fantasy date? A sunny day, the man she—

She sat straighter. She didn't love Dakota. She couldn't love him. She was safe with him. She trusted him. Safe and trustworthy didn't equal happily ever after. She doubted she'd ever trust any male of any species enough to share her life with him. She was a woman meant for moments. Stolen glimpses of contentedness. Like this leg of the ride to Selena's hometown.

Britt adjusted the air conditioning vent away from her face. They were heading into the gloom of the forest. She wasn't going to relinquish the sun's heat to cold air blowing on her.

"Why are you fidgeting?"

"I'm not fidgeting. I'm trying to get comfortable."

"Sore from last night?"

Her face heated, and not from the sun beating through the windshield. "No."

"Have you ever had sex that many times in one night?" She considered his question for a moment. Did he need reassurance? He was new to sex, so yeah, given her history, maybe he did. "Nope." A one and done was precisely that.

And Judd before them, who sometimes preferred drugs to sex.

"New record, huh?"

"I guess. I'd call last night a nice time."

"Only nice?"

"Understatements sometimes say more than superlatives."

He laughed. The dark sound drew shivers throughout her body. "Okay."

"How about you? Are you sore?" She wasn't the only one in their bed.

"Some," he admitted. "You're worth the discomfort."

Who was she trying to kid? The best sex of her life was with him, and he claimed he was a newbie. What would he be like with practice? Maybe she'd keep him a while longer.

If they could manage to stay alive. Maybe she should move to Colorado with him after all.

"How many children should we have?" He changed the subject. "Lycan females have a hard time getting pregnant, but sapien females have lots of babies. I'd like at least two, maybe four."

"Wait a minute." She cleared her throat. "I'm not a baby-making machine."

"Of course you aren't." He sounded hurt. "But imagine the good times we'll have making babies."

"Are children a deal breaker for you?" She hoped they were.

"What? No? There are no deals in mating. There are...degrees. Degrees of happiness."

"Isn't your goal to make me happy? Didn't you tell me you have to make me happy and not hurt me?"

"The first time, when I marked you."

"Shouldn't the standards apply to our relationship all the time?"

"If you had female elders, they would tell you the same thing." He didn't sound quite as positive. "Selena will tell you."

"Selena doesn't have any older relatives either."

"Then her mentor. Ethan's great-aunt. The old female healer." He lurched from unsure to snapping at her.

The moon was visible, even in broad daylight, not quite a perfect circle hanging in the sky. One side appeared gnawed by the stars. A constellation. The damned dog. Sirius. *Canus Major* and *Minor*.

"Are you always this cranky before the full moon?" She tried to remember her years of living with Selena. All she recalled was *it's that time of the month*. Double meaning.

"Lunacy is a fact of my life. How many kids do you want? As many as we're blessed with?"

He always changed the subject when he didn't want to discuss something.

"I'm not committing to anything." *Especially not a future beyond this nightmare.*

Dakota was silent for approximately a mile. She relaxed. The road was curvy, hilly, and not something she, a native, wanted to drive, especially come winter. He was confident behind the wheel. He was a professional. She trusted him.

"Our mating is not something you can negotiate, commit, ponder, or deny." He sounded calmer. "We are a couple. Period. As much as you don't want to spend the rest of your life with me, you're stuck."

"I know," she admitted softly. "Your actions reinforce your words. I'm not trying to hurt you. I'm trying to protect me."

"Protecting you is my job."

"I don't want to be someone's job. I want to be a woman who commands respect. A woman in control of her own life."

"What makes you believe I don't respect you? Don't I consider your opinions when making decisions?"

"Why do you get to make the decisions? Didn't you listen? I control my life."

"You? In control? Babe, I've never met anyone more out of control than you are."

She twisted in her seat to glare at him. His lips were curved in a smirk. A damn smirk. Was he implying she was a hot mess? She was, but he had no right to judge.

"My life, my definition of control."

"Tell me how you've controlled your life this week."

"I brought you home with me."

"The only smart thing you did."

"Jamming a tree limb into a maybe-vampire wasn't smart?"

"Brilliant survival instinct."

The light dimmed as the road entered the forest. Ancient trees hovered around them. Britt shuddered. Why would anyone want to live in the near-constant darkness?

"What's wrong?" As if Dakota sensed her mood shift.

"This place." She had no words to describe the foreboding closing in on her, threatening to crush her.

They'd left the light and ventured into darkness. Darkness consumed. Darkness housed vampires and other creatures of the night. Like werewolves. And Dakota freely admitted he was a werewolf. Freely admitted he preferred the night.

"Yeah, I don't like being here either. Ulvskog is not my home. Bad scat happens in these woods. I witnessed the aftermath of the massacre. I smelled the corpses rotting, as bad as any vampire reek."

Britt didn't know how to react, so she said nothing, and stared into the undergrowth lurking in the ditch on the side of the road.

Dakota slowed and left the main road for a gravel track. "I have nightmares featuring Ulvskog." He downshifted. "But the village is important to Selena and surprisingly, Ethan's grandfather feels invested. Both packs were slaughtered in cold blood, and the Peters political dynasty was behind the massacres."

"Wait a minute." Her chest tightened, making breathing more difficult. "Back up. What happened to Ethan's grandfather's pack?"

Dakota's knuckles whitened on the steering wheel. "Liam Peters' grandfather, also a congressman, tried to eliminate the Limmikin pack. They didn't have a treaty with the government. He couldn't control them. Ethan's grandparents escaped. That's why it was fitting for Liam to—"

He stopped. She wanted to kick him. "Fitting for Liam to what?"

"Die in these woods. The woods that sheltered both the Varulv and the Limmikin."

They arrived at the rough clearing with the half-built shacks. The scent of sawdust filled the cab as Dakota opened the door and hopped out.

Britt didn't want to be alone. As much as she loathed and feared Ulvskog's atmosphere, she couldn't stay in the SUV.

BRITT DRESSED IN HONKYTONK angel mode. Her tight jeans showcased her long, slender legs, legs she'd wrapped around his waist last night. Legs that bore his weight as he fucked her from behind. Legs that clamped his head as he lapped from her source. *Ancient Ones*, he loved her legs.

She also wore a long-sleeved white shirt and a pale purple vest that glittered silver when the light caught the fabric a certain way.

He could have watched her all day.

Britt had to open her mouth. Had to try to make him feel bad for being a lycan who understood revenge was a necessary part of life. Was he supposed to ignore her suffering when she told him what Byrne, DiNardo, and possibly Peters had done? Turning the other cheek was not a lycan option. She had a lot to unlearn from her pastor papa.

He waited for her to catch up with him. They found Restin and Rand, along with members of the Varulv, working on walls.

"We weren't expecting anyone but Parker," Restin greeted them.

"We have a situation," Dakota shot back. Restin's ego didn't allow for social niceties. "My gut is telling me we need a pack at Ethan's house on the full moon."

"What does Ethan say?"

"He echoes his mate."

"Who is an alpha." An unnecessary reminder.

"Of her pack. Not of the Loup Garou." Dakota jutted his chin and waited for Restin, with all his ambition and jealousy of his cousin Tokarz, to swallow the bait.

The Varulv stopped working. As did Rand. Ethan was his son. Family came first. His loyalty lay with Ethan. "Aren't you too insignificant to ignore an alpha?" Rand inquired.

"Regarding my mate's safety? There are no degrees of significance."

Restin studied Dakota as if he were hiding something.

Except for Britt's revelation, Dakota was an open book.

An old woman hobbled into sight. Dakota recognized her as Ethan's great aunt and Selena's teacher, Old Olivia. A contemporary of Hatch, she had mated with Hatch's brother, who had been murdered in the Limmikin Massacre.

"Selena needs us?" she asked Dakota.

"Selena doesn't want help." Britt stood apart from the others, as if marking the distinction between sapien and lupus. "Hi, Olivia. Good to see you again."

"Britt." Old Olivia acknowledged her with a nod. "Why does Selena need help?"

"She doesn't," Britt said. "Except for the vampires at the end of the block. Dakota theorizes a pack of werewolves on the full moon can take them on."

Dakota fumed as Old Olivia studied him. Britt should have let him tell Old Olivia why they'd come to Ulvskog. The crone ignored him in favor of Britt.

"Selena was sick after she tangled with a vampire. Maybe she knows what she's doing," Old Olivia suggested.

"Dakota was comatose for a while after he tangled with one. He recuperated quickly," Britt continued. "Of course, he didn't kill the creature. I did. Selena gnawed her way into a vampire's chest and chomped out its heart. Maybe ingesting vampire heart is what made her sicker than Dakota was."

"Not a bad theory."

"I'm a scientist," Britt explained. "I examine raw research data objectively. We have only two samples, but we see the differences in the study group situation."

What was she blowing on about?

Except Old Olivia was nodding, as if Britt's babbling had merit. "What's your idea?"

"You're past shifting age, right?"

How did Britt become in charge of the conversation? When had she commandeered his negotiation?

"Yes, although legend says I can still shift if I need to."

"I can't shift at all, being sapien. We could recruit Helga, too, as the stake squad. We let the werewolves distract the vampires then stake them while they're otherwise occupied—"

"You're not getting near any vampires," Dakota interrupted. His female was crazy. "Once was enough."

"I'm not supposed to have your back?" Britt's falsely calm tone reminded Dakota of the eye of a hurricane. Whatever mischief she had in mind was poised to destroy all his carefully planned arguments.

"Not the same," he snapped.

"Why?" she thundered back. She whipped her head. Static electricity crackled in her flowing yellow hair. "How is me protecting you different from you protecting me? Okay, I'm not lycan. My senses are inferior. My speed is lacking. But I'm also not a victim. I'm not a victim of old lovers, I am not a victim of my upbringing, and I sure as hell am not a victim of the moon."

The world hushed. Even the insects and birds didn't respond.

"I can adapt," she whispered a moment later. "Evolution. I've reinvented myself three times in my life. If you and I are the life mates you claim, I need to adapt to life with shifters, a culture I never knew existed until a few days ago. You can't adapt, so I have to."

He'd adapted to accommodate her. Hadn't he?

"None of you can evolve. You shift on the night of the full moon, whether you want to or not." Her voice warbled, either from her powerful words or fear.

"She's right." Old Olivia spoke in her quiet way. "The gods of our elders are forcing us to evolve. Limmikin with Varulv, Loup Garou with sapien. The next generation will exhibit new strengths."

"Survival of the fittest," Britt mused. "We are fitter working together. Dakota is right. A werewolf pack does need to confront the vampires on the full moon. In the moonlight."

Suddenly her mouth gaped. She blinked rapidly, as if blinking provided more energy to her brain cells.

"In the moonlight," she repeated. "Moonlight is nothing except reflected sunlight, and vampires, if the legends are true, cannot abide sunlight."

BRITT CLEARLY REMEMBERED HOW the creature she'd staked staggered in and out of the patches of moonlight. How a raised arm protected its eyes from the quicksilver beams.

"Moonlight is reflected and weaker sunlight."

"Now you're talking crazy," one of the Varulv said. "The moon is our friend."

"The reflected light illuminates your world enough for your inherent vision to work. But vampires can't tolerate sunlight."

The concept prompted a slew of other ideas. Other questions. Such as how she, a puny geek, was able to ram a tree branch into the creature's heart. Vampires inhabited human bodies. Human bodies needed Vitamin D to strengthen the bones. Sunlight kickstarted the body's ability to manufacture Vitamin D. Therefore, would vampire bodies not be vitamin D deficient? Lack of the vitamin would make their bones either soft or brittle and easier to exploit.

"We can make their vulnerabilities work for us," she murmured.

"Vampires and lycans are both creatures of the night," the Varulv continued.

"No, they're not."

Dakota, Restin, and Ethan's father stared at her as if she'd lost her mind. Maybe she had.

If vampires suffered a vitamin D problem, maybe lack of other vitamins were at play, too. Like vitamin C. Wouldn't they lose their fangs to scurvy? So one didn't necessarily lead to the other.

What other problems could lack of nutrition, needed to maintain a human body, cause for the undead? Or did vampire cooties, for lack of a better term, mutate what had been human into something else?

The *being* that attacked her might not be a vampire. Dakota believed it was, and his battle was more intimate and personal than hers. He claimed to recognize the smell. Why hadn't she smelled anything?

"I know what I observed." She spoke slowly. "The creature I killed last night was avoiding the moonlight."

Dakota stared at the treetops and the ragged-edged clouds peering around the leaves. "She's right," he agreed after a moment. "It didn't register at the time, but the vamp stuck to the shadows. I thought it was trying to hide from me."

"The creature tried to shield its eyes, too," she added. "Maybe it was a new vampire, supersensitive to any light."

The vampire wasn't Judd unless DNA could prove otherwise. If vampire cooties changed the composition of the host body, would they also mutate the DNA?

Though the scientist in her was fascinated, no way was she going back to Elysian Estates to gather DNA samples. Besides, without the original DNA, she had nothing for comparison.

Britt continued to muse aloud. "Werewolves are not creatures of the night. If you were, you couldn't be building new houses on a sunny afternoon. Sunlight doesn't bother you. You might *prefer* moonlight, but it's only a preference. You prefer the light to darkness." She glanced at Dakota. "What happens on the new moon?"

"Nothing. Shifting is impossible."

"So you need light in order to shift."

"Well, scat," someone muttered.

Britt didn't know where her hypothesis would lead, but the data had to mean something, if nothing more than werewolves needed light in order...to be werewolves. Therefore, werewolves could not be creatures of the night. Their nocturnal habits were nothing more than customs. She had a similar one. She preferred her nighttime life, too. Hitting Holsters after dark for a drink and maybe someone to share a good time.

"Your theories are fascinating." Restin's voice was heavy with sarcasm. "But what do crackpot ideas have to do with anything?"

"Other than supporting Dakota's theory a pack of werewolves on the full moon can destroy the gaggle of vampires trying to kill them? The theory opens dozens of avenues for thought."

"Did you come here to convince us to leave our rebuilding project in order to deal with a clutch of vampires? Why can't you take care of them yourselves? You claim to have killed one last night. Kill them all with my blessing."

Dakota growled, low and deep in his throat. "Do not speak to my mate in that tone. She is trying to help us. Rebuilding Ulvskog is not part of your mission to Minnesota. You were sent to Ulvskog only to deal with the dead."

Restin froze. Light flared in his wide blue eyes. "Are you trying to usurp the mission, tau?"

Dakota squared his shoulders. "I don't presume to be a leader, especially when Tokarz is such a worthy alpha."

Whoa. Something intense was happening.

"I'm only stating what my alpha told me as he ordered me to transport you. The dead have been handled. We should be heading back to Loup Garou."

Restin snorted. "If we'd headed back after dealing with the dead, would you have met your mate?"

"Yeah." Dakota hooked his thumbs in his jeans pockets. He suppressed the urge to leap at Restin and claw the smug expression off his face. "I would have. She's Selena's best friend. Why? Worried you won't ever find yours?"

He couldn't believe the words left his mouth. Thinking them was one thing. Giving them air could be dangerous.

Even Rand Calhoun, one of the steadiest males Dakota ever met, froze at the challenge. Because Dakota *had* challenged his beta.

Several of the Varulv slunk away. They were the ones who survived the massacre. They recognized the sound of a destructive force.

Restin placed his hammer on a nearby piece of lumber. His bright blue eyes never left Dakota's face.

Ancient Ones, he was going to have to shift, and he wasn't sure he had the strength.

"You shouldn't have brought mates into your pissing match," Old Olivia scolded.

Dakota had forgotten she was present.

"Tau doesn't speak to beta in a threatening manner," Restin growled.

"Excuse me." Britt waggled her fingers for attention. "I don't pretend to get the nuances of your cultural structure, but would a leader bait an underling suffering from an illness?"

"And what illness would Dakota have?" Restin was on the verge of attacking.

"Vampire cooties."

"He has vampire cooties?" Old Olivia sounded appalled. "How?"

"Last night. He fought the vampire for a long time."

"And he's upright? What are you thinking, Tau?" Old Olivia demanded.

"He's not," Britt lied. "I'm afraid I talked him into presenting his idea. Clearly he hasn't recovered."

Dakota opened his mouth to contradict her, but Restin spoke before he could form a word.

"Vampire cooties? What kind of scat are you talking?"

Old Olivia squinted at Restin. He wasn't her beta, but she was a pack elder. "Selena was sick for several days after tangling with a vampire. I wasn't sure she'd live."

Restin narrowed his eyes.

"Unless you've discovered something new about vampires?" Old Olivia stood her ground.

The elderly she-wolf had embarrassed Restin. Other than what Selena learned in her confrontation, vampires were mysteries to the lycan world. Selena's specifics were vague. Because Dakota hadn't been infected as badly as Selena, the details were vague for him as well. Vampire cooties covered a lot of ground.

"I should be taking notes," Britt muttered. "I could switch my focus from cosmetics to the supernatural, be the world's first expert on vampires."

Dakota hoped she was speaking for Restin's sake. He didn't want her anywhere near vampires again.

Restin didn't respond. The insects and birds still didn't speak. The light breeze ruffling the tops of the trees ceased, as if Ulvskog held its breath.

Britt turned to Old Olivia. "Are they still having a pissing match?" she whispered, as if not a single lycan present couldn't hear her question.

"Yes," Old Olivia replied.

Movement behind Restin drew Dakota's attention. Two Varulv males emerged from the forest. Dakota recognized the bright blue plaid shirt one of them wore. He'd been one of the workmen who'd vanished at the first sign of conflict. Apparently he'd gone for reinforcements.

Or they were going to revolt against Restin. Dakota couldn't pick a better candidate for mutiny.

The two males strode past Restin to stand at Dakota's side.

"Is Selena in danger?" Blue Plaid asked him.

"Possibly."

"She battled a vampire?"

Dakota hesitated. Britt still wasn't aware exactly how Liam and DiNardo had died or how many lycans participated in their deaths. "Yes. Before," he finally answered. "Before the night of retribution."

"Are vampires still stalking her?"

"Keeping her prisoner in her house at night," Dakota clarified.

"Will she be able to return home for the full moon?"

"If she leaves in daylight."

The two Varulv exchanged a glance. Blue Plaid acted as spokeswolf. "No one should be a prisoner on the night of the full moon."

His partner grunted in what Dakota could only assume was agreement.

"We're going back with you."

"Selena wants you to stay in Ulvskog." Rand entered the middle of the mess.

"She's our alpha, and she's a night prisoner. Not acceptable. You may be heir to the Limmikin alpha, but we're not Limmikin."

"I didn't come to recruit Varulv," Dakota said. Two recruits were better than none. "I hoped the Loup Garou would help me protect my mate."

Except the only Loup Garou in Ulvskog was Restin, who could request backup from Tokarz before the full moon. They had a day. Dakota had gone and stuck his foot in it by challenging Restin.

"I came to my beta to request his help." He rephrased the insult. "You're my witnesses."

He grabbed Britt's arm and pulled her toward his SUV, unaware Blue Plaid and his shadow followed until they climbed into the back seat.

"Wait for me." Old Olivia scurried as quickly as her ancient bones would let her.

He reversed the SUV and nearly hit Hatch who materialized from nowhere.

Hatch motioned for Dakota to open his window. "Do you want me to contact Tokarz as a favor, alpha to alpha?"

Was Hatch offering an alpha strategy? "Can you?"

Hatch's face folded into deep creases. "Maybe. I've only recently acknowledged my alpha heritage."

"Test the waters," Old Olivia suggested. "Come on, *Hache-Hi*. Hitch a ride with us."

Chapter 26

"Ulvskog was fun," Britt quipped as brightly as she could as Dakota left the track from Varulv and hit the paved road again.

"Restin has issues," Dakota muttered. "We will discuss your behavior later."

She wasn't worried. She could always claim ignorance.

"Why do you need to wait until the full moon to take on the vampires?"

Old Olivia broke a couple of miles of awkward silence. "The moon is waxing. We grow stronger every night. If your mate's theory is right, the vampires are growing weaker. Maybe they're expecting something on the full moon. An earlier strike on our part could put the surprise factor on our side."

"Especially if the vampires aren't aware reinforcements are here," Blue Plaid added.

"Have any of you ever met a vampire?" Dakota asked.

"I smelled them the night after the massacre." The second Varulv lobo spoke softly. "Their stench is hard to miss."

"They were around after the massacre?"

"Yes," Old Olivia said. "The night we spent in the old town, before you arrived from Colorado."

"Right around the time the suckers started congregating at the end of Ethan's block," Dakota murmured.

"Yes. We'd relocated to Warwick. They followed us."

"I remember." Britt inched her seat forward to give the tall werewolf behind her more leg room. "We planned to blend our products for Night Shift in the basement until you moved in."

"We needed a place to recoup and decide how to move forward," Old Olivia said. "Ethan was kind enough to offer his cellar."

"So why are we waiting until the full moon to attack?"

"That's when we're strongest," Dakota replied. "We need every advantage against them."

"Olivia's idea of attacking the night before is better," Ethan's grandfather put in. "I agree with the element of surprise. We need every weapon at our disposal. Besides, if we need to, we could shift."

"You can shift?" Britt glanced at Old Olivia. "I thought the ability disappeared as a werewolf got older."

"Only with the females. Once we're past childbearing age, we can't shift. Nor can we shift when we're gestating. Our vulnerability is what makes our males overly protective of us."

Britt never considered the reason for Ethan and Dakota's highhandedness. Old Olivia's perspective made weird sense. Still, she would hate having restrictions on her life. Thank Lucifer's stepchild she wasn't a werewolf.

"Hey," Dakota protested, "I'm not a leader. I'm not a strategist. I had an idea, nothing else. Hatch, you're alpha. If you want to band together to attack the vampires on the night before the full moon, I'm with you."

Too many bodies crammed Ethan's house.

Night had fallen shortly after Dakota drove into Warwick. The two Varulv hunched in the back of the SUV, hiding as Dakota left Oak Street for Ash. Britt shivered when Dakota drove into the crowd. They were going with the element of surprise. Sneaking the Varulv into the house was easy.

Until Selena saw them. A couple minutes of ugly followed. She wanted her pack safe in the woods.

The woods, they'd pointed out, wasn't any safer than the city. *Remember?*

Too many now packed the Ash Street house. Britt slipped out the back door. Restlessness jittered in her blood, along with the shivers she couldn't shake. Her feet hurt. She hadn't followed Parker's instructions to rest them. She could only take so many repetitions of planning *Operation Full Moon* before she lost control of her need to scream. *They* could howl at the moon. The only release open to her was screaming. Shrieking. Especially since she couldn't go dancing.

Dancing. A hurricane in her hand, country music in the air, and the dance floor of a honkytonk for her feet. Her poor, aching feet. A cure for everything that ailed her.

Moonlight spilled onto the landscape, silver seeping between every twig of the hawthorn hedge and the huge tree in the far corner. Patterns of shadow and light decorated the lawn. Dew glittered on the grass. Lightning bugs pranced in the air. The scene, she mused, would make a great fabric for a skirt. She had to think shallowly; otherwise madness lurked.

Why couldn't she live a quiet, nerdy life, without drama following her? She must have been a wicked person in a previous incarnation. She was given a brain and curiosity meant for science, yet the restlessness inherent in her personality kept inviting disaster. Had she been crazy before her mother's illness? She couldn't remember.

Before the rage her father's faith created, increasing as her mother's health deteriorated, life was a blur. Britt cared for her siblings. She resented always being at church. She'd sensed her faith-based home schooling was lacking. She was never meant to be a passive geek.

She wandered across the grass, displacing beads of dew as she passed. She shivered and rubbed her arms. Maybe she could convince Ethan to put speakers in the windows and they could transform the lawn into a makeshift dance hall. Everyone in Ethan's house needed to loosen up. Dancing would warm her.

The neighbors might not appreciate Toke Lobo and the Pack blaring. Maybe some would want to join the party. A block party. Wouldn't that be fun? Of course, Helga the alleged witch was the only other person who lived on the block. Britt imagined others from neighboring streets would want in on the fun. Ash Street wasn't some highfalutin McMansion development.

The night grew chillier. She should have brought her jean jacket outside with her. She paced the length of the yard to the big tree—mulberry, according to Selena who was investigating possible healing properties. Britt could have told her. Silk. Silk undies could fix a lot of woes.

"Britt?"

Who followed her outside? She'd been adamant about needing alone time.

"Behind the tree." The disembodied voice drifted from the back hedge.

She left the cover of the tree and inched toward the shrubbery. "Who are you, and why are you hiding?"

"Me."

"I'm not in the mood for games." Her teeth wanted to chatter.

"Neither am I."

"Where are you?" Bad vibes bombarded her. The rear stretch of the hawthorn hid in deep shadow, and the shadow was colder than the lake in January. Darkness shrouded the back-neighbor's house.

"A few more feet. Climb into the bushes."

She stopped. "I'm not fond of thorns."

A finger of moonbeam crept around the hedge.

"You owe me, bitch." The words switched from cajoling to vicious. Moonlight glinted off red hair. A fang. A hand, a forearm, thrust through the shrub and grabbed for her. Touched her.

It howled as thorns tore into flesh.

Judd. She recognized the voice stalking her nightmares.

Judd was on the other side of the hedge. Britt did what any woman would do. She screamed and ran for the house.

THE BACK DOOR SLAMMED open. Dakota's feet barely touched the ground as he rushed toward her. "Britt!"

"Judd is here!" She could barely gasp out the words as she sprinted across the lawn toward Dakota, and safety.

How had Judd found her?

"Where?" Ethan was right behind Dakota.

"In the back-neighbor's lawn," she gasped, as Dakota's arms circled her. He was warm. So deliciously warm. He swung her between him and Ethan. "He was calling me. I didn't recognize his voice at first. I saw his hair." Her teeth chattered as she buried her face in Dakota's chest. His wonderful, broad, warm chest. "A f-fang."

"You're as cold as an iceberg." Dakota rubbed her arms. "And you stink of vampire."

"He reached for me." She wasn't going to cry. She wasn't going to let go of Dakota's solid presence.

The cold. The soul-chilling cold. She should have recognized the atmosphere, should have remembered the arctic weather from the previous evening.

"You told me this house was vampire proof," Dakota growled at Ethan.

"The address is vampire proof. The block is vampire proof. The house behind us isn't on the same block."

"Scat! Doesn't that matter when vampires have targeted my mate?" Dakota roared.

"Why don't you tell the vampires at the end of the block?" Ethan retorted sharply.

The edge wasn't honed enough to cut Dakota's fury. He lifted Britt from her feet, tossed her across his shoulder, and stalked toward the house. "Hot shower," he muttered, "before you die from hypothermia."

She was shaking. Dakota's warmth hurt. "Run water in the tub," he snarled at Selena as he carried Britt to the guest room. "As hot as you can make it."

He tore her clothes from her as if they were made of tissue paper. The few words she'd uttered to him depleted her strength. He yanked a blanket from the bed and wrapped her in it. The scratchy material didn't matter. The blanket wasn't warm. The blanket wasn't Dakota.

He carried her to the bathroom, where Selena stood next to the tub. "The water is as hot as it gets. What's wrong with her?"

"Vampire cooties, sapien style."

SELENA'S MOUTH GAPED. "I have no experience with vampire cooties for sapiens."

Dakota squatted next to the steaming tub. "Would Old Olivia? Isn't she a healer?"

"She heals lycans, not sapiens," Selena pointed out.

Dakota removed the blanket he'd wrapped around Britt before he slowly immersed her into the steaming water.

She whimpered.

"Parker hasn't left for Ulvskog yet." Selena's face folded into lines of concern. "Isn't he an EMT?"

"Not Parker." His packmate didn't need to see Britt without her clothes.

"If he's an EMT, he might know more about sapiens than I do," Selena tried to reason. "He's not going to lust after your female. You're being ridiculous."

Britt wouldn't let go of Dakota's neck. "W-Warm." Her teeth chattered. Her legs blushed pink from the heat of the water.

"Give the bath a minute," he murmured before kissing the top of her head.

"No. You." She tightened her hold. "You're warm." She wanted him? Pleasure momentarily replaced worry.

"The water will thaw you."

"I c-can't f-feel the water. I c-can only f-feel you."

"Let the water warm you," Selena urged.

"I wasn't this c-cold last night," Britt complained.

"You didn't smell the vampire?"

"C-cold. Last night, too. No smell." Britt closed her eyes and whimpered.

"I smell vampire," Selena insisted.

"Me, too." Dakota unwound Britt's arms from his neck. She winced when he touched her. He twisted her arm until he could see a fresh burn mark on the tender flesh inside her wrist. "What's this?"

She stared at the mark. "Judd touched me. So c-cold."

"Freezer burn?" Selena suggested.

Dakota nodded. The mark could explain why the cold wouldn't leave her body. Maybe it was some kind of vampire curse.

"Let me get Old Olivia." Selena hurried from the bathroom.

"The water isn't working," Britt whined. She sounded sleepy; Dakota knew the symptoms of hypothermia included sleepiness.

"Stay awake," he ordered. "I don't want you drowning."

"I didn't get much sleep last night. I'm not c-complaining."

The chattering of her teeth lessened.

Old Olivia entered the bathroom. She dipped her hand into the water lapping at Britt's lusciously naked body. "This water is barely tepid. She needs hot water. Oh, and I spoke to Helga, who suggested tea."

Dakota trailed a finger across the surface of Britt's bath. The water was rapidly cooling. "A hot bath isn't working," he admitted. "Let's get her out."

Britt managed a weak smile as she raised her arms. Old Olivia used the discarded blanket as a towel to wrap around Britt's slick flesh as Dakota lifted her from the water.

Britt snuggled her face into the crook of his neck. "You're so warm."

Even her breath was cool against his skin.

"Maybe you should share your body heat while we wait for the tea." Old Olivia nodded toward Britt. "She's responding to you."

"Mmm," Britt murmured.

He carried her to the guest room, water dripping on the floor and soaking his clothes. Old Olivia drew back the covers on the bed while Dakota briskly rubbed the rough blanket against Britt's skin.

"Body heat works best if you're both naked."

"You only want to see my body, old woman," Dakota accused, half-joking, as he tucked the bedding around Britt, who curled into a shivering ball of female.

"Of course I do. I'm old, not dead, and you're as fine a lobo as they come, regardless of status." She snickered.

She was trying to get him to relax. How could he relax while Britt suffered?

"Why don't you make love to her?" Old Olivia suggested. "Sex ought to heat her blood."

He didn't point out Britt's physical frostiness might shrivel any erection he coaxed into being.

"I'll leave you some privacy." Old Olivia winked before leaving the room. The door closed behind her with a quiet snick.

Dakota stripped off his wet shirt before sitting on the edge of the mattress to remove his boots.

Selena tapped on the door. "Hi. Sorry to interrupt." She carried a steaming mug of something fragrantly fruity. "Helga brought some tea she said will help Britt."

Selena's gaze caught Dakota's as she extended the mug. "Wild berry tea."

Berries. At last he was offering berries to his mate.

"Thank you."

Britt wasn't interested in tea. "Hurry," she whispered. "So c-cold."

"You need to drink," Dakota stressed. "While the tea is hot."

"You're h-hot."

"Thank you for nothing. Flattery will get you nowhere." He helped her into a sitting position. "Drink." He supported her back with one hand while he held the mug to her mouth with the other.

She sipped. Made a face. "Not coffee."

"You're right. Helga recommended berry tea to warm your insides. The sooner you finish, the sooner we can resume getting naked."

She emptied the mug in a series of swallows.

"Atta girl." Dakota settled her against the pillow before setting the mug on the floor.

Jeans, socks, and boxers followed. Dakota eased beneath the covers. Britt had no body heat. He braced himself to wrap around her.

"Oh, you feel good." She moaned as his skin surrounded her. She moaned a couple of more times as he repositioned himself to be effective but comfortable.

He'd barely stilled when Britt twisted to face him. Her legs uncurled and her arms went around him.

Maybe his imagination was working overtime, but she didn't feel as cold has she had. Instead of pressing her face to his chest, as he expected, she stretched to kiss him. Her lips were cold. She slipped her tongue into his mouth. Cool, but not icy. His penis stirred. Apparently, she wasn't cold enough to dampen his desire.

He let his hands roam her body; the smooth skin of her back, the firm muscles of her ass.

"Yes," she whispered, as he squeezed her butt cheeks. She parted her legs, as she touched him in ways to stir his cock.

He was getting hard. Really hard. The chill of her palms didn't diminish his arousal. He wanted nothing more than to pound his heat into her.

"Make me hot," she whispered in a break from kissing him. "Nobody makes me hot the way you do. I need you so much."

Who was he to ignore a needy mate?

He slipped his hand between her thighs and found warmth in her. Genuine warmth. He stroked her core and found more heat. Wet heat. As if her body was thawing from the inside out.

Her next moan wasn't from pain or cold. Every instinct he owned assured him she was aroused. Her legs splayed, then rose as she planted her feet on the mattress. A few fumbling moments later he thrust into her waiting heat.

Her breath whistled sharply between her teeth. "I need you so much."

One part of him worried he would hurt her. She was having none of that. Her nails dug into his shoulders, her thighs clasped his ribs, and her answering movements echoed his urgency. He cupped her ass as he thrust into her. Her climax nearly undid him. He slowed his pace, gentled his force. He wanted the moment, the connection to last, at least until she was room temperature.

He brushed his lips across her forehead. She was thawing.

She needs me to help her heal.

I'м тоо stupid to live.

Britt should have known better than to answer a voice coming from the hedges. Even if someone refusing to identify himself hadn't been a clue, the increasing cold should have warned her. If the others banned her from their strategic planning meeting, she wouldn't blame them.

She wore a pair of Dakota's black sweat pants, was cocooned in a blanket, and perched on his lap. His legs and arms surrounded her. While she wasn't as cold as she'd been before Dakota rid her of Judd's touch, the room still chilled her.

She shared one end of the sofa with Dakota. Old Olivia occupied the other end. Due to the lack of furniture, most of the werewolves present either sprawled on the floor or leaned against door frames or the wall closest to the windows. Strategic lounging.

"What we've learned," Ethan was saying, "is whatever magic protects our part of Ash Street doesn't extend to our neighbors on other streets. A couple of us sniffed around after the attack on Britt. There's no mistaking vampire stink."

"Judd is a vampire." Britt couldn't wrap her head around that one. He was going to push the boundaries of the undead. Whoever changed him was going to regret it. Judd couldn't be controlled.

"They're getting bolder," Parker said. "The vampires," he added, as if anyone might be confused.

"The person he was before he became a vampire ignored the rules." Britt rubbed a patch of the blanket between her forefinger and her thumb. "Rules won't mean anything to him now. How did he find me here?"

"Selena's address was on the business forms." Ethan narrowed his eyes, as if thinking. "Another possibility is the vampires at the end of the block told him."

Vampire networking. Great.

"Why is he after you?" the Varulv wearing the bright blue plaid shirt asked.

"I'm responsible for his being incarcerated. He—I reported him to the police. I testified against him at his trial." She shivered; Dakota tightened his clasp on her.

Ethan and Dakota exchanged a tense glance. "She knows," was all Dakota had to say.

What was the big deal? Her darkest secret was way worse than killing a rapist.

"You believe because I reported Judd to the police I'll do the same to you? For killing Liam and Curtis or for being werewolves?"

No one answered.

"I don't have a history of betrayal."

"I wouldn't claim that," Selena muttered.

"What did I ever do to you?"

Selena didn't respond. She couldn't. Britt had been a loyal friend to her since college.

"I've never gone public about how my father was responsible for my mother's death," Britt reminded Dakota. "I told you how he wouldn't let her seek medical treatment, how he was going to heal her with faith. Information smearing his name could destroy Pastor Paul. I had good reasons to call the cops on Judd. I didn't get my chance at Curtis. I want my chance at Judd."

"Difficult to do being only a sapien," Blue Plaid Shirt pointed out.

"Ed," Selena warned. "You're out of line."

"We need to go after them before the full moon, when they least expect a counterattack," Dakota insisted. His arm tightened around Britt's waist.

"And they don't know Ed and Harry are here," Selena added.

"You have stakes, right?" Why else would a house with no fireplace have a stack of wood in the basement?

"Of course. My pack armed themselves while they were here."

"I say we go in on full moon eve." Old Olivia's voice cracked. "We're closest yet still building toward our full power."

"I agree."

Britt squirmed out of the hurt place the others' opinions placed her. She could lick her wounds later. After this clusterfuck was history. The situation was going to end one way or another, and soon.

She listened to the lycans plot their strategy, with Old Olivia keeping the non-shifters involved in the action. At her suggestion of recruiting Helga as a staker, Selena agreed, while the guys pooh-poohed the idea.

Selena put her foot—or was it a paw?—down. "We need all the help we can get. Helga has proven herself our ally on more than one occasion. We invite her, we don't draft her."

Selena's voice rang with authority. For the first time,

Britt glimpsed what being an alpha werewolf meant.

Hatch tried to argue. "I'm not comfortable putting females in danger. Risking their safety is against everything we believe."

Selena bared her teeth. "I appreciate your concern, but as the alpha of my pack, I make the final decisions."

"You are Limmikin now," Hatch insisted. "You mated into Ethan's pack. That makes me your alpha."

The two Varulv males would have bristled had they been in wolf form.

Britt let the werewolves have their pissing match, while she tried to pinpoint the cause of a niggle of caution bothering her. Something was missing. Something crucial.

Her restlessness magnified. She could blame the jitters on her need to drink and dance all she wanted, but boot-scooting up a sweat only masked her problems. Swilling her way into oblivion delayed the need to face and hopefully conquer them.

She was one messed-up woman. She had been for years. The only time she was genuinely happy was in the lab, making her concoctions work. Putting the factors together to create something new and good. Two plus two always made four, no matter how often she was told differently.

She needed to approach her disquiet the way she would a problem in the lab.

Every scenario she conjured circled back to missing something big. Important. Vital. Yet she sensed the key wasn't a mystery.

Background events happened whether or not she was aware of them. Ethan went to Congressman Bryant Peters pretending to represent Night Shift and brought Selena as well as Britt to the forefront of his attention. Where was the connection?

She wanted a whiteboard, a large, wall-mounted surface, to diagram her thoughts. One hung in the basement, purchased before Selena decided to back out of Night Shift.

"Britt?"

Dakota looked at her as if he expected a coherent answer.

"We're missing something."

"What?" Selena asked.

She and Selena had worked well together perfecting the formulas for the Night Shift products. Britt trusted her.

"I wish I knew."

Surprisingly, no one scoffed. More shocking, a few of the others took her seriously. Selena. Old Olivia. Dakota. Ethan remained unreadable.

"I need to think," she muttered as she clambered off Dakota's lap. No one stopped her as she headed toward the basement stairs.

Helga sat on the sofa in Ethan's living room. Her bright blue eyes shone like supernovas in a summer sky. "I would have been hurt if you hadn't invited me. Those vampires stink up the whole neighborhood."

Could everyone smell vampires except Britt?

"Besides, I resent having to drive around them on my way to Hy-Vee. Oh, I can see the daytime thugs aren't vampires, but the gamut is still unnerving for a woman my age." She settled into her seat. "I've noticed the cops a couple of times. You should get the law to take care of the thugs, and we'll handle the vampires. I've never killed a vampire before. Is it hard?"

"More debilitating than anything else," Selena replied. "At least for lycans. Britt managed okay, as long as she avoided physical contact."

"Vampire cooties are unpredictable." Old Olivia sounded as if she spoke from experience.

"Vampire cooties?" Helga snickered. "Now I've heard everything."

Old Olivia arched an eyebrow at Helga. "The term fits. They affect lycans differently than they do sapiens. Britt suffers from the cold."

"Vampire-induced hypothermia." Helga scrunched her face, as if thinking. "Hot berry tea combats the curse. Hot tea cures almost anything. Except vampire stink. I haven't found a solution to the smell."

Dakota tuned out the silly female chatter. He wanted to rid the world of vampires, commencing with Ash Street in Warwick, Minnesota. If Luke could manipulate his obsession with sapien porn into a gig with the FBI, why couldn't Dakota become a vampire exterminator?

Stupid question. Luke loved his computers; nothing he did changed, whereas Dakota preferred driving the band tour bus. He liked the control. This situation with the vampires put him on edge. The creatures were unpredictable. Life was simpler when all he had to deal with were lycans and sapiens. Loup Garou and honkytonks. Currently stuck in an unfamiliar world filled with vampires and Wiccans—and whatever scat Helga was peddling—unsettled him.

He was done listening to alphas, future alphas, and alpha wannabees discuss how to best defeat the vampires. His plan, as amended by Old Olivia, was the best idea so far. If they continued their current pace, they'd be debating until the Wolf Moon in January.

"When you guys get your scat together, give me a howl." He left the room. He'd rather hang with Britt.

He followed her scent to the basement. She stood in front of a whiteboard, marker in hand. She'd written down names. Circles, lines, and arrows.

"What's this?" He gestured at the chart.

"Analytical mind mapping." She focused intently on the scribbles and scrawls.

"Explain it to me." He stood behind her and studied the schematic.

"Nothing happened until Ethan tried to meet with Congressman Bryant Peters using Night Shift as an excuse. My name and Selena's names were attached. The only clue not fitting to make the situation a neat puzzle is Judd contacting me right after you and I hooked up. He's the wild card."

"We didn't hookup." How long before she admitted they were more than a one-night stand?

"At the time, I didn't know." She spoke absently, still focused on her scrawls. "Bryant Peters' suicide. Liam Peters' disappearance. Curtis DiNardo's vanishing act. You and me. Judd. Our separate visits to Connor Peters. How did Judd get into the mix? I don't buy the Curtis connection between Judd and Connor. Too tenuous. We're missing something."

Dakota slipped his arms around her waist. "Maybe we should sleep on it."

"Not a bad idea," she murmured, as she leaned into his embrace. "If you ponder a problem right before you go to sleep, your subconscious takes your thoughts as a cue to work on the problem while you're sleeping."

"Sleep isn't what I had in mind." Dakota nuzzled her ear. She smelled sweet and fresh, like the outdoors. The Night Shift products were a huge improvement over some of the stinks he'd encountered on sapien females during his honkytonk years.

Her responding laugh was throaty and full of promise.

Chapter 27

Britt woke, dislodging Dakota's arm as she bolted upright in their bed. He grumbled something in a sleepy voice. Outside their window, birds welcomed the rising sun.

"I need my mother's cross."

Dakota responded with another unintelligible vocalization.

"Seriously. We need to go to my apartment. I need my mother's cross."

Dakota rolled onto his back, flung his arm across his eyes, and groaned. "Wake me in an hour."

His erect penis created a tent with the sheet. "Tell me another one, Bus Boy." She patted the pole.

"Easy."

"Oh, right. Your dick doesn't have a brain."

"It still has needs. Right now, it wants you to be nice."

"I need my mother's cross." She slowed the patting to a caress. "Am I being nice enough?"

"Almost. Why do you need your mother's cross?"

"Vampires are allergic to crosses and to silver, and her necklace is silver."

"Oh. You mean a necklace."

"What did you think?"

"No clue." He raised his hips so she could caress more of his erection.

She yanked the sheet to the foot of the bed, exposing him in all his naked glory. "If I'm real nice to you, can we go to my apartment this morning?" She lowered her head and let her breath trickle across his sensitive skin.

"Are you trying to bribe me?"

"Yep." Her lips brushed the tip of his penis.

More male noises—or maybe they were werewolf sounds—escaped Dakota's throat.

She licked the length of him.

"Not this morning." He jackknifed upright and clasped her waist with his huge hands.

"I need the necklace today," she said, as he flipped her onto her back.

"I didn't mean your mother's cross." He plunged into her. She was ready for him. She usually needed a lot of foreplay before intercourse. Dakota eliminated the need. She climaxed almost immediately, clinging to him as if only his presence could keep her from disappearing into the ether.

A moment later he shuddered and held himself still.

"Good morning," she whispered.

"Sure is," he muttered.

"Can we sneak out and head toward my apartment?"

"Give me a minute to recuperate, will you? You discombobulate me."

She discombobulated him again in the shower.

An hour later, Dakota drove them toward Britt's apartment, after a stop at Caribou for coffee. "Maybe we should call your cop buddies to meet us."

"We'll be in and out. I know right where the necklace is."

Dakota parked in front of Britt's apartment.

"Why doesn't my apartment feel like home anymore?"

"I have fond memories of your bedroom," Dakota admitted.

"Fond as they are, I don't want to live here."

"You're right." She opened the door and hopped out of the SUV before Dakota could dash around the front to do the honors.

He clasped her arm. "Let me go first."

"No argument here."

The stairs were empty.

She scanned the dusty rooms. "Nothing is out of place."

"How can you tell?"

She wasn't as meticulous at home as she was in the lab. So what? She was a well-rounded woman. She pushed past Dakota without saying anything and headed straight for her closet.

"The room smells like vampire," Dakota muttered. "Only worse. I didn't know worse existed."

A funk clung to the air. The smell wasn't as bad as Dakota claimed. She ought to open the window and let in the cool morning breeze. "If we find a vampire sleeping in my closet, run the broom handle through the corpse."

She didn't store the few mementos she had of her mother with the rest of her jewelry. Seeing them made her too sad. She didn't have a lot, only what she was able to sneak out of the house before she left: a small silver cross on a fragile silver chain; a cheap handkerchief printed with violets; a tube of rancid, barely pink lipstick. She kept everything in an old Valentine Day candy tin.

"What the—? Don't you smell that?"

Obviously not as potently as he did.

Britt was certain the heart-shaped tin was on the top shelf of her closet. She opened the closet door, stumbling over a pile of dirty clothes as she reached for the upper shelf.

"*Oh, scat.* We have to leave."

"Hold on a second." Britt dislodged battered purses and an old college logo duffel bag. A wide-brimmed straw sun hat fell on her head.

"This is Dakota Towne. Are you awake?"

"Who are you talking to?" she asked, as she blindly groped the shelf.

"I'm calling your cop friends."

There. Her fingers brushed the cool metal.

"Anderson, you better come to Britt's apartment."

She dragged the tin to the front of the shelf, then turned to gape at his next words.

"Based on the bloodstains, I'd say someone was murdered in her bed."

THE STENCH WAS UNBEARABLE. Dakota recognized vampire stink, but this stink was worse. Terror. Feces. Blood. Decay. He hadn't called Anderson because Britt's bedroom reeked. He'd called because blood saturated Britt's bed.

He cherished his memories of that bed. He considered the befouling a double desecration.

"Lucifer's stepchild." Britt stared at the body-shaped stain drenching the bedding as she clutched a metal box. Her face blanched to the color of the sheets before they'd been defiled.

"Yeah, let's wait for your pals someplace else." He grabbed her upper arm and steered her out of the bedroom.

She shook so badly, whatever was in the box rattled. "I could have been sleeping here," she whispered.

As if he didn't know that. As if knowing she could have been murdered while she slept didn't infuriate him.

"Can we wait in your car?" Her voice was small.

"Great idea." He wished they could wait someplace else altogether. Colorado. Home. He opened the SUV door for Britt, then boosted her in.

She clutched the box so tightly she dented the cover.

"What's in the box?" he asked, mostly to distract her from the imitation Shroud of Turin upstairs.

"Mementos of my mom. I managed to snag a few items before Pastor Paul booted me."

"Let's have a look."

The metal of the box was cheap. The top didn't come off.

"I'll get it." Dakota took the box from her. He was a lot stronger than she was and was able to pry the top from the bottom without too much damage.

The contents were sparse, wrapped in a purple and white square of thin cloth. Lipstick. A fragile black chain with a tiny black cross.

"The silver is tarnished. I'll have to get some polish."

"Doesn't matter. Silver is silver, and a vampire repellent."

"According to legend."

"Let me." He took the chain from her.

She lifted her hair off her neck as he fumbled with the clasp.

Maybe they had time to buy garlic.

Anderson and Clerkin arrived. Clerkin's scruff hinted he'd been yanked from bed. His bloodshot eyes glared. "This better be good."

"I wouldn't have called you for good news," Dakota snapped. "We came to retrieve some of Britt's stuff, and, well, you go in the bedroom and tell me if what you find is good."

He handed Clerkin the key. "Lock the door after you're done. We'll be at Ethan's."

"You wait here," Anderson ordered.

"We should have left before they arrived. No one needs a key to get in anymore." Britt's sullen tone blended with her narrowed glare as the cops vanished inside her house. "My life has gone to hell. Exactly like Pastor Paul predicted."

"Your life, my life—temporary slumps."

"Slump? You have a funny definition of slump."

A few minutes later, a black-and-white cruiser pulled to the curb in front of the house.

"This is going to take all day," she said.

"Do you have other plans?"

"I wanted to practice staking vampires."

"What?"

"I plan to make some targets in the back yard and practice jabbing stakes into them."

Another black and white parked behind Dakota. The uniformed officer climbed out, a roll of yellow crime scene tape in hand.

"Great," Britt groused.

Dakota's cell phone rang. "Yo."

"Where are you?" Ethan asked.

"Britt and I are running errands. Why?"

"Helga is here. She's right. We either need to pay attention to the radio or watch television."

Dakota's chest tingled. His saliva curdled. "What?"

"Connor Peters vanished from the hospital."

The tingling spread to his arms and legs. "Repeat that."

"Connor Peters is gone."

Dakota strung together a list of sapien curses.

Britt's eyes widened, and she inched away from him.

"Wow. Some vocabulary. I'm impressed. I might have you teach me a few new cuss words," Ethan said.

"How the *fuck* did Connor disappear?"

"What?" Britt's voice squeaked. Her pulse fluttered in her neck.

"He was supposed to have a police guard," Dakota snarled into the phone. "I should have finished him off while I had the chance."

"He *did* have a police guard. Who didn't see or hear a thing."

"Will he change into a werewolf?" Britt's knuckles whitened on the metal heart. "You bit him, and—"

"No. Bitten or born is a myth." Dakota turned on her. "I've explained this to you. You are either born lycan or not."

"Uh-oh." Britt pointed.

Anderson and Clerkin were headed toward them, their faces grim.

"I gotta go." Dakota disconnected the call. He opened his window while Anderson approached, not liking the way Clerkin split off and headed toward Britt's side of the SUV. "Well?"

"Something died in Britt's bed, all right," Anderson said.

"We figured."

"What are you doing here?"

"The apartment is still in my name." Britt leaned toward the driver's window. "Still my legal address. I needed to fetch some personal belongings."

"You didn't spend the night here?" Anderson prodded.

"Nope." She didn't elaborate.

"Are you getting ready to leave?"

"I am. I'm moving in with Dakota. We're visiting his hometown. Rumor claims the politicians in Colorado aren't as crooked as they are in Minnesota."

"I wouldn't leave town any time soon," Anderson suggested.

"You're contradicting what you said the last time we talked. Am I a suspect?" Anger battled with the fear shaking in her tone.

"We may need to speak to you again."

"Can I have my house key back?"

Anderson handed the key to Dakota.

"I'm being framed."

No comment from Anderson.

"I may not be your missing dead bodies, but I'm a victim."

The cop didn't blink. "Don't leave town. Either of you."

BRITT SAT ON THE back steps of Ethan's house and stared at Dakota as he whittled sharper tips on the stakes from the basement.

"Whose blood do you think it was?"

"I'm not going to speculate." Dakota focused on the blade in his hand.

"Connor vanished. Like Liam."

"Not like Liam. I told you what happened to Liam. I don't know what happened to Connor." He dug the blade of his knife deeper into the wood.

"If he doesn't resurface soon, he'll become a martyr. I do mean soon. Martyrs are never held accountable."

"I'm worried, too."

"You don't know what happened to him?" She wanted to believe Dakota. Needed to believe him.

"I don't."

"Okay." If she ever found out he'd lied to her, she'd drive a stake into his heart.

"Do you know what happened to him?" Dakota kept his eyes on what he was doing with the knife.

His question surprised her. "How would I know? I don't get all this supernatural, paranormal stuff. I'm only a preacher's kid gone wild."

"Who was raised to believe woo-woo. You're wearing a cross around your neck."

She touched her mother's necklace with the tips of her fingers. "Are you referring to Christianity?"

"Any religion. Whether or not the tenets are true, faith is still supernatural."

She'd never considered the core of her previous religion before. He was right. Accepting anything on faith instead of demonstrable fact was paranormal or supernatural.

"Besides," he continued, "maybe a Christian vampire would fear the cross because it symbolizes his beliefs. Would a vampire of another faith react the same? I'm homo lupus. If I were to become a vampire, your cross would mean nothing. The symbol has no meaning to me."

"I'm all for using any tool we can get our hands on. I'm even swiping the rope of garlic Selena has hanging in the kitchen." She wasn't joking.

"Okay." Chips of wood fell from the end of the stake.

The door behind Britt opened. "Hey Selena, I just told Dakota I'm going to steal the garlic rope from your kitchen for tonight."

"Stealing garlic now? You are a bad ass." Tom Anderson, not Selena.

Britt jumped. Thank goodness she hadn't said anything more damaging. "Hi, Tom. I wasn't expecting to see you."

"I figured."

Dakota kept working at the point on the stake. "What do you want?"

"We need both of you to be fingerprinted."

"Sure," she agreed, as if she didn't have a care in the world. "I do have a hot date later, but if fingerprinting won't take long, we can go now."

The late afternoon sun threw sharp shadows across the lawn. Although the early summer sun wouldn't set for hours yet, Britt wanted to practice wielding a decent stake.

"No." Dakota continued whittling while Tom remained inscrutable behind his aviator sunglasses.

Britt's chest grew tight. She had nothing to hide, and for a moment, forgot Dakota did.

"We need to eliminate your fingerprints from any others in the apartment."

"I had a roommate until a few days ago. Kathryn. Kathryn Becker." Britt found herself babbling. "She moved, though. Wouldn't tell me where. She works at a big wine and spirits distributor."

Fortunately, until she'd dragged Dakota home, she had never let her one-and-dones know where she lived.

"We're not requesting DNA, for God's sake, only your fingerprints."

"You're not getting either," Dakota stated. He kept running the blade of the knife against the wood. Shavings and chips continued to fall to the ground.

"If you don't have anything to hide, what's the problem?" Tom's tone was mild, even if his intentions weren't.

"Do you blame anyone for being paranoid in the current political climate?" Ethan asked from the doorway.

Tom's phone vibrated. He headed for the privacy of the mulberry tree in the back of the yard.

"We're all on board," Ethan reported softly. "Cooperate."

"You sure?" Dakota asked.

"Yeah. Don't do DNA. DNA could be disastrous."

Britt couldn't imagine living with the fear of an unusual DNA. How different was a werewolf's DNA than a homo sapien's?

Tom headed toward the house, his phone call brief. "We've identified the blood on your bed."

"As long as the blood isn't mine or Dakota's, should I be worried?" Her cheeks hurt as she stretched her mouth into a smile.

"Maybe," Tom said.

Judd. Someone had killed Judd in her bed.

"Connor Peters."

OF ALL THE PEOPLE Anderson could have mentioned, Connor Peters was the last person Dakota expected.

"Peters' blood is in Britt's bed?"

Britt stared at Anderson, her mouth agape. "How?"

"That's what we need to determine." Anderson's tone was grim.

"We were home all night." Dakota couldn't prove where they'd been. The cops would believe his friends lied for him. As would the Varulv lycans. Even Helga would lie. No one needed to lie. He and Britt had not left the house.

Ethan cleared his throat. "Who's your superior officer?"

Anderson stiffened. "Captain Hilleran," he replied tersely.

"Can you get him on the phone?"

Anderson's mouth thinned ominously as he pulled out his cell phone and dialed a number. "Captain Hilleran? Someone wants to speak to you." He placed his phone in Ethan's outstretched hand.

"My name is Ethan Calhoun, and I need you to call a guy named Mitchell Jasper. After you have spoken to him, call Officer Anderson back." Ethan recited a phone number, disconnected the call, and returned Anderson's phone to him.

Mitchell Jasper was the werewolves' former government contact. Something must have changed if Ethan was having the locals call Jasper.

Senses pinging, Dakota resumed whittling the tip of another stake.

Britt lifted the one he'd finished and made a show of jabbing the point into the ground.

"What is she doing?" Anderson asked after several moments of watching Britt repeat her action.

"Practicing," Dakota replied.

Anderson's phone vibrated before he could inquire further. "Anderson." He listened, his lips growing thinner, tauter, and paler as the conversation continued. "Yes, sir." His voice was even tighter. He disconnected.

"You should have told me you were a fed."

I've been promoted?

"I'm not a fed," Dakota began. "Ethan's the fed—"

"Don't play word games with me," Anderson snapped.

"Okay, I'm a fed." Maybe he was. Feds needed drivers.

Cool. He was a fed. "Being a fed doesn't change the fact I contacted you and Britt sought you, the local guys she trusts. She's having problems. Byrne is a local problem. Nobody tried to butt into your jurisdiction, so don't get all territorial on us."

"Byrne is not a local problem if a U.S. Congressman was behind getting him sprung from prison." Anderson didn't try to hide his anger.

Britt jammed the stake several inches into the ground. "Well, shit."

"Which U.S. Congressman?" Dakota asked.

"You're the fed. You tell me."

Okay, Anderson wasn't cooperating. He was pissed off, and Dakota couldn't blame him.

"We'll follow you to headquarters for fingerprinting," Dakota conceded. "Only so you can eliminate us from Britt's apartment."

Britt's apartment. Where they'd had sex. More than once. Unprotected sex.

Scat! His DNA lingered on the same sheets Connor Peters died on.

HURRY UP AND WAIT. What shouldn't have taken more than an hour took several. Britt was not happy to be stuck at the Warwick Police Department for any length of time. She didn't have the hours of daylight to waste.

The cops were being social and nice. Many had gone to high school with her, although she hadn't run with their crowd. She'd hooked up with a couple later, not realizing they were cops. She barely remembered them.

A lot of the officers were country music fans who wanted to hear Dakota's Toke Lobo and the Pack stories.

Daylight continued to hover as they left the station. Britt donated a strand of hair, including the root, to ensure they'd have her DNA. Several officers were on dinner break and wanted to drag Dakota to the Steak Out for a meal and pump him for more Toke Lobo insider tales.

"We have plans," Britt reminded Dakota.

"Fish," he said, and she understood. The guy wanted red meat.

The Steak Out was crowded. Service was slower than usual. Darkness shrouded the landscape by the time they left.

"We are so screwed." Britt pulled the shoulder harness across her breasts after locking the door of the SUV.

"I enjoyed it." Dakota shrugged. "We needed normal."

He started the engine and reversed out of his parking spot.

"Thanks for refusing the beers the guys tried to buy you," Britt said. "You're a great designated driver."

"Lycans can't drink. Alcohol screws with our ability to shift."

"Seriously?"

"Yeah. Weird for the brewers of Moonsinger, huh?"

"Ironic," she replied.

"I'd better not get a speeding ticket." He threw the SUV into gear and spun out of the parking lot.

"If we'd left sooner, the sun wouldn't be an issue." Yes, she was peeved.

"I needed normal."

"Except our lives aren't normal." *Mine may never be again.*

"We'll be fine."

The moon had not yet cleared the horizon, but the eastern edge of the sky grew brighter by the moment.

"I hope they don't start without us," Britt muttered.

"We'll be the unexpected. Relax. Arriving after dark is our normal. We'll lull the vamps into thinking all is well."

She grimaced at her reflection in the window, longing to be done with her past. She wanted Judd in prison with Connor as his cellmate. She wanted to rid the world of vampires. *Regularly scheduled life, here I come.*

They had no problem driving through the hoard at the end of the block. Dakota slowed so she could count heads at the corner of Oak and Ash. She shivered from the cold front. From her vantage point, the same number of vampires continued to guard Ash and Hawthorn.

And who was to say they were all vampires? Staking a living being would create a whole new set of issues. As far as she could tell, they might all be alive. Except for the suffocating cold and Dakota's insistence the smell was going to make him lose the fine slab of red meat he'd eaten at the restaurant.

"Where have you been?" Ethan asked as they entered the front door. He sounded pissed.

"With the cops," Dakota replied. "As you ordered."

His audacity amazed Britt. She shrugged at Selena, as if to say, *it is what it is.*

She opted for a conciliatory attitude. "I should have called or texted."

"We developed a plan while you were gone," Ethan continued, as if Dakota hadn't spoken. "I could have used your input."

"Then you shouldn't have sent me away."

Ethan ignored him. "We attack at midnight."

"How original."

"You don't need to be sarcastic," Selena growled. "Maybe you should listen to what Ethan has to say."

"Ethan is a smart lobo. I agree with his decisions. Let's see-we attack at midnight. Old Olivia, Helga, and Britt will be the rear guard with the stakes. Hopefully attacking one intersection will draw the bloodsuckers from the other corner. They'll need to go around the block, giving us additional time to subdue the first batch. When the second contingent arrives, the Varulv attack from behind. All these plans assume not one of us will contract vampire cooties or be hurt."

"Yeah."

"As I said. You're a smart lobo."

Britt was tired of the posturing. Another pissing match as far as she was concerned. "I want to practice with the stakes."

"Too late." Selena scowled at her. "If Judd tried to breech the back hedge last night, he might succeed tonight. What if exposure to hawthorn creates an immunity?"

Chapter 28

Britt stood with Helga and Old Olivia, away from the windows. One by one, Selena and the males morphed from human shape to wolf form and slunk from the house as silently as the shadows they mimicked. Her heart beat a cadence against her eardrums she hoped would go away during battle.

Dakota was the one who suggested the three women dress all in black. Black wasn't one of Britt's colors. She borrowed jeans and a turtleneck sweater from Selena.

"You look hot," Dakota told her. "Don't give the clothes back."

Britt managed a smile, although her face was numb.

She was terrified. Practicing to be a warrior-vampire-slayer was a fun fantasy. To brave the soul-sucking cold and drive a wooden post into a body that had once breathed and bled was something else. She discovered a new appreciation for soldiers. Talk was cheap. Plotting strategies was game playing. Reality was soul-destroying.

The moon splashed milky light into every available crack and crevice. If Dakota hadn't told Britt the moon wouldn't be full until the following night, she wouldn't have been able to tell. The brilliant glow bleached the nearby stars into near nonexistence.

The vampires would see them coming. Hiding wasn't an option.

"We're not the ones they want," Old Olivia reiterated. "They want Selena. Liam Peters was supposed to call them off. He disappeared before he could."

"Liam Peters used vampires?" Britt tightened her grip on her stake.

"His father did. Mercenaries. Bryant Peters assembled an army of mercenaries. He used everyone...vampires, rogue shifters, the scum of the earth."

"He was an evil man," Helga added.

Most people in the district, Britt included, were blissfully ignorant of Bryant Peters' true nature and shocked as the truth surfaced.

"He killed my daughter." Helga's tone lacked emotion, as if she were saving her pain, her rage for the upcoming confrontation. She swung her stake in an arc. "The least I can do is kill a few of his minions. I only wish vampires felt pain."

"Bryant Peters blackmailed the Varulv into annihilating the Limmikin. He blackmailed other mercenaries to eliminate the Varulv. They killed my mate." Old Olivia's bitterness was enough for both her and Helga. She eyed the point Dakota had whittled on the end of the stake before jamming it into the ground. "I survived both massacres. I've vowed no one will survive tonight."

"I can't figure out who wants to get me," Britt confessed. The Peters family wasn't responsible for the death of any of her loved ones, so her reason felt insipid compared to Old Olivia and Helga's need for retribution. "One of the Peters arranged for my ex to be sprung from prison. Believe me, my ex has a lot of reasons to hurt me."

If not kill me.

"We're going to win." Old Olivia hefted her weapon.

She was so old, so fragile-looking, Britt worried she wouldn't survive the battle. Helga wasn't in much better shape. Her teammates.

They probably had concerns about her fitness, too. She still limped, despite Selena's comfrey concoction.

"And they're off." Old Olivia's whisper drew goosebumps on Britt's arms.

She could barely make out the wolves' movements. They stayed low to the ground, clinging to what shadows they could find as they slunk toward Oak Street.

The night smelled of someone's freshly mowed lawn. Night insects continued their performance, not betraying the werewolves' advance. Even the lightning bugs cooperated.

All hell broke loose.

The wolves sprang at the vampires. *Surprise!* Seven werewolves took on five bloodsuckers. Britt's sapien eyes barely made out the blurs of dark shapes as the two species battled.

"Let's go." Old Olivia gave the signal for the stakers to join the melee.

The cold hit Britt first. Her bones flash-froze to icicles. Although she'd expected the arctic blast, the suddenness of the ache blindsided her. In the dark, she couldn't tell the werewolves apart—not that she would recognize the individuals if she met them on Main Street on a sunny day.

Growls and hisses filled the night air, silencing the insects. Fangs flashed reflected moonlight. The scent of freshly churned earth replaced the cut grass. The vamps tried to take the fight to the shadows, while the lycans favored the moonlight.

Helga raced into the melee, her stake raised high with two hands. She shoved the wooden weapon with a force Britt hadn't expected, driving the point into the back of a vampire's neck.

The vamp screamed and abandoned the werewolf he'd been fighting to swipe at Helga with long, curved claws. Britt sprang into action and drove her stake into the vamp's back, into its heart. The splintering of bone as the point impaled the body vibrated against Britt's hands. Bones cracked loudly in the stillness. Snapped like a tap dancer. The creature exploded into icy ash.

"Cool," Helga murmured.

Another vampire exploded as a wolf, muzzle deep in skin and bone, found its heart.

Two down, three to go.

Except the vamps from the other end of the block arrived at the showdown.

The moonlight glinted off red hair.

Oh, Judd's going to be next.

She knocked the vampire debris from her stake and launched toward the red-headed one.

Someone grabbed her arm. "Not a good idea." The voice was familiar.

She whirled and came face-to-face with Connor Peters. He grinned at her, new fangs flashing in the moonlight. "I'll be kinder to you than Judd. He has plans for you. Ugly plans."

"You're going to vanish the way your brother did." Britt hoisted the stake above her head with her free hand. "I hope mutating into a vampire hurt like hell. I remember how much you hate being bitten."

"You're not going to like changing, either," Connor threatened as he feinted left then right. "I can't wait to make you scream."

Britt jabbed at him with her stake.

"Coming on your face was fun, but I've always wanted to fuck you, especially in the ass. Every time your father's name is mentioned, I remember that night."

He spoke from behind her, his speed turning his movements to blurs.

She twisted to face him.

"If I bite you, you'll be mine to do with what I please. I can't wait to force your father to watch me defile you."

"Too late, Connor." Her growl was worthy of any werewolf. She stabbed at him again, but Connor's new speed worked against her. He snatched the stake and tossed it away.

Something screamed. Maybe her.

His grip was strong, painful, and cold. He didn't have fully-formed claws yet. Maybe claws developed with age. But his fangs? He'd been fangless the last time she'd seen him. He bared the new scalpel-like weapons at her. He tried to pull her toward the far end of the block, but he couldn't cross to Ash Street.

Her arm bone ached from his frigid touch. Her feet shrieked in agony.

"What the—?" He continued to tug on her arm, nearly tearing it from its socket.

"Sacred triad." Britt forced her teeth not to chatter. "Ash, Oak, Hawthorn. Keeps out the evil. I guess you didn't pass the test." She ignored the throbbing in her feet to kick him.

He twisted her arm behind her back, wringing tears from her eyes. Steam rose from the hot saline hitting the frigid air.

"I have plans for your mouth, so don't provoke me into hurting it before I make you sorry."

"I've been sorry since the first night I met you." She spat at him, her saliva turning to hail midair, then falling short of his face.

He pivoted and tried to thread his way around the battle, hauling her in his wake.

She strove to dig in her heels, but the scraggly grass along the verge of the street offered no purchase.

His touch burned like ice. He'd frozen her flesh. She had to do something or die. Distracting Dakota—or any other fighting werewolf—was unthinkable.

"Peters. You've taken what's mine." Judd's voice rang loudly above the scuffling around them.

"I snatched her first. You'll have to wait," Connor gloated. A stray moonbeam bounced off his fangs as he swung Britt behind him. "If I decide to let her go after I've fucked her into oblivion."

"You having her first is not the deal." Judd's fangs were longer. Sharper. Deadlier. His claws curved like scimitars.

"You've never known your place, Byrne." Connor tightened his hold on Britt. Contempt dripped from every syllable. "You can always be sent back to prison."

Judd circled them.

Connor pulled her with him as he evaded Judd, moving so quickly Britt thought she would come apart at her seams.

"Just like a politician with empty promises," Judd sneered as he lunged.

"I'm with Connor at the moment," Britt taunted Judd.

Judd hissed, moonlight glinting off his fangs. "You are going to get yours."

"I've already got mine." She jerked her arm again, but Connor maintained his grip. She couldn't let them scent her fear. *Stay angry.*

Connor dragged her deeper into the shadows. Judd followed.

She was going to die, all because she'd hooked up with the bad boy in high school.

"Being a vampire is great." Connor preened for her, as if he believed she preferred him over Judd. "I'm faster and stronger than I was before."

"Hand over my bitch." Judd stalked behind them into the dark fringe of the street.

"Ash," she shouted, hoping for a magic word. "Hawthorn. Oak." If only she could get away from Oak Street, back to the safety of Ash Street. "Garlic."

Judd giggled, the incongruous sound still haunting her dreams. "Are you chanting an incantation? What would your beloved father say about witchcraft?"

"I don't have a beloved father."

"You loved him enough to rat me out for robbing him."

"I called the cops because you hurt my brother. Bartholomew never did anything to you." She spat another hailstone at him.

"That sniveling brat? He's the next person I go after." Judd inched closer to her.

Connor still clutched her arm. If he didn't release her soon, the cold would enter her veins and chill her blood to slush.

She brought her free hand to her throat, where her mother's tarnished silver cross rested. What she needed was a patch of moonlight. A scrap. Enough to reveal the cross.

Mamma, if you ever loved me, don't desert me now.

Something overhead cracked. A branch from one of the tall trees fell, hitting Britt's shoulder before it smashed onto Connor's wrist and forced him to release her.

A weapon. A stake. She grabbed the limb, tightly gripping the wood, although her arm ached from shoulder to fingertip. Moonbeams broke into the gap the fallen branch created.

Connor and Judd shrank from the light, their arms raised to shield their faces.

She flipped the branch until she held the leafy end, leaving the jagged end for either Judd or Connor. Preferably Judd. Definitely

Judd. Of the two, Judd was more evil. Britt focused on him as he clung to the shadow of the tree.

"You can't take on both of us," Connor jeered.

"I only need to stake you one at a time." Making sure she stayed in the fractured moonlight, she swiveled in a semicircle, brandishing her weapon. Her breath hovered in white puffs. "Come and get me."

Connor laughed and faked a lunge.

"Oh, I wouldn't be so amused, if I were you." She tightened her grip on the branch. "You have no idea what you've unleashed by pissing me off."

Both vampires edged toward her. "Or we can face off till daylight. I don't care." She checked her position again. Silvery light splashed her hand.

"The moon will move," Judd predicted, as he advanced.

"And I'll flow with it." She waved the branch as she tried to catch her breath.

Judd tested the moonlight, like a swimmer testing the water one toe at a time. His body shook as the silver washed over him. He hissed and retreated.

Connor laughed harder.

"Shut up," Judd snarled.

"Who's going to make me?" Connor jeered. "You? You're the tough one. Go after her." Connor goaded

Judd, who was stupid enough to take the bait.

Judd showed his fangs before he leapt at Britt.

Her aim was true, but her angle was all wrong to fully penetrate his chest with the broken limb. She got enough of him to make him scream.

She sensed Connor rushing toward her and dropped to the ground. He stumbled over her and hit the branch still wobbling in Judd's chest. Judd vanished in a puff of ash.

Connor hissed. "Oh, you are a smart bitch."

She remained motionless in the splash of moonlight. His eyes darted, as if searching for her. Couldn't he see where the heat of her breath collided with the frigid air his existence created? She exhaled cautiously.

"Where did you go?" Connor whirled so fast she was surprised he could see anything. He never peered into the bluish puddle of moonlight at his feet.

"Britt?" Old Olivia's voice drifted like mist through night. "Has anyone seen Britt?"

"No," Helga shouted back. "Not for a few minutes." "Scat. Where could the girl have gone?"

Britt didn't dare answer. If she spoke, Connor could locate her. She was weaponless again, except for the blackened cross dangling at her neck.

"Dakota." Old Olivia's tone was as sharp as the end of one of the stakes penetrating the night. "We can't find Britt."

If Dakota came this way, he would be able to see her. Dakota would be able to scent her. Dakota would find her.

If Old Olivia and Helga are talking to him, it means his strategy worked.

Which also meant the vampires were now flakes of icy ash. Britt wanted to close her eyes in thanksgiving but didn't dare let Connor out of her sight.

A snuffling sound alerted her. Dakota, tracking her?

Connor cursed. "Don't tell me I'm the last vamp standing."

Someone growled. The fine hair on her nape rose.

She slowly turned her head toward the wolf. He stood at attention, his ruff bristled. Curled lips bared formidable teeth.

"Get ready to join your brother." Britt whispered.

Connor's head jerked. He winced at the light as he located her. "There you are." His body blurred as he swooped to attack her.

Dakota lunged.

Britt clutched her mother's cross with numb fingers as Connor covered her like an avalanche—cold, heavy, suffocating. His fangs against her throat were shards of ice. The heat of Dakota's wolf made an aching contrast.

Agony exploded in her throat.

She pulled her mother's cross from her neck and pressed the silver into Connor's cheek.

Another poof, and ash drifted like fat, dry flakes of snow.

Searing heat surrounded her. Inhaling mimicked the way a dragon exhaled flame. The pressure in her head threatened to implode her sinuses.

Dakota, now human, sprawled on top of her. "Say something," he muttered, his voice hoarse.

"I'm c-cold."

BRITT'S FLESH WAS BLUE with cold. Dakota didn't want to leave her long enough to brew a cup of wild berry tea. He'd lost sight of her during the battle with the vampires and blamed himself for her hypothermia. Peters had punctured the skin on her neck with his fangs before Dakota managed to gnaw through his spinal cord.

One vampire, beheaded.

The proximity to the full moon must have protected the lycans from vampire cooties. Now terrifyingly cold, Britt hadn't fared as well.

He tried to pry her mother's necklace from her hand but her fingers were frozen around the broken silver chain dangling from her clenched fist.

Maybe she still needed protection, since Byrne had vanished.

"We should all shift back and sleep in a huddle with her in the middle," Selena suggested. She sat at the kitchen table, buttoned to her chin in a flannel shirt.

Dakota considered Selena's idea as Helga pondered solutions.

"All she needs is hot wild berry tea and sex," Helga finally said. "If you used the microwave, you could heat the water a lot faster."

You, a voice inside his head echoed. *Remember? She claims only you can fix what's wrong with her. She said you. Only you.*

That was consent, wasn't it?

He carried Britt to the guestroom and deposited her in the center of the bed. Helga followed with the steaming mug.

He took the tea from her; she closed the door behind her as she left.

Dakota supported Britt's back and fed hot wild berry tea to her. Britt was less cooperative the second time.

"Finish this cup, and I can make love to you. Remember how I warm you up? You need to let me thaw you from the inside out."

She finished the tea, then buried her face against his bare chest. Her nose was ice cube cold.

"Okay," she murmured. "Now, please."

"You're in no condition to consent to letting me have my wicked way with you."

"Not wicked. Good. Please."

How could he resist? His mate wanted him, even if she was stupid with cold.

He covered her. Thrust into her. Something clattered to the floor as she clung to him with both hands. Her thighs clamped his ribs. All he had to do was use his penis to draw her inner heat to her outer body.

All he had to do was love her, even if she didn't love him back.

Chapter 29

"I don't want to go to Ulvskog. I just recuperated from being sick." Britt knew she was being a whiny brat, but she hated Selena's hometown nearly as much as she loathed Judd. She didn't want to get out of bed, and she didn't want Dakota relinquishing his body heat.

"A forest is the safest place for us on the full moon."

Stubborn werewolf. "Most of Ulvskog's inhabitants were murdered the day of the full moon. That's not my definition of safe. Besides, Tom suggested we not leave town."

"They didn't mean visiting Ulvskog. They were referring to Colorado."

Colorado lost its appeal. Judd was a pile of ash, blowing in the wind. She was finally safe.

"I should have stayed an icicle," Britt muttered. She swung her feet out of bed. She needed the bathroom.

Her bare foot landed on something pointed and hard. She yelped, then cursed at the new insult to her still-damaged feet.

"What?" Dakota's concern was sharp and immediate.

"I stepped on something." She leaned to retrieve the culprit.

Her mother's cross. The one she'd pressed into Connor's face. Except the metal was no longer tarnished. The silver gleamed as pure as the dawn.

Her hand trembled, still weak, still recuperating from vampire cooties.

Dakota peered over her shoulder. "What happened to the tarnish?"

"I don't know. I…" A vague memory, a dreamlike sequence, a scary movie half forgotten. She didn't remember most of the battle. "I pressed the cross into Connor's face. Maybe at the same moment you did whatever you did. Together we killed him."

"Teamwork," Dakota murmured after a long pause. "Right." Britt tried again to stand. Her legs gave out.

She collapsed on the bed. "I'm not going with you today. I'll be perfectly safe here. Helga can stay with me, if you're worried about me being alone."

"Helga won't be much protection."

"The vampires are gone. You guys ashed them all last night. Great job, by the way."

"You sent one or two on their way yourself," Dakota pointed out. She'd told him what happened to Judd.

"We proved the magic triad works. Connor tried to drag me onto Ash Street but couldn't pass the Oak Street intersection. Because of that, I'll be fine."

Dakota scowled. "I don't like leaving you unprotected."

"I can barely stand." A slight exaggeration.

"I'll carry you."

"And after we get to Ulvskog and you don't have arms? No, I'm safer in civilization. I'm not going anywhere, except maybe Helga's. You can carry me to her house. First, though, you need to carry me to the shower."

CLEAN AND WARM AT last, Britt still draped a blanket across her shoulders as she curled in one corner of the sofa. Clouds billowed in the sky, obliterating the sun. The gray day was chilly, but the chill was normal, not the teeth shattering cold of a vampire night.

"I can't shift, the full moon lodge isn't ready yet, and there are no young ones to mind," Old Olivia lamented from her corner. "Addy should be here with us."

"Her mate will protect her." Selena stood at the window overlooking the back lawn, Ethan at her side. "They survived the massacre. The offspring she carries is the future of the Varulv."

"If more vamps do come, they won't show up tonight. They need time to regroup. Assuming any escaped. Since they sleep all day, they haven't had time to assess the damages," Ethan said.

"You make them sound smarter than they are." Selena's breath clouded the windowpane.

Ethan snorted. "Smart vampires would do as you say. The stupid ones—and they all must be stupid, or they wouldn't be vampires—will congregate again until whoever is currently head of the Peters clan tells them to back off."

"Nola," Britt and Selena said at the same time.

"I met her and her fiancé, Rick Tuttle, at the reception the other night," Britt added.

Ethan turned. "Rick Tuttle?"

"His father is the senator. He was at Nola's party, too."
"Richard Tuttle is the highest-ranking senator in congress. He's in town?"

Britt made a face. "He was. I'm not privy to his schedule. Don't you guys have to leave soon?"

"We're all set." Ethan massaged Selena's shoulders. "The Peters family are all dead. Your pack is fine. This month is not going to be like the Milk Moon."

Being separated from Dakota for an evening was good. Sometimes his demanding presence overwhelmed her. Neither Old Olivia nor Helga were the chatty type. Britt would have the space and time she needed to consider everything happening, most notably her future as a werewolf's mate. She liked Dakota. A lot. The sex was a bonus. Even if he'd been the worst lover in the world, she still wanted to be with him, though the werewolf thing scared the spit out of her.

A while later, Dakota loaded the others into his SUV and headed toward the Ulvskog forests, where they could wander at will in their wolf shape.

"They won't see much of the moon tonight," Old Olivia observed.

Helga stared at the sky. "We could use some rain to flush the debris from the street."

"Freeze-dried vampire," Britt muttered, and the other two laughed. "Let's hope rain won't reconstitute the bloodsuckers."

Helga missed her television set and wandered home.

"Do you have any questions for me about living with a lycan?" Old Olivia asked.

"No."

"Then I'm going to take a nap. I don't like daylight hours, even on overcast days."

"Pleasant dreams," Britt murmured, as Old Olivia made her slow way to the pack dormitory in the basement.

Britt crawled into bed, too.

The rumble of thunder woke her. She reached for Dakota before remembering he'd gone off to the woods for the full moon. How could her life have changed so drastically in the course of a single week, that she reached for a man the moment she awoke?

Lavender lightning lit the windows. Electricity hummed in the air. Static crackled in her hair as she sat up. Full dark had fallen.

Her stomach rumbled. She climbed out of bed, tripped on a pile of discarded clothes, and stumbled to the door. She flipped the wall switch. Nothing happened. The power was out. She would have to get dressed in the dark.

She located Dakota's discarded T-shirt and yanked the garment over her head. His scent clung to the fabric and comforted her. She wondered if the storm reached Ulvskog and how the werewolves coped.

She limped to the kitchen, stumbling in the dark. No power meant she couldn't cook; she didn't share Selena's obsession with sashimi. There had to be something she could eat cold.

Lightning crashed into the ground nearby. The house vibrated; the windows rattled. Britt jumped, and banged her head on an open cupboard door. The storm emoted directly above the house. Thunder pummeled the air, lightning strobed in the darkness, and rain slashed at the orange walls. Britt found a bag of what smelled like popcorn in an upper cabinet.

She stared out the front window as she munched, admiring what the lightning did to the glittery purple paint on Helga's house. The rain streaking the windows added a psychedelic aspect to the view. Or a Salvador Dali perspective.

Storms didn't bother her. They were how the world expressed anger, something she'd never been allowed to do.

Someone banged on the front door. Maybe Helga wanted company since she couldn't watch television.

Britt unlocked and opened the door. A tall man pushed past her.

More angry than frightened, she snapped, "Wait a minute. Who are you? You can't burst in here uninvited."

"I've come to send you home."

The voice was familiar. Sickeningly familiar.

Daddy?

"How did you find me? What do you want?" She forced the questions from her too-tight throat.

"I've come to send you home," Pastor Paul Hauge repeated.

"What are you talking about?" Had he been keeping tabs on her? That was nearly as creepy as Judd's texts from prison.

"You have not repented. I prayed for you after you helped the authorities arrest and convict the man who robbed me, but you are too evil for even my prayers to redeem you. You can never be forgiven for your latest transgression." Rainwater dripped from his coat.

As if his forgiveness mattered. Not that she knew what he was talking about.

"I will never absolve you for my mother's death." Her hand touched the silver cross she'd refastened at her throat. "I will never forgive you for letting her die when science might have saved her. I guess we're even."

"The Lord would have saved her had she been worth saving."

"I'm not worth saving either. Get out."

He took a step toward her. His eyes glittered in the darkness, a beast of prey on the hunt. "You are my one failure. My one embarrassment."

He was finally telling the truth, not some fanaticism induced fantasy. In reality, his concern was for himself.

"Tough. I live with the embarrassment that you're my father."

As usual, he ignored her. "God has plans for you."

Everything in her stilled. Only her heart continued beating. "What are you saying?"

He took another step toward her. "I'm saying your ability to survive must mean God has bigger plans for you. He's instructed me to send you to Him."

"Only the good die young," she reminded him. His words stymied her. "According to you, I'm not good."

"Word is you're creating a line of potions suitable for cancer patients. You're dedicating the potions to the memory of your mother, who needlessly died of breast cancer." He choked on the word *breast*.

This conversation was getting weirder by the word. "Are you stalking me or something? How do you know what I'm up to? What's your point?" Britt retreated, wondering what happened to the unused vampire stakes.

"You're dragging my name into the public in a negative manner."

Of course. His world revolved around him. Nothing changed. But how did he know? "Don't worry. I won't mention you."

"Too late. Our names have been linked."

"Not my doing. I swear. I'm married. Changing my name. No one ever need know we're father and daughter."

"There's been a change of plans."

"You've got no say." She stubbed her heel on the metal strip separating the foyer floor from the kitchen vinyl.

"Congressman Peters told me all about your so-called marriage. How your husband is a beast. You're having sexual congress with an animal." His disgust reverberated around the room. "You were a whore when you were with the devil-haired person from high school. Now you're consorting with a beast. You must be sent home." He followed her at a leisurely pace, as it trying to draw out her fear.

She was more angry than afraid.

Lighting flared, shining pale blue on her father's face.

"Which Congressman Peters are you referring to, Dad? The one who killed himself rather than be exposed as a pedophile, his rapist son, or the one who turned vampire? Oh. Wait. You preach to your congregation to support the Peters dynasty. The individual doesn't matter."

"The good they do outweighs their sins."

"What good?"

"They kill the evil beasts who would have our government's blessings to run wild in our Christian nation. Service for sanctuary is nothing more than allowing Satan's minions free run of our sacred country. A sin."

"Patriots," Britt countered.

She backed away as her father advanced.

He might have said something else. Thunder masked his words.

Finally reaching the kitchen, she fumbled behind her back and pulled open a drawer. Her fingers rummaged through the contents, searching for a knife or any other type of weapon. *There.* Something wooden. Slender and round. Maybe a spoon. She explored the length. A meat mallet.

"I cannot continue to allow you to embarrass me or my mission," her father intoned.

"Will you sic more vampires on me if I don't?" A shot in the dark.

And...bullseye.

"Judd Byrne was supposed to avenge your betrayals in exchange for his freedom from prison."

"*What?*" She could not believe her ears. Her father was the one behind Judd's release?

"Congressman Peters needs my continued support, especially after his son's sex scandal. We assist each other. I have access to money and campaign volunteers. He has the clout to arrange favors."

"You wanted Judd out of jail to kill me?" Her voice squeaked.

She'd known her father despised her but trying to kill her launched his hatred into the surreal. The man was unhinged, confusing the generations of the Peters' dynasty. Damn them all. Now she knew how her father had learned about Night Shift.

"If thy right eye offend thee, pluck it out and cast it from thee."

"You already cast me out. You don't need to kill me." She crept toward the back door. "Besides, there is no Congressman Peters. They've all committed suicide or died in other nasty ways. Connor Peters changed into a vampire the other day. I can't believe a servant of God like you is dealing with nasty, stinking vampires."

Lightning flashed again. This time, the light flickered on something shiny in her father's hand. A knife? Her father was going to stab her? Gut her?

"You are a sinner who refuses to repent. You don't deserve to live. Your death will gain me much sympathy."

His words shouldn't hurt, not after all the years of their estrangement. Her own father meant to kill her.

"Killing me makes you a sinner, too," she flung at him, as she whirled and sped toward the back door.

Too late she remembered escaping the backyard without risking serious injury in the hawthorn hedge was impossible. The soles of her feet throbbed with every step. The back stairs were slick. She lost her footing and tumbled to the wet grass.

Her father reached for her; she swung the meat mallet. The hammer bounced off his hand but didn't dislodge the knife. The action bought her a few precious seconds.

Rain pelted her. Wind whipped her hair into her eyes. Dakota's shirt clung to her in clammy folds as she headed toward the back of the lot.

Jagged bolts of lightning split the sky. The air smelled of mud and rain. Her father stood at the bottom of the steps and scanned the yard for her. If she didn't move, maybe he would mistake her for a shadow. Dakota's dark shirt hid everything but her fish belly white legs and her fair hair. The sky in the east paled, despite the heavy cloud cover.

"Don't make death harder on yourself. Surrender to your fate," her father shouted. He stumbled forward, rain plastering his hair to his skull.

"I'm nobody's damn sacrifice. Search for a ram, Abraham!" Britt screeched the scrap of scripture at him before she plunged into the hedge. Thorns snagged on her shirt and bit into her bare flesh.

"And Abraham lifted up his eyes, and looked, and behold behind him a ram caught in a thicket by his horns: and Abraham went and took the ram and offered him up for a

burnt offering in the stead of his son." Her father paused and raised his hands toward the sky.

"Instead of his child!" she shouted. "I'm your *child*!"

More lightning flared, giving his actions a jerkiness reminiscent of old monster movies. The monster was after her.

The lightning also let her see the length of his knife blade. She was so fucked.

Her father resumed sloshing toward her, not hurrying, drawing out her terror. She was trapped. She raised her face to the weeping sky. *Mamma. Mamma.*

"You have embarrassed me for the final time."

Britt left the hedge and dove behind the mulberry tree. "You cannot hide from God." He ran into one of the Adirondack chairs clustered under the tree.

"I'm hiding from you, you sanctimonious false prophet." If she ever escaped his wrath, she was going to every newspaper, every TV, radio, and cable station she could find and expose him for what he was.

First, she needed to get out alive.

"Britt?" Old Olivia stood framed in the back doorway. "What's going on? Who's with you?"

"Run!" Britt screamed, betraying her hiding spot. "Call 9-1-1!"

Rain pattered on the leaves of the mulberry tree as her father regained his footing. "You cannot hide from God! God will guide me to you."

Lightning rent the sky. The resulting crack as a bolt struck nearby was deafening. Thunder bellowed simultaneously. The air reeked of ozone and burnt wood. The ground beneath Britt's bare feet quaked from the impact.

As if in slow motion, half the tree split off. Tumbled earthward. Her father froze. Stared at the falling branches as if they had nothing to do with him.

Britt screamed.

The tree struck her father's head, before teetering to the ground. He stumbled, knocked off balance by the blow. Then lurched, slipping in the wet grass. His arms wind-milled as he tried to regain his footing. The knife flew from his hand.

He fell into the quavering mass of leaves from the shattered tree.

And didn't get up.

Chapter 30

DAKOTA'S EXHAUSTION DRAGGED AT him. A lobo was supposed to sleep after singing to the moon all night. He couldn't. He'd needed to get back to Britt. She'd been in danger. Maybe they'd killed Byrne and Peters, but she was still at risk. She didn't answer her phone.

Except she hadn't needed him. She'd handled everything on her own.

Now she sat next to him on the sofa, wrapped in several towels, while the police commandeered the back yard.

Her father was dead, impaled by a broken branch from Selena's mulberry tree.

Neither Dakota nor Britt had killed him.

Dakota couldn't wait to learn the whole story. Until the authorities finished removing Pastor Paul's body, Britt's uncensored version needed to wait.

Anderson and Clerkin were present, cranky and suspicious as always. They didn't buy the idea Pastor Paul was skulking around Selena's backyard with a knife during a storm. Britt stuck to her story. Old Olivia puttered around, offering hot herbal tea. The cops' scowls deepened.

"They drink coffee," Britt told the old woman, as she sipped her wild berry tea.

Post-full moon exhaustion, fearing for Britt's safety, sensing her terror yet not being able to do anything, added to treacherous road conditions and made the drive from Ulvskog the worst ride of Dakota's life.

Eventually everyone left. The cops. Nosy neighbors. The congregated press reporting Warwick's own mega-church pastor dying in the backyard of a tacky house in a seedy part of town.

"Your father was behind everything?" Dakota failed to understand a father killing his child. Aborting that child from his life for no reason other than a difference of opinion.

"He and Congressman Peters made a deal. My father was appalled to learn the government has service for sanctuary treaties with supernatural beings. Called them an abomination. In exchange for my father's financial support, as well as a base of docile believers, the Congressman promised to rid the country of werewolves."

Genocide of lycans wasn't news to Dakota. They'd known the Peters Dynasty secretly condoned the systemic annihilation of the homo lupus.

"Then Selena and I started Night Shift. I was focusing on lotions for cancer patients in remembrance of my mother. My father was furious. Probably afraid the story would get out, of how he wouldn't let her seek medical treatment so he could faith heal her. The truth would taint his ministry."

Britt sipped her tea, her fingers wrapped around a yellow mug, as if trying to absorb the heat.

"How does Byrne fit in?"

"Pastor Paul knew Judd was livid with me. His sentencing was the top news story of the day, and he proclaimed his intention to get even with me. My father figured he could get Judd out of jail to deal with me. He didn't plan on Connor's interference."

"He didn't know about the night Judd shared you."

"To make matters worse, I connected with you. Once he learned you're a werewolf, he lost his sanity. I was embarrassing him by consorting with a beast. He decided to inflict the wrath of his God on me."

"Backfired." Dakota had seen the tree branch protruding from the man's body. "Why did you run to the back yard instead of out the front door?"

"He was blocking the way."

"It's done," Dakota soothed. "Anticlimactic now."

"History," she echoed. "Mostly. We don't know who killed Judd and Connor before making them vampires. The authorities are going to keep searching for Judd and for Connor's body. We can't do anything to stop the waste of taxpayer money."

They sat, not talking, for several moments. Had they been in Loup Garou, a fire would be crackling in front of them.

"The Peters Dynasty has ended. Ethan's grandfather will be glad."

"Maybe not. My father mentioned the old congressman. The retired one. Plus, you forget Nola. The sister. The one engaged to the son of the most powerful senator in Congress. That has to mean something."

"Not to us." He was determined they stay out of the negotiating business. "I'm in Warwick because I drove Restin, Parker, and Ethan's elders. My part in this fiasco is finished."

"We can't move to Colorado."

He suspected she'd been leading to this moment. "Connor bled out in my bed. I'm still a person of

interest."

She might not be a formal suspect, but she was right. The authorities would want them both accessible for years to come. Unless he could get Mitchell Jasper to do something. Except Jasper's hands were tied until the fate of the sanctuary treaties was settled.

"Too bad there aren't any other houses on this block," she mused. "I trust the sacred triad now."

"It's finished," Dakota insisted.

"Should we hold off having children until the treaties are secure?"

Dakota's heart grew until it filled his entire chest cavity.

"You accept me as your mate?"

Britt rested her cheek against his pecs. "My one-and- done turned into a one-and-only."

I HOPE YOU ENJOYED Dakota and Britt's story.

Sign up for my newsletter, where subscribers are always the first to learn my news: titles, covers, release dates, sneak peeks of my works in progress, and occasional bonus material for subscribers only. When you signup, you will receive a FREE short "origin" story about Toke Lobo & the Pack.

So why wait to subscribe? Click HERE for the form.

Next up: Parker & Phoebe's story, BESIEGED BY THE MOON.

Also By MJ Compton

COLUMBIA GEMS BASEBALL ROMANCES
PARANORMAL ROMANTIC SUSPENSE (Shifters)
THE WRITE PLACE RETREAT ROMANCES
Visit my website (www.mjcompton.com) for more info.

About the Author

MJ COMPTON GREW UP near Cardiff, New York, a place best known for its giant—a hoax so successful, P.T. Barnum duplicated it. The tale of the "petrified man" convinced MJ that inventing stories could be a career.

Although her 30 years working in local television included such highlights as being bitten by a lion, preempting a US President for a college basketball game, giving a three-time world champion boxer a few black eyes, and meeting her husband, MJ never lost her dream of creating her own stories.

MJ still lives in upstate New York with her husband. Music and cooking are two of her passions, and she enjoys baseball, college basketball, and sitting on her patio on summer nights to count lightning bugs, but she's primarily focused on writing.

www.ingramcontent.com/pod-product-compliance
Lightning Source LLC
Chambersburg PA
CBHW030740310726
48969CB00005B/1268